THE
NAKED
DRINKING
CLUB

THE
NAKED
DRINKING
CLUB

RHONA CAMERON

EBURY
PRESS

1 3 5 7 9 10 8 6 4 2

Published in 2007 by Ebury Press, an imprint of Ebury Publishing

Ebury Publishing is a division of the Random House Group

The Random House Group Limited Reg. No. 954009

Addresses for companies within the Random House Group can be found at
www.randomhouse.co.uk

A CIP catalogue record for this book is available from the British Library

The Random House Group Limited makes every effort to ensure that the
papers used in our books are made from trees that have been legally sourced
from well-managed and credibly certified forests. Our paper procurement
policy can be found on www.randomhouse.co.uk

Printed and bound in Great Britain by
Mackays of Chatham plc, Chatham, Kent

ISBN 9780091901837

For all my drinking partners, in the very best and very worst of times.

Especially Willie Gunning and John Crowe
wherever you are x

I have such beautiful people in my life now, and I am lucky to have had so much help and support. To all those who have helped me with my life and the writing of this book.

A massive thank you to:

Jake Lingwood and everyone at Ebury;

Kirsty Fowkes for being such a good editor;

My little pal Sarah Boyall;

Jeff Savage for all his help and generosity at BP Gardens;

Tad Chong and Philip Skinner at Shaw Walker and co;

The lovely Gerda Von Posch;

David Morgan;

Rebecca for her love and patience, and for her help, which allowed me the time and space to initially, create this;

My mum for my lovely writing time back home in the late summer;

Charlotte Leaper, for her invaluable support and kindness;

But most of all to Deb who saved my ass big time. I was a nightmare, I know. Thank you from the bottom of my heart.

A change in the weather is known to be extreme
But what's the sense of changing horses in midstream?
I'm going out of my mind, oh, oh,
With a pain that stops and starts
Like a corkscrew to my heart
Ever since we've been apart

'You're A Big Girl Now', taken from
Blood on the Tracks by Bob Dylan

1989

I danced around within the confines of the plane toilet, trying to change my clothes without removing my Walkman. I felt nicely drunk and sexy. Beyond the Gipsy Kings, I could hear the captain saying something over the tannoy. Someone knocked on the door. I pulled on my vest and finished off the rest of my whisky miniature before unlocking the door. An air hostess scowled at me, indicating to me to remove my headphones.

'G'day,' I said, blowing her a kiss and buttoning my denim skirt, one of only three items of summer clothing I'd brought with me.

'Return to your seat immediately, please. We are landing very shortly,' she said abruptly.

'Are we well into our descent?' I asked laughing. She moved me along a downward-sloping aisle towards my seat. I felt all eyes on me and I blew kisses back to all the dirty looks. I climbed over the merchant seaman I'd sat next to for twenty-three hours, who drank solidly but hadn't spoken a word since Paris, and shoved last season's clothes underneath the seat.

Terry, whom I kept calling Tony, shook another two miniatures at me and laughed.

'Nice work, man,' I said, hugging him.

The plane turned on its left side down towards the water, causing everyone to point and take pictures through the tiny windows now that the Sydney Opera House was in full view.

I took Terry's two-way adapter and attached both our headphones to my Walkman. We toasted one another and drank our last in-flight drinks down together. The seaman stared ahead as he had done since Dubai, while Terry and I danced an upper body dance to 'Bamboleo' by the Gipsy Kings for perhaps the thirtieth time since London, and then snogged furiously, Terry touching my tits as I felt him up under the blanket. The jolt of touchdown caused us to stop. We cheered and joined in the passenger round of applause for the captain. The cabin monitors played a video of Australian celebrities, mostly made up of the cast of *Neighbours*, singing a song about Qantas. We were last to disembark.

'No hurry, man,' Terry mumbled, getting us both a cigarette out ready for lighting. He was an electrician whom I'd met at the bar in Dubai where we stopped to refuel. He was already on the flight from London but was sitting in a different seat. We began talking and drinking together and back on board he moved to an empty seat beside me.

We missed the queues in immigration as we'd spent so long in duty-free. Like me, Terry had no one to meet him in Sydney, but unlike me he did have a place to stay, so I took up his offer of going there with him.

That afternoon we drunken-fucked in his room in Annandale, a suburb close to the city, in a house that belonged to a friend of his brother. We opened a bottle of vodka from our duty-free and I played my Gipsy Kings' tape over and over, which we decided would always be our music in years to come.

A week later, I was still there. I had no concept of where the time had gone since landing, but was aware that the first two days were lost to drinking until we had gone the full circle and drunk ourselves sober again. We went to a few bars nearby, then went back and fucked again, then slept a lot. I began calling Terry 'T', because I would still accidentally call him Tony.

Then T's brother came over and started hassling him about getting his shit together for a job he was starting on a half-built office block the following week. Our party came to a close and we started to feel awkward in the few sober hours we spent together. That's when I thought it was time to move on. Anyway, I wasn't worried. I got people easily. I was attractive, petite and slim, with a nice mouth, and dark brown eyes that everybody I slept with went on about. I was twenty-four years old and I didn't get hangovers.

The next afternoon when T was out buying work boots and the house was empty, I left him my Gipsy Kings' tape with a note saying thanks and good luck and that I hoped I'd run into him again, and headed to a place called Glebe nearer town, where I had an address for a friend of a friend from home, whom I was told could put me up for a few days if I was really stuck.

The one big problem about Australia was I couldn't sign on. I had only a few hundred pounds to last me until I met someone, or found some way of supporting myself. I would need money to fund my search, ideally from an easy job that wouldn't interfere with my drinking. On the bus to Glebe, I picked up a Sydney newspaper that I found on the seat next to me. The paper was folded a few pages in, and there was an advert on the upturned page. It read:

Want to earn $300 in two to three hours?
Call 357-0927

CHAPTER ONE

I was immediately drawn to Scotty. He was wearing a baseball hat that had 'SHITHEAD' printed across the front. He was showing off to two Scandinavian-looking blonde girls who had laughed at everything he'd said. He was the Australian weather-beaten-face surfer type, but was a little skinny and short. He punctuated his story with the word 'chicks'. His voice was hoarse like he'd been caning it for a long time. He looked older than he was, I was sure of it. I said hello, he looked me up and down, checking me out, before introducing himself.

The blondes smiled but didn't volunteer their names as they were engrossed in Scotty's lame attempt at a story. We all stood around in a large flat in William Street, Woolloomooloo, a downtown area of Sydney, waiting for things to start.

I surveyed the other people in the room. A man older by about ten years than me sat quietly on a sofa, shaking his head and smiling at Scotty's banter with the girls. A queenie guy with over-the-top gesturing talked with two English girls who looked marginally duller than the two blondes. A couple of other nondescript male and females drifted in and out with bags of shopping.

Then the door opened and a man came in with major atti-tude. He was followed by a sexy, intriguing girl with a swagger that was instantly annoying. The guy had his sunglasses on indoors, which I took to mean a personality defect.

'All right, g'day, listen up.' The sunglasses man clapped his hands loosely a couple of times. 'My name's Greg, I run this outfit, and it's great that you all could make it today. I see we have a few newcomers that want to work and that's great, so

I thought we'd start by telling you a little bit about what we do, and why we do it.'

Scotty laughed a little, like he'd heard Greg's routine a hundred times before.

'This is my girlfriend Anaya.' Greg casually gestured to her with his hands in his pockets. Anaya waved at everyone and said hi. I could see that she could be a complete bitch.

'Now, we call ourselves ART,' Greg went on. 'We essentially take artwork around to people, instead of them coming to see us, which is usually how artwork is sold. It's on this basis that we do well, and let me tell you, we do very well.' He pushed his cheek out with his tongue at this point. For a guy that did well he dressed down: his T-shirt was baggy and faded and he wore a pair of shorts and was barefoot. He had a beer gut and didn't look like he had ever exercised, but he was cleanly shaven and his hair looked recently washed.

'This is how it works.' He pointed to a large portfolio folder against the wall in the kitchen. Scotty jumped up and brought it to him.

'Every day at four o'clock we meet here and we form two teams, or one team, depending on how many of us there are, and we put you in a couple of cars and we give you these.' He kicked the portfolio. 'And we take you out to the suburbs, just in time for tea.' He looked over at the English girls with his eyebrows held in the raised position until he got the reaction he felt he deserved, which was a slight giggle. 'Then we set you loose on the lovely Australian public.'

The newcomers, except me, looked perplexed.

'And you ring the doorbells, knock on the fly screens, whatever you want to do, and you take your little folder and you charm the pants off them. They feel intrigued, you show them these lovely paintings, and guess what happens next?'

Scotty shouted out on cue: 'They buy them and make me plenty of money to buy beer and cigarettes!'

Everybody laughed politely. Scotty got out the paintings and laid them round the room turned to the wall so we couldn't see what was on them, while Greg went on about money. He explained that mostly the paintings sold for around the eighty-dollar mark, but we could charge more if we thought it was possible. The company took fifty dollars per painting. We would be issued with Visa forms and had a phone number to call to verify people's bank details – we had to ask permission to use their phones. But we were encouraged to offer a discount for cash purchases.

Someone asked how many was a good amount to sell, and Anaya replied in what I took to be a German accent, 'How many's enough?'

Then Greg told us that he had sold the most on a coastal trip, where he offloaded ten in one house alone. He ended his talk by telling us we would be back in the city by nine thirty at night, leaving us enough time to get drunk.

This all sounded perfect. I didn't say anything because I didn't need to. This was right down my street. I knew I could do it.

There were ten paintings, all oils, most of them still drying, which Greg insisted people liked because it made them real. They were all the same size, done on artist boards without a frame, although the company could arrange to have them framed at an extra cost. They were made in Bali by someone with painting skills looking for extra money. We would all start with the same ten paintings each in our folders, and nearby Scotty would be waiting in the car with a whole fresh supply to replace the ones we'd just sold. We were told to be discreet and to move from one house to another as quietly as possible, under no circumstances letting any of the residents see us with our supervisors replenishing our stores. We were selling our paintings as 'original works of art'. All except the queenie guy, Nigel, who made it known to the group that he didn't have the stomach for deception and walked out early. After that, Greg spoke more frankly.

'Look at it this way. This is not illegal. These *are* paintings, look!' He tapped a canvas. 'People want pictures to put on their walls. You don't force your way into their homes. They let you in. How you manage to get in is down to you, there are so many different techniques. But once you're in, chances are they will buy from you.'

I felt geared up; this looked easy. I was already multiplying paintings by dollars in my head.

'Listen, somebody painted them 'cause they needed the bucks. And you are selling them 'cause you need them too, and somebody's buying them 'cause they have the bucks and they like what you're selling, so where's the harm in that?'

'No harm!' I shouted out, keen to get going.

'Excellent stuff,' Greg said to me but smiling at Anaya first. 'Excellent stuff.'

Anaya brought Greg a beer from the fridge as he moved up a gear.

'Now then, you need to familiarise yourselves with the actual paintings, and I'm going to start with my personal favourite, and it is my favourite because in my experience it's always been a great seller. And here it is at number one …' He swigged his beer before he bent down to pick it up. 'Ladies and gentlemen, I give you Peter Stuger and his beautiful boat composition.'

We looked at it not knowing how to react. Scotty laughed, which broke the ice, so we all managed a round of sniggers.

Anaya reined us in. 'Yeah, guys, you can laugh but like Greg said, this is a good seller, it's one of our best paintings.'

'Where's Peter Stuger from? You tell them.' Greg pointed at the older man on the sofa. He had a kind strong face and big hands, and I liked him at once. He was in his mid-thirties by the look of him and we'd already caught each other's eyes and smiled during the talk. Now he looked embarrassed and rubbed his brow, trying to suppress his laughter.

'By the way,' Greg went on, 'I should introduce you properly. This is Jim, he's your new supervisor, and you couldn't melt butter in his mouth. Look at this honest face, folks.'

We all laughed again. I could tell Greg was really enjoying himself now and that the beer helped.

'Hello, there.' Jim was shy in front of the group, and spoke in a soft Yorkshire accent.

Greg proclaimed, 'Peter Stuger is, of course, from Holland. He's a Dutchman and, like Van Gogh, one of our best painters. And the Dutch love painting boats.'

This was my favourite line so far. I'd done art history at school the year I applied for art college and I didn't remember anything about the Dutch loving boats.

The picture itself was a mass of dripping oil forming a cluster of old-fashioned boats, which I took to be moored together at a harbour. The main boat, which was moored at the front of the others, had a creamy sail that dripped all the way down the boat through a porthole into the water. There were lots of ropes tying the boats together. The painting looked as though it was done in a matter of minutes, which of course it was. We all stared at it intently, nodding politely like the good pupils we were, as though there was so much more to this lesson than a drunken conman teaching us how to sell shite.

'Who owns the company, and how is the artwork distributed?' asked one of the blonde girls.

'I'll be coming on to that.' Greg raised his eyebrows in an 'and your name is?' fashion.

'Karin. I'm from Denmark.'

'Then you'll know Peter Stuger?' came back Greg.

'Is he for real?' Karin was such an innocent.

'He is as real as you make him,' snapped Frau Anaya, never missing a trick.

'He's Dutch, right?' piped up the other blonde girl.

'So they say.' Greg was unfazed by any interjection; instead he just lazily smoked away taking it all in his stride, for all these comments and questions had no doubt been made a hundred times before.

'Karin and I are from Denmark, not Holland.'

Jim and I suppressed laughter.

'Trust me, sweetheart, people over here will not know the difference. As far as they are concerned, you are European and Europe is where all great art is from. OK?'

'OK,' said the girls in sync.

'Right, let's move on to the triptychs,' said Anaya, over-smiling in an attempt to keep the atmosphere light.

Jim and I had started a non-verbal communication about everything going on: eye-rolling, smiling, head-shaking in disbelief.

'Scotty?' Greg gestured to the other paintings against the wall. Scotty, mid-cigarette, gathered three of them up, bounded over and handed them to Greg, taking away the boats.

'Thanks, mate. Oh, Scotty's the other supervisor and nobody, and I mean nobody, apart from me of course, can sell more than this fella.'

Scotty took off his baseball hat and lowered it to the group. Anaya encouraged a round of applause which everyone except Jim reluctantly joined in. Greg drank the last of his beer and went on to the next painting.

'Now this is more your John Constable sort of thing.' It was a very dull landscape of some watery green hills and a couple of distant trees. 'It's naturally very beautiful but there's more to it. The artist has not been able to capture his subject in its entirety because there's not enough room on the board, so ...' He bent down and turned round the other two paintings to reveal pretty much the same as the one he'd been talking about, except there was a bigger hill in the background and the start of a distant fence in the second one.

'He's created a triptych, which in artistic terms means three, one of three, you see?' He moved the three paintings together. 'Hence enabling him to paint all of the countryside before him that he loved so much.'

This was surely the limit, I thought. Who could buy this stuff? I turned to Jim with a look of disbelief but he was already nodding at me, confirming all that Greg was saying to be true.

'The trick with the trip is to slowly tease the customer with the background to it.'

'Are you joking? Are we both looking at the same background?' I couldn't resist and said it without meaning to. Jim laughed immediately, then Scotty, then the Danish, but the English didn't really go with it. Anaya and Greg looked at each other again and Anaya took a long slow inhale on her cigarette.

'Very good,' she said, as I imagined her in an SS uniform. 'I think you're going to do well.'

I tried not to start really laughing and felt told off. Greg went back into relaxed teacher mode.

'Yeah, like it. Sorry, didn't get your name?'

'Kerry.'

'Kerry. Well, when I say background, I mean, of course, the

story I told you that led to the creating of two other paintings to join this one. And the beauty of it is, Kerry' – I wanted him to stop using my name and for Anaya to ease off on the staring – 'the beauty is, that if you get it right, nine times out of ten they buy three and not one, which means you can buy us all a drink afterwards.'

Without instruction this time, Scotty took away the land-scapes and brought out another two paintings. Greg clicked his fingers, prompting Anaya to go to the fridge to get him a refill.

'Got two beauties for you now, folks.' He held two paint-ings facing away from us. 'This one,' he said, turning the one in his left hand round, 'is a bit bland for me but a lot of older people like it. Two ladies in the field.'

We stared at a canvas made up of largely two shades of green and two small white figures with what I thought were brown hats on.

'And this one, which some of you might be familiar with already.' He proudly revealed the painting in his right hand. 'Australia's very own Blue Mountains, everyone.' He showed us a purple blur that could have been painted with a potato. 'For those of you who have not been in our fair land very long, the Blue Mountains are a big tourist haunt a couple of hours north from here. They're a large range of mountains and are remarkably blue in appearance, caused, of course, by the foliage covering them.' I looked over for Jim's response, but he was already adopting the fake 'Oh really, is that so?' look for my benefit.

'And a big favourite with the oldies,' added Greg.

Jesus. I panicked for a moment. I hadn't thought about conning old people, and thought immediately about my grand-father, the one family member I cared about, and the one reason for returning home once my search here was complete. I wouldn't rip off old people on any account, no matter how desperate I was. Greg's comment threw me as I'd imagined all the people in the suburbs to be rich and annoying. Scotty did his bit again, giving Greg a chance to get a few good gulps in. He could feel us all looking at him enviously.

'Sorry, thirsty work all this talking,' he said, lighting up in addition to drinking. I was desperate for a beer and couldn't wait for the lesson to finish. 'Now, a portfolio wouldn't be complete without a couple of experimental pieces of art thrown in.' He seemed half cut by now, not noticing that some ash had fallen on to a blue mountain.

'This is abstract. The Chinese favour this stuff, they like it 'cos it's modern and clean, and they like all that minimalist stuff. Last year I hit a Chinese area, and they just bought in bulk, mate, they just can't get enough of those bloody abstracts. I sold out the whole bloody car, and some others. And if you can get a Chinese family that have just moved in ... bloody gold mine, mate, I'm telling you.'

We all stared in silence at the three abstract paintings. One was a red square in the centre of the board with a background in two halves, half of the board coloured orange, the other half brown. The second had a yellow background with three blue circles overlapping, and the third was basically just a board of fawn with what looked like an oatmeal handkerchief painted over it. Jim was staring ahead in a joke trance with his mouth open, and I burst into laughter.

'Sorry, I just ...' I said apologetically, trying to contol my giggles.

Anaya deliver me a cold, controlled smile. 'It's OK. I was the same. But if you get it right, people buy this. It is Art, after all, Carrie.'

'Kerry.' I pulled myself together. 'It's Kerry.'

'Ah, you don't like Carrie?'

'Hate it.'

'Sorry, Carrie, let's get it right, uh?' That bitch wouldn't let up, so I composed myself to shake her off, as I could tell she liked to get at people.

'Don't take it personally, mate, Anaya is useless with names.' Greg tried to soften things again while Anaya outstretched her arms in the 'I'm innocent' position.

Jim made a small O with his mouth.

Greg took a quick break in order to finish his second beer and light a new cigarette from the one he was just finishing. As there was only one painting left, I had the feeling that Greg was going to pull something special out of the bag. I wasn't disappointed.

'This, my little travellers –' as he slowly turned the painting round, he began to laugh himself at what he had just said; his laugh went into a cough until he gained control of it – 'this is something very special. I know I've said it before but I really mean special.'

He revealed the last picture, which featured a unicorn drinking from a lake, surrounded by mist, in front of an oriental-looking mountain like you see in pictures of Japanese golf courses.

'Something for the single ladies of the suburbs. And the bikers love it.'

'Bikers!' I laugh-shouted.

'Don't knock it, mate.' Scotty jumped to its defence. 'Loads of bikers in the some of the suburbs round here.'

I looked to Jim for confirmation of this. He was nodding again.

Greg said, 'The thing to say is, this art is for everybody. You got that?'

The Danish nodded with complete absence of humour. I was still coping with the biker info.

'The whole idea with this and all these paintings is – and this is the bottom line, and they love to hear it – We. Bring. Art. To. The. People.'

'Art for everyone!' shouted the Frau, rallying the troops.

'Now let's all grab a beer for five and come back, when I'll fill you in on technique with my good man Scotty here.'

Scotty rubbed his hands eagerly, and Anaya threw out the beers.

We all shuffled towards the kitchen area. Scotty lit up a joint on the patio. He gestured to offer it out but nobody was interested. He made gasps of relief as he sucked on it for the benefit of the Danish girls who were predictably impressed. Jim and I drank a beer and got talking.

'So, you been here long?' asked Jim.

'Few weeks. What about you?'

'Around eight months – seems like nothing, though. Been doing this lark for six months.'

'What did you do at home?'

'I was an English teacher.' He drank from his beer. 'Far too sensible, was worried I was becoming boring so thought I'd try something completely different.' He laughed in a self-conscious way. He was an attractive, big, solid man. 'What about you?'

'Oh, this and that. But I've not really found what I want to do yet.' I peeled the label off my beer.

'What part of Scotland you from, then? I went to uni there, you know?'

'Oh yeah?' I was envious of people who had studied, and was more often than not the only person in a group who had never gone to college or university.

'Yep, I'm from Leeds but studied in Glasgow. You've an east coast accent though, haven't you?'

'Yeah. Edinburgh.'

'Where are you staying in Sydney, then?'

'Just crashing at a friend of a friend's, you know, but I can't be there for long. It's kind of a favour on their part to someone else and I don't want to take the piss.' I felt awkward about disclosing details of my shambolic life.

'Not tying yourself to anything, eh?' Jim seemed to detect my unease.

'Yeah, something like that.'

'Well, that's the idea of travelling, isn't it?' He was kind and reassuring, and I felt grateful for his presence in the group.

'What about you? Where do you stay?' I asked.

'Moved in here. They do that, you know, they just knock a bit of money off to cover your rent. It makes it easier.'

'What's it like?'

'Not bad. I've got a room to myself, people come and go, it's easy really. So you staying much longer with these friends in Sydney or what?'

'I plan to be kind of moving around.'

Jim nodded. 'I see.'

I nodded back.

He said lightly, 'If you stick with this for a while, you could move in. There's room just now.'

Anaya bounded over, tying back her hair at the same time. 'You telling Kerry about how nice we are to you, Jim?'

'No, I'm telling her to run away while she still has a chance.'

Anaya was irritating but sexy in her looks; she had light-brown long hair, blue-green eyes, great cheekbones and a heart-shaped face. I had felt her eyes on me the whole time since I'd made a couple of light remarks about the paintings. I decided to try to find out more about her.

'So how did you come to do this then, Anaya?' I found it hard to look at her properly.

'I was travelling when I met Greg. He's a Kiwi. I met him in Auckland.'

'Where's that?' I hadn't a clue about anywhere and wasn't ashamed to admit it.

'New Zealand. Oh my God, you haven't been?'

I shook my head like it was no big deal.

'It's beautiful, totally boring but beautiful. Anyway we met there. Greg's half-Maori.'

'So you see, that's why he wants to fuck over the Australians.' Jim laughed at his own remark, but I didn't get it.

'Not at all, he loves it here. So, Kerry, you think this is for you? It's really easy money, you know.' She looked right at me, I held her gaze.

'I'll give it a go. I really need some cash as soon as possible.'

'Excellent. It's exciting. And I love it when we have a new team,' she said, chain-smoking, with no expression, just far-away eyes.

CHAPTER **TWO**

Sydney was humid, and got dark quickly. I liked the combination. I hated the five-till-seven slot of the day anywhere, so I was happy to be plunged into darkness early, unlike at home where far too much was made of hours of summer evening light. Dusk had always been a good marker for the onset of drinking, which I was concerned about being compromised by the new job.

Jim parked up a big old Holden Kingswood at the edge of a suburb called Dover Heights, close to North Bondi. It was nearly six o'clock; I had been asleep for most of the journey out of the city, which had taken an hour in commuter traffic. I sat in the back with the two Danish girls. Scotty sat in the passenger seat with his bare feet on the dash, his baseball hat over his face. The Danish girls smelled clean and fresh like the nice girls they were, and a slight, warm breeze blew through the car.

I felt lonely. I didn't know the others yet. I knew I would know them in time, but I was growing tired of constantly moving around in my life, of things being so short-lived. I could have let myself slip right down, had not Scotty turned on the car radio and passed round some gum.

'How you feeling, girls? Are you up for making some easy bucks?'

'What time will we finish the work?' asked the Danish called Andrea.

Jim turned round and smiled.

'Depends, but we usually tend to call it a day around nine-ish. But if someone is selling after that we wait for them.

Sometimes you could be in your last house around eight thirty but it could take you an hour to close.'

'What's close?' asked the other.

'It's like, finish the transaction, complete the sale,' Scotty answered, stretching his arms out as much as he could.

I hadn't asked much, I didn't feel the need to. I had a feeling I knew exactly how to play things. As always, just as I was slipping down, my arrogance kicked in and saved me, setting tightly in my jaw.

'Right then, let's make a move,' said Jim.

'Yep, better get on with it,' added Scotty.

'Are you selling too, Scotty?' I asked.

'No, I'm just helping out, seeing how you guys are doing and helping Jim with the areas.'

'What about you, Jim?'

'No, thank you very much. I've earned my place of supervisor so you lucky people can earn my money for me.'

'Oh yeah, how does that work, then?'

Scotty laughed and looked out the window.

'Well, I've sold for lots of time, six months in total, but they need someone to run the teams so I'm the obvious choice for now. But if we do a trip away, I might go back to it a bit.'

'So you earn commission off us?'

'Exactly. Tough, eh?' Jim laughed.

'It will be when I'm supervisor.'

'Maybe if you turn out to be so good at selling, you won't get the chance, eh?' He turned round and looked at me smugly.

'We'll see.' I was beaten.

'Come on, you lot, let's get the stuff out the back.'

The Danish said nothing, unable to understand our mock sparring, with its serious undertones.

Scotty opened the boot and dragged out the portfolios.

'All right, help yourselves, people.'

Jim reached into the glove compartment and grabbed a bunch of leaflets. 'Here you go.' He handed us out some each. 'Those are your bank-card slips with the credit-card authorisation phone number. Try to encourage cash but some will want to pay by card, especially if they are buying more than one. You just fill in this form and ask politely to use their phone to call.'

The three of us looked blank.

'It's OK, it's straightforward. You just call and ask to authorise a payment. This other number here is our merchant number, that's the company's registered number. They'll ask for that and the amount, and that's it. OK?'

'Where will you two be?' I asked.

'We'll be nearby, in the car. When you come out you'll be able to find us and we'll pick you up when you've finished or when you need more paintings. Any questions, just find us between houses, and don't worry, guys.' Scotty handed out the folders as he spoke. Jim looked at his map.

'Karin, I'm going to start you off here. This is Hunter Street. You stick to this side for the time being, and it's unlikely you'll get further than this tonight unless no one's home.' He pointed to the houses. 'Andrea, you just start here on that corner.' He pointed with the other hand on her shoulder. 'Then move round to Myunda Road, do you see it round the corner?'

'Yes, I understand.'

'OK, good luck, guys.'

'Mind the dogs, yeah?' Scotty laughed.

Andrea turned back looking concerned. 'I fucking hate dogs.' I was glad she swore.

'Talk in a high voice and they won't bite you.'

'I mean it, Scotty,' she snapped.

Scotty waved her on, laughing more than was necessary.

'Scotty, don't wind her up like that,' said Jim.

Scotty lit up. 'Proven fact, mate, dogs don't mind a high female voice.'

'Shut up and get in the car, you lunatic.'

I was getting a little irritated with the banter and Scotty was starting to grate on me even though I could see through his act.

'Hey, Kerry, we need to get back in the car. We're dropping you somewhere else.'

'Whereabouts?'

We all got in and drove off slowly; Jim had the map in his teeth while looking at the houses.

'Think we covered this street about six months ago,' said Scotty.

We'd only moved a minute away to a wider street with bigger houses.

'Yip, this is it. OK, Raleigh Street, let's go.' Jim and I got out while Scotty stayed in the car fiddling with the radio.

'You've got the whole street, OK?' said Jim. 'Both sides, yeah?'

'Yeah sure, thanks. Have a nice evening, boys.'

Jim patted me on the back.

'Think of the beers afterwards,' Scotty said, leaning out of the car with 'Uptown Girl' playing in the background.

'Turn that bloody thing down, Scotty. Jesus, nothing like telling them all we've arrived.' It looked to me like Jim had never really left teaching.

'I *was* thinking about the beers,' I said to Scotty.

I walked off in the direction of a large white house at the corner of a crossroad, wondering if my Peter Stuger painting was dry or not.

I knocked on the fly screen of the white house with palm trees lining the front path. The main door was open. The house was called 'The Cove'. It was written on a piece of wood that hung above the door; it really annoyed me. I could hear some people noise from through the back of the house. A woman came to the fly screen with a glass of wine in her hand; she was wearing smart office clothes and no shoes. She was relaxed and friendly and smiled when she saw me. I was already smiling from when she first came into view. She opened the screen and leant against it.

'What can I do for you, love?' she said, still smiling but looking at my folder. A small child ran down the hall towards us and grabbed her leg. I had no interest in the child but I pretended.

'Hello there, you,' I said in a playful voice. 'Hi there, my name's Kerry. I'm from Scotland and I'm here showing the artwork of some people I'm working with.' I hated Greg's coached words coming out of my mouth, but it felt like the right thing to say.

'Oh, yeah? Artwork, you say? Is it yours?'

'Mummy!' shouted the child, competing with me for her attention. The woman played with the child's hair as he swung around her leg.

'Baby, don't pull Mummy's skirt.'

'One of the paintings is mine. It's the only one I have at the moment, the rest of the work belongs to other painters from the same group as me.'

'Mummy! I don't like pumpkin.'

'I know you don't, darling.' She looked over at me. 'Sorry, we've got our hands full at the moment.' The child was pushing the woman against the wall. 'Mattie, watch Mummy's glass.'

'I can see you've got a lot on, it's that time of night, I know. But that's why we come to you, so that we bring our work to you in your home, in your time.' I'd lost the thread at that point, I knew it. Then the husband appeared from down the hall. He looked tense.

'What's happening, honey?' he asked.

I smiled as the woman talked to the child about pumpkin, telling him he didn't have to eat it, but the child went on and on. The husband frowned at me and looked perplexed, and I wanted to speak to him before she did but it was too late – she got to him first.

'What's all this?' he asked.

'She's selling paintings from Scotland.'

'Well, I'm from Scotland ...'

'Oh yeah, which part?' he asked, interested.

'Edinburgh.' My cheeks were sore from smiling; at this rate I wouldn't last the night.

'My brother married an Edinburgh girl. Marie Jamieson.' He said the name in a special voice that I suspected he only got out for dinner parties. I appeared really interested and made a deep-in-thought expression, as if I might actually know her.

'I know you won't know her, it's a big place, uh?'

I had lost the woman to the child, and she was knocking back the wine. I had to bring focus back in somehow. 'It's not as big as Sydney. Sydney's massive, I love it.'

'Our neighbours are from Glasgow!' The man said 'Glasgow' in an awfully bad Scottish voice and pointed in the direction of houses across the street with his wine glass.

That was it. I decided to take control and to do so, I'd have to take some risks, otherwise we'd be here all night. I turned to the opposite houses. 'That one, there? I forget the number.'

'Yeah, forty-eight, with the boat in the drive.'

'Oh yeah, they are a lovely couple.' That was it, too late to turn back. I didn't know the name and I didn't know if they were even a couple but if my instincts were correct, he would tell me and I'd go along with it.

'The Gordons, Pam and Michael?'

'Oh my goodness, really? I was calling Pam Anne all the time – how embarrassing! I mustn't have heard them.' I fiddled with the ties on my folder, not wanting eye contact.

'You went in there and met them, did you?'

The woman walked away down the hall carrying the child.

'I couldn't get away. They're a lovely couple, aren't they? Some characters.' Amazing newfound bullshit, I thought, as I eased into the con like an old hand.

'Oh yeah. Michael likes to talk. We all went on holiday a couple of years ago and it was a hoot, I'm telling you.' He laughed to himself and took another drink of wine.

It was then that how to play him came to me – how to get in the house and what to sell him. My heart was pounding and I was becoming increasingly edgy at us talking on his doorstep, as I feared it might attract the very neighbours that I was lying about. I had to get inside during this next chunk of conversation.

'Yeah, they're great people, and I have to say I agree entirely with their taste in paintings.' I remade eye contact for this.

'Oh, right.' He sipped from his wine. 'They liked your stuff, did they?'

'Not all of it – you don't expect anybody to like all of it – but they really went for one in a big way.' I appeared as nonchalant as possible.

'They bought some, did they?'

'Yes, they did. It looks good there, and they've got a lovely place.'

'All right, let's have a look at what you've got then. Come in.'

The thrill I got from running the show and not knowing what was going to happen set my heart thumping.

The hall wasn't ideal as it was a little narrow to set out all the paintings and to allow him space to stand back and see them, but at least I was in. I had already planned that if the Gordons came over, then I would either make out that it was another couple I had met, or, if really pushed, I would come clean about the whole thing, which wouldn't be the entire whole thing. I'd leave the bit out about the paintings being mass-produced and completely shit, but I would admit I was a struggling artist who was desperate for money. As I worked through my emergency back-up plan in my head, I felt calmer.

'My name's Kerry, by the way.' I put out my hand to shake his, which as a gesture felt really out of place alongside my jeans, vest and torn sweat top.

'Pleased to meet you, Kerry. My name's Jeff and that's my wife Kim. Kim, love, come here for a minute, please!' he shouted through to the back of the house. I started to feel like I had a conscience and that what I was doing was wrong, but then I convinced myself that I would probably never live in a house like this, and that these things were technically paintings, and that, like Greg had said in the training session, no one was forced to buy them; they bought them because they liked them, and they had the money to.

'Kim!' he shouted again. I didn't want the wife around; she'd only bring the child with her, who was a potential hazard.

'What? I'm trying to finish dinner.' She appeared with the child, who was sucking a dummy and thankfully sedate. I started getting the paintings out of the folder, hiding my nerves at what I might find.

'Tell you what, Kerry, bring them through here where there's more room.'

'For goodness sake, Jeff, back and forward,' said Kim, as Jeff led the way into the kitchen and out through the back into a conservatory. The back garden was massive and all lit up with candles. Kim sat down on a basket chair near the door, while Jeff refilled her glass. I was desperate for a drink, having gone way passed my usual start time.

'Do you want to have a glass with us, Kerry?' Jeff asked, on cue.

This was going ridiculously well.

'Em ...' I play-acted a dilemma out of politeness. 'Yes, all right, thanks. Just a small one.'

'So what do we have here, then?' asked Kim.

'Hey, love, she's just been over Pam and Michael's,' said Jeff, pouring me out a glass of red wine and handing it to me. 'They bought a painting. She says they were a real laugh.'

'Oh yeah? God, that's not like Michael to be frivolous. He must have been pissed.' They both laughed.

I just smiled, not wanting to laugh at someone having to be pissed to buy my paintings.

The wine tasted good and only fired me up even more. I fantasised about selling Jeff and Kim three pictures and then just staying there until nine o'clock, drinking with them before returning to the car. Easy.

'Now then, I'm going to show you a few paintings. Jeff, you just sit down there and take it in. Don't be rushed; you have to see what you like.' I put my wine down and returned to the job. I rifled through my folder and made a decision to hold back the triptych till last, all the time worrying about Kim and Jeff suggesting we get the Gordons over.

I laid the other paintings round the conservatory. The child fell asleep in its mother's arms. They both said nothing. I stood back and took another drink from my wine, planning at speed what to say next.

'They are very eclectic,' I said finally. Eclectic was good, I thought. It's a word arty people use.

'Mmm,' said Jeff, seriously giving them some thought. 'What do you think, love?'

'Not my cup of tea. Quite like that one.' She pointed to Peter Stuger's boats. Bingo. I quickly did the biog routine about him, the Dutch angle, said he came from a long line of artists dating back to the eighteenth century, hoping there would be no questions about that part of things, or about why the mast of one of the smaller boats in the picture was clearly glistening with wetness. I was desperate to pee but knew that if I left the scene they would confer among themselves or, even worse, call their neighbours and I wouldn't be able to control things. So I persevered.

I went through every one with them. I told them that the abstract wasn't for everyone, said Stuger was our most popular artist, told them the Blue Mountains had never been painted with such love of their beauty and such understated simplicity. Jeff refilled the glasses.

'OK, Kerry.' I saw him look at my tits a bit as I bent down to pick up my wine. 'What did bloody Pam and Michael buy?'

'Well, I'll show you.' I pulled out the bland, green, hilly triptych.

'Oh, OK.' He looked surprised.

'Hey, how come they bought them if they're here?' said the wife, who was obviously less drunk and less stupid than her husband.

'This isn't the actual painting they bought, but it is by the same artist and it is related to theirs.' They looked at each other, then looked back at me and laughed; I joined in, not wanting to seem defensive.

'This is what we call a part of a double triptych.' I laid it all out as I talked. 'It's very unusual to be done in this way, but the artist, who is a Welsh woman, painted this in a set of six. This would be one half and the other, obviously from a different angle, is the set your friends have bought.'

'How much is it?' Jeff was first to ask.

'Each part is a hundred and fifty dollars.'

'Jeff, you're mad – it's nice but you're mad,' Kim laughed. He ignored her. 'They bought the other three, you say.'

'Yes, they did, which I think is rather extravagant. I mean, if you like it, just get one. Who needs three?' I knew where I was going with this.

'Nope, if they bought it, then it makes perfect sense that we have the other set, don't you think so, love?' Jeff swung round a bit too hard, which was an indication of how much wine he'd drunk.

'No, it makes no sense. I like them but it makes no sense, you're crazy.' She laughed lovingly. He lapped up the crazy part.

Oh yeah, I thought, you're fucking crazy, crazy suburban office guy. I finished my second glass of wine, and decided, despite it being my first night on the job, that if I sold this I would retreat early to the car and call it a day at one house.

Jeff walked round the pictures looking at them, moving his head from his ear to his shoulder at either side.

'We've got all that space in the study, Kim, you have to admit. They'd look nice there.'

'Yes, I can see that. You've got a point there. It's just, what … four hundred and fifty bucks!' She threw her hands in the air and slapped them down on the outside of her thighs for dramatic effect, but Jeff wasn't fazed, and I helped things along with one final relaxed push.

'It is a lot of money, but it's cheaper this way though, me bringing it to you. A gallery or even a coffee shop would charge double. But it's still a lot, I couldn't afford that.' I sounded so reasonable, I believed myself.

'No, fuck it, let's do it,' said Jeff, covering his mouth with his hand afterwards for the kid's sake, mouthing 'sorry' to a disapproving wife. 'Come on, love, you gotta admit it, it is kinda cute, and we have spoken about getting some real art in, haven't we?' He sidled up to her, until she bore a half smile. I wanted to vomit on their immaculate tiling.

'OK, Kerry, my little Scottish mate.' He put his arm round my shoulder and pulled me in. Kim rolled her eyes at me. At this point I would have felt guilty had it not been for the Mercedes in the drive out front, and the Ducati I could see out the back by the garage. I nodded back at Kim, smiling. I wanted to rush for the credit-card forms but knew I had to appear relaxed to the very end.

Jeff walked out of the conservatory through to the kitchen and picked up the phone. I felt the blood drain from my face.

'The cards are in the drawer in the study, love,' Kim shouted, which gave me a second to think.

'Yeah, I'm going to phone Pam and Michael.'

I was fucked. I couldn't move from the spot. I tried to keep a smile going and lifted up my glass for cover, then remembered it was empty. I turned to Kim. 'Hey, it would be better as a surprise, you know? Imagine their faces when they come over next.'

'Jeff!' she shouted, and the kid woke up. 'Oh shit, I've woken Mattie. Jeff!'

I'd never been so pleased to see a child start to cry.

'What?' Jeff came back in with the card.

'Don't you think we should surprise them?'

'Oh, yeah, I suppose we could. Here, give Mattie to me.' He picked up the kid and rocked him about a bit while I got the payment forms out from the bottom of the folder. 'Yeah, you're right.' Then he got completely distracted with the child. 'Come on, little Mattie.' He took the boy off down the hall.

'I just need to use your phone to call an authorisation number.'

Kim yawned; the atmosphere felt flat. 'Yeah, sure. The card's there. Let me get you the phone.'

I felt full of dread, convinced that the wine that once worked for us was now working against us. Jeff came back without the kid. I proceeded to dial the number on the slip, trying to hide my hands, which were shaking. I began chewing on my lip. I dialled, listened to it ring at the other end, and then a Chinese-sounding voice answered.

Jeff and Kim started cuddling; they were talking but I couldn't make out what they were saying. I was worried they were pulling out. The Chinese voice asked me for the credit-card number. As I read off the card, Jeff asked me would I mind if he took the paintings into the study. I nodded for him to go ahead. Kim followed him until they were completely out of my sight. I felt sick and panic-stricken as the voice asked me for the merchant number. I read it back, straining to hear Jeff and Kim. The voice confirmed payment. I put down the phone, picked up my wine and toasted my reflection in the conservatory glass. I looked out into the garden and breathed deeply.

I was packing up a few minutes later when Jeff and Kim came back.

'They look great,' Jeff said.

I smiled. 'You know it makes me happy to see people

appreciating art, especially when I've played a part in bringing art to people and not making them come to some stuffy, pretentious, overpriced gallery.'

I shook hands with them both. They showed me back to the door. I couldn't wait to join the rest of the 'team' in the bar, and brag about my exploits.

'Enjoy them,' I said as I left.

'We will,' Jeff nodded.

'Is Pam and Michael's light off?' asked Kim, leaning on Jeff.

'Yeah, guess they must have gone to bed early.'

My back was already turned to them; I looked up at what was a perfect evening sky and felt warm with the wine.

CHAPTER **THREE**

Scotty drummed away on the bar while he waited for the drinks to come. The Danish girls stood next to him. I sat at a table with Jim. He was laughing at my story; no one had ever sold a triptych on their first night.

'I'm bloody impressed,' he said.

'Yep, so am I, but, you know, I was genuinely shitting myself at one point.'

'And you wouldn't have wanted to do that in their toilet, otherwise there'd definitely be no bloody sale.' We both pissed ourselves laughing.

'Alrighty,' said Scotty, as he and the Danish put their drinks down on the table. We all sat together in the Honest Irishman, a block from the ART house. Things felt really good. Jim and Scotty seemed familiar already despite the fact I'd only known them for one day. Now the drinks were about to flow and there was, in my experience, no better way to speed up getting to know people than by drinking with them, but also no better way to know what people don't want you to know about them. I was good at latching onto people, and I was equally good at dropping them again; both came quite naturally to me. I forgave myself for these personality traits that others might find callous. It was just what I had to do – my life was about moving on. I felt confident and cocky on the back of my sale; I was going to do well in this, I knew it.

'Well, I think we've got to raise our glasses to Kerry here for a bloody superb first night,' said Scotty, clinking his glass against mine. I clinked with everyone after him.

'And to Andrea and Karin,' added Jim. The Danish had

sold two each, which I found utterly perplexing given that they hardly said anything.

'It is really fucking addictive, isn't it, though?' I felt cheerful and light and far away from my darkness. Jim and Scotty nodded as they gulped their schooners, the Danish just smiled blandly. I couldn't stop smiling. It turned out that Andrea and Karin went to college together in Denmark, and were here on some kind of gap-year thing. They told me a little about their course, after I felt I had to ask something, and I nodded politely throughout, but felt completely uninterested in their lives. Scotty and Jim, however, hung onto every word they said. I didn't dislike the girls, I just found them to be lacking in the essential qualities that make me really want to know someone. Plus, they were just so snowy-white and boring.

I thought about Anaya, and wondered why I found her annoying yet compelling. All the time I was hoping that she would turn up so I could boast about my triumph.

By the time she and Greg arrived, we were all fairly drunk. Scotty had shown us how he could take a cigarette inside his mouth on his tongue and completely close it. I pretended it was the first time I had seen it done. And for the Danish it genuinely was.

'Hey, I believe you have had an excellent first night, Kerry, congratulations,' said Anaya.

'Yeah, mate, really well done, especially on your first. You've all done very well,' said Greg.

'What happened to the English girls?' I asked.

'They couldn't stand the heat, mate!' shouted Scotty, overexcited by the company paying him attention.

'Yeah. It's not for everyone this job, some people just couldn't do it for the life of them.' Jim wiped lager froth from his top lip. I was glad that the team was limited to two mousey girls, rather than four. That would have been too much.

Anaya stood with her back against the bar, resting on both elbows, in a cocky I-own-the-place fashion. She had washed her hair and done herself up a bit in evening mode. She looked good, but she was so cold. I wanted to know more about her, but I'd leave it for now; leave it until they needed me more, and needed the money I was going to bring to them.

Jim was still shaking his head and laughing. He did impressions of me doing my routine at the house.

'Well, I couldn't afford it, but it's cheaper that way, me bringing the art to you.' His Scottish accent was terrible. Everybody laughed except Anaya. She looked at me, as though she was trying to figure me out.

Jim went on, 'Excuse me, can I use your toilet? I think I'm going to shit myself.'

We all laughed.

The bar was buzzing and it felt exciting. I put two dollars in what I considered to be a perfect jukebox. Sentimental old songs were my favourite and this jukebox was one of the best I'd ever seen. Even the old bars back home down in Leith couldn't top this. My money got me three tunes, 'Seasons In The Sun' by the Fortunes, 'This Old Heart Of Mine' by the Isley Brothers, and Peter Sarstedt's 'Where Do You Go To My Lovely'. It was all too good. I came back to the bar singing along with the Fortunes. The chorus came and the entire bar including Anaya belted it out.

Jim ordered the two of us a couple of shots of JD. I grabbed him by the shoulders with both hands and fixed him to the spot, straining my voice above the double chorus of the last verse.

'LISTEN TO ME!'

'WHAT?'

'THERE IS NOTHING, AND I MEAN NOTHING, QUITE AS GOOD AS THIS, IS THERE?'

He nodded, then threw his head back and laughed.

'I FUCKING LOVE ALL THIS!' I shouted, all fuelled up and on top of the world.

We hugged and toasted 'the new team'. After checking with Greg and Anaya, I told everybody I was moving into the company flat the next day. They all cheered, and then the Danish announced that they were doing the same, and we all cheered again. Two more schooners were brought to us by the barman, who shrugged and pointed over to an older man who had been playing pool for most of the night, or sitting at the end of the bar on a stool and watching us. We raised our schooners at him, and he raised his back. I felt so happy and content, and hopeful about this job, and where it would lead me. It surely meant that I'd get enough money to travel around and find what I was looking for.

While the others were talking, I looked in the zip section of my purse and checked that my piece of paper was still there. It was my only copy and I carried it everywhere. I looked at the notes I had made on it two years before I came here, and then put it back in my purse for safe keeping.

CHAPTER **FOUR**

I stood on the corner of Tulley Street and Mulberry Way, a pretty *Neighbours*-style area an hour out of the city. The car had just pulled away; Scotty made a clenched-fist sign out of the car window for my benefit. I surveyed the streets in either direction. The houses looked the same: they all had matching driveways and plots of front garden surrounded by lush vegetation. It looked like a new development.

I decided to start to my right, in Mulberry Way, because my portfolio was hanging over my right shoulder. I walked up a drive, pausing before I knocked on the fly screen to compose myself and to practise smiling. There was no answer so I rang the bell. A few seconds later, an old man, possibly in his eighties, came to the door followed by an old woman. My heart sank. They looked at me through squinted eyes.

'Sorry, love,' said the man, smiling. 'We don't hear so well. Had you been knocking for a while? Everybody stands there for the longest time until we hear them.'

'No, not at all. Listen, it doesn't matter, I was just ... I'm showing some artwork but ... it's OK, I won't bother you.' I didn't feel comfortable selling to them, it seemed wrong. I was counting on the people I sold to annoying me with their wealth and happiness, but not this – not kind, vulnerable, old people. I decided I wouldn't go any further.

'What's she doing, love?' asked the old woman from behind her husband.

'She's an artist.'

I felt really bad. 'Well, I am kind of, but I don't need to ... don't worry.'

'You'd better come in then, love, and tell us all about it.'
They both chuckled, in that way old people do at young
people. I felt it would be rude not to go in now, so reluctantly
I did. They guided me through to the lounge where they had
been sitting at a dining table still not cleared from dinner.
This made me feel even worse. I thought about my dear
grandfather, the one reason I had stayed in Edinburgh for as
long as I did. I thought about his life now, his tiny room in the
nursing home, his miserable tray dinners, a life of watching
Countdown with the heating up full blast and nobody ever
bothering to tune the radio in the communal lounge to a
station. I hated his second wife for what she did to him, how
she put him in the home while she lived in his house and
spent his money. If my grandmother had lived, they could
have had a life together like the sweet old couple with me now.

'Oh, I'm sorry, were you having your dinner?' I asked.

'Don't you worry, we've had plenty dinners.' The old lady
chuckled some more. They were ridiculously nice. 'Now then,
take a seat and we'll get you a cup of tea.'

'No, no really … it's fine.'

'You can put that thing down there.'

I felt awkward with my enormous folder of deceit taking up
what felt like most of their lounge. The old man pointed to an
area of wall beside the sofa.

'There, that's it,' he said, as I lay down the folder. The old
woman left to make some tea. I felt exhausted with politeness
even though I had only just begun.

'It's a lovely area, isn't it? And this is a very nice house,' I
said, looking around. The place was full of ornamental cheese
dishes; they crammed the glass cabinet in the corner of the
room, and the top of it, and the windowsill. Three were on the
television, and two more on the table we were sitting at. Some
were plain, and others were decorated with various woodland
creatures hanging onto the handles; one had a china mouse as
the lid, another had two Australian flags sticking out on top.

'It is lovely, we're very lucky,' said the old man.

'How long have you lived here?'

'Oh, it must be coming up for fifteen years now. Before that
we lived nearer the city beside my wife's sister Madge, but

after she passed away, and we were getting on a bit, we decided to get a smaller more manageable place for us both.'

I'd already decided to ask about the butter dishes next; by that time, the tea would be ready, and I'd talk a bit about Scotland because everybody loves that, and then I would thank them and leave, not wasting too much time not selling. I had to be firm. I needed money and I had to make some cash tonight. There was nothing left for me to pawn. Coming to Australia with only around two hundred pounds was always an insane thing to do.

The old lady came through with the tea. I was surprised to see a tea cosy. They must be from Britain originally, I thought, despite those Aussie accents.

'How long is it, love?' asked the old man. 'The girl's asking how long we've been here.'

'Oh now ...' She put down the tray, while the husband cleared stuff away and laid out the cups and saucers. 'Madge passed away in 1975 in the April and we moved here in the November. Fourteen years, next year will be fifteen.'

'Yes, next year will be fifteen years,' added the husband.

'My name's Kerry.' I decided not to shake hands as it was too formal and salesman-like for old people.

'Well, Kerry ...'

'That's a nice name, isn't it?' said the lady, pouring with a shaky hand that broke my heart.

'I don't think I've heard that name before,' said the old man, taking over the pouring.

'It's not really my real name.'

They chuckled again, as they did with almost everything I said.

'Do you take milk and sugar, Kerry?' asked the lady.

'Just milk, thanks.'

The old man said, 'I'm Norman and this is my wife Barbara.'

'Hello again.' This time we all chuckled.

They offered me a plate of Garibaldi biscuits, which prompted me to ask them about the photos everywhere of a man in uniform.

'That's our son, Tom. He was in the army but he's retired

now,' said Barbara, picking up a picture. I took a Garibaldi and put it on a side plate. Tom looked handsome, and was pictured with a woman and two children. 'And those are our grandchildren, Thomas and Norman.'

'There's your glasses, love.' The old man passed his wife a case.

'Thanks, love.' She looked closer at the picture. 'That was taken the Christmas before Tom left the army, that's at Kirundi RSL.'

They passed it to me. I politely held it for a time I thought to be appropriate and smiled before I handed it back to Norman.

'He's very dashing, isn't he?'

'He gets his good looks from his father,' said Barbara.

'What's an RSL?' I asked.

'Royal Servicemen's League,' said Norman.

'It's for men and women who served in the armed forces in Australia. It was set up after the war, wasn't it, Norman?'

'Yeah, that's right, just after the war, and you become a member if you were, or are in the forces, and your family and friends can go there as guests.'

'Yes, but you have to sign them in, Norman.'

'Yes, you sign them in. They limit the numbers, but you can sign people in.'

'What's it for? Is it like a British Legion kind of thing?'

'Yes, of sorts.'

'And sometimes they use it for other things, social events. We had a bingo night at our local one recently, Norman, didn't we?'

'We did, and they do discos for the younger ones like you as well. We didn't go to that,' joked Norman. We all laughed.

They explained that their son Tom had moved to New Zealand and that they only see him and their grandchildren at Christmas and in the summer holidays from school. They missed seeing them terribly as they used to be nearby and would visit them most Sundays.

They told me about how they met during the war. Norman was originally a Londoner who worked as a postman, but was later sent to Devon, and it was there he met Barbara, who was working as a housekeeper. They came to Australia on the 'ten-pound package'.

'Yep, we're ten-pound poms,' said Norman.

'And proud of it,' added Barbara.

They told me that at first they were sent to Elizabeth, a place in South Australia, where all the English newcomers went. It was named Elizabeth after the queen. As I talked to them, I realised how Australia provided the perfect escape for so many people from back home, and the chance to start life over again. I was beginning to understand how easy it must be to take up and leave for a place that is vast enough to allow a person to hide from everyone they knew and the secrets that may haunt them back home.

Barbara made a fresh pot of tea. I looked at my grand-mother's watch. I'd been there an hour and I couldn't go on devoting so much time to one house each time I went out, unless I sold three per house each time, which was asking far too much. I made my peace with the situation by telling myself I could put the time spent here down to my own personal research for information, down to the real reason that had brought me here.

But now it was time to go. I thanked them both for being so kind and offered to take the cups through to the kitchen.

'Don't be silly, we need something to do when you've gone.' One more chuckle all round.

'Now then, love, what was it that you were selling?' said Barbara, looking over at my folder.

'Yes, come on then. We'd better take one,' said Norman.

'What? No, really, you don't have to.' I couldn't believe what I was hearing.

'Come on, let's have a look, we'd better have one,' he said, putting on his glasses.

'You don't have to, really. I didn't stay because of that, and I really liked talking to you both, honestly, that's all.'

'Don't be daft, you've got to earn a living, don't you?' insisted Norman.

'Well, yes. But you're different. Thank you but it's OK, really.'

'At least let us look.' Barbara laughed again.

I reluctantly went over to my folder and began getting the paintings out, deciding not to bother with the abstract ones. I laid them around the room. They both surveyed them, the same painting at the same time. I watched them both, doing everything together. I wanted to rush out and phone my grandfather but I couldn't really afford it, and besides, there was a time difference problem, made even worse by the ridiculous regulations at the home restricting you to calling during office hours only.

I began to talk about them, but on the second one I stopped and let Norman and Barbara pick what they liked.

'We've already got that one, haven't we, Barbara?'

'What?' I said, panicking.

Barbara looked closely at the boats. 'Yes, we have, yes. Haven't even put it up yet, have we?'

'No. I keep meaning to, though,' said Norman, leaving the room.

'Sorry, how come you have this picture? I mean, there could be one similar but it can't be the same.' I was embarrassed but Norman and Barbara didn't seem to find the situation odd or awkward or dubious.

Norman came back in the room with a picture under his arm.

'Is this it?' he asked, turning it round to reveal another Peter Stuger identical to mine, except dry. At that point I realised that there was no need to express shock or disbelief, no further need to bullshit and lie, for Norman and Barbara simply didn't care.

'Go on, you pick one for us,' said Barbara.

I started to feel that there was little chance of me leaving now without selling them a painting, as they were so insistent and it seemed to make them genuinely happy to do so. Perhaps Norman and Barbara enjoyed my company as much as I did theirs and this was just their way of showing it. Maybe they missed visitors, and they see helping me make some money a fair exchange for a chance to be visited and talked to. I felt less bad as I processed these thoughts and came to the conclusion that all three of us got something out of this, so I agreed to sell to them.

'No, you tell me what you would like, but honestly you don't have to.'

'I like the one of the fields, that's pretty.' Barbara pointed.

'Right then, how much do we owe you?' asked Norman, taking off his glasses.

'Erm, they sell for seventy dollars each.'

'OK, just a moment, love.' Norman left again, taking the Stuger with him.

I stood in silence, mesmerised by the proceedings. Barbara smiled and cocked her head to one side.

Norman returned with an old wooden cigar box, counting some dollars from it.

'Let me see now, that's it ... forty, there's fifty ... that's sixty, and what did you say, eighty?'

'No, seventy.'

'Do I have a ten there? Yes I do, here you go, love.'

'Are you sure, Norman?'

'Course we are, aren't we, love?' He turned to his wife.

'Yes, don't be silly now, we are very comfortable. Don't worry about us, and it's been lovely meeting you, dear.'

I took the money and packed away the rest of the paintings. Norman and Barbara showed me to the door. I thought about making polite conversation on the way about them managing to hang that one on the wall and not leave it in a cupboard like the first one, but there was no point, it would only spoil the honesty of the situation. They knew the score; they knew what I had to do.

I stood on the step on the front porch.

'Well, all the best, love,' said Norman, touching my shoulder.

'Yes, we hope everything works out for you, love,' Barbara said, holding onto Norman's arm.

'Can I just ask you something?' There was something I was really curious about.

'Course, love.'

'Who sold you that other painting, and can you remember how long ago it was?'

'Oh now, let me see.' Norman and Barbara looked at each other, trying to think back.

'It was a young girl, Norman, wasn't it?'

'Yes, she was young, about your age I should imagine. I can't remember where she was from now.'

'Was it not Holland or something like that?'

'Yes, it might have been Holland. Oh now, when was it?'

'Must have been a year ago now.'

'Yes, around that time.'

'You don't remember her name, do you?' I asked.

'Oh dear, I'm afraid that's asking a bit too much of us these days.' They chuckled again.

'Not to worry, I thought I might know her, that's all.' We all chuckled one more time before I thanked them and left. I promised myself that I would buy a phone card by the end of the week, call the nursing home and check how my grandfather was.

CHAPTER FIVE

'Get in, we're moving,' said Scotty, gesturing to the back seat of the Holden with his thumb. I was surveying a house a couple of doors down from Norman and Barbara when they pulled up. Jim was in the driver's seat with a map spread out over the steering wheel.

'What's the problem?' I asked, hauling my folder into the boot.

'Fuck's sake, Scotty, this is really slack,' Jim said, still examining the map.

'Just move out the area, mate, then we'll sort it out. Just hit some carpet for now.' Scotty was serious for once, biting his nails and spitting pieces out of the window. The Danish were in the back seat talking manically to one another in their own language. They were excited, punctuating their dialogue with gasps and screeches.

Jim passed the map to Scotty and put his foot down.

'What the fuck's wrong?' I was forced to talk to the Danish.

'Oh my God,' said the lighter-shade-of-blonde one. 'You have no idea, Kerry, it was sooo funny but scary, you know?'

'What?'

'I was in a house and I brought out my folder to show the people the paintings and when I turned round one of the pictures the lady said, "Hey, wait a minute, I have this picture!"' The other Danish laughed and shrieked at this point.

'Then what?'

'Then she goes into another room and brings out the same one, the Blue Mountains, and shows it to me.' We all laughed.

'What did you say then?'

'I said, "Yeah of course," and I thought, oh my God, what am I saying yeah of course for?' We all laughed again.

'Then I say, "Well, you know, the Blue Mountains are a very popular attraction and they are painted by many different artists."'

I could see Jim shaking his head as he drove, his shoulders moving with laughter.

'And I am thinking, yeah, well done, Karin, you got yourself out of that one all right.' Both the Danish were in hysterics. 'Then she says, "Oh yeah, they paint the Blue Mountains a lot, do they?" Then she brings in another picture and turns to me and says, "So how do you explain this, do they all paint the same boats as well?"'

'She's only got two fucking pieces already, eh, mate,' said Scotty, with his feet back on the dash.

'Oh fuck, what did you say?' I said.

'Well, I am looking at her and smiling, you can imagine.'

'I can.'

'I look at her and I say, "Yes, the boats are also very popular, I mean."' We all laughed.

Scotty beat the car roof with his hand. 'The boats are also very popular, very fucking true, very fucking true,' he laughed.

'So how did you get out of the house?'

'I just had to say that there was no point in showing her the rest because she had probably already seen it.'

'You said that?'

'Hey, after we were both standing there with the same two paintings, there was no point in any bullshit, you know?'

'Well, that makes two of us,' I said.

'You're having a laugh?' said Jim, who'd only just composed himself.

'Nope, mine had one already as well, but it wasn't a big deal because they were very relaxed about it, as though they knew how it all worked. They seemed happy to buy another one from me, in exchange for a bit of company, I suppose.'

'Yep, the olds are good once they let you in, once they trust you, they just like to chat away.'

I hated Scotty saying 'olds' and was on the verge of asking

him to be more respectful, when Jim started some half-pint philosophising.

'Listen, the trouble with Australians in general is they are too bloody trusting for their own good, don't you think? I mean, there's no way you could get away with this back home, they'd be out chasing you down the bloody street. Everything's so bloody new and OK here. They're not pissed off and cynical enough yet, so they get ripped off.'

'Hey, I asked mine if they knew who sold them the other painting and when, and they thought she was Dutch, maybe,' I said, hoping to help with the mystery.

Scotty slapped his hand repeatedly on his forehead, and then looked at Jim. 'Dutch, my arse, bloody German more like, and probably called Anaya!' he said, in an entertaining fashion for all our benefit.

'Guys, guys, I'm innocent!' said Anaya, joking around and holding her hands up. She was sitting on a bar stool in the Honest Irishman back in the city, smoking.

'Like hell you are, you crafty little minx.' Scotty had it bad for Anaya, and I suspected that it had been that way for a long time.

'It was a bit of a wasted trip, Anaya,' said Jim, trying to make the tone more serious.

'Listen, guys, mistakes happen. Anaya was supervising that area a year ago maybe, and she should have remembered.' Greg glanced over at her and she shrugged. 'Sometimes the logbook doesn't get filled in for whatever reason, and when it doesn't, it's bad, I know. Shit happens, you guys, really sorry,' he said. 'Won't happen again. Now let me make it up to you and buy you all a beer.'

'Not for me, thanks,' said Jim. 'I'm going to hit the sack. Got some letters to write.' He stretched and rolled his head round. 'No bloody waking me up, you lot, OK?' he said jokily to me and the Danes, and then left looking worn out.

'Sorry, guys, I really fucked up with the area, yeah,' said Anaya, swinging her legs around on her stool and catching my eye every so often.

'So how long were you supervisor, Anaya?' I asked, just wanting to say something to her but not knowing what. Greg began talking to Scotty and the Danish, leaving Anaya and me to ourselves.

'Why? You after the job, Kerry?'

'Might be. We'll see. Only just got here.'

'You have to sell a few more first.' She stared right at me, blowing out smoke and picking her little finger with her thumbnail.

I reapplied my lipstick to cover up my unease, thinking that it would be easier to talk to her when I was drunk. I was apprehensive about being around her and the others too much in the daytime, now that I had moved into the ART house. I had problems with the day in general, much preferring to be alone until the evening, that brought with it music and drink to ease my discomfort. I had left Glebe that afternoon, packing up the few items I had with me into my rucksack and heading downtown to the flat in William Street. Greg had offered me the smallest room, next to Jim's; it was barely big enough for the single bed and small chest of drawers, but it was fine, especially as I didn't know if I'd be stopping long, and cheap. He and Anaya had the room next to the office, in the basement directly underneath me. The Danish were in a room with a pair of single beds, two rooms down to my left, next to the bathroom. There were two other spare rooms with two bunk beds each. Scotty lived at home with his mother in another suburb. So for now it was just the six of us, and I wanted it to stay that way.

'So, you settling in OK, Kerry?' Anaya asked, with her head tilted to one side. I was very good at reading other people's gestures, and from where I was sitting Anaya's was very obvious. She liked me. And the overuse of my name was also a dead giveaway.

'Yeah, it's fine, thanks, it's good.' The Danish, Greg and Scotty faded into the background for now. 'How long you lived there, Anaya?' I thought I'd start to use her name more; my drink was kicking in slightly and loosening me up.

'Mmm, let me see, about maybe a year.' She put out her cigarette, while still holding my gaze. I looked for signs of anything I could interpret in everything she did.

'Not long then, uh?'

'No, not long.' She laughed a little, confusing me as to what amused her. Perhaps she was laughing at my dumb questions, which would get better and longer the more I drank.

'Well, I hope you will like it with us.' She smiled warmly for once. 'I'm sure we will all have some real fun.' She finished off her drink and checked the time on her watch. I looked down into my glass, giggling slightly at her use of the word 'fun' in her drawn-out, flat Germanic accent.

'Would you like another drink, Anaya?' I hoped she would stay and see me looser and more entertaining, but she declined and left, saying very little except a goodnight to us all with an open-hand circular gesture, to which I stupidly did the same back. After I watched her leave, I thought about walking back to the flat with her, but decided against it this time. After all, there there would be plenty of other nights, and besides, I didn't want to go to bed yet.

The old guy playing pool, who'd bought Jim and me a drink the first night I came here, caught my eye again. He was chalking a cue when he winked at me; I winked back, which made him laugh. He took his dollar off the edge of the table and gestured for me to join him. I went over and picked up the other cue.

'All right?' I asked.

'Yeah, kiddo, all right. Drink?'

'Go on, then.'

He clicked his fingers at the barmaid who opened two bottles of VB, a local lager I was starting to enjoy. He didn't pay – which meant he kept a tab, which meant he drank there all the time, which I liked. He set up the balls in the triangle, spinning the black before breaking. We kept silent for a while. His hair was greying and he had a moustache. He was clean in his appearance and I would have put him in his mid-fifties.

'So,' he said, after potting a stripe.

'So looks like I'm on coloureds, then?'

He smiled. He liked me. He was attractive for an older man, in a Sean Connery in *The Man Who Would Be King* way. Just below the neckline of his T-shirt I could see the top of a tattoo.

'So you with the art company lot, then, are you?' He smoked constantly and spoke through squinting eyes from the cigarette smoke permanently coming out of his mouth. It was hard to make out his accent at first. It was all mixed up, transatlantic, maybe Canadian or Anglo-American, but as I heard more, I figured he was originally Scottish.

'My name's Kerry, and yeah, I've started selling for them.'

'Have you now?' He was playing around with me, and I knew enough to know that most of what he found amusing was down to his evident drunkenness. 'Offloading Greg's works of art on the endearing Australian public, are you?'

'Yip. What's your name?'

'Mac.'

I put my hand out to shake his. He stubbed out his cigarette before shaking mine, making me wait with mine outstretched.

'Mac. You Scottish, then? I'm working with a guy called Scotty.'

'Well, I was certainly born there, but that's going back a bit.'

'What part?'

'Dundee. Why? Think we might know the same people, do you?' He laughed unnecessarily again.

'No, I'm from Edinburgh. Only been here and there.'

'This is some journey here, is it not? Doing the backpacking bit, are you?'

I could hear much more of his Scottishness now. 'Not exactly. I'm on a young person's work visa because I'm under twenty-five, so I wanted to make the most of that while I could.' I'd almost finished my beer and shook the bottle to ask him if he wanted another.

'Val will get us another.' He finished his beer. 'Val!' He clicked again. The barmaid turned round, rolled her eyes and brought us a refill. I had potted two, he was on his last ball; Mac had put aside some serious pool practice in his time. With another cigarette in his mouth, he slammed the ball off the top end of the table and doubled it back to knock it into the bottom left-hand corner pocket, just where I was leaning.

'Oh yes, got to make the most of things, very important,' he drawled.

'So what do you do then, Mac?'

'I play pool a lot.'

'What, professionally?'

'No, not professionally, for fuck's sake. Among other things.'

'Such as?'

'I have a job.' He set up another game, intermittently looking me up and down. I felt good; I was getting a tan and my legs looked good in my denim skirt.

'Well, what do you do?' I persisted.

He stopped before he hit the ball and looked up at me; he made me wait for everything. 'Well, I'm a sports journalist for the *Sydney Morning Herald*.'

'You don't strike me as very sporty.' Now it was my turn to laugh.

'I cover the horses, the track. Have you ever been to Harold Park?'

'No.'

'Well, maybe I'll take you one time.'

'What, if I'm good?' I felt like playing around with him now that my beer was kicking in.

'That's right, if you're good.'

'And what if I'm bad?'

He was leaning over the table; he dropped his head onto it and laid it there for a moment. Then he looked up and belted another ball, which slammed off the end of the table and bounced up in the air, landing on the floor, causing the barmaid to shout over, 'Mac. I'm warning you!'

'Well, answer my question. What if I'm bad?'

'Then you'll be sent to Dundee, and I wouldn't wish that on anyone.' He took a packet out of his pocket and lit up his last cigarette.

'I'll have one, thanks.' I said, putting out my hand. He slammed some coins onto the table; Val threw him a new packet from behind the bar.

'Tired of pool,' he said, drawing up two barstools. I joined him, lighting up the cigarette he gave me. I looked over at the others and waved to them. Scotty waved back.

'Is that your boyfriend?' Mac sniggered.

'No, it is fucking not!' I was embarrassed, quickly turning the questioning back towards him. 'Where do you live?'

He pointed to the ceiling.

'Here?'

'Yep, upstairs.'

'Why do you live here?'

'What do you mean, why do I live here? Because it has everything I need, and I don't have to go far to get here, do I?' He tapped the bar. I liked him; I didn't know why because he wasn't exactly friendly. I knew he was dangerous and slightly attractive, if beat-up looking around his face now that I examined him closely. I also knew that his difficult and evasive manner was down to years of boozing and being alone.

'Are you married?' A predictable question, I thought, just as I'd asked it.

'What do you think?'

'I think you were and now you're divorced, and you spent so much time in this bar during your marriage that after you left it, you thought you may as well move in. Am I right?'

'What are you, a fuckin' detective?'

'I love the idea of being a detective. Can I see your room? If you showed me it, I could tell you things about yourself by looking around at the things you own. I'm good at that.'

'You won't tell me anything I don't know already, and I don't have much stuff.'

'I could still tell you things.'

'OK, one time I'll show, but it'll be a warning to you.'

'What?'

He didn't answer. He just looked at me again for long enough to make me feel uncomfortable. I decided that then would be a good time to show off my trick. I jumped down from my seat and went to the pool table. I put my hands on the end of it, gripping the edge, and leant forward taking my weight on my arms and chest, and lifted my legs slowly up until my body was perfectly horizontal.

'Look!' I shouted, getting the attention of almost everyone at the bar.

'Very impressive,' said Mac sarcastically.

'I'm strong, you know?' I said, pleased with myself.

'I don't doubt it,' he said.

I lowered myself back down, winked at him and headed to the toilets. I felt buzzy and warm and fairly happy. I was carving out a life in Sydney, having only landed a few weeks before, and felt pretty pleased with myself. I had a way of making cash with no need for an alarm clock (one of my main aims in life) and some people to drink with, plus my interest in Anaya to keep me from getting bored. I could perhaps settle in Sydney, making trips away every once in a while to continue with my investigation. Who knows, maybe I'd stay for ever. I could marry someone and get a passport. Fate had led me here and it would all take shape eventually. I felt confident and relaxed about my journey, untouchable, unreachable and numbed by the drink.

I sat on the toilet wondering about things, and whether I wanted to have sex with Mac or not, and what he was to me. I had only just met him, but had those feelings I'd had before with various others, of accelerated intimacy despite very little conversation or time together. I had been close to an older man in the past; he was a newsagent I had worked for as a teenager. At the time he'd acted as a bit of everything for me, particularly when my useless father was absent from our lives. But it hadn't lasted long.

Was I going to have sex with Mac? I wondered. I wasn't sure but thought it was inevitable at one point. Then I thought about the group and put them in order of shagability. That fucking annoying Anaya would be up the top for some reason that I couldn't work out, and Scotty down the bottom. I put Jim in second place, but knew I felt something different for him than the others. I flushed and left the cubicle.

Tonight I wanted to get absolutely bladdered. I wished Anaya had stayed and drank with me. Perhaps I could have told her why I was here, though why she would possibly be interested, I had no idea. But I just felt warmth for everyone when I had a drink in me. Warmth and hope. It was, after all, hope that I'd find the answers that I was looking for that kept me going. If I thought about it too much, I would sink down, and I didn't want that. I was in a world full of strangers, so I would take what I could get, and right now I wanted to get shit-faced with someone interesting and willing. Money was tight, but it had never stopped me before.

I saw a Tampax machine on the wall. I opened the door to the toilets and checked that no one was coming. I had to be quick. I was breaking one of my rules: don't shit on your own doorstep. If this was going to be my local, then this was going to have to be the one and only time I do this here. The coast was clear, so I got underneath the machine, then pushed it upwards with my shoulder until it came off its hinges. I carried it into the cubicle and locked the door. I put the toilet seat down, resting the machine on top. This had to be done quickly in case Val were to come in and notice it missing from the wall. I turned it over and placed my two middle fingers into the plastic drawer at the bottom where the money rested in and nudged it upwards. I shook the machine until dollar coins spilled out into my hand and onto the floor, coughing to cover up any scattering noise, then, when it was as empty as I could possibly make it, I stood it up on the toilet as I scrabbled about on the floor picking up the change.

I put the money in my pocket and took the machine out of the cubicle with me, wedging my foot against the outside door as I hooked it back on the wall. It had been a while since I had done a machine and had vowed to give it up in Sydney, but fuck it, tonight was one of those nights.

I went back out to the bar where Mac was chatting to Val. She left when I approached him.

'Fancy a whisky, Mac? My round.'

'Rum, thanks. I don't fuckin' drink whisky.'

'Suit yourself.' I leant one foot on the bar stool and counted up my money: I'd got nineteen dollars from the machine. That would be about seven pounds at home. The Australians have slightly less in their Tampax machines than the Scots, I thought, as I clicked my fingers to get Val's attention.

CHAPTER SIX

Mac hailed a cab on the corner of William Street.

'Where you taking me?' I was excited and giddy, hanging onto his arm; the street and traffic a soft blur.

'To a decent fucking bar in the Cross.'

The cab driver played Indian music.

'Turn it up!' I shouted.

King's Cross was dirty and full of junkies sitting in doorways. Mac stopped at a newsagent to buy some cigarettes. The man behind the till served people while threatening someone on the phone and he had a baseball bat beside him. I didn't care, I liked everything. The night was full of possibilities. I felt in love with Mac, and sure we would be partners of some kind or another. We walked along King's Cross Road into Earl Street. There were junkie trannies everywhere, and teams of lads coming and going in and out of strip joints. Mac walked ahead of me, saying hello to people every so often.

I hadn't been to the Cross district before. At first, when I was in Annandale with the electrician from the plane, I ventured down to Bondi for an occasional swim. Since my brief stay in Glebe, I'd moved straight to Woolloomooloo to the company flat and I hadn't been on any tourist jaunts. I would take in all the sights eventually but I wasn't in a hurry, and I wasn't here as a tourist.

We took a left off Earl Street into a small opening. Blondie's 'Atomic' blasted from a bar called the Star. We went in. A woman with very short hair and a painted-on moustache was taking money at the door. She waved Mac and me in and we headed straight for the bar.

'OH MAN, THIS IS GREAT. I FUCKING LOVE THIS MUSIC!' I shouted after Mac, who was making his way through the crowd. The bar was tiny. On the counter, in the corner, a dog slept on a blanket. Mac nodded at a man with pure white long hair and a dramatic black hat; he waved back then spoke to the barman. We positioned ourselves at the end of the bar. Mac hadn't spoken to me for ages. Two beers were sent across to us from the white-haired man via the barman, and Mac toasted him, and he toasted back. The bar was full of an assortment of characters, no particular types, but there was a distinct absence of regular Aussie-guy types in shorts and baseball hats. There were fewer women than men, and few people, if any, around my age group.

'WHAT'S THE SCORE HERE, THEN?' I asked Mac, getting slightly frustrated at his lack of communication.

'There is no fucking score, for fuck's sake. Why do you have to ask so many questions?'

'Because I'm younger than you.'

Mac shook his head and downed his beer; he was getting really drunk by now and his eyes were narrowing. I didn't know how long Mac had been smoking at the rate he was tonight, but I was amazed that he was still alive. I had already noticed the way he shuffled along the street, an indication that the cigarettes were affecting his circulation.

The music had switched to early Beatles; it was so loud there was no point in trying to talk any more.

A man with no top on leant over me at the bar and gestured to the barman to kill the music. His armpit stank and was directly over my head. The music faded slightly.

'Mr Wilson,' said Mac, cigarette in hand, thumb resting behind his front teeth.

'Mr Mac,' said the topless man.

'Excuse me,' I said, sick of armpit.

'I'm afraid you can't be excused, you'll have to stay until you've made a complete arse of yourself,' said the Wilson character in an extremely upper-class English voice.

'Shouldn't be a problem,' I said back.

'Excellent stuff, highly amusing.' He winked and turned his attention back towards the bar.

'Who's he?' I said to Mac.

'He's all right,' Mac said back. He'd enjoyed my exchange with his friend.

The Wilson man moved away from the bar back through the crowd, carrying two schooners of lager that were spilling all over the place. I turned round to watch him, which was difficult because in the short time since we'd arrived there, the place was packing out even more. I realised I could see his bare arse jostle through the crowd. He was completely naked except for a pair of Blundstone boots which I'd noticed on almost every Australian man I'd seen.

'Who the fuck is he and what is he doing?' I asked Mac. He laughed and laughed, which went into a cackle then some kind of serious bronchial episode. I banged him on the back.

'He runs the club,' Mac said, spluttering. 'Oh fuck, that's funny.'

'It's not that funny. Jesus, you're going to have a fucking heart attack.' Mac was just laughing at anything now, he'd lost it. 'What club?'

'This one.'

'What one? This is a club?'

Just then I heard a PA cranking up and a microphone being tested. Mac nudged his head towards the back of the room. I turned round to see Wilson standing on a chair in a tiny carved-out DJ pulpit area. The Beatles stopped.

'Good evening, ladies and gentlemen. Firstly, I'd like to point out that you're all a bunch of cunts who deserve none of this.' The crowd cheered and various people shouted for him to fuck off. 'Secondly, I'd like to welcome you to The Naked Drinking Club, and I'd like to add that if you're not naked now, then you fucking will be.' The crowd went mental again. 'If this is your first time here, then you've only got yourself to blame. Now then, I'd like to point out that we have provided a paddling pool to my left here on the dance floor, should you require it for vomiting purposes. Right then, let's kick off with some of your very own shite. You should be so fucking lucky.'

Kylie Minogue's 'I Should Be So Lucky' piped out and was appreciated with irony by most of the crowd who started dancing. Wilson, a big public-school type, towered over everyone, and jokingly pushed others out of his way in order to maximise the dance floor for his own ludicrous dancing, which nobody seemed to mind.

I loved this place. I loved the atmosphere. Nobody cared about how anyone behaved, it was friendly and perfect, and had none of the pretensions that had put me off going to clubs before. I felt into my pocket and examined my change.

'Let's get some tequila slammers,' I said to Mac, getting close to him. I could have kissed him but I didn't. I wasn't sure yet how I felt about him, and I wanted to jump up and down with the music. Mac just watched me in that way I was growing used to. Either he was very interesting or just a boring old fucked-up drunk, but he'd brought me here and I loved it.

'Mmm. Shall we?'

'Your call.'

'Yee-es.'

I ordered a couple of tequilas from the white-haired man who was helping out behind the bar; he poured and Mac and I slammed. I went to the dance floor and started dancing near Wilson, who seemed to have an assistant of sorts. The woman, with the short hair and painted-on moustache from the door, had joined him in nudity and similar carefree dancing. Wilson grabbed me.

'I'm sorry but you're going to have to strip,' he said, getting into the next song, which was an old Suzy Quatro/Chris Norman duet I hadn't heard in ages. Wilson knew all the lyrics, which he sang along to as he attempted to remove my top.

I looked over at Mac, who was engrossed in conversation with the white-haired man.

I took off my T-shirt and bra and swung them around a bit, thinking nothing of it.

'Good tits,' said Wilson.

'Thanks. Good cock,' I said, pointing at it.

Lots more people were naked by now and nobody seemed to bat an eyelid, we were all much more concerned with dancing away to the music. 'Come Up And See Me, Make Me

Smile' caused a surge of enthusiasm from the crowd. I took off my skirt, and danced around in my underwear for a while, before removing everything and throwing my pants at Mac. Mac just picked them up and carried on talking to the man. It felt very easy to remove my clothes, and I loved the feeling of no boundaries, of limitless debauchery.

I danced between Wilson and the moustached woman who rubbed her tits in my face every now and then. We danced however we wanted, with no emphasis on trying to look good whatsoever. It was just about moving around in whatever way we felt like. The moustached woman brought out a bottle of poppers and offered it to me, just as the music changed to Black Sabbath's 'Ace Of Spades'. Wilson ran over to the DJ box, grabbed a crash helmet and put it on. I hadn't had poppers for a while and they made my head rush to what felt like the point of bursting, as Wilson ran head first, repeatedly, at the back wall. I looked into the sea of naked, drunken and vastly different bodies that surrounded me and felt fantastic.

I danced for about an hour with beer breaks every so often. I went to the toilet at one point and took some coke in a cubicle with two naked men, with whom I had bad kissing, and a goth girl. When I came out of the toilet, Mac was gone. I found the white-haired man, who was topless, and asked him if he knew where Mac was.

'He's gone to play in a poker game, he won't be back now.'

'Where's my clothes?' I slurred. I felt sudden, intense concern for my clothes.

'Steve's got them.' He pointed to the barman who gave me the thumbs-up.

Mac must have given my clothes to Steve to look after and told Whitey to look out for me, I thought with drunken logic. That means he must care for me. I've only just spoken to him today yet I feel I've known him for a long time. What does that mean? And was the poker game just an excuse? Did he leave because I was so off my head and naked? What does my nudity mean to him? Is it wrong because he is protective of me? Does he get naked? Why does he come to this club? Why did he bring me? Maybe he can help me with what I'm looking for through his contacts in the *Sydney Morning Herald*. Maybe that's why our paths have crossed. Everything happens in my life for a reason. Oh, fuck it.

I stopped questioning myself for the time being, because I was in no fit state to answer. The barman poured us both tequilas. That's when I snogged him across the bar. And that's how I ended up in his bed.

The thirst woke me up first. I was dreaming I was eating watermelon. I woke up scratching my hand; I thought there were eggs planted in it. I thought an insect had laid four small jelly eggs under my skin that were about to hatch. I felt sick, and my legs felt trapped. I tried to move them but they were weighed down. Then I came to and found the weight was a pit-bull terrier lying across me at the foot of the bed. I twisted my body round; a large, muscular man slept on his side away from me. It wasn't Mac. I strained to see his face, which caused the dog to growl and the man to stir. I didn't know him at first.

On the floor was a crumpled-up Durex. I tried to make out whether it was full or not but couldn't see. I lay back down again, defeated by the dog and nausea. I needed a drink of water so badly; the Australian heat added a tricky new element to the morning after.

I had to give in; it was too hot and dry. I thought hard about where I could be. I remembered dancing naked in a bar and later being in the room I had slept in, and a barman asking me what Branston pickle was. I thought I had fucked the man next to me in a toilet, that I had sat on top of him and someone had come in, a woman with a moustache, but I couldn't be sure. I remembered being in a cab with Mac before that, then I could hear Blondie's 'Atomic' but the gaps were really big this time, bigger than usual.

I went back to sleep for a while, and when I awoke I was less drunk, and the barman had gone. I sat up in bed, my numbed head, resting on both hands which were killing me from showing Mac my pool-table balancing. I put on my clothes and left.

The street was all lively and bright and full of more couples than usual. Then I remembered it was Saturday, and we were going out selling early just after lunch. I stood at a bus stop, trying to focus on the route information on the sign. I put my hands in the back pockets of my denim skirt to find some soft folded paper. I took it out and examined it. It was three pages from the Sydney phone book, all of the name Duffy. I had two of them on the first page scored out, which made me worry that perhaps I'd called them the night before.

Back at William Street, things were fairly quiet. Only the Danish were up and about. I still felt slightly drunk when I walked in. I didn't care whether Anaya saw me like this or not. In fact, I was rather hoping I would bump into her. Maybe I would ask her to come for a drink with me or something. I wouldn't care what I said to her. I looked at the Danish eating breakfast cereal and laughed.

'Hey, Kerry.' Karin laughed back, not really understanding that I was laughing at them.

'Heeeeyyy,' I said, looking in the fridge. I bent down, putting my hands on my knees, staring in at our divided food sections. The Danish had a joint section full of fromage frais, yogurts, ham and cheese. Jim's was mostly ham, cheese, eggs, and jam and some salad. Mine was completely empty. 'I dunno …' I mumbled.

'Is that you just back, Kerry?' asked Andrea who was tying her hair back with a band, sitting beside Karin on the sofa.

'Yep. 'Fraid so.' I shut the fridge, took a glass from the draining board and filled it with water, turning round and leaning against the sink, gulping it down.

'So, party, party, yeah?' said Karin.

'Party, party,' I said in a sing-songy voice.

'Did you go off with that guy in the bar?' Karin asked, between enthusiastic mouthfuls of cereal eating.

I poured another glass of water. 'Mac?'

'Do you know him?' asked Karin.

'Kind of.' I thought about telling them everything but what would be the point? They'd only say 'cool' or something annoying like that.

'Yep, we went to a club in King's Cross, and I just crashed with someone there.' I pushed the patio doors open with my foot, and lit up a cigarette from a packet lying on the kitchen worktop.

'Cool,' she said.

'Whose are these? Do you know?' I asked, already lighting one up.

'I think they're Anaya's,' said Andrea.

'Cool,' I said, sniggering. They began speaking to each other in Danish. I sat on the step, with my back against the doorframe, half looking outside, and half looking at the Danish, sucking on the cigarette, which I regretted within seconds.

Andrea began licking stamps and putting them on post-cards. That's when it was time for me to leave. I stamped out the cigarette and retreated to my room, feeling nauseous. I was too fucked to shower, and decided to have one later. I lay down on my bed, looking at my clothes on the floor, and made plans to tidy and settle in more. I lay on my side, trying to find a position that felt better for what I had to admit was a hangover, and replayed the night before, trying to figure out what kind of sex I'd had with the barman, or what his name was. I couldn't remember much. Instead I felt envious of the Danish, and longed to be simple like them, up bright and early, making the most of the day. We were both here in Australia for very different reasons though, mine much more complex than theirs. I felt sad and panicky for a moment, but told myself that it must be the come-down and that it would pass. I took all my clothes off and got under the covers. My body smelt of the stale sweat of the barman and me. I wondered if Anaya was still asleep in the room beneath me, and felt certain that she, of all people in this mixed troupe of players, would understand my darkness. I listened for sounds of her, and drifted off.

CHAPTER SEVEN

Within a week, I quickly learned all there was to know about selling the paintings. It was so easy to read people, the ones that were likely to let you in and the ones that weren't. I learned little tricks of the trade through Greg, reporting back to him every night in The North Angel about the things I'd encountered during that evening's work.

'A good one is,' he told me, 'to make out you're thirsty, say if you could just have a glass of water, that way you stand a chance of at least getting into their hall.'

One time I had asked for a beer from an approachable-looking man who answered the door with a joint in his hand. I ended up there the entire evening, just smoking and drinking a couple of beers, and shooting the breeze about this and that. By the time Jim turned up with the others, I hadn't even opened up my folder once, and was so wasted I couldn't explain why without laughing. In the car on the way home, things were quiet and Jim was angry with me, I could tell, but he didn't know me well enough to chastise me. Instead he just said, 'Well, it's your own bloody time that you're wasting.'

That only made me laugh even more. A slack approach, I thought in hindsight, after my first week of work.

Greg also told me not to waste time on the chatty partner, for it was always the silent one that held the purse strings. It all sounded bollocks at first, but when put to the test, Greg's tips paid off every time. Even the stuff he'd said on day one that sounded ludicrous, all fell into place in various houses. I would never have believed the notion that because people are Chinese, they would buy the abstract paintings, until I encountered my first Chinese household, when they did exactly that.

'Could I please show you in there?' I had said, pointing to the clean white empty hallway behind the two men, which smelled of fresh paint and was just screaming out to be filled with my paintings. They looked at me, and then said something in their own language to one another. Neither of us could understand what the other one was saying, but within five minutes they had picked out two abstracts at one hundred bucks a piece. I was lucky, their house was new and empty and I just happened to be in the right place at the right time. Greg told me later that there was a certain amount of luck involved, but ninety-nine per cent of it was confidence. He felt I had more confidence than the others. I suppose in some ways I did.

We all got given our dollars on the same night we earned them, if we made cash transactions, but most of it slipped away on endless rounds of drinks in the bar afterwards. If customers bought more than one painting, they would always pay by cheque or bank slip – most people liked to have the safety net of a cheque, to allow them to back out. It didn't happen often, but once in the first week Andrea had a sale fall through. It was frustrating and worrying to wait for these transactions to clear, but I guess I saw them as savings to put towards my journey. I kept a notebook of money owing to me, and the paintings I'd sold. So far, I was in the lead with ten paintings in my first week. I had earned myself four hundred dollars, around two hundred pounds. With rent money knocked off, that left me with a total of three hundred and twenty dollars, or one hundred and sixty pounds.

Karin was in second place with eight sales, and then Andrea with six. Scotty made the odd sale to keep things ticking over for him, but mostly he drove and sorted out the painting stock. Jim supervised everything, and liaised with Greg over areas and routes. When it got busier Scotty would take another team out, but for now he stayed with us.

I'd made more of an effort to settle in at the flat. I bought some groceries, although most days I ate breakfast out at a café on the corner. I'd also done some laundry and tidied up my tiny room, putting up a Bruce Springsteen poster that came with Sydney's *City Limits* magazine, and a photo of my granddad in an effort to make it more homely. I bought a pack of airmail letters, and had already written two and sent them off. One to my grandfather and the other to Maggie, a friend of mine back home who was looking after my records while I was away.

The mornings and afternoons were quiet. We often ate burgers together in a greasy type café a few blocks away, before we left for work just ahead of the rush hour, heading out to the suburbs. Sometimes I would lie sunbathing in the yard out the back from lunchtime onwards, reading a paper, scribbling thoughts in my notebook, or making little sketches of the others as we lay around. The rest of the time I would lie in my room, looking up and wondering when I would do something concrete about my search, and not understanding why I didn't. The late mornings were spent watching terrible yet addictive American soaps on TV. There was a whole new world out there, but I just didn't seem to care.

Apart from the non-selling-night blip, I was being good, and had drunk very little more than the others each night. But by the following weekend I was growing restless again, as usual, and the all-too-familiar empty feeling was beginning to set in. On the Friday night, I started to drink a bit more, and made efforts to look for Mac whom I'd seen very little of since our night out together, as he'd been in Perth working. I was disappointed with his absence, as I had hoped we could hit King's Cross together again, or something similar.

Plus Anaya had been on holiday down the coast visiting people since the weekend before, and I found the company of the others limited, especially while trying to adhere to moderate drinking.

On the Friday night I was looking forward to Anaya being back, and getting paid what was owing to me. I showered after we got back from selling and put on some make-up, and a top I thought I looked good in. But neither Anaya nor Greg showed their faces in the bar, preferring instead to have dinner together somewhere in town, according to Scotty, and then have an early night. I wondered how much Greg loved Anaya, and how Anaya could possibly love Greg, before sinking too many Jack Daniel's to care.

CHAPTER **EIGHT**

I was growing tired of my introduction already and would have to find another one soon. I was having difficulty switching on my usual patter, and had forgotten to smile, due to my head vagueness and drowsiness from the JD the night before.

I was in – what I was told – a mostly Greek area, late Saturday afternoon. The houses were older than most of the ones I had visited so far, and surrounded in white fencing. A woman answered a door.

'Hi there, my name's Kerry and I'm from Scotland. I'm travelling around showing some people my artwork.'

'Yes, my husband will talk. Please.' The woman shouted a name I could not understand and a small hairy man with a newspaper appeared at the door.

'Yes, how can I help, please?'

I couldn't bear to go through it again.

'I'm showing my paintings.' They both looked blank. 'I have some artwork, can I show you?'

'Yes, please come in.' The woman said something, which I assumed was in Greek, to the husband and left the scene. While most people would consider being allowed into a home that quickly a positive sign and an almost certain sale, I was rapidly learning that that wasn't the case. For the easier it was to gain entry into a house, the harder it was to sell once there. Bizarrely, the harder it was to get in, the more likely a sale would take place. My way of reading it was that the people who kept you outside didn't trust themselves with buying stuff, while the ones who were happy to have you waste your time entertaining them for half an hour or so, were confident that they wouldn't do anything reckless once you were in there.

I arranged the paintings throughout their lounge, while the husband watched me. Ornaments in cabinets rattled from the washing machine vibrating in the kitchen. It was a hot afternoon. I asked him for a glass of water. He shouted after his wife who brought me one, smiled and left again. The man was dirty, I could tell straight away; I had a feeling about people like that, a sense. He had shorts and a vest on and bare feet, and constantly looked at my crotch. Every so often he yawned, unaware that he was expelling a gust of halitosis as he did so. He looked at my tits as I bent down to take out the last painting. He was revolting but somehow, with the hangover, I liked him looking at me. He asked me to sit down whilst he spent some time examining them. I took a chair and deliberately sat with my legs open. I was wearing cut-down Levis and a green striped T-shirt that I'd cut off at the arms.

'You like them?' I asked, with my legs still open.

'Yes, very much,' he said, glancing at the kitchen to check his wife couldn't see him.

'What do you like?' The situation was starting to turn me on, so I decided to up the play a little.

'Yes, I like, they are very beautiful.'

I rested one hand on my thigh, fanning myself with my other. 'It's hot today, isn't it?'

'Yes, hot.'

I blew my cheeks out. He sat back in his chair, his crotch growing bigger. He had a thirsty, dry mouth with nerves and kept swallowing and looking over at the kitchen. I got up, picked up a painting and stood over him, my crotch at his face level.

'Now, this one I think would look nice here.'

'Yes.' He swallowed.

'The colours would look nice in this room with the green. You see.' I moved my fingers over the hills, and bent down to give him a good look down my top.

'It's OK to touch it. It's oils, you know, but it's dry. Would you like to touch it?' I leant in, looking towards the kitchen myself, hearing the washing machine on spin. I could see the wife out the back hanging out washing. I leant further in, allowing his arm to brush against my breast. He had a full-scale hard-on by now and tried to lean forward to hide it.

'Yes, very nice,' he said over and over like a fucking robot. He was annoying me now because he was so easy. I went back over to my chair, which gave him a chance to pull his T-shirt down over his shorts and look more closely at the kitchen.

'It's OK,' I said, bringing the whole thing out in the open now.

'What do you want me to do with painting?'

I nearly snapped 'Buy it, for fuck's sake and we'll sort something out' but I just said, 'Buy one, if you like it.'

'How much?'

'One hundred and fifteen bucks.' Bucks was a little rude, and after I said it I regretted it, but in the circumstances I guessed it wouldn't make any difference; the standards had been dropped, after all. I sat back down. His chest was moving up and down as he looked at my legs and crotch, then down at his hard-on. I put my hand inside my shorts and moved it around a little. The wife came back in from the kitchen and went upstairs, and I quickly pulled my hand out while he covered his erection with the painting of the two ladies in the field. I went back over to him.

'Do you want it, then?'

'Yes, I want it, very nice.'

'Do you want that one you're holding?'

'Yes.' I took his hand, put it in my shorts and let him feel around, while touching his cock over the fabric of his shorts. He moaned and swallowed, bits of white saliva gathering in the corner of his mouth. The wife came downstairs again; we separated and went back to robotic polite chat.

'Please go to the bathroom, I will look from window,' he whispered, his eyes darting back and forward at the kitchen. He got up and showed me through to the bathroom, then spoke in a deliberately loud voice for the wife's benefit.

'Yes, you can use the bathroom. This way, please.'

I didn't know why he wanted me to go there but I did. I went inside and locked the door. I could hear him speaking with his wife. In the bathroom was a window covered half in opaque glass, in the corner was a chair. I dragged the chair over and stood on it in order to look out. I could see him hiding behind his garage wall in the garden, with a door open, which I presumed was obscuring the wife's view of him from the kitchen. He was already unzipped with his cock out, moving his hand up and down it. I lifted up my T-shirt and bra to fully display my tits to him; I leant in and pressed them against the cool glass. With my other hand, I masturbated. Nothing lasted for more than about thirty seconds for either of us. He put it back in his trousers and closed the garage door. I got down off the chair, splashed some water on my face, browsed in their wall cabinet, flushed and went back into the lounge.

He was standing there, counting his money.

'You like it?'

'Yes, very much.'

'Good,' I said, taking the money and packing away the rest of the paintings.

The wife came through and put some folded linen into a drawer. They spoke in Greek to one another.

'It's pretty, yes?' I asked her while packing up.

'That is nice. Yes,' she said, before going out again.

I felt detached and cold already, forgetting what had taken place, with my mind on a cold beer and a cigarette.

'Well, I better be going then, thank you and I hope you enjoy it.'

'Yes, enjoy very much,' he said, smiling for the first time. He walked me to the door. Just before I walked out onto his step, he gently grabbed my elbow.

'Please, I want your telephone number, to meet with you.'

'No, I don't have a number and that's just mad. Thank you and enjoy your painting.'

CHAPTER NINE

'Truth or dare!' shouted Scotty at Anaya.

We sat drinking beer in a circle on the lounge floor back at the house, which on nights like this felt more like a youth club.

'Truth,' said Anaya, smoking like a French actress.

'I'm trying to think of a really good one, hang on.' Scotty was so excited.

'Is Greg the one for you?' said a Danish.

'Oh please, that's really fuckin' girly and boring,' said Scotty, just beating me to it. Jim and I looked at each other and shook our heads.

'Have you ever got it on with a girl?' Scotty asked eagerly.

'Scotty, you're so predictable,' said Anaya.

I just shut up and watched and listened. I was enjoying it too much.

'Of course.' She looked over at me first, then inhaled. 'I'm from Germany, we're much more open-minded than you guys.'

'Cool,' said Scotty, trying not to look too pleased. Jim and I laughed out loud. We were all excitable and half cut.

'What about you guys?' He turned to the Danish, his eyebrows raised.

'Perhaps,' said Andrea.

'Oh, you'll have to come and visit to find out, won't you?' Karin said.

'Is that an offer, is it?' Scotty leant in closer to Karin. The girls both laughed.

'Fuck's sake, Scotty, you're obsessed. Leave them alone, it's not even their turn.' I grabbed the bottle and span it. It stopped at Jim. He looked embarrassed.

'I'm too old for this shit,' he said, taking the obligatory swig from the communal vodka bottle that went with the game.

'Never too old, Jim,' I said.

'Exactly!' Anaya winked at me, which was unusually playful for her. I winked back.

'Fucking dare,' he said reluctantly. Jim could tell that we were all pleased that it landed at him, which only added to his embarrassment. He was the one we knew least about, the one that was hardest to know and the one I suspected with something to hide.

'Dare you to get your dick out and put it in the vodka, mate.' Scotty was cracking up at everything he said.

'There is no way I'm doing that, Scotty boy, no way. Sorry.'

'Yeah and there's no way I'm drinking it afterwards,' added Anaya.

'It's the game, mate, if you can't stand the heat and all that.'

'I have to, on this rare occasion, say that Scotty has a point, Jim. You agreed to be in on this so you can't back down, it's morally wrong.' I spread my arms out.

'I don't have a problem with that. We wouldn't be here if any of us had morals.'

We all laughed.

'Come on, Jim, don't be such a square,' said a Danish, much to my surprise.

'Go and …' He turned to the Danish. 'Excuse my language. Go and fuck yourselves.'

'Is that a dare?' I said. The others laughed.

'I don't do dick stuff for your own little sordid amusement, Scotty. Sorry, mate, pick on someone else.' Jim grew serious again.

'Mate, the bottle picked on you, not me. It's the rules of the game.'

'I tell you what, I'll swap it for a truth. Can I do that?' Jim looked round for group consent.

'Mmm,' I said, taking control. 'We'll have to all agree, and it also depends if you are prepared to really answer truthfully, Jim. I mean, are you?'

'Kerry's right, you gotta give us something.'

I liked Anaya saying my name. She was looking very sexy: her hair was tied back and she had on a bit of lipstick. The evening felt good in the company of the group; I felt content and happy at the start of the fun ahead.

'Yes, we will accept your swap of a truth in place of a dare.' I spoke in a wise-old-judge kind of voice. 'And it has been decided that I shall provide you with the question.'

'Yes. Otherwise it will just be about sex if Scotty does it,' said Anaya. The Danish pissed themselves laughing.

Scotty pulled his baseball cap down over his face and held his hands up. 'Can I help it if I'm a sexy guy?'

'You're so fucking embarrassing, it's beyond belief,' said Jim, taking another drink from the vodka.

'OK, Jim, here's the question,' I announced.

'OK, give it to me.'

'If you had to sleep with someone here, who would it be?'

'Hey, how come she can ask about sex?' Scotty screamed, all red-faced as usual. Jim was cross-legged on the floor; he dropped his head and held the base of his skull with both hands.

'Karin,' he said.

The Danish looked pleased with herself. Jim spun the bottle; at last it landed at me. I was delighted; I would show them a thing or two. I was unafraid of any direction the game might go in.

'I love all truth and dares, go ahead.'

'I'll do this one,' Anaya said straight away. 'Mmm, truth or dare, Kerry?' She definitely fancied me. Using my name this many times was a sure sign.

'Dare, thanks, and don't waste it.' I drank my beer and lit up one of Scotty's cigarettes, looking forward to whatever lay ahead.

'OK. I dare you to kiss someone in the group, anyone you want.'

'What kind of kiss?' I was delighted with her choice.

'A proper kiss.' She sat back, leaning on her hands. Scotty clapped.

'Oh, here we bloody go,' said Jim, rolling his eyes and

taking a drink. 'Like a slow train coming down the bloody track.'

I thought about kissing him but I knew he would be too embarrassed and refuse, and that would make me feel stupid. I knew that Anaya was such an obvious choice, but felt I would be foolish to overlook the opportunity. I put down my beer and licked my lips, warming up my mouth to entertain the others. I leant in, pulled Anaya's head towards me and kissed her.

The kiss was too good for the game, and Anaya responded immediately with the same enthusiasm I had. I didn't want to be too soft and slow with the others staring, so I kissed her hard. We went on for far too long for anyone to find it amusing. I wanted the others to disappear and to be alone all night in a room with the mysterious, cool, sexy but annoying Anaya, continuing the kiss which she seemed to be enjoying as much as me.

'All right, you two, this is getting boring.' Jim intervened at last. 'I'm going to go to my room and read if this gets any worse.'

We broke apart. I avoided looking at her, so had no way of telling if she was looking at me.

'It's only a game, for Christ's sake, and a game about ridiculous behaviour,' I said, for the sake of saying anything to appear relaxed and nonchalant after the kiss, even though it had caused a surge of excitement to course through my body.

'Yeah, loosen up, Mr Crown,' Anaya croaked, then coughed to clear her voice.

'Where's Greg, Anaya?' asked Scotty, stirring the shit.

'Greg's away tonight doing some business, he'll be back Monday, and no, he wouldn't mind this if that's what you mean.' She lit up, dragged on the cigarette and tidied her hair.

I could feel my obsession growing.

'All on your own tonight, Anaya?' Scotty joked, looking over at the Danish girls to check whether they were listening or not. Jim sat quietly, watching Anaya and me. I leant over Scotty to get a new cigarette as mine was nearly out, and glanced over at Anaya. She gave me a cold intense look, her head and eyes completely still, which was enough.

'So, Scotty, who do you want to sleep with in the group apart from the— Andrea and Karin?' I'd nearly said 'the Danish'.

'I never said nothing, mate, that's your own idea.' He got really defensive and red in the face. I felt sorry for him.

'Only pulling your leg, Scott.' I tried to hug him but he pulled away.

'Anyone up for a bong, yeah?' He began compulsively flicking his lighter on and off. There was a general reaction of no interest. But he got it out all the same and we all had a turn on it.

Later Karin, the Danish who spoke more than the other, stood up.

'I know, we'll play this thing where everybody has to tell the group something about themselves that the others don't know, yeah?' She swayed, then sat down.

'OK, you go first,' said Anaya, who was more sober than the rest of us.

'OK with me. Mine is about school.' Karin paused. We all listened intently.

'Get on with it,' heckled Scotty, who was the most wasted I'd seen him.

'When I was at school, I ran the school … What is your name for it? Selling the sweets for the children at the school breaktime, in the shop, yes?' She looked down at her friend and conferred in Danish.

'Tuck shop,' shouted Jim.

'Yes, tuck shop, and I stole some money from it every week, and with it I bought myself a record when I had enough money.' She giggled to herself.

'And that's why you find yourself here today, my dear,' said Scotty. There was little reaction to her confession, but Anaya made a comment on our behalf, out of politeness: 'Naughty you.'

'OK, I go next.' Anaya straightened her shoulders back. 'OK, mine is that my father is a high court judge.'

'Fucking hell!' said Jim and I at exactly the same time.

'Does he know you do this?' I was impressed.

'He knows nothing about me, I don't tell him.' She took a drink. Scotty was too far gone to feel anything about it, but Jim and I were amazed at her declaration.

'OK, you next, Kerry.' She shifted the attention away from herself. I wasn't sure how to treat this. I could tell them any number of bad things I'd done which would outdo anyone in the room, but it might be too much, so I decided to keep it light and innocent.

'Kerry's not my real name. I changed it from something else.'

'So what's your other name?' asked Jim.

'That's my other secret.'

'I hope you haven't been in big trouble.'

'No trouble, it's to do with something else.'

Anaya blew out smoke and looked at me. She may be cold but she was getting hooked in, I thought. I was pleased with my announcement and the mystery it added to my presence in the group.

'Now, Jim, what about you? What don't we know about you?' I asked, taking over from Anaya.

'Well, I don't believe you know anything about me, do you?' he replied.

He was right; out of all of us, he was the hardest to fathom. He was moody and often silent, but when he was interacting, he was engaging and genuine. He'd also landed the super-visor's job early on, which meant he was trustworthy and reliable, but I knew enough by the age of twenty-four to tell when a person was carrying something big inside them. I knew, because I was too.

'Tell us something, Jim, come on,' I pleaded.

'Yeah, go on, mate,' said Scotty, with slits for eyes.

Anaya and I had another quick look at each other.

Jim sighed. 'All right. I used to be a woman.' He burst into fits of laughter, the Danish roared, and Anaya and I joined in half-heartedly, still looking at one another.

'Tell us something we didn't know, mate.'

The Danish laughed even more, perking Scotty up with their reaction to his remark. He shouted, 'Tell us about the bloody enormous big scar on your side. What the fuck is that?'

Everybody went quiet.

'It's not a big scar, Scotty, calm down, love,' answered Jim calmly.

'I might be pissed off me nuts, mate, but I know scars and that is a fucking big knife wound, isn't it, eh, big boy?'

The rest of us were still, unsure of what to do and feeling the tension from Jim's awkwardness.

'It was an accident, a stupid accident. That's it. There's no bloody great story, ye daft Aussie twat.' Jim took a drink, his eyes never leaving Scotty for a second. Scotty lunged forward at Jim and tried to pull up his T-shirt.

'Right here.' He winced as Jim grabbed his wrist and held it tight, leaving Scotty unable to move. Scotty was completely oblivious to Jim's anger; he just laughed and crumpled on the floor.

'All right, Scotty, that's enough,' said Anaya, reining him in.

'What's your secret, Scotty, uh?' I said, trying to steer the attention away from Jim.

'Oh fuck, there's so many.' His words were muffled as the right-hand side of his face was pressed into the floor. 'OK, I killed a dog last week in my car.'

'NOOO!' cried the Danish as one.

'Aw, Scotty, mate.'

'I know, it was shit, but what could I do? It was the bloody dog or me.'

'In the Holden?' asked Anaya.

'Yeah, the bloody Holden. I cleaned it all off though, poor little thing. Sorry, ladies. Really sorry.' Unbelievably, Scotty lit another bong and gurgled away.

'OK, that just leaves you, Andrea.' Anaya smoked in the direction of the Danish.

Andrea had drank steadily all night but had said very little, if anything at all. I couldn't remember anything she had said since I met her.

'Well, mine is also about a dog. When I was sixteen, I let my boyfriend's dog, Bengy, lick me.' It was a mixture of the fact that it was Andrea who said it, and that she was obviously thinking about it during Scotty's confession, and the fact that she named the dog, and the fact it was named Bengy, that caused us all, Jim included, to hit the floor and laugh solidly for what felt like an hour.

The nurse annoyed me with her tense, nasally Scottish accent. I tried sounding sober but could hear myself slurring.

'What time is it there?'

'You've already asked me that, Mrs Swaine.'

'Miss!'

'You've already asked me. It's two o'clock in the afternoon.'

'All right, OK. I just want to speak to my grandfather, that's all.'

'I'm afraid we can't, it's not possible. There isn't a phone in his room and we don't have the staff or the facilities—'

'How is my grandfather, for fuck's sake?'

'I'm sorry but I'm going to have to terminate the call. I can't tolerate swearing. If you'd like to call back another time – meantime I'll pass on your regards.'

'No, wait!'

'You're shouting, Miss Swaine.'

'K-e-r-r-y. It's not my real name. I need you to do one thing, please, I promise, just one thing for me. I'm in Australia, I'm miles away and I don't have a phone. It's my birthday, that's why I'm drunk.' I thought the conversation needed a socially acceptable reason for my behaviour.

'What can I do, Miss Swaine?'

'Tell my granddad I'm thinking about him, that I love him. OK?'

'I will do. Now, if you'll excuse me.'

'One more thing.'

'I'm afraid I'm putting down the phone now, Miss Swaine. If you'd like to call back another time.'

'Please. PLEASE tune the fucking radio right, will you?' The line went dead. I replaced the receiver, and went back inside the flat, creeping around so as to not wake the others.

CHAPTER TEN

It was warm despite the downpour. Neutral Bay smelled clean and good with a coastal breeze blowing in over the houses of Montpelier Street. The rain had made me melancholy; I was thinking about the past and my constant need to search for answers as to why I felt the way I did: lost, drifting and drinking far too much.

Nobody wanted to see paintings when it was raining. No one wanted some stranger dripping wet in their hall. Plus it was Sunday, and Sundays were probably the same all over the world. People wanted to be left alone to read the papers and go for walks in looser clothing than usual, or have dinner with their family. All my life, I had hated Sundays; they seemed to intensify all my feelings of loneliness and fear.

I stood sheltering in a phone booth with my folder. I was wearing a cagoule that I'd found back at the base left by a past seller, but my hair was dripping wet. I lit up a Benson & Hedges Light. I wasn't up for this today, and felt weary. Perhaps I would stay in the phone booth and accept defeat until it was time to get picked up. But Greg and Anaya wouldn't let up when sales figures were down; and they had been, for all of us. The last month had been the wettest month in Sydney's history. This job had been an easy ride at the start, but on days like this I could see why it was hard to hack for some.

The street looked dead, no cars moving, nothing. I finished my cigarette, flipped a coin and went left up towards Premier Street where the houses were whiter.

I was drawn to the house from where Astrud Gilberto music was coming. I rang the bell. A voice shouted, 'Round the back!' so I went up the side of the house and through a wooden door into a garden. Six people, seated round a dinner table on a patio covered with a corrugated roof, looked at me.

'Can I help you?' said a man about my age, standing up.

'Hey, how you doing today?' I began the act, remembering never to start with an apology for my presence, never to assume a low-status position from the outset, but feeling like a total dick for asking how people were, having just arrived uninvited on their own property. I took in the table of six, three couples by the look of it, and remained smiling despite the fact I was getting nothing back.

'I guess we'd like to know who you are and why the hell you're here,' said an underweight woman in bright red lipstick and sunglasses. I wanted at once to punch her repeatedly in the head.

'Hi, I'm from Scotland, my name is Kerry and I'm just going round your neighbourhood today showing some paintings, that's all.' I kept smiling away like a dummy. The man who first stood up, moved towards me with tongs in his hands.

'How many of you are there?' The group round the table laughed. 'How many other little Scottish people are there out there?'

I was at a crossroads early on. I had to decide how to play this, if indeed to play it at all, or – for my own satisfaction but at the risk of making no money and possibly ruining anybody's chances in this neighbourhood again – just telling them to fuck right off and die.

I decided to carry on. 'Well, I'm just the scout, they send me on ahead of the others, but they will be here soon.'

'Let her stay for a bit,' said another equally annoying man. 'Might be a bit of a laugh.'

'No, Hugo, we've got to get going soon. Max is at my mum and dad's, remember?' said another thin woman whom I took to be his wife. I felt stupid in my cagoule and the pumps that Scotty had drawn smiley faces on the night before. A woman who seemed less neurotic than the other two, drank white wine and watched me.

'Paintings, you say?' she said, speaking from the glass she held at her mouth.

'Yes, Robin, let's see what you make of them. Maybe you could get some inspiration,' said Dick One.

'Shut up, I'll be the judge of that.'

They all laughed again. I could see the way this was going. The white wine drinker was a painter and I was in big trouble, and this was going to be my biggest challenge so far.

The first man kicked the folder. 'Come on then, get them out, wee lass.'

The others found the bad Scottish voice hilarious.

'Be careful with the folder, otherwise I'll have to pay for anything damaged,' I said.

He retreated, miming treading on eggshells. I still had no idea of what line I was going to take but I knew I couldn't do the usual one. It just wouldn't work with this lot.

'My name's Kerry, by the way.' I'd already said this, but I was buying time.

'G'day, Kerry,' said Dick Two. I felt the confidence drain from me and had an overwhelming urge to give up or just beg them to all chip in and buy one piece of shit from me.

'Here you go, Kerry, have a glass of wine,' said Hugo.

'Yeah, why not, lass?' said Dick Two. They were all half cut from afternoon drinking; the table was strewn with the remains of a Sunday dinner.

'OK, OK, let's go,' said the one who'd kicked the folder, clapping his hands and hurrying everything along.

'Someone should tell her,' said Dick One. They all stifled giggles.

'Leave the poor girl alone,' said Robin. 'Red or white, darl'?'

'White, please. Bit early for red,' I said, in a bid to appear cultured.

'Tell her!' shouted Dick One.

'No. Now shut up!' Robin snapped. 'Kerry, just ignore them and show us the paintings. I'm genuinely interested.'

What could I do? I would have to get the paintings out some time, even though the crowd would rip me to shreds. It didn't matter how good I was at reading the situation – in a group like this, the paintings would speak for themselves, and that meant I would be humiliated. After all, this entire gimmick was designed for the dumber, unquestioning people who lived in the suburbs, not the cynical sarcastic personalities of urban types. That's why we didn't sell in central locations such as trendy Paddington, which was awash with bookshops, delis and gay couples. Or Surrey Hills, home to media people, fashion designers and hairdressers.

I sheepishly pulled out the Peter Stuger. They all clapped and roared with laughter.

'Guys, guys, come on, seriously, give the girl a break,' Robin cried over the noise.

Guys, give the girl a gun, I thought, but Robin was on my side and that meant something.

'Look, maybe I should just leave it. They're obviously not your cup of tea, and that's fine. You can't please everybody.' I knew they'd urge me to stay for their own amusement.

'No, no, we promise to behave,' said Dick Two, pulling up a chair for his feet.

I pulled out the ladies in the field.

'An absolute classic!' applauded Hugo. I remained looking relaxed and moved slowly to give myself time to work out what to do. I had no idea why I didn't leave and spare myself the effort of trying to get them to like and want what I had, other than I was becoming addicted to the risk of losing and the challenge of winning – and the realisation that it was me I was trying to sell to people.

'Sorry, I can't let the girl go on; I've got to help her out here,' said Dick One.

'What?' I made myself look as though I was enjoying their game as much as they were enjoying mine.

'This is Robin Bullivant, one of Sydney's most up-and-coming young painters.'

I gulped my wine. 'Yeah, really?' I turned to Robin. She was a fairly attractive woman, perhaps a few years older than me, with cropped blonde hair and glasses. 'Great. Are you currently exhibiting? Sorry, I don't know anything about the Sydney scene. I haven't been here long.'

'Yes, I am actually, in Paddington. Do you know the Signs Gallery?'

'Nope, sorry. Like I said, I've only just kind of got here.'

'Pleeease, can we see more of your terrible paintings?' begged Dick Two again. He had dry white bits in the corner of his mouth.

'Well, I do have to sell some at the end of the day. It's my living and you're just blatantly taking the piss.' Although I was direct I didn't lose the casual relaxed tone.

'Did you pick these up in Bali on the way over?' asked the woman who had wanted to leave earlier. I took off my cagoule as a bead of sweat ran down the side of my face.

'No, I didn't actually. I painted them.' I drank more from my wine, and took a cigarette Robin had offered to me, allowing them time to laugh then feel the silence afterwards as they realised what I'd said. I was cranking up, I had found some direction. I stepped purposefully over to the folder and dragged heavily on my Marlboro.

'Do you honestly think I like trying to get rid of this shite? Of course not, but I'm an artist and I have to make a living.'

'Seriously?' asked Robin.

'What do you think? I mean, look at this stuff.' I pulled out the unicorn drinking by the lake. They erupted, except for Robin and the couple who wanted to pick up Max from the wife's parents. 'It's a fuckin' unicorn, for fuck's sake.' I had them howling. 'But I'll tell you something, it sells.'

'I don't believe you,' said Hugo. 'Not round here, please. Maybe over in Redfern.' I didn't know where Redfern was. 'So, is this a tourist rip-off thing or something? I mean, Nick's right, they're from Bali or Hong Kong, yeah?'

'It's a long story,' I said, finishing my wine and wondering what my long story was going to be.

'Sit down, sit down.' Nick slapped a seat next to him and Robin. 'Tell us all about it, wee travelling lassie.'

'That's a really good Scottish accent by the way,' I said, toasting him with my empty glass and winking at Robin.

'More wine?' asked Dick Two.

'Why not? It's Sunday.' I smiled at the gathering. Then I continued, directing most of my spiel at Robin and at Max's parents, who seemed to be the dullest of the bunch. 'No, seriously. I graduated from Edinburgh College of Art last year.' I felt much more confident out of my cagoule.

Robin said, 'Oh OK. In?'

I could see she was genuinely interested and not doubting my credentials in the slightest. 'Oh, fine art, painting mostly.' I worried that it was wrong to say 'painting mostly' and that 'fine art' should have covered it.

'Right, right. I also did fine art, but I graduated four years ago now.'

'Sydney?' I presumed they had an art school in Sydney.

'Mmm.' She nodded and smiled. I tried to ignore Nick unravelling a small piece of folded paper, which I knew would be coke. He fumbled around, spilling a little, mopping it up with his finger and sucking it.

'Nick! Come on, eh?' Hugo gestured to me. I looked up, pretending just to notice.

'No, it's fine, really, it's totally all right, go ahead.' I turned back to Robin, my only real hope.

'So you were saying, you graduated,' she prompted.

'Yes, I graduated but my trouble was—'

'Kerry?' Nick offered me the first line. There were six chopped out on a table mat with pictures of different kinds of fish. This surprised me, given that Max had to be picked up from his grandparents.

I sniffed it up my right nostril, for only the third time in my life. Robin went next.

'You were saying?' she asked when she'd finished and passed the mat on.

'Yes. You see, my father was actually a famous artist.' I offered Robin and the others a Benson & Hedges. They all declined in favour of Marlboro and Silk Cut.

I scanned the area for ideas of my father's name. I thought about the child called Max, waiting on his mum and dad. Then I thought about *Mad Max* and how it starred Mel Gibson who was Australian, then I put Mad and the ax from Max together and I formed Maddox which sounded like an artist. In fact, there was an artist called Conroy Maddox who was part of a surrealist group of British painters. I remembered him from sixth-year art studies, the one subject that kept me at school for my final year. The discovery of the name excited me and caused my heart to pound as my brain raced for another name which was to be his second, which had to go well with the first but it had be quick; I mustn't take too long, otherwise I would give myself away.

On the table was a lighter with a Harley-Davidson on it, and so my father was named.

'Maddox Davidson. He was part of a group of Scottish painters from the sixties. No?'

'No, doesn't ring any bells.'

'Well, he was very well thought of. Not by me, though.' I added some criticism of my father for authenticity.

'So it's in the blood, then?' asked Nick, grinding his teeth.

'Must be. Unfortunately it's not the only thing, though.' I tilted my wine glass to the side. Some of them nodded like the suckers they were becoming. 'Yep, unfortunately my father died a penniless drunk.'

'Oh no, that's so sad,' said the thinner of the two thin girls, the one with the lipstick and the sunglasses.

'Yep, everything we had, all the fortune he'd acquired, the lot, all gone. He was just mad, destructive. He got called Mad Maddox, that's how Edinburgh knew him.' I was really pushing it now, surely.

'So when was that, then?' asked Robin sincerely, pulling her knees up under her chin and wrapping her arms round her legs.

'In my final year at art school. He didn't even make my graduation show.' I quickly scanned the group to see if anyone was going to pick me up on 'show'. I didn't know if one had an art show or not.

'So you decided to get away and start afresh. I can understand that.' Hugo spoke slowly, trying tentatively to guess my life story.

I nodded to encourage him. 'I was tired of living in my father's shadow. He was a very powerful character and extremely well thought of on the British art scene. I mean, he was a terrible father, but a great painter.'

'Maddox Henderson,' muttered Robin.

'Maddox Davidson,' I corrected her. Nick laid out another batch of lines.

'What sort of stuff did he paint?'

I should have prepared myself for Robin's question but I was concentrating on Nick chopping out another six lines. It felt like seconds ago since he was chopping out the last lot. How long would this go on for? How was I going to tie in my father's death with me being here trying to flog a group of well-educated people some tacky piece-of-shit paintings for a couple of hundred dollars? One thing at a time. Right now, I had to explain what sort of stuff he painted.

On the table were the remains of some cantaloupe, which made me think of antelope.

'One of his most famous pieces of work centred round his trip to Kenya, in the late fifties, where he photographed antelope, which he later worked with on his return to the UK. The antelope period was fairly abstract. I mean, he was an abstract painter, drifted into it after the Kenya trip.' I lit up another cigarette for something to do and to cover up the panic at the end of each new bullshit sentence.

'Really?' asked Robin, while the others listened attentively to my increasingly odd story.

'He was really a surrealist at heart.' Absolute silence prevailed. 'But became abstract for a while.' Oh my God, I thought. Is it fucking possible to be surrealist and then *a bit* abstract for a while? Did I say a bit abstract? Or just abstract? Because a bit is very poor.

'Right.' Robin kept nodding. 'Sounds a bit confusing.'

Acknowledge confusing, I thought. Don't deny confusing, you'll only look as though you're being defensive and that will convey dishonesty.

'Extremely confusing, that was him, and that was life with him.' I felt clever for building on confusing and making something of it rather than letting it bring me down.

'Pretty amazing story.' Dick Two was still with me.

I took another line, this time up the left nostril. I didn't want to use too much of the right, I wanted to balance it with the left. Also, I had turned left out of the phone booth and that had brought me here, which was where I was meant to be for some reason, so left is good, I thought, hoovering up.

'Not being funny or anything, but your dad is this great

painter in Scotland, yeah?' Fucking Nick was on to something.

'Yeah.' Now I'd joined the nodders.

'Well, how come you're painting this shit?'

I took the longest drag of my cigarette I could possibly manage in order to stall. 'The Girl From Ipanema' stuck on 'looks straight ahead, not at me', which I took as a sign, which reminded me that Robin had an exhibition at the Signs Gallery in Paddington. Which made me think about Paddington Bear, my childhood favourite, which made me think of Paddington's favourite food, which was marmalade sandwiches, which reminded me of my poor old granddad who lived on marmalade sandwiches before he moved to the home, which made me feel sad, which I feared I would be unable to smoke off as it was exacerbated by the Santana CD that Nick had just put on. I felt myself slipping into a rare melancholy and I wanted to hold Robin's hand. Instead, I attempted to answer the question.

'Well, I wanted to get far away from Scotland and where I was from and all the reminders of my family name. I have a brother out here, so I decided to follow him and start a life here.' That explained the personal journey. 'In terms of my work, I want nothing more than to exhibit here in Sydney, but I'm a long way off that right now because this is just the start for me.' Nodding all round. 'Incidentally, my brother is a sculptor.'

'Cool,' said Robin.

My pathological dislike of people who said 'cool' brought me momentarily out of my depressive slump.

'My brother and I and a couple of his mates, who're painters as well, want to hire a big studio down by the docks to work in, but it's so pricey and I've got to pay rent where I'm living, so I decided to do some basic stuff to earn me some cash while I work on my real art.'

Fucking brilliant, I thought. But my made-up story, I noticed, was as sad and difficult as my true life, which I regretted. I could, after all, have made things a little better and happier in my fantasy life. I was battling against 'Samba Patey', which Nick had turned up with a remote control from where he was sitting on the patio. The wine tasted like apple juice that I couldn't stop drinking to quench my thirst. My larynx was numbed out from the coke. I must pace myself and not bombard them with too much of my sad fantasy life, I thought. I looked down for a while, feeling the music, but my shoes made me sad. I looked under the table at the other shoes on display; the others mostly wore flip-flops, which seemed happier.

Then the thin woman spoke for the first time in ages.

'But there are other paintings like this going round the suburbs. My cousin's got some; she's become a real westie.'

Her boyfriend and the other thin girl sniggered.

'Westie. What's that?' I asked.

'It's someone that lives in a daggy part of town and dresses really daggy, and like, I suppose, well ... What would you say, Rod?'

'Common, I suppose. The pommies would say common.'

Oh, please, not the colonial jargon coming from some rich city-boy twat, I thought, stubbing out my cigarette with regret.

'Yeah, common, you know, white patent shoes, really westie.'

'Schemer.'

'What?'

'I think you mean schemer – that's what we say in Edinburgh.'

'Schamer.' Robin struggled with its pronunciation.

'Schemer, yeah. So your cousin's a schemer?'

'Yeah, she is, and a couple of summers ago some people came round like you and sold her some tacky picture of the Blue Mountains, or something.'

'Right.' I overnodded.

'So, is this an organisation? That's what Penny's asking,' said the boyfriend. Which was a real shame because I was banking on taking all the praise for the paintings and the idea that there must be a market for them out here, away from the city.

'Yeah, it is an organisation called ART, it's based in Sydney, and me and the other painters use the studio space they have to paint in, and they supply that and the materials, and we bang them out very quickly – the same eight or ten scenes that are recycled with each group working there. Then we go round trying to sell.'

They looked blank.

'It's all a means to an end for the time being.'

That was it. I was spent. It took all my powers of concentration to hammer that out under the coke, which was making me feel increasingly withdrawn and in need of silence from all talk.

This was only the third time I'd taken coke, the night in the Naked Club being the second. The first time I tried it, I was nineteen and worked in a hotel. The head gardener, Dougie, let me try some at the end of my last day. We sat in the greenhouse listening to Frankie Goes To Hollywood's 'Two Tribes,' and Jerry, whose slight coke habit I hadn't noticed until that day, explained how close we were to nuclear war with Russia. Then we hugged and I got on my bike a bit horny and cycled home with great vigour.

It was only now that I noticed the various reactions that different personalities had to the drug. The quietest of the group – the thin girls and Hugo – seemed to become more talkative, whereas Robin and I seemed to quieten down.

'So, why can't you use the studio space to paint your own stuff as well as the tacky stuff here?' asked Hugo.

'Mmm,' agreed his wife.

'Yeah, why don't you do that?' said Robin.

'Yeah, I do.' I couldn't concentrate; I was worrying whether I was too young to have a heart attack.

'Then you wouldn't have to get your own place to paint,' Robin finished.

I wanted to correct her. She was confusing everything; it was all wrong.

'Yeah. I do. I do paint there.'

Robin had taken off her glasses and put on sunglasses even though it was overcast, and was moving with the music. Nick was making a square on the table with matches.

'Yeah, Kerry, why don't you do that?' asked Hugo again, taking over the cocaine preparation.

'Do what?'

'Just use the gear at the ART place, or whatever it's called.'

'I'm only there because of the shit paintings, aren't I?'

They looked at me, four of them in sunglasses now. I'd left mine in the car because it was raining and I didn't think I'd be taking coke with a bunch of strangers.

I went on, 'If I wasn't selling this to get money I wouldn't be needing the money. No wait. I wouldn't be.' I started drumming on the table with my fingers as the song built up some pace. 'I wouldn't *have*! I wouldn't have the place to paint the shit stuff, if I wasn't doing the job, would I?'

The four with the glasses were laughing at me. The two without glasses weren't. Would I be like them if I had worn my sunglasses?

'I get it,' said Hugo.

'Well, thank fuck for that,' I said accidentally, barely able to force a smile.

I had planned a good while ago, during our initial conversation, that I would confess to selling mass-produced, tacky art, and lie about painting it, but would profess to have painted what I considered to be good and sellable art which I also carried about with me. I had settled on the abstract pieces because they were simply less recognisable as shit to most people. Unfortunately, I had now confused myself with my own story, which I was starting to believe – or at least the part about me painting the tacky stuff. I knew the coke was running the show now but I couldn't stop. I also couldn't stop with the obsession that I had to sell them a picture. I was fucked for the rest of the day and night, I couldn't move on to another house in this state. I couldn't afford not to sell.

'Hey, Kerry?' The coke was passed to me once again.

'What?' I took it up the right nostril, and planned to do only one more up the left to balance my nose abuse, and then I'd stop. Pleased with my decision and with a self-imposed end in sight, I found some reserve positivity.

'What?' I asked again.

Hugo was crippled over laughing and unable to complete his question until he'd got his breath back. 'You're a great girl and all that, but we're not going to buy your shit paintings. You know that, don't you?'

'I am,' said Nick, putting up his hand. I felt instant compassion for him.

'No way, Nicky boy.'

'Yeah, I fuckin' am. Look great in the fuckin' salon, that unicorn.'

I was stunned into further silence.

'You fuckin' cocksucker, Nick,' laughed Rod.

'Rod, don't talk to him like that,' said Penny, his girlfriend.

'I don't mind. I'm used to it. I don't care.' Nick stood up, wiping his nose on his sleeve. 'How much is it, Cathy? I fucking want it.' He slammed some notes and loose change on the table.

'Look, I come here, I drink your wine, you share your coke with me, I can't charge you. Nope, not right.' I genuinely meant it, but only because I had convinced myself that I wanted to sell my own work – i.e. the abstracts – rather than the mass-produced stuff. I hadn't spoken to Robin for a while, losing her to her trance, so I said, 'What do you think, Robin?'

I felt, based on nothing, that Robin and I had a rapport.

'Let him buy it, he wants it. He's Kylie Minogue's hairdresser, he's loaded.'

I liked everything Robin said.

'I cut her hair *once*, Cathy, before she was famous,' protested Nick.

'Kerry,' I muttered.

'ONCE, KERRY!' He boomed, sticking up one finger.

I was lost now. I was beaten. I would accept defeat and go with the flow. 'Take the unicorn, it's yours.' I swung on my chair, and picked up a pair of sunglasses from the table and put them on without asking.

'I've got ...' He counted his change. 'One hundred dollars here, but only because my dealer didn't show. I thought it was you, by the way.' He touched my shoulder. He was becoming increasingly camp. 'One hundred bucks and fifty seventy cents. Here, take it.'

I gave him the double thumbs-up, and cocked my head towards the unicorn. He cheered and ran towards it. It didn't make me happy, though; I wanted to sell my abstract art.

'What sort of stuff do you paint?' Robin picked up a camera from the table and began taking shots of me as I talked.

'Abstract. I've got some with me. Do you want to see?'

'Yeah, go on.'

I went over to the folder and brought out what I considered to be the best two out of the three. I placed them against the wall of the house and stood back. Robin squatted down and looked at them for a while. I poured myself another glass of wine, as it had gone well past the politeness stage by now, and lit up. I walked over to join her, dragging on my cigarette, tapping my fingernail on my tooth and taking it all in, like I was at an opening.

'Well? Be honest.'

'Hmmm. There's not much going on with it – I don't feel it. But I think I like it.'

'There's not meant to be much going on. I mean, that's the idea, isn't it?'

'It's banal, I think.'

I didn't respond to banal; I couldn't, I didn't know what it meant.

'I feel empty,' I said instead.

'It's very empty.'

'Very, yeah, it's meant to be, it's how I feel.'

She snapped away some more.

I stayed still behind the sunglasses I was wearing. The others chatted away in the background, oblivious to us.

'But you know something?' She kept clicking, not looking up from her camera.

'What?'

'I'm going to buy it.'

'Really?'

'Yeah. But I want you to sign it.'

'It is signed.'

'I want you to sign it.' She looked up from the camera and over the top of her sunglasses. I didn't feel the need to say any more on the subject. Everything fell into place for me at that moment; I understood exactly what was happening. The sunglasses made the wearer have more insight into what was going on, and a sense of power; that's why I sold when I was wearing a pair, and that's why Nick bought the unicorn when he was without them. And that's why Robin had found me out only when she put her sunglasses on. I didn't want to take off whoever's glasses I had on, in case things started going wrong for me.

Robin went to remove her glasses. I put my hand out to stop her, but it was too late. She too would be weakened now.

'How much?'

'One hundred and fifteen bucks.'

'One hundred and fifty, there.' She pressed money into my hand. 'I'm giving you a bit more because my brother should have; he can afford it, trust me.'

'Let's take a bottle and go inside,' I said, nudging her.

'OK.'

We walked through the patio doors into the lounge area; nobody noticed us or seemed to care what we were up to. There was no need to say any more; all feelings of nervousness had disappeared, and we had both joined the same altered reality and felt connected for what would inevitably be a short time.

We moved with drinks in our hands. She walked backwards as I pushed her towards the kitchen, away from view. The moment we got through the kitchen door, I pushed her up against the worktop and started kissing her. She went to take off my sunglasses but I wouldn't let her. We kissed intensely for about ten minutes without stopping. Then we had a break for wine.

'Whose house is this?' I asked.

'My parents. Nick's my brother, my mum and dad are away, we're house-sitting.'

We started kissing again.

'Let's go upstairs,' I said, when we broke off.

'There are no stairs,' she said, laughing.

'Other room, then.'

She took my hand and I took the bottle of wine. Then I stopped. 'Wait. No. The pictures, I can't leave them.' I didn't want to leave her for a second; I didn't want anything to change for now, for her to go away, but I went back out to the patio.

'You better look after my sister,' shouted Nick, who was

chopping out five lines. I grabbed my folder, hoping that Nick wouldn't offer me some more coke because I couldn't say no, but at the same time I didn't want to unbalance my nostril distribution – if I took another, I'd have to take another one after that.

He didn't offer and I went back inside to find Robin as I'd left her, drinking her wine, leaning against the kitchen unit. We kissed more; the kissing was better than at the beginning. She took my hand and we went into a small bedroom with a single bed and a painting of a flamenco dancer. The blinds were half closed, making lines across Robin's face as she sat on the bed and leant her head against the wall. She pulled me into her and we kissed for the longest time yet. I stopped it eventually to drink more wine. She would have kept going had I not, but I wanted my wine as much as the kissing. After all, I would not be kissing if it was not for the wine.

We took off our clothes. She had a piercing in her belly button which I fiddled with. We could hear the others laughing and talking outside, and someone had turned up Grace Jones's 'La Vie En Rose'. We rubbed around a bit. I wanted more coke, more wine; I wanted to go back to the start with Robin. And although it was my idea to go into the room, I didn't like it now that I was there. I didn't understand why. I went down on her, whoever she was.

After a while she pulled my head up and brought my face close to hers. We both stared at one another without talking.

'I'm off my fucking tits,' she whispered.

'Me too.'

'Take the fucking glasses off.' I let her do it. Then I lay on the bed beside her.

'I don't usually like Sundays,' I said, but she wasn't listening.

CHAPTER ELEVEN

'Is that Mr Duffy?' Mosquitoes hummed round the phone booth. It was Monday night, a night we usually got off, but it was a public holiday and Greg wanted us out. I'd just finished my last house; I'd sold two in the evening, both in the same home to two different couples who were having dinner together. I drank some wine with them, and felt all loose and happy and cured of my hangover, so I bought a phone card and decided to make a start to my enquiries, before meeting up with the others. However, now that it came down to it, I was extremely nervous.

I was holding the second page of Duffys from the phone book and had chosen a number at random.

'Mr Duffy, does live here but I'm just a visitor,' said an older voice.

'Hello, my name is Kerry, and I'm trying to contact a possible relative of mine. I'm in Sydney just now but I live in the UK. His name was John Duffy and his wife is called Madeline, they moved here in 1965 or '66, I think.'

The man laughed. 'Well, Kerry, that was a while ago, and it's certainly not me. Not unless I've inherited any money.'

I laughed back out of politeness. 'Look, I'll be honest with you, I've just torn a few pages out the phone book and I'm making a start going through all the Duffys.'

'There are other ways you could do this, you know, easier than that.' He sounded a pretty relaxed and open type, which I liked.

'Yeah, but I want to do it this way for now, you know?'

'I do, yes. Who is this relative, if you don't mind me asking?'

'He's a man that might be related to my mother, and I promised her I'd try to look him up when I got here. It would mean the world to her if I could trace him.'

'I see.' He sighed and half laughed ironically.

'Sorry, am I wasting your time?' I tried to move things along; at this rate it would take me a year to get through all the names.

'No, not at all. It's just weird, that's all.'

'How come?' I breathed on the glass and drew a D on it.

'For a number of reasons, but I may be able to help you a little more than you had hoped.' He was really dragging this out.

'How come?'

'Well, I have my own radio show for one thing.'

'No way.' I stopped drawing.

'Yep, got around twenty thousand listeners.'

'So, you're a DJ?'

'Among other things. I'm a qualified physio, the radio thing is more of a hobby, local radio, really. I'm a big country fan and that's what my show is about, country music, it's a show for old cowboys like me.'

'I didn't know there were any cowboys in Australia, apart from the ones I'm working with.'

He laughed at my joke. The dollar sign changed to fifty cents, so I put another one in.

'How many names have you tried already?'

'I think I tried a few before, when I first came here, but I can't remember because I was drunk. Tonight I just picked one out and it was you.'

'Well, that's incredible, kid, because like I said I'm not technically a Duffy. In fact, I'm not a Duffy at all, my name is Hank White, although my real name is Frank.'

'Who is the Duffy, then?' I traced over my old D.

'This could all be a coincidence, see, but this isn't my house, it's my sister's. She's the Duffy. I'm down visiting from Brisbane, where I live.'

'That is pretty strange, isn't it? You answering and offering to help with your radio show?'

This was starting to feel like the rest of my life, all of it a series of bizarre coincidences which, I believed, would eventually lead me to my answer.

'I've gotta tell you, kid, this must be fate.'

'Yes, yes, it must be, it always is.' I was excited and speedy. I lit a cigarette and took in a massive drag.

'Sounds like you've needed some help if you can't remember who you've been phoning.' He laughed again. I could tell that he fancied himself as a bit of a character – but then again, all the best people do. 'Well, what are the chances? You phoning the Duffys, and getting me, when it's not even my house. I answer the phone because my sister happens to be away tonight, and it turns out I'm a radio DJ with access to listeners through my show, who might be able to help with what you're looking for. Think about it.'

I had to agree with him, nutcase or not. 'So what do you think I should do then?'

'Well, just to add something even more bizarre into the equation, my brother-in-law down here, the Duffy part of things, is a minister!'

'Oh right, OK, so you mean he could put out a call as well? In his church?'

'I was more thinking his parish magazine. He could reach quite a few people in Sydney.'

'Uh-huh.'

'Were they church-goers, these relatives, or relative?'

'Relative. I don't know. Doubt it.' I couldn't see, in the circumstances, how she could go to church.

'Well, it's worth a try, kid.'

'What's next then?' I was dizzy from oversucking on my Marlboro, a brand usually too strong for me.

'I could take more information from you on what you know about John Duffy, talk to Bob, my sister's husband, and I could put out a call on air for anyone who might know of him, and ask them to call the station. How does that sound to you?'

'Good, yeah. Good, thanks, but that'll be in Brisbane and I don't know if he's there or in Sydney.'

'Sure, well, it's a start, and it's covering two more areas than you were five minutes ago, isn't it? And you really don't know for sure if it's Sydney or Brisbane or Melbourne even, by the sounds of it, do you, love?'

'No, I don't. I don't know much at all.'

'Exactly, and Australia is a big place.'

He spoke to me as if I was about ten years old; I finished my cigarette in record time and stamped on it.

'OK, so tell me, what you do know then?' I could hear him scrabbling around looking for a piece of paper.

'John Duffy was in the Australian army around 1965. In 1966 he met a woman called Madeline Thomson. She was a nurse and they married and moved to Sydney or Brisbane, not sure. I think she came on the ten-pound package, maybe – don't know – but more than likely because I don't think they had much money, and she was from Newcastle.'

'Newcastle, England, not Newcastle, Oz?'

'Yeah, England. I didn't know there was one here.'

'Oh yeah, they've got everything English here, except the weather.' He amused himself no end. 'That's all you have on this, kid?'

'Yeah, that's all I know.' I liked his corny detective talk.

'Do you have a phone number, Kerry? Do you know I haven't even asked where you're calling from?'

'I'm in Sydney, I'm working here. But Hank, there's one more thing.'

'What's that?'

'It's very important that you tell them a Joanna Thomson is looking for them.'

'Is that your mum?'

'No, but I can't explain that right now, it's a long story.'

'So I'd better take your number, then.'

'Yeah, sure, there's a phone at the place I work but we can't really receive calls too much, it's more for emergencies. I'll give it to you just in case but don't overuse it, will you?'

'No, I won't, unless I have something concrete for you, but I'll give you my number. I'll be going home tomorrow and I've got my show on Wednesday night, so I'll put something out then.'

'What will you say?' Despite my eagerness I didn't want to completely fuck up someone else's life unnecessarily.

'Just that there's a person trying to trace someone by the name of John Duffy, and all the stuff you gave me; I don't want to go upsetting anyone's life now, Kerry. You understand, don't you?'

'Why did you say that?' It was almost as if he knew more than he was letting on.

'Just making sure, kid, that's all.'

'OK, thanks.'

The car pulled up alongside the phone booth, with Jim tooting. I signalled that I would be one minute.

'Hank, can you play a tune to go with the message?'

'Well, that might be stretching things a little, but I'll do my best. It's a country show though, so I wouldn't be playing any of your pop crap.'

'Good, I hate that myself.'

'What do you want then? But I can't promise, mind you.'

'Can you play Bob Dylan's "You're A Big Girl Now", please?'

'Well, that's not pop, but it's not country either. I tell you what, I'll do my very best.'

'Please, just play it, Hank, will you?'

'OK, just for you, love. I'll see if I can dig it out from somewhere.'

'Thanks, I really appreciate this.' I was trying to turn round and shield my eyes from Scotty, who had his arse pressed against the phone box; I could see the Danish rolling around in the back of the car in response to it. I tried to ignore him as I took down Hank's number in Brisbane on the inside of my Marlboro packet.

'Got to go now, Hank. I've got people waiting for me outside.'

'OK, love, I'll be in touch whenever I have any news.'

'Uh-huh, thanks now.'

'Take care, love, see ya.'

I hung up, folded away the phone book pages again and got in the car, laughing reluctantly with the rest of them. From a random phone call in six minutes, I'd come further in my search than I had in six weeks. This all felt right.

CHAPTER TWELVE

It was warm and turquoise out there. I didn't miss the Edinburgh buildings, the austere gloomy Georgian sandstone, and the pasty tight-lipped people that lived and worked behind it. Fuck that, I thought, as I drank a pineapple and guava smoothie outside a café, updating my 'Paintings Sold' list in my notebook. I liked the mornings alone; there was always enough chatter with the others during the car journeys in the late afternoon to exhaust me before I even knocked on a door. I had quickly learned to pace myself, and was beginning to feel like an actress exhausted all day from putting on a show every night.

I was feeling positive again after my call to Hank, and fairly pleased with myself, a rare occurrence. Things felt as if they were being dealt with better. I was happy walking along the street, I saw the good in people; I smiled at a child who passed by who was humming the *Batman* theme. The sun seemed a good thing for a change, the slight breeze was perfect and the day felt as though it had a sense of purpose. I had decided, when I woke up, that I would start my life again.

I was full of promises. Big and small. Small ones like: I must get fit, I must write to my granddad, I must eat better, and I must save more money. And big ones, things that were harder to change: I must stop having sex with strangers, I must stop drinking, and I must start to have a life plan.

The queue in Hercus Loan, the pawnbroker, was longer than before. I stood behind a man in stained trousers that smelt of layers of drink. Everybody was quiet. There was a real absence of angry people in Sydney. Even the odd drunk would just wander along aimlessly. Back home everybody was always shouting, all the tramps and winos were raging against the world all the time.

The man behind the counter took the optic out of his left eye and finished off the cigarette in the ashtray on the counter.

'I'll give you one hundred and seventy-five dollars, mate, and no more.'

'It's a bloody good watch that, reckon it's worth more.'

'Well, fair play to you, mate, if you can get it elsewhere, but that's my price, end of, I'm afraid.'

'Go on then.' The man shuffled a little in embarrassment.

I waited my turn and then handed over my ticket. I hummed a tune under my breath while he searched the drawers beneath the counter for my item, happy to be a collector for a change. I paid him the cash, putting my grandmother's ring back on my finger for what I had promised to myself was the last time. It wasn't coming off again.

Greg and Anaya called me into their office when I returned. Greg had been away for the last three Saturday evenings on some kind of business trip. I had never been asked into the office before. It made me nervous.

Greg stood behind a desk surrounded by at least twenty Blue Mountains, with lots of credit-card-authorisation forms and ashtrays strewn all over it. There was a small storeroom off the office behind him, with more paintings piled up in their landscape groups. Anaya was sitting on the edge of Greg's desk, swinging her perfect legs and eating a sandwich, which she shared with Greg. I sensed a problem, as Greg appeared slightly tense.

'Hey, Greg, how was your trip?' I asked, keeping it light, but sneaking a look over to Anaya, hoping she'd reciprocate, which she didn't.

'Yeah, good, thanks, mate, good. I'll tell you about it later maybe. It was interesting.'

'What have I done wrong?' I asked to pre-empt any awkwardness.

'It's bad, Kerry, we're gonna have to let you go,' said Anaya, pursing her lips and raising her eyebrows.

'What?' My heart started thumping. Now I was fucked, but at least I had the ring, I thought.

'She's taking the piss, mate, just ignore her.'

Anaya laughed and ate her sandwich. I just didn't understand her game with me, and found her a curious mixture of hostility and flirtatiousness. She had practically ignored me in the weeks that followed the kiss episode.

'Sorry, I'm joking, yeah?'

'Yeah, ha fucking ha,' I said, trying to be offhand.

'No,' Greg went on, 'it's just your folder's missing a painting?'

'That can't be right.'

''Fraid so. We check the folders every morning. We left it yesterday because I was away overnight and Anaya forgot, but we've been through them now and yours is short. What happened Sunday?'

'Nothing.' I felt my face and neck go red-hot. 'It was a quiet area, didn't really work for me but I sold two. Two in two houses.' I lied to cover the amount of time I was with Robin.

Anaya looked me up and down slowly, and then held my gaze. She knew exactly the kind of thing I'd been up to, and she was loving my awkwardness. Greg didn't notice; he began rummaging around in the paperwork and maps on his desk. While he did, she upped her flirtatious looks towards me. So that's what kind of day it was today – a flirty Anaya who liked teasing me.

'Neutral Bay, yeah?'

'Yep, but Sunday and raining. It was a bit shit, really.'

'Hey, guess what?' said Anaya. 'Andrea and Karin had their best day, Andrea sold four and Karin five.'

'Yeah, they did well. So what happened to you, then?' Greg backed her up.

Those fucking Danish with their pretty little features and mermaid-long hair, and soap-smell skin.

'What's this, a trial?' I imagined Anaya in a German uniform.

'No, of course not.' Greg laughed to relax things a little.

'You're missing an abstract painting,' Anaya said, keen to get back to the issue.

'Which one?' I asked, remembering that before I left Robin's house in Neutral Bay I'd given Nick a painting in return for the coke I'd used.

'The cube overlapping.' She drew in the air with her finger. My mind went back to the kiss we had, and how I'd been able to tell how much she wanted to take things further, but didn't dare.

Then I realised I'd be so shit scared if she did.

I said, 'I don't see how I can be missing one, it must be an error. I genuinely don't know.'

I wasn't sure why I didn't just tell Greg and Anaya that I got wasted with some customers and lost track of things. I was sure they would understand – after all, it wasn't as though they ran a typical boss-employer relationship, and Greg was out of it most of the time anyway – but I felt instinctively that I had to protect myself against any future uncertainties involving customers. I was also planning in the back of my mind that if I did stay on here a while, then surely I'd want to end up a supervisor, and losing paintings wouldn't help my plans.

Anaya lit a cigarette, took a drag and gave it to Greg.

'Look, we're pretty relaxed here, aren't we?' she said, exhaling.

'Yeah, of course.'

'V-e-r-y,' she drawled. I didn't understand Anaya or what she was on. She was just so odd all of the time, like she was playing the part of a *femme fatale* in a really bad amateur production. 'We have a good laugh, don't we? I mean, it's fun work, isn't it? And it's bloody easy, right?'

'Yeah, of course.' I relaxed a little.

'And look, we know the score; it's a bit rock 'n' roll out there at times.'

'Sure.' I had already gone back to the pawnshop in my head.

'But you can't lose the paintings, you know. Otherwise you'll just get yourself in debt to us and it won't work out.'

I kept nodding.

'Got me?'

'Yeah, sorry. I really don't know what happened.'

'Look, forget about it, it's happened before. But I'm going to have to charge you, mate, sorry.' Greg did look genuinely sympathetic.

'Or you can just work it off on another sale,' added Anaya.

'Yeah, why don't you do that?'

'OK.'

'Well, it's eighty bucks. Sorry, but that's the score, yeah?'

'Yeah, don't worry about it. I'll work it off, and I'm sorry, it won't happen again.'

Greg didn't seem too bothered now; he opened the blinds as the sound of a truck pulled up in the street.

'Better not,' said Anaya. 'Or we will have to be bad to you in some other way.'

The doorbell rang. Greg left the office to answer it, and I was left alone with Anaya, my heart racing.

'I'm sorry.' I twisted on my grandmother's ring, which felt tighter with the heat.

We looked at each other for a while in silence, before she said in a stern voice that brought me out of my trance, 'Don't let it happen again.'

I channel-flicked the portable TV on the kitchen worktop, while waiting for my toenail varnish to dry. Jim was alone outside on the back patio writing an airmail letter.

I watched some of the news, and wondered when Hank would call with any results. I was desperate to hear anything. How long would it take to find her? I wondered. Without looking very hard? I had never stopped to consider that she could be dead – that just wasn't something I could cope with considering for one second. That would truly be the road to madness for me. Besides, I felt that she was very much alive somewhere. I wondered if she had children, and a job. I wondered if she smoked or drank like me. I wondered if, since I'd been here, she had watched the same Australian television programmes at the same time as me. Perhaps we were both watching the same news now, or the Joyce Cane carpet sale ads that seemed to come on television every five minutes.

'Kerry!' shouted Jim from the back yard.

'What?'

'Get out here, I want to show you something!'

I hobbled out, carefully trying to avoid toe contact with the ground.

Jim was stroking a small animal the size of a cat, with a grey coat. It was fat like a koala, and had big eyes. It was sitting on the wall.

'Check this out,' said Jim, with the letter in his other hand.

'What is it?' I put my hand out to touch it.

'It's a possum, I'm pretty certain.'

'Why is it here, is it lost?'

Jim laughed. 'No, it's not lost, they live all over the place. They're tame like koalas, just like we have squirrels. It's just one of the things they have floating around Australia.'

'Fuck, there's so much stuff here, isn't there? It's so different from home. It's weird, don't you think? How far away we are?'

'That's the idea, isn't it? To be as far away as possible?' His voice tailed off at the end. He seemed unusually wistful for him.

'Have you come to travel round then go back or have you come here to stay?' I put my hand out to the possum.

'Probably the latter. No plans. How about you?'

'Same. I've technically only got six months with my visa. If I wanted to stay, I'd have to get married, I suppose.'

The possum chewed a branch and seemed quite happy with the two of us stroking it.

'Don't you miss teaching?' I asked.

Jim was thirty-five and looked fit and healthy. He gave the impression that he liked his solitude above the company of others, and so I could never work out why he ended up in that particular job.

'There's this misconception about teachers, that we all feel so passionate about teaching and that we're all so earnest and feel so fulfilled by educating young people, that we're all fucking Sidney bloody Poitier. But we're not. I regret the day I set foot in teaching; it was a fucking nightmare from beginning to end. It nearly cost me my sanity and there's never a day goes by when I'm not glad to be away from it.'

'Don't you feel like a teacher here with us? Being the supervisor, driving us around, planning where we go, keeping us in line?'

'Different this. It's a laugh, isn't it? I mean, it's not a proper job, is it?'

'No, it's like a show or a game.' I felt we were just using the possum by now in order to have our conversation, and if it moved away we would have to stop.

'It's a game all right. I would never have imagined me ending up in a place like this, two years ago even.'

'Where were you two years ago?' My hand felt grubby from the possum coat.

'Two years ago I was playing a very different game from this, that's for sure.' He broke up his sentence with forced laughter.

'What game was that, then?'

There was a loud bang from the street and the possum scurried away.

'I'll tell you one time, if we go away. There'll be plenty of time to get drunk together.' Jim wiped his hands on the jeans that he was never out of despite how warm it was.

'Away where?'

'The Gold Coast. Greg might have a trip planned. That's what happens every so often, apparently, don't know much more than that just now.' He shook his airmail letter. 'Got to catch the post.'

CHAPTER THIRTEEN

'It is nice.' She hummed and hawed. 'And I do agree with you, the other two just set it off nicely.' The lady tried to get her husband's attention.

I felt myself trying too hard, so I eased off a bit. I learned that trying too noticeably hard will get you no sales.

The lady had three paintings laid out that she fancied; predictably, it was the triptych. Her husband sat on the sofa watching the prime-time news. He was completely uninterested but seemed happy allowing her to choose what she liked.

It was my third day in a row of selling only one painting, despite the fact that I was adhering to another new healthier life plan. I had drunk only three or four beers each night, had made a considerable effort to eat well, and had cut out cigarettes until midday. However, my new approach didn't seem to be helping much, so by the time I'd reached the second house in Magic Cove in the suburbs of Clifton Gardens, I'd already decided that I'd exercised enough self-control for this week and that it wasn't paying off.

I had heard nothing from Hank, which was a total disappointment. I would have expected a response from anyone with any information almost straight away, but to me a week without hearing anything meant I would have to give up on him and pursue some other angle of the search.

'Colin. What do you think? Come on, love, help me out.' The woman clicked her fingers, and rolled her eyes at me.

Colin was watching a report on Channel 7 about a Christian movement led by some freak called the Reverend

Fred Neil, who was leading a march in Sydney against what seemed like absolutely everyone who wasn't a Christian. I tried to watch the item, bored with the situation. The husband wouldn't look up from the screen. He wore top half office-worker clothes, bottom half sweatpants, which was a sign to me that he was tired and just wanted to be left to the television. He grunted in response to his wife's plea.

'I'm just not sure.'

I eased right back. 'Would you mind if I sat down for a moment and left you to take this in your own time?' I asked, already sitting down. The husband looked up, which I knew was a bad sign.

'No, go ahead, love.' She scrutinised the painting. 'Is it meant to be wet? The paint's all sticky over here by the trees.' She pointed to the three brown strokes on the left painting.

'Yes, it's very normal, it's the nature of oils,' I said, as the man glanced over again. 'They will dry over the next few weeks.'

'I do think they would look good above the sofa.' She held one up. 'Actually, I might take it over there and just get an idea.'

'You do what you want, and only buy it if you are sure. It's no good me telling you what I think and what I like, when at the end of the day you know what you like.' I pulled some easygoing bullshit out of my bag.

'Would you mind helping me just hold that up?' She pointed. 'Just above where my husband's sitting.'

I obliged, trying not to disturb the husband in any way despite the fact we were holding the paintings directly above him.

'Colin, just have a look. It does look nice.'

Colin looked above him, but wouldn't budge further than that.

'Up to you.' My spirits lifted. I detected a green light. I figured they would be card buyers or possibly cheque, but not cash. Office workers rarely had cash as opposed to manual workers or ethnic groups.

My arms were getting sore from holding the paintings up. The wife had me up and down to the sofa five times. She was hopelessly insecure without her husband's backing, and although he'd given her permission to do what she wanted, I could see that in reality she couldn't.

'OK, how much?' she said eventually, now that we were off the news and on to the ads before *Emergency Ward 901*.

'The oils cost one hundred and fifteen dollars each.' I never ran the price together for a multiple sale straight away; that would come next. I didn't want to overwhelm the customer with a large sum straight away.

'And for the three?'

'Well, that would be three hundred and forty-five dollars for three oils.' I thought I heard the husband laugh from his sofa.

'Can't you sell me them at a reduced rate as I'm considering more than one?'

I had already weighed up the pros and cons of bartering with them in my first ten minutes in their house, and decided that it would work against me. This was a fairly educated, well-spoken couple with a stable income, judging by their house and clothes, and experience had taught me by now to know that people like to think they want a bargain but they don't really. The moment the painting is brought down in price, they immediately distrust it. I would have felt confident bartering with a builder, or cab driver, but not these people. I would have to teach Colin and his wife the value of my beautiful works of art.

'I'm sorry but the reduction in price has already been accounted for with the removal of the gallery aspect. If you were to find these paintings in a small gallery, let's say, or a café, you would find that they would fetch this plus another fifty dollars just for the privilege of hanging there.' I felt Colin turning towards me, but when I looked at him, he glanced away.

'It's just a lot to pay out unexpectedly.' She laughed tensely. 'I wasn't planning to buy a painting tonight.' She had a simple and honest point, and as usual I was going to have to think of an effective comeback.

'I know, you're right, but often the most spontaneous things in our lives are the best, don't you think?' Predictably they said nothing to that. 'Look, they are paintings done by artists who want to live and work as artists.'

'Oh, I know that, I'm not arguing with you there.' She started stroking her throat, which was a cry for help, and I was about to give her some.

'I'm sorry if I get carried away at this point, it's just I feel very strongly about the amount of money and commission galleries take from artists. That's why we formed this way of working.' I became so strident, I believed myself again. 'And yes, it is technically door-to-door selling, but it's what we believe in. We believe in bringing art to the people.' I made the inverted commas sign with my two index fingers, to reinforce our motto.

'I understand and I agree with you about the price of them elsewhere. I'm just not sure if I should pay all that tonight, that's all.'

'Entirely up to you.'

Colin got up and left the room.

'Take your time, honestly. I like it when people take their time,' I said.

'Let me have a word with my husband.'

'Sure,' I said cheerfully, knowing that Colin would never, despite his passivity while I'd been there, allow his wife to use any of their money to buy my or anybody else's paintings. While they were both out of the room I slumped in the chair momentarily, running my hands over my face with the kind of body language that you don't want your customer to see. The Joyce Cane carpet sale ad came on as usual, boasting further and final reductions on all carpets in her Parramatta Road showroom. The couple came back in; I sat upright and changed my tired face to neutral. I could already tell by her expression that she wasn't going to buy.

'Sorry, but I don't think so. Sorry about that, really.'

'You don't have to apologise to her, you didn't ask for her to try to sell you stuff,' Colin said, pulling the ring on a can of Foster's and falling back into the sofa without even looking at me.

I had a real problem with him now; I would have to deal with him. At moments like this, it was hard to contain my rage, for the rage I felt against the people rejecting my selling technique had become indicative of the rage I had felt most of my life against the world and most of the people in it, and inevitably the rage I felt against my mother. It would be so easy, just once even, to let myself go and tell Colin, or whoever I was working my arse off in front of, to fuck right off. But it would be so wrong, and I had vowed that, no matter what lows I would experience in this game, I would keep control of the urge to lose it. I could play games with these people, I could politely express my disappointment, but I wouldn't allow myself to lose it.

Colin was, in my opinion, about as rude and annoying as anyone I'd come across so far. I was going to sell him a painting – fuck the triptych, even if I sold him one I would be happy. But it had to be him I was winning over now, not his pathetic, insecure, can't-make-a-decision-for-herself wife.

'Sure, no problem, I'll just pack up.' I began going through the motions of leaving. The wife looked guilty while the husband looked more relaxed and pleased with himself, which made my blood boil.

'It's interesting.' I casually set my trap.

'What is?' she asked, as I'd hoped.

'It's just interesting all the different people you come across when you do what I do. You think you have a sense of people and what they like, but you've just proved me wrong.' I slowed down my packing, careful not to run out of paintings to pack away before they bit at my bait.

'Why's that, then?' She still spoke for the both of them.

'Well, based on what I would call instinct, like, you know, the surroundings, your colour scheme, everything, I would have thought that you'd have gone for a very different kind of painting to this one, which is, in my opinion, rather bland.' I waved goodbye to the triptych sale, but I had to scapegoat it in favour of hooking them in on something else.

'No, I liked it, I really do. I just think it's too much money.'

The husband still fixed his gaze on the television. I couldn't be sure whether he had listened to anything I had said, but if I was reading his type correctly then he was hanging on my every word.

'I would have thought that you'd like this one.' I held up the Peter Stuger, and, right on cue, Colin turned his head away from the television and on to the painting that I had the audacity to tell his wife that she should have liked.

'No, I don't like that one so much,' she said.

He just sneered. I was counting on him saying something but the sneer reaction would have to do.

'Oh, you don't like that?' I said, with deep warmth and charm in my voice despite the tightness of my jaw.

'That is awful, look at it,' said Colin suddenly. He was engaging with me, right where I wanted him to be.

'You don't like this?'

'No, I bloody don't.' He wasn't angry or aggressive, just dismissive and sneering.

'You are obviously someone who knows exactly what kind of work they like.'

'Yes I do, and it's not that crap.'

There were proper sentences being exchanged between us now, and that was something I could work with. The wife had sat down, taking a back seat, leaving it to me and Col to battle it out.

'OK and you don't like this.' I brought out another nondescript landscape.

'That's not so bad, but the other one's really bad. I mean, anyone can see that, you don't have to be a bloody art expert.'

'You like all the ones I don't. This one.' I picked up the one that he'd just said he quite liked. Neither of them noticed that I was unpacking all the time I was talking, and arranging the paintings round the room again.

'This one, for example, is painted by an older man, and these ones, the ones I prefer, are painted by a young woman. Amazing that, isn't it?' How anyone could agree to being amazed at this point even out of politeness was beyond me, but they did.

'Yep. I prefer the older guy's stuff – it's just a bit bolder,' he said importantly.

Of course you do, you fucking clown, I thought.

I said, 'There's one painting here I've been trying to sell for a while now. It's by the same guy.'

'What's his name?' asked the wife. The initials were just a squiggle and I frequently made up names to fit them on the spot. On the way into the house there had been a lawnmower on the front porch with Victor written across the front.

'Victor Duffy comes from Melbourne.'

'Oh, yeah?' he said, getting right into it now.

'Well, this painting I can't stand. Victor loves it. I just don't get it, but I keep carrying it around with me when really I shouldn't bother. But you see, that's an example of how different all our tastes can be, one person sees something that another just doesn't, and that's how I feel about that thing.'

'Let's have a look, then.'

I could already hear celebratory music in my head. 'No, honestly, it's a waste of time, trust me, it's going nowhere.'

'Come on, we'll have a look.'

I sighed like it was a pointless chore and brought out a painting I genuinely rarely sold of some golden hayfields and an ominous-looking sunset. I held it up and even shook my head slowly.

Colin nodded his head in response and pointed at it, smiling with his mouth twisted into one corner. 'Now, you see, I like that.'

'*No*! You can't, no way. I don't see it at all.'

'How much is it?' he asked proudly.

'Oh please, no. What about the lovely triptych? Come on, guys.'

'I agree with Colin. I like it too,' announced his wife happily. I had them both.

'I am shocked.' I threw my hands in the air.

'I don't care; I don't bloody like these other ones. I like that one. How much?'

'Hundred and fifteen.' I appeared even more in despair. 'Are you sure?' Never thinking for one moment that they weren't.

'Cash?'

'Cash is fine by me, but I can't say I agree with your choice.'

I win.

CHAPTER FOURTEEN

Mac broke first and potted two stripes. I hadn't seen him for a while, as we had mostly been drinking at the house or in the Red Star, a few streets away.

'So where have you been, kid?'

'I like it when you call me "kid".' I broke the rest of the balls up, to give us options.

'I know you do.' He played with a cigarette between his lips but never once let any ash fall onto the table.

'Have you got children, Mac?'

He sighed deeply and loudly for my benefit in protest at the question, then belted the white, making it double back and pot another one. He then stopped and looked at me, playing with his tongue in the corner of his mouth.

'Oh yes, I do.'

'Where are they?'

'Take a shot, kid.'

I chalked my cue to stall time, hoping that he would answer.

'Are they in Australia?'

'She. Take a shot.'

I missed all the balls.

'Your mind's not on it.'

'It's only a game. I want to know more about you.'

'There's nothing to know, I've told you, what you see is what you get. It starts here, it finishes here.'

'Do you know that you're intriguing?'

He just looked at me again in that way that was increasingly drawing me in.

I potted two. I felt sexy. Australian life suited me; I was brown with the sun, and had enough cash to afford some new clothes from the Saturday markets at Paddington. I was wearing my new dress; it was tight, red, and made of Lycra. I'd borrowed a pair of Karin's boots that laced up the front, and had my hair styled differently by pushing it to the side. I reapplied my lipstick while Mac took his shot, and lit up my cigarette with my new Zippo.

'Hey, what about that Naked Club? That was fantastic. Can we go there again?'

'Ah, Mr Wilson, eh? I knew that would be right down your street. Yes, gets a bit out of the ordinary down there.'

'Why do you go there?'

'The man with the white hair, Charlie, he's an old mate of mine, it's his bar. The lunatic that runs the club, that's Mr Wilson. His father's a cultural attaché.'

'No way.'

Mac softly lined up against the cushion, sending the white rolling softly close to the edge all the way down, nudging in another. 'He's one of those disinherited characters, roaming around the place.'

'A dropout?'

'Of the highest order.'

This was the most straightforward conversation I'd had with Mac since I met him.

'He hires the place once a month, or something like that.'

'Can we go out again one time, Mac?'

'We'll see, shall we? Take your shot.' Mac clicked his fingers and pointed down to the table when Val, the barmaid, looked over.

'Where is your daughter now?'

'Oh, for fuck's sake, you don't give up, do you?'

'Just interested.' I propped myself against the wall, leaning on my cue, while Mac cleaned up.

A boy brought our beers over.

'Val wants to remind you about your tab. She told me to tell you that.'

'Oh, did she? Well, I'll deal with Val later.' The boy went back to the bar.

'What did you do before you came over here?' I asked, taking my beer.

'I was at sea most of my life. I've done a bit of everything, really.'

'What about your wife?'

He was about to pot the black but stopped and rested his forehead on the pool table.

'This is normal; it's called getting to know someone.' I laughed, trying to lighten things a little. He walked over to me, looking into my eyes at close range. I could smell his cigarette-beer breath. It reminded me of the dirty old newsagent I worked for as a teenager on a Sunday job.

'OK, listen.'

I nodded slowly, looking back at him, matching his intensity.

'I never married her, not the first one, never got the chance. Never see the daughter, don't know what happened to her, and don't know her fucking name for fuck's sake. Her mother saw to that. The second one I married, she divorced me over here. That's it.'

'That's really sad,' I said, trying to hold back from throwing my arms around him.

'That's what happens, kid. You do stuff and you live with consequences.' He potted the black, then the rest of mine and placed his cue on the edge of the table, like I suspect he'd done every night for quite a while.

'Hey, you know who you remind me of, Mac?'

'Don't tell me.' Mac perked up, grabbing the chance to deviate from his life story.

'Well, you talk like Humphrey Bogart in *Casablanca*. Have you seen that film?'

'Course I've seen that fucking film, I remember when it came out the first time, unfortunately.'

'You remind me of him, all wounded and washed up in a bar where you feel far away from anyone who can hurt you again.' I felt confident and insightful; I potted another spot, pleased with my analogy and my pool playing. Mac, however, didn't look impressed.

'Well, of all the bars, she's not going to fucking walk into this one.' He finished his drink and looked over at the bar to catch Val's eye for a refill.

'Very good, very good.' I loved our banter on the *Casablanca* theme. I had that exciting, carefree big-night-out-ahead feeling in my stomach. 'Why wouldn't she?'

'What?' He waved at Val. Val shook her head and mouthed for him to fuck off.

'Why wouldn't she come in here?'

'Because she knows I'm here. Now can we finish this?' Squinting against the spire of smoke that constantly trailed up from his mouth he belted his last ball, accidentally taking the black with it.

A few beers later, Mac suggested we leave for somewhere else. I wasn't fussed but got the impression that he didn't like Val and his cronies seeing what he got up to too much. Not that I was sure what he was up to, but I had the feeling that something would happen between us tonight.

Outside, Mac hailed a cab with a two-fingered whistle, which always impressed me.

'Don't you ever walk anywhere?' I asked, straining my voice above the late-night traffic.

'Not if I can help it.'

Inside the car he didn't smoke, which gave him nothing to do but look at me. I was laughing and sticking my head out the window, messing up my new parting.

'You look different from before,' he said.

The cab driver was playing some weird, overpowering classical music, which was totally inappropriate to my playful mood.

'I've got a tan,' I said, playing down my sexiness. 'Everyone looks good with a tan. Turn it up, man, that's fab.' I leant forward. Mac laughed. I turned back round to look at him. He looked at my tits, which looked big in my dress. I felt young and light and strangely full of fun for me. I leant in to kiss him, touching the side of his face; he shaved well and smelt of nice aftershave. I was too drunk by now to notice any of the bad smells I noticed earlier. He was all good. We kissed. His lips felt thin and soft, and he kissed half-heartedly without any force.

'What's wrong?' I asked.

'Have some fucking decorum,' he mumbled.

'Fuck you,' I said, turning round the other way. I looked out of the window for the rest of the journey, which wasn't long, and got no reaction from Mac, who instead smoked and tapped on his leg in time to the music.

As soon as the car stopped, I stormed out, still playing the part of the stroppy female, leaving Mac to pay the fare. I liked our row: I felt safe and married and belonging to someone.

'Where are we?'

'Coogie.'

We were near the sea; I could hear the waves lapping.

'Here we are,' he said, walking across the road. He went into a bar blasting out some live sixties music followed by a round of applause and whistles.

'A lot of English people drink here,' he said as we walked in.

Inside it was heaving and I forgot instantly about my huff. Mac loved the music and uncharacteristically even began singing along.

We got some drinks without paying from a friend of his behind the bar, another older guy. Mac said something about him and introduced us but I couldn't hear. I just smiled and raised my glass to him, mouthing thank you. The band was a perfect pub band: nice, simple, tried-and-tested covers that pleased all. They played a mixture of Kinks, Beatles and Stones. I sang my head off to 'Waterloo Sunset' with Mac standing behind me, both of us facing the band. I reached down a couple of times to hold his hand, only to get burnt by his cigarette, which made him laugh. Three tracks passed, and we drank a whisky and Coke for each song. The room became more and more packed, causing Mac to press into me. I said nothing except thanks for each new drink.

The band played 'A Whiter Shade Of Pale'.

Mac leant down to my ear. 'So sad. This is so fucking sad.'

I let my head rest back on his shoulder, and he played with my hair. I decided I must be in love with him, because it was too odd to be anything else. I couldn't keep my head there for long as it gave me the spins, which was a sign to slow down. So I slowed down everything.

I kissed a random man on the way to the toilet, as usual. The back door of the bar was open; I went outside for a moment to get some air. The door led on to a narrow passageway, which led on to the street. At the end of it was a pay phone. I had some change in my bum bag round my waist. I took out the crumpled piece of paper with Hank's number on it, but I couldn't read it. I tried calling the number which I was convinced was right, but the voice on the other end claimed not to know him. The voice was patient, considering the time, but him not being, or not knowing, Hank angered me, and I accused him of lying. He put the phone down. I soon forgot to be bothered, took deep breaths of air and went back inside.

I was very drunk for me. I didn't notice if Mac was any more drunk than usual but he must have been, because when I went back inside he grabbed me and started kissing me quite hard. We alternated between that and singing along to Rolling Stones' hits. We leant up at the bar for some time; it was difficult to keep track of what we were doing, or saying. His friend at the bar spoke to him while I held onto Mac, more drunk than ever.

'Let's go back, you're drunk,' he said.

'You're drunk,' I said back.

The cab driver had his radio on unnaturally loud. Mac asked him to turn it down as soon as we got in the cab, but he ignored him. Mac sat simmering, tapping his legs and I didn't say anything. I just stared out at the streets. Just as we hit Darlinghurst, the voice of Joyce Cane came on saying all carpets were slashed by sixty per cent. At that point Mac leant forward with his head down, clutching his hair in his fists.

'What's going on?' I slurred.

He lunged forward towards the radio.

'TURN THAT FUCKING THING DOWN, MAN, FOR FUCK'S SAKE!' He grappled with the cab driver who grabbed his hands from the radio. The car skidded to a halt and we were thrown out.

We walked the couple of remaining blocks in silence. I tried to talk to Mac about why he was so pissed off, but he just smoked a little faster than usual and ignored me. It didn't bother me much; he was a moody bastard and nothing would change that.

When we got back to the Honest Irishman, Val was still up smoking and drinking with a couple of regulars. The doors were locked, but they saw Mac at the window and let us in.

'Oh, here he is, then,' said Val, as I followed him across the floor to the back stairs that led to his room. He didn't acknowledge her, and hadn't spoken since he shouted at the cab driver. The stairs were old, wooden and narrow. He gestured to me to be quiet as we walked passed a closed door. He paused outside what I took to be his door and looked at me, tidying his hair from the mess he'd pulled it into. He got a key out of his pocket attached to a curly piece of plastic that stayed linked to his belt loop, and opened the door.

'All right, kid, all right.'

The room was very small with a single bed that was neatly made to military standards, the window was open and a blue curtain blew in the breeze, while late-night traffic going to and from the Cross roared and tooted from the street below. I surveyed its contents. His wardrobe doors were slid along open; in it was one black suit, one of crumpled linen, one pair of shiny good shoes, four white shirts and two pairs of trousers. There were no books, no radio and no pictures. On the table at the window, almost a foot high, was a pyramid of Bic lighters, each one perfectly and meticulously placed to add to the structure. Mac sat down on the one chair and lit up.

'You see, I have everything I need downstairs.' He blew out smoke from what was surely his last cigarette of the evening, and carefully added his current Bic to the pyramid. He mumbled something but I couldn't make him out. I had removed Karin's boots, which were killing me by now, and lay down on his bed. He sat there motionless for the longest time. He looked so sad, and I was well past sexy. But I wanted to see the whole night through with him. It didn't seem right to leave.

I looked at the different colours of the lighters until I fell asleep.

CHAPTER FIFTEEN

'G'day folks, tell you what. We've got some true blue bonza bargains down here, we really have.' Joyce Cane walked amid a mix of hanging carpets in her downtown showroom. 'Like this Persian.' She stopped at one, stroking the corner with some non-speaking extras who smiled inanely. 'Feel that quality.'

The extras nodded, still stroking.

'I'm not kidding you. I would have to be mad to cut these prices, but I am, so I will. But only at my massive end-of-winter sale, where reductions are as much as sixty per cent.'

I stood eating cereal, leaning over the breakfast bar in the communal kitchen area, watching the ad.

The cameras followed her outside her showroom where she was joined by a cross-section of the Australian public in the forecourt.

'What's the name?' she shouted.

The camera panned up high above them all, she stood at the front, and they all waved.

'JOYCE CANE!' they shouted.

'You'd better believe it,' said her voice, before 101 Parramatta Road flashed up on the screen.

Joyce Cane was a warm, bubbly, tanned, trusting-looking woman, with big highlighted curly hair, frosted lipstick and lots of sparkly jewellery. She seemed to be constantly selling all her carpets at half price in a furniture showroom on the Parramatta Road. I wanted Joyce Cane to be my mother. She was perfect. I imagined Christmas day in the Cane household, bursting with lively family, drunken wheezy uncles with Brylcreemed hair, cuddly aunties constantly bringing over food, cute children running around. I would sit next to Joyce at the table – I was her first born on Australian soil, only nine months after she arrived in the mid-sixties. I imagined a happy life as the daughter of a carpet mogul, working contentedly away in the family business for many years before inheriting the entire empire for my own family.

In comparison, I thought about my own family Christmases back home and how bleak they were. How unhappy my mother and father were, and how my father's mood swings overshadowed our lives. How he and my brother would shout and fight, how my mother would drink heavily to cope with it all. I had spent last Christmas in the nursing home with my grandfather, in an attempt to avoid my father. A small thin man, who was husband to one of the nurses, dressed up as Santa Claus and gave out presents to the old people, who were mostly stroke victims or disorientated through dementia. I dressed my grandfather in a suit and shirt and tie and sat at the table with him, pulling crackers and wearing these pointless paper hats. When I left him at the end of the day, he held my face close to his when we hugged. He pulled me in with his working hand until our foreheads pressed firmly together. The stroke had left him unable to speak, but he didn't have to. I understood what he was thinking and feeling, and I wanted to help him leave his overheated hell, but it wouldn't be right.

After my grandfather was admitted to the home, there was no reason for me to stay. He would have wanted me to come here, to find what I'm looking for, and perhaps carve out a better life for myself. And become the only one in my family to escape.

My trance was interrupted by the Danish about to hang out their hand-washing.

'Hey there, Kerry, how's it going?' said Karin, always the more talkative of the two.

'Yeah, all right, what are you up to?' I was glad of their arrival in the kitchen, for I was entering a massive slump brought on by my thoughts of back home. I pushed them away. They would lead me nowhere.

'Hey there,' said Andrea, which was almost all I had ever heard her say. But at least Andrea had admitted to letting Bengy the dog lick her, which made her marginally more interesting.

They pulled open the sliding patio door and began arranging their washing in the yard.

'Yeah, Andrea and I are going to the botanical gardens, I think. Have you ever been there?'

Fucking botanical gardens, who gives a shit? I thought. 'No, but it's supposed to be beautiful,' I said.

The Danish were the perfect tourists. In the short time I had known them, they had taken a day trip to the Blue Mountains, climbed Sydney Harbour Bridge, visited Taronga Zoo, done a guided tour of the opera house and been to see an art exhibition. They had taken hundreds of photos, written millions of letters back home, which they seemed to be constantly posting, and kept a journal each day of what they'd been up to. I, in comparison, had been to several bars and the pawnshop twice.

I envied the Danish. I didn't really know them, but I envied them. Although they were boring and weak, they had happy lives without darkness. They were the only ones in the happy troupe of sellers that were like this. People always say everybody has got their problems, skeletons in the closet, nobody's perfect, etc., but that's bullshit. There are also many people who have had an easy life, with a happy mother and father who loved one another, and a happy schooling, and a life they feel relatively comfortable in; these people inevitably glide through life effortlessly as a result. And Andrea and Karin of Denmark were a prime example.

I had never met anyone from Denmark before and knew nothing of the country itself. I thought it might make bacon, but I couldn't be sure. I should really make an effort to ask them things about it, I thought, finishing off my Kellogg's Multigrain, the cereal of athletes.

'Morning, girls.' Jim was in his shorts and vest, covered in a post-jog sweat.

'Morning, sir,' I joked.

'What's happening here then?'

'The Dan— Karin and Andrea are going to the botanical gardens, and I'm not sure what I'm doing yet.'

It was ten o'clock, which was late for the rest of Australia to get up, but early for me. The night before I had been hot, and slept badly. I was constantly dehydrated from drinking, and the intensity of the weather was starting to give me what I feared were my first hangovers, which would be a major blow.

'You should come out on a run with me,' said Jim, stretching out, making it possible to see under his vest to the scar that ran from the middle of his stomach right round to the side of his abdomen.

'I know I should.' I gulped some apple juice from the fridge.

'Right, then.' He clapped his hands together twice. 'Anyone fancy Bondi? It's a bloody boiling-hot day out there.'

'What time? We're going to the botanical gardens,' said Karin, hanging out the last of their perfect whites.

'Well, to hell with that, grab your togs all of you, I'll see you out the front in ten.'

Bondi is Sydney's most famous beach. It is the busy, bright-blue metropolitan seascape always used in holiday brochures, or adverts for Australia. It was an easy bus ride from town, and was always full of surfers. The beach was quite small, but the water could get really wild and choppy, full of treacherous rips and curls that could drag the most accomplished, experienced surfer out to sea. Consequently, it was manned by muscular lifeguards who sat on high chairs positioned between flags that indicated safe areas to swim and surf. Bondi had its own pavilion at the back of the sand, a large white fifties building, with a café seating area and changing-room facilities. Behind it lay a parade of restaurants, bars and shops. This was where all Sydney's teenagers did their first dating, which if you were a girl, consisted of watching surfing, and if you were boy consisted of showing off your surfing to the watching girls.

Everybody in Sydney looked like they had a modelling contract. The boys were so good-looking it was ridiculous. They had blond wiry hair from surfing and enormous golden shoulders, with tiny hips and waists to die for. It was such a shock coming from Scotland where most people were fat and white, with faces broken up with red veins, due to the cold or excessive alcohol consumption, and where nearly all men were bald before thirty.

Jim was in good condition, tall and broad and solidly built.

We all took off our clothes and settled down on the sand. Jim wore fairly baggy shorts, while the Danes and I wore our bikinis. Karin and Andrea had matching bodies, with long lean legs and small tits. They too were broad and healthy in their frame. I was shorter than them by about two inches and my tits were bigger, but my frame was petite, and without paying much attention to what I ate or drank I never seemed to put on weight, which is why I knew I would never venture out jogging with Jim, and had no plans to exercise until I was in my thirties. The Danes wore baseball hats to protect their pretty little pale faces and fair hair from the sun. I, on the other hand, was blessed with good skin, which was almost Mediterranean in its ability to turn brown without getting burnt. I covered myself with olive oil that I'd taken from the kitchen in an effort to get even browner. After a while I got bored and became curious about Jim's scar, now that it was in full view.

'How did you get this, then, Jim?' I asked, tracing it with my finger.

'Got involved with some stupid big Yorkshire men, back home, in a long-running feud.' He spoke from behind his sunglasses.

'Who came out worse, then?'

'My little brother did.'

'What happened?'

He began filling his hands with sand by his side and emptying them again.

'Life deals you blows, terrible blows, and it changes everything, and then you become someone different.' Jim spoke slowly in a monotone. 'It can all change, in a matter of minutes.' He clicked his fingers. 'Madness.'

'What happened?' I fixed on his scar.

'Aw. It's too much for now.' He sighed, and tipped sand out his hands again.

'I've told you, when we go on this bloody trip we'll learn lots about one another, don't you worry.' He dusted sand off his forearms and started tidying around him, even though there was nothing to tidy. He moved a Coke can and flattened out the beach towel he was lying on.

All the time the Danish had been listening to Jim, they never said a word in response to his story. How could they? This was way out of their league.

'Christ's sake, listen to me going on, what a miserable bastard.' Jim stood up, took off his glasses and stretched. 'Pull yourself together, Crown.' Jim was always telling himself off in the third person. 'Come on, let's get in. I'll race ye, ye daft Scottish bastard!' He sprinted off.

I ran screaming towards the giant foamy waves, Jim already waist-deep punching the water and roaring with laughter before I'd reached the edge.

Greg and Anaya called a group meeting back at the flat, half an hour before we left for the suburbs.

Jim and I sat drained and sunbeaten on the sofa waiting for Scotty to arrive. Anaya and the Danish drank herbal teas in the kitchen, while Greg paced up and down smoking. We all laughed at Scotty's car screeching to a halt outside, for he drove all the time like it was an emergency. His stereo stopped and he burst in.

'Guys, guys, how you doin'?'

Despite what a see-through dick he was, I had to admire him for his constant attempts at humour and friendliness.

'Yeah, in your own time, Scotty, mate,' said Greg, who, despite his casual, relaxed, constantly stoned persona, was always keen that we maximised our selling time and rarely allowed any excuse for lateness. Scotty winked at me and sat down on the floor. I noticed that he had two different shoes on.

'Right then, guys.' Greg brought out some envelopes from his pocket. 'First of all, I've got some money cleared from various people's credit-card transactions. Scotty.' He gave one out to him.

'Cheers, mate.' Scotty gave him the thumbs-up.

'Karin, here you go. Kerry.'

'Thank you.' I took the money and counted it before putting it in my pocket.

'Finally, Andrea.' She smiled sheepishly taking the money; I was mystified as to how she sold anything. Perhaps they just found her look trustworthy and honest and her pretty little pale face spoke for itself.

Anaya took over. 'Yeah, guys, I know you know this but do try to get cash. I know it's hard but try. It's better for all of us, especially when you go up the coast.'

'Yeah, the coast. Looks like we're all set for next week,' said Greg, handing Jim an envelope which I took to be his percentage of our credit-card sales. 'Basically, we think the middle of next week would be a good time to go. You'll all take the Kingswood. We'll load it up and off you go.'

'How long?' asked Andrea.

I couldn't have cared where we went or how long we went for. I could call Hank from wherever if I wanted to. I had no interest where we would be staying when we did, happy to go with the flow. I didn't bother with the usual questions; I left that to Karin and Andrea.

'Two weeks is what we usually do. You stay in caravan parks and motels.'

'Yeah. Watch out for redbacks,' said Scotty.

'What is redback?' asked Karin.

'It's a spider with a lethal bite and if it's miles to the nearest serum store you're fucked.'

'Scotty! Enough now!' shouted Frau Anaya.

'Yeah, yeah, there's spiders, and snakes and sharks, but none of them will get you because you lot will be in the houses of the lovely people of the Gold Coast, OK?' Jim scrunched up his envelope paper, threw it at Scotty and said jokingly, 'I'll bite your flamin' arse if you don't shut up.'

'Really, you'll be doing the same thing as you do here except you'll get to see some of the coast and countryside, which is wonderful.' Greg lit up. 'Jim and I will go through the maps and routes before you go and sort you out some good areas, and that's pretty much it. You will seriously love it, guys.'

'What will you guys be up to when we've cleared off up north?' asked Scotty, which I suppose we had all wondered about, for there was a part of all of us that was suspicious of Greg and Anaya's true intentions.

'We will be here dealing with stock and things,' said Anaya.

'How will we fit all of us and the paintings in the Kingswood?' was Andrea's contribution to the questions.

'You won't take much stuff of your own,' replied Greg, without hesitation.

'Yeah, the girls will have to leave their make-up. That takes up far too much room.' Scotty looked round the room for the recognition he felt his joke deserved. Karin delivered him a mock slap on the back of the head.

'Seriously, doin' all the way up to Brisbane, yeah?' asked Scotty.

Suddenly I was very interested. 'Brisbo? Brisbane, yeah? Is that where we'll be staying?' My stomach turned over.

'That's the plan,' said Greg.

'Right, guys, let's get going,' said Lady Macbeth. 'Make good sales, you guys. Later tonight, we're gonna cook for you a proper Aussie barbie. Well, Greg is, he's the cook.' She laughed.

'Yeah, we're going to enjoy ourselves. It's been a good month for us and it's going to get even better,' said Greg. Anaya winked at him.

I sank down into the sofa, trying to get my head around the prospect of perhaps some kind of showdown very soon.

CHAPTER **SIXTEEN**

The evening dragged. I wanted it over so we could go back to William Street and party. I had been in three houses so far, all of them on Ocean Drive in Diamond Bay. Two of them were time-wasters, and the third were time-wasters who at least offered me a drink. Three female friends sat around drinking cocktails and were more than happy to let me in almost immediately, always a bad sign. They talked about the paintings, laughed at the unicorn, and got me to bring various ones over to each of them so they could examine them at close range. They asked me plenty of questions about the paintings, and even more about myself and where I was from. But they didn't buy. It would be a rare occurrence to have women buying any paintings without their male partners. They fell into the 'things for the house' category, and that was usually a joint decision, I had found. I knew all this but it was hard to get away from them. I was washed out from the sun and the beach, and they offered to make me a strawberry daiquiri, which I couldn't refuse as I had never tasted one before. Afterwards I thanked them and left, preoccupied by the notion of joint decisions, wondering whether I'd ever experience such a thing.

I quit Ocean Drive, and took the next left into Leamington Terrace. I was immediately drawn to the corner house, where from the street I could see into the lounge, which was packed full of children in what seemed to be a meeting of the largest family known to man. I suppose it was wrong of me to interrupt a 'family' occasion, but you do what you have to do to get by.

I wasn't sure where they were from; their English was very limited. The man who answered the door was old, with a short beard and yellow teeth. Most of the men had thick dark stubble or moustaches. I took them to be Arab but I wasn't sure; I'd had no experience of any countries other than the one I had escaped from. Children weaved in and out around us as I attempted to explain what I was doing.

'Paintings,' I said, opening up the folder.

'You show,' he said.

'Do you like the paintings?' I said, bringing out the Stuger.

'No, you come, you show.' He indicated for me to stop showing him and to follow him into the lounge.

There were about thirty people packed into the room, which was full of heavy ornate furniture laden with an enormous buffet, with food on it I didn't recognise. They all spoke very fast and smiled at me, while the men smoked and drank from strange little glasses with a fancy design round them. The women wore baggy sheet-like dresses and had material covering their heads.

'Hello.' I smiled at the whole room. The women seemed friendlier than the men.

Most people nodded back.

'How are you today?' I asked, not knowing where to start.

'Hello, how are you? Welcome,' said a chubby man in a white shirt, with a chest as hairy as a rug.

'Good. Good.' I wondered if I should open the folder and get my paintings out or wait a while. Most of the people broke out into chat of their own again, which I didn't sense was about me, so I thought it would do me no harm to light up and join the rest of the smokers. I reached into my back pocket and pulled out a soft pack of Marlboro Lights, the brand I had now switched to, influenced by my visit to Robin's house in Neutral Bay.

'No, please. You take, welcome.' Six moustached men leant forward with their cigarettes. I took one from the man next to me, the same one who answered the door. I felt stupid taking his cigarette because it too was a Marlboro.

'My name is Kerry,' I said before my inhale.

'Yes, welcome.' They liked to use the word welcome.

'I come from Scotland,' I said on my exhale.

'Yes, welcome to our home,' said the one who answered the door, again.

'Where are you from?'

'Jordan.'

'OK, right, yeah.' I had no idea where it was.

'Please, try this.' One of the men handed me the small fancy glass. So far none of the women had spoken, although initially they seemed friendlier. They just smiled and nodded and chatted among themselves. I toasted them all and said cheers, they said something back. I drank the fiery drink down in one because the glass was so small and I thought it might be the correct way to do it. This caused them all to laugh quietly. The drink was foul, and what I had imagined meths to taste like. I made a noise after I swallowed it and clutched my throat.

The children started to open the folder and got out some of the pictures.

'Careful now,' I spluttered, taking a painting back quickly. I stretched my hands out and rubbed my fingers together in an effort to explain that the kids' hands might be dirty. One of the mothers pulled two children towards her.

It didn't take long for the fiery drink to relax me and make me not care about anything again. I also hadn't eaten much and had just sampled a do-it-yourself daiquiri, which no doubt was stronger than one made in a bar would be. I was enjoying the language barrier, and the room full of Jordanians who felt little need to try to talk with me.

I sat looking around the room at everyone; there seemed no sense of urgency. I decided to enjoy myself for a while before getting to work. Usually I would have begun directing the conversation, but the strange drink had an overpowering effect on me. Some children lingered by the folder, still in anticipation of its contents.

'You want to look in here?' I spoke like a zombie. The kids giggled and looked back at their mothers. A woman stepped forward with a dish of olives.

'Please.' She offered them to me. I wanted some of the food on the table rather than the olives, but I politely accepted.

'You can eat if you want,' said the chubbiest of all the men.

'Mmm, thank you.' I was offered a plate and led to the table.

'What is this?' I picked up a green thing.

'This is vine leaf,' she said.

I filled my plate, sampling almost a bit of everything. Some of the others did the same. I sat back down and ate in silence.

'I want to see!' shouted a little boy with big ears and glasses.

'OK, little man, I'll show you.' I felt momentarily happy and playful.

The men started lighting up. I was offered another cigarette but declined in favour of one of my own. I bent forward to take a light off a man two seats to my right. He looked at me and then looked down my vest top. I gave him a quick look back, taking a little longer than necessary with the lighter.

I brought out the paintings, displaying them wherever I could find a space between the furniture and where people were sitting. Once I'd finished, the chatter increased, everybody helping themselves to a closer look, some picking them up and passing them around. There was absolutely no point in me saying much, they would either want to buy or not. Meanwhile I was happy accepting an offer of another shot from the man who looked down my top. I sipped it a little, learning from the last time.

'Yes, you must take slow,' he said, looking at me in a much dirtier way than before. I felt differently towards this one than the Greek one from a few weeks earlier. He wasn't so pathetic – desperate all the same, but not so nervous. I wondered how many men there were wishing that a bit of spontaneous action would appear on their doorstep and break up the monotony of their married lives. It didn't bother me. The way I saw it, was I was offered drinks and things happened; it had always been that way. For me the language barrier was a plus, the less said the better.

A man, who'd been out of the room since I'd arrived, came into the lounge and said something to the others, pointing back outside to the garden. I wondered when the eye-contact man would make his move, as the situation was very restricting. The man from the garden sat down, given a seat by a woman who went outside. The eye-contact man got up.

'Come with me, I show you.'

I downed the shot, feigned a questioning look to the rest of the room and followed them both out.

At the end of the garden behind a hut was a wooden fence with a corrugated roof, which contained some kind of enormous grill-cum-barbecue facility. The woman was using tongs to turn over a huge piece of flat bread. I couldn't have given a shit about the bread or whether they were frying a kangaroo out there, I knew what this was all about.

'Wow, you make your own stuff here?' I asked, playing along.

'Yes, we cook Arabian food. This is our bread, you try some,' said the woman. She took the piece off the heat and put it on a plate. The man said something to her. She took the bread and went inside. I leant up against the fence with my leg folded behind me, waiting until he said something.

'What is your name?' he asked slowly.

'Anaya.'

'My name is Faleed,' he said, glancing over to the house. I had gone into a trance in anticipation of him touching my tits. I had no concerns over the people in the house coming out at any time, it wasn't my problem, and neither did I care about the paintings for a while. He smoked and looked me up and down; I hated myself for starting to ache, but had no control over it.

The woman came back out from the house carrying something. I stood up from the fence and looked alert and interested in the grill. So did the man, who had grabbed some tongs as soon as she appeared.

She handed him a plate with some red meat on it. He laid the meat on the grill, which sizzled and spat. I took the tongs from him for the benefit of the woman. Then she left, seemingly without any idea. I put the tongs down, and moved back against the fence out of view from the house. I looked at his crotch intentionally so that he would see me doing so. Without looking at me, but with his eyes on the house and one hand on the tongs, he pulled my nipple with his free hand. His hard-on was massive and brushed against the edge of the grill. I unzipped him and brought out his cock. All the time he looked inside the house, then back to the grill. I moved my hands up and down, he made no sound. He grabbed my breast more firmly then rubbed his hand on my crotch outside my jeans.

'Open this,' he whispered.

'No,' I said. I leant back against the fence and unbuttoned my jeans just enough for me to slip my hand in, intentionally keeping just too far for him to reach me without losing a full view of the house. The meat sizzled away near his cock.

'It's burning,' I said, moving my hand around.

'Very sexy,' he said, not noticing the smoke.

'The meat, look.' I gestured to the grill with my head. 'It's burning, you must turn it over.'

His eyes had glazed over; I felt my face flushed with the drink and the excitement. He took the tongs and turned the meat over, to reveal a burnt topside. I moved over to him and put his hand down my jeans. He moaned.

'Yeees.'

I moved his cock up and down some more, before moving back against the fence. A female voice shouted out from the back door. He shouted back, turning his body round towards me more to fully conceal his exposed erection behind the grill. When he turned back towards me, I was touching myself quickly, aware that there was little time.

'Let me see,' he said.

I opened my jeans more, unzipping them right down to give him a full view. I was surprised that I was able to come given the effect of the drink, but I did. I made no sound, just shut my eyes and pressed my head into the fence. He came about ten seconds after me, shooting his load onto the ground and spilling some onto the cooler box. He tugged at his penis making sure he'd emptied everything before zipping it away. I had already lost interest. He mumbled something, smiling at me. He attempted to touch my face. I pulled away, feeling that we were both pathetic. He put the meat, which I'd now decided was lamb, onto the plate. I took it from him, saying nothing and headed for the lounge, wanting one more of the shot drinks before I hit the road.

Inside, three people stood round one painting.

'You have others of this one?' said the chubby man, holding up my favourite painting of the unicorn drinking from a lake in a background of hanging willow trees and a distant waterfall.

CHAPTER SEVENTEEN

Greg placed the biggest prawns I'd ever seen on the barbecue, while Anaya smoked and prodded the coal with some tongs. We all sat round the patio out the back of the house, every so often going back inside to help ourselves to the contents of the enormous fridge designated entirely for cooling beer.

Scotty sat on the step, skinning up as usual, holding centre court.

'Hey, so this guy's getting on with this girl, yeah?'

We all reluctantly say yes or nod.

'And he starts proper fucking her, yeah?'

Some of us nod.

'So he starts getting into it, yeah, and her toes curl up.'

The Danish giggle, Jim and I roll our eyes.

'So, he's well into it by now, trying to ignore what's happening, when her feet start to curl up.' Scotty dragged it out, being the type of person that can't complete a joke for laughing at it. 'So he's beyond the point of no return when suddenly the entire fucking lower half of her body starts curling.'

Andrea Danish had to cover her mouth up in case she spat out her drink.

'And finally he says, "What the fuck's happening?"' He finished his JD and kept some ice in his mouth, which meant he mumbled during the next bit. 'And she says, "Ye flamin' idiot, I've still got my bloody tights on."' He spat out his ice and slapped his leg, collapsing about the place.

Then Karin asked, 'What are tights?'

Jim and I started laughing harder than Scotty.

'Scotty, mate,' said Jim, 'I'm afraid you lost the girls on the tights reference.'

'Say again, mate?' I could see Scotty was growing tense.

'Well, you don't get tights here, do you? And it's obviously another word in Denmark.'

Scotty tried to laugh it off but he hated being teased by Jim. Jim didn't let up.

'Sorry, mate, I shouldn't laugh but your whole joke was resting on tights.' Jim spluttered into his schooner.

'Yeah, well, it was a bloody pommy that told me that joke.' This only made Jim laugh even more.

'Poor Scotty,' said Anaya, stroking his head.

'Poor Scotty nothing, there's nothing wrong with me, it's you lot, you're too bloody serious.' Scotty's face was always red and sunburned but now it was the reddest I'd seen it.

'Jesus, it's going to be an interesting trip for you lot,' said Greg, all slow and half cut as usual.

'Yes, when would we be back in Sydney?' asked Andrea, no doubt hoping that everything fitted in with their student plans.

'The trips last around two weeks, and they are unforgettable, aren't they, Scotty?' Anaya brought Scotty back to us, which cheered him up.

'Oh, mate, I tell you, they are awesome.'

'Why are they awesome?' asked Jim, much to Scotty's annoyance.

'Just a real laugh and you get to see some nice parts of the coast.'

'What about that Italian girl, Scotty – will you being seeing her again?' Anaya leant on Greg and winked at Scotty.

'Who, Daniela? No way, she was a fucking nightmare.' Scotty pushed his baseball-hat peak further up his head as though he was overheating.

I felt sorry for Scotty because although he seemed a happy guy who enjoyed life to the full, I could see behind his act. Here was a man who could not stop joking and boasting about his conquests with women, which I doubted in reality had been more than about two. I wondered if I'd find out more about him and what he was hiding. The same with Jim, and with Frau Anaya. As for the Danish and Greg, there was nothing more than what you saw on the surface. I agreed with Greg, the trip was going to be very interesting.

'Hey, Greg, I was thinking that you might want to give Bali a call and order some more unicorns before the trip. Might be lots of non-Aussies along the coast,' said Jim.

'Yeah, mate, I just might.' Greg didn't turn round. Then he began laughing and spluttering in my direction. 'Mate, I've gotta fucking hand it to you. Once again, you've outdone yourself! Four fucking unicorns.'

Everybody laughed.

'I know, I know, it's mental, I couldn't believe it. How does it happen?' I played along with the shock factor for entertainment purposes. I mean, it was a triumph, but I understood how it happened.

Jim shook his head as he peeled the label off his Victoria Bitter. 'What's the most of one painting you've ever sold, Greg?'

Greg turned round, sweat pouring from his face, eyes like piss holes as usual. 'I remember when I first started out, I sold to a company who had just bought some massive office block and I convinced them that they should buy a ton of abstracts for their corridors, and I think I might have sold around twenty, but I've never had more than one unicorn sold at a time. That is pretty amazing.'

'And very strange,' added Jim.

Fucking Greg and his office story topping my triumph. I looked over at Anaya, who was watching me the whole time Greg was talking. What the fuck was her problem with me?

'I told you this business is fascinating, really bloody fascinating; you learn so much about people.' Greg turned back to putting the prawns on a plate.

'Is that why you're in it, Anaya?' I asked, really pushing it.

'Maybe, yeah, why not?' Anaya was floundering and began helping Greg distribute the food to take the heat away from her.

'Do you ever wonder about the people that paint the shit we sell? Do you think that they might be having a beer somewhere, laughing like we are about it?' Jim was still picking at his label, searching for the deeper meaning as usual.

'Oh mate, nah, nothing much goin' on there. Just normal people, trying to make a buck without doing too much, just like you and me.' Scotty picked more stray tobacco out of his mouth and offered his joint around. Greg accepted.

'You reckon?' asked Jim, unconvinced.

'Fuck, yeah.'

'Maybe some of them are really brilliant painters, maybe they hate having to do this shit. I mean, they can really paint, can't they?' The truth was I had often wondered about the people who supplied us with all our artwork or, more to the point, who supplied us with the names signed at the bottom. I'd asked Greg and Anaya, and they insisted that the names were genuine. Although the only clear one was Peter Stuger.

'It's a simple operation, they do what they do best and we do what we do best.' Greg drew in the joint then passed it to Anaya.

'Exactly,' she said, inhaling and then blowing it out.

'Why don't we toast the painters?' I said, standing up and lifting my bottle.

'And the unicorn,' said Andrea.

Jim, Scotty and I stood up; we all moved over to Greg and Anaya beside the barbie. I cleared my throat.

'OK, raise your drinks, folks, to Peter Stuger and the other signatures we're unable to read.'

'And the unicorn!' shouted Karin.

We all clinked bottles to various mumbles of 'Peter Stuger'. Anaya and I clinked each other's last and with some considerable force.

The evening turned into drunken dancing. Jim was the only one reluctant to join in. I tried to drag him up a couple of times but he just wasn't having it.

'No, fuck off! I'm really not a dancer, OK?' He stood against the wall watching me and Scotty throw each other round in an attempt to do some kind of jive to 'My Baby Just Cares For Me'.

'No one really is. Come on!' I tried grabbing both his hands.

'It's not going to happen.'

Karin came over and grabbed his other hand, helping me to try to drag him up. Eventually he gave in.

'OK, OK, but it won't be pretty.' He reluctantly got to his feet and swayed around making a figure of eight with Karin and me dancing beside him. Scotty danced with Andrea, and Greg and Anaya were pressed up to one another even though the music was fast.

I took off my vest and danced in my bra and denim shorts. Scotty clapped and whistled using his two fingers. Andrea did the same, then Karin. Anaya looked over at us, took off her T-shirt and threw it behind her, causing it to land on a branch in the tree that hung over from the adjoining wall. A fairly poor portable stereo that mostly stayed on the kitchen worktop supplied the music. I ran inside and turned it up as far as it would go so that the sound distorted badly, but I needed all it could give. When I got back outside, Scotty had taken his T-shirt off, and Andrea was attempting to remove his long baggy surfer shorts. Jim was avoiding the entire thing by sitting back down on the step, picking at a new label and drinking fast. The Danish and Anaya began dancing round Greg, who looked gross thrusting into Anaya. I removed my bra and threw it towards Anaya's suspended T-shirt. Anaya removed hers next and she switched partners to dance with me. Some chart-topping shit belted out, and then changed into Rainbow's 'Since You've Been Gone', which caused an upsurge in madness. The Danish were topless too and began a double pelvic grind with Greg, who was far too out of it to notice anything.

Anaya and I danced round one another shouting out the chorus and playing air guitar. Then she pushed into me, rubbing her tits against mine. Scotty cheered and poured beer over himself. I put my hand round on to Anaya's arse and pulled her into me. We stayed like that for the duration of Rainbow, checking out Greg every so often just to make sure things were OK. We looked right into each other. She had the most piercing blue-green eyes, and her blue eyeliner was slightly smudged, making her look damaged and fucked up and even sexier.

'I see you,' I said dreamily.

'WHAT?' she bellowed.

'I SAID, I SEE YOU!' I immediately regretted shouting it. She said nothing back, just laughed for the first time ever.

I was completely fucked again. It had been a slow, steady climb since the daiquiri way back in one of the first houses to the fiery shots with the Jordanians to the VBs here. Fuck the prawns, I thought, as I pressed into the warm sweaty groin of the woman I hated but wanted. Scotty had paired off with Andrea and was dancing behind her, his hands on her hips. The song finished, I swung Anaya round to find an empty step where Jim had sat.

I pressed my forehead against the door in the phone booth, convinced that I was making sense but finding it hard to remember the last sentence the nurse had spoken to me. I only had eight dollars in coins and had already used half saying God knows what.

'His name is Joe. Joe Swaine, don't call him Joseph, he hates it, it's Joe, yeah?'

'Kerry, we know his name is Joe, and I appreciate that you are far away, but there really is nothing to worry about ...'

'He hates it there, not-there, that-he's-like-that-there, you know?' I caught myself slurring.

The nurse sighed. 'The last time you called up, you were drunk and abusive to the staff.'

'FUCKSAKE!'

'I won't tolerate bad language. Perhaps you should call back. I'm going to terminate the call.'

'Terminate? Come on, look.' I had a point to make but couldn't remember it. 'OK-OK-OK, OK, listen, when it's late at night here it's the right time there, so that's why I'm like this, you don't like me calling the other time I've called.'

'We can't accept calls all of the time, we have to organise meals and that uses all the staff.'

I could hear her whispering my name to someone else in the background.

'Like a fucking zoo, feeding time,' I mumbled under my breath.

'I beg your pardon.'

'Nothing.' I sighed and pressed my whole face into the door. 'I need to speak to him, he's my only family left.'

'That's not true; your mother has been here to visit your grandfather.'

'I don't talk to her. I want to talk to him, why can't I?' I heard Radio Forth come on in the background, seeping through from the inmates' lounge to the warden's office.

'We don't have the facilities to do that but we can pass on a message.'

'Do you have the facilities to change the station or at least put it on one properly?' I laughed entirely through my nose.

'I'm going now, Ms Swaine.'

'Please, please, when can I speak to him? He needs me.'

'If you call back another time when you are sober, between our hours of nine and ten am we can perhaps come to some arrangement—' The beeps went but I'd used all my dollars and the line went dead. I stood there for a while, blowing out through my mouth, before calling it a day and going back inside to bed.

CHAPTER **EIGHTEEN**

It had been a baking hot day, perhaps the hottest I had experienced since arriving in Sydney. It was 1st October, the start of the Australian spring. The time had moved so quickly since I began selling paintings, and I was starting to feel more settled than at any other time in my life. However, the fear of never achieving what I'd really come here to do in the first place was beginning to eat me up. I had called Hank a couple of times, but he'd had no luck. He told me I could call any time and just talk about things, but I backed off. I was also worrying about my drinking, which was starting to feel like a monkey on my back. I was growing tired of managing it, of watching it, of measuring my abstinence from it on the odd occasion when I would try turning over a new leaf. I had promised myself that once I had found what I was looking for, I would quit drinking for good, which would automatically stop me sleeping with so many strangers. One day the strangers would have to stop, and turn into one person.

But I didn't feel that I could move on in any shape or form until I found her. Then, when I thought deeply about it, I came to the conclusion that I only looked for her when I really wanted to, when it felt pressing. The rest of the time I was just following the course of my life, whatever that was. Anyway, I was convinced that things happened for a reason; thinking the whole thing over panicked me, then the emptiness would set in again, and I would have to push it down for my own survival.

I had additional practical worries to consider as well; my work visa would run out in two months and then I would have to make some serious decisions. I didn't know if I could sell paintings long term, I needed to have a proper career some-where down the line. My money passed through my hands each week, my plan to save amounted to nothing as usual.

I rested my head against the back-seat car window and looked up at the Sydney sky, disappointed in myself as a tourist. We passed the green and white road signs leading us out of the city. The car was quiet, the Danish were snoozing. Karin had drifted off, causing her leg to lean against mine, which was making me sleepy. Scotty sat up front, his baseball cap covering his eyes, his head way back against the headrest. Jim was at the wheel, and had hardly spoken a word all after-noon. I leant forward and massaged his shoulders.

'All right, love?' he asked.

'Yeah, just thinking,' I said, not sure whether to share any of my feelings with Jim. I had the feeling since the barbie that he was off with me. I wondered if he thought my behaviour with Anaya was out of order. I was sick of Anaya, she was full of shit and games. I was looking forward to the trip away, to put some distance between us. I decided against discussing her with Jim.

'And, how're you doing?'

'Just knackered. It's too hot for this, isn't it?' he said, blowing out.

'What were you like when you were my age, Jim? Were you happy?'

'Huh.' He coughed. 'Thought I was, I suppose, but things are better now.'

'So they get better as you get older, do they? All that shit is true, is it?' I spoke softly, not wanting the others to hear. I had drunk with these people until late into the night, most nights since I had met them, and I had got to know them, but I didn't talk to anyone about why I came here, or what I got up to in the houses. That was my business.

'Well, you've got to put in a bit of effort, you know. It doesn't just all fall into place, like.' He looked at me over his sunglasses in the driving mirror.

'Do you think there is such a thing as the right person for us all?'

'Ooh, don't know about that, but I've been burnt. Do you?'

'I hope so,' I said, half laughing and resting back on the seat again. 'Or I'm fucked.'

This was the last night of selling before the coast trip. We had tomorrow off to get our things together, and I promised myself to give myself a sober day before our departure. The last thing I wanted was to be hungover in a car on a long, hot journey.

It was nowhere near dark when Jim dropped me at Watson's Bay. I couldn't wait for dusk to take the sting of the day away. I surveyed the houses with my now expert eye. There were many people not home from work yet, few cars outside and most doors and fly screens closed. The street was long and wide, I felt exposed, standing on the corner with my big black folder of lies.

I walked up a path belonging to a house that had a dog barking round the back. A woman answered.

'Can I help you?' She appeared cautious.

'Well, my name's Kerry, I'm travelling around with my paintings.' I knocked on the folder. 'Showing them to people, trying to raise some interest in my work.'

'I don't want to buy any paintings, thanks.'

She was right of course, but her directness irritated me.

'I'm not necessarily selling them—'

She cut me off. 'So you're just wandering around are you, showing them to everyone just for the sake of it?' She laughed a little.

No one had spoken to me like this before; she was bang on the nose.

'Well, it's really a different approach from the galleries that take so much from the artists. We have decided to bring art to people, just ordinary people like yourself.'

She pulled her hair behind her ears, her eyes darting all over me, the folder and the rest of the street. 'I don't think so.' She began closing the door, which had happened many times. It was one of the hazards of the job, and I'd learned to let it quickly wash over me and move on to the next one, not wasting too much time with the no-go areas. But tonight I pushed it.

'You could at least give me a minute.'

'I don't have a minute.'

A car pulled up outside, then reversed carefully into the driveway. We both watched it. She became increasingly anxious. I was turning away slowly, calling it a day, when the engine stopped and a man got out. I thought he was pointing down at my folder and mouthing something when he first pulled up, but then I told myself I was being paranoid. Turned out I wasn't. His face was vaguely familiar, which could mean only one thing. He quickly got out of the car.

'You don't remember me, do you?' He was tall and dark with cropped hair, and he moved his car keys in and out of his fist. He didn't acknowledge the uptight woman, choosing to stare me out instead.

If I had sold to him, I couldn't deny it, for he may have been a credit-card customer and everything would be recorded in a paper trail that would lead to my name and the company. Anyway, I wasn't breaking the law, I said to myself, trying to feign relaxed and perplexed at the same time.

'Amazing that I should run into you, don't you think?' He was milking it.

My mouth went dry. 'That depends on the circumstances in which we met before.' I tried to empower myself with my casual response.

'Bruce, what the fuck's going on?' The woman changed the tone immediately with her use of fuck, bringing a sense of urgency that hyped us all up, each for our own individual reasons.

'Bruce?' I shook my head. 'Nope, sorry, I still don't remember.'

'Well, I suppose you meet so many people on your little travels, it must be hard to keep track of who you run into.'

This was the point of no return.

'Bruce, can you get inside?' The woman had another agenda. I remained perplexed, lost for words for once.

'No, you go inside, I've still got some questions to ask our little rip-off artist.' Bruce thought he was Columbo. I wondered how long he was going to dance round the situation before charging me. He took a step nearer to me. I heard a heavy old engine with a meaty exhaust that I prayed was the

Kingswood. It seemed to be coming from behind the house on the next road down, but I was unable to see through a thicket of trees to ascertain whether it was or not.

'Bruce!'

Bruce turned to look at the woman who gestured furiously at the other houses.

'Linda, get back inside. I'll deal with this.' The woman left, shaking her head and waving her arms around.

'Listen, mate,' I said reasonably, 'whatever you're worked up about, don't take it out on me, I've done nothing wrong, I've just obviously sold you a painting that you no longer like, sorry, but ...' I was talking with a wobbly half-laugh voice, which I realised must be irritating but my nerves were taking over.

'Let me see inside your folder, please!'

'It's a bit late for "please", isn't it?'

'I'm going to go inside and phone the police if you don't let me look. I have friends in the police force, you know.'

'I don't have to let you look, it's my property.' It was time for Bruce to back down. Through a small clearing at the back on the left, I could have sworn that I saw the creamy roof of the Kingswood getting closer.

'You're trespassing.'

'What, on your land?'

He was about to say something, but changed his mind at the last minute. I knew from the moment he arrived that it wasn't his house. It was time for me to be Columbo now.

'OK, Bruce, what did I do to you?'

'You sold me two paintings under the pretence that they were originals.'

'Uh-huh.' I nodded.

'Then I bloody find out that there's about four other people in the same street as us that have the same ones – so I want my bloody money back.' Bruce had gone white round the lips by now, and a dark red in the face.

Of course he was completely within his rights, but that didn't mean I was going to comply with them. Besides, I was about to win this case, because he'd made one fatal mistake.

'I'm sorry if you feel I misrepresented the artwork I was selling but they are genuine paintings—'

He cut me off. 'BULLSHIT!' He looked around the street, moved even closer to me and clenched his teeth, trying to control the volume at which he was talking to me. 'I paid you around three hundred dollars and I want it fucking back. Now, I want to see inside the folder, and I'm calling the police.'

'Inside is a bunch of paintings. Some of them are the same designs as the ones I sold to you, but you know that, so why don't you fuck off?' I regretted the last bit, but at the same time it was so satisfying. This guy was being way too heavy with me. I began walking off. He strode towards the door to go inside and, I guessed, use the phone. The woman was at the curtain, and he pointed to the door for her to open it.

I got to the end of the drive, my heart pulsing, adrenalin rushing around my body, then I turned back, rushed to the door and knocked on it. She opened it, and I could see him on the phone in the background. I couldn't let him do it. I remembered Greg telling us that we should never leave customers uncomfortable, or any untied loose ends that might have the company investigated, except he didn't say investigated, but I knew that was what he meant. And that was where this was heading.

He dialled. I moved in for the kill. I put my folder against the outside wall, leaning into the house. He looked up at me.

'You take one step in this house and I will have you prosecuted.' He shook with rage, and was clearly dying to punch me, as I was him.

'I'm not in your fucking house, I just want to sort this out, because you are being so heavy about this.' I think I was as red as him by now. I put one foot inside the house, keeping the other on the step.

'RIGHT, YOU CROSSED THE LINE!' He slammed the receiver back down and lunged towards me. The woman rushed forward and grabbed him.

'Bruce, for God's sake! What are you doing?' She restrained him slightly by pulling on his arm and standing between us. I had a quick look round the windows to check the neighbours' situation, but remarkably nobody was about. I wanted him to shut up, but I also wanted him to push me, so I could push him back. He was a smug, uptight bastard and I wanted to kick his fucking boring little head in.

'Tell her to get out and show me the folder, she's a bloody liar!' he snarled through gritted teeth, and an even madder face.

'Will you show him the folder, if it makes things easier?' she snapped.

This was out of hand, but that fucker wasn't going to get me. I decided to do what I do best – bluff him.

'Listen to me. I haven't been here before. We cover different areas each night, so if, like you claim, I ripped you off' – I said 'ripped you off' in a heightened voice – 'then it wasn't this address. So if this isn't your address then it's hers and she isn't your sister, is she?'

In my head I was wearing a trenchcoat, pacing around the room with an old cigar.

'It's no business of yours who I am!' The woman had just shot herself and Bruce in the foot.

'What the hell has that got to do with anything?' He was standing, slightly calmer, with his hands on each hip, in that arrogant prick way. I ignored his questions and continued in the direction I'd decided on.

'I know it's not your sister because of the way you spoke to her.'

'I don't know what you're talking about,' he said, just before I was about to charge him.

'Look, you're both wearing wedding rings. This isn't where you live; you argued with her like you're going out together. She was tense from the moment you arrived, and you backed down that drive cautiously as though you haven't done it very often, so that rules out family visits unless she hasn't lived here long. And there's just one more thing.' The Kingswood arrived at the end of the street, Scotty was driving. I turned so he could see me and flagged him manically to come over.

'What are you saying?' Bruce paused.

'And do you know what?'

'What!' he shouted.

'I have never sold to a single male, they are all married.' I raised my eyebrows, really playing with him now.

Scotty pulled up outside and leant out the window.

'Everything all right, mate?'

'Not really.' I said, turning towards him for a second then back to Bruce. I wasn't out of the woods yet; there were still some loose ends.

'You see, just as you can trace me, I can trace you through the sale. I could get your address and come round and apologise to you and your *wife*!'

'Bruce, for God's sake, let's go inside and leave this silly little girl to whatever she's doing.' The woman tried to pull him away again, but Bruce stood defiantly.

Scotty walked up the path towards us gently and slowly, his hands in his pockets, unsure of what was going on and how to approach us.

'You've got a bloody cheek,' Bruce said, trembling slightly.

'Can I help at all, mate?' Scotty sounded the most serious I had ever heard him.

'There's just been a misunderstanding, but it's OK now, just put my folder in the car, please, and I'll be out in a second.'

'Sure, mate, whatever. I'll be here if you need me, OK?'

I nodded. Scotty gave Bruce a don't-fuck-with-me-mate look, picked up the folder and walked back to the car.

'Look, I've got a job to do, OK? And it's selling these paintings, right?' I spoke in a quieter voice to calm things down. 'Yes, they are not all original. But they are paintings and they are painted by people who genuinely need the money and are sold by people like me who genuinely need the money as well, and they are bought by people like you and your wife.' The woman walked away down the hall. 'And the original reason why you both bought the paintings still stands – you liked the look of them. And to be fair, there was no cause to tell you that I wasn't going to sell another one to one of your neighbours. Why should I? And as for the song and dance about you all having the same paintings, why not?' I flung my arms around, I was enjoying it now, and I was well back on dry land. 'You've got practically the same cars, the same fucking houses and the same clothes, so why not have the same paintings?'

'I could still report you and get my money back. I'm sure

there's a lot of other people like me who would like to hear about this.' Bruce thought he was gaining points again.

'Listen, Bruce. I'm leaving now, you are not going to call the police or mention this to anyone because it's not worth the trouble. Now, give me a break and I'll give you one, OK? Otherwise I'll be turning up on your doorstep and having a talk with your wife.'

'That's blackmail, and that's a very fucking serious thing to say!'

'You said it, I didn't, but now you've given me an idea, haven't you? Want to test me and see if I'm playing or not?'

He leant right into me. I didn't budge, not one part of me. I heard Scotty open the car door again.

'If I ever, ever see you again, or any of your friends, I swear, I will get you.' He stayed near to my face, awaiting my response.

I could have said many things, but I decided at that point that the guy had been through enough so I simply said, 'Fair play.'

Which made him back off.

'Get out of my sight and off this street.'

'Sure. That I can agree to.' And that felt like the best I was going to get in terms of a deal. I walked down the drive and into the passenger seat of the Kingswood.

'You all right?' Scotty put his hand on my thigh and patted it.

'Just let's get out of here, Scotty, I need a drink.'

The wheels spun, causing a screeching as we tore down the street. I turned around to see Bruce close the door, and then slumped down in the seat, glad of Scotty's hand on me.

Scotty and I stood at the bar waiting to be served. I kept shaking my head in disbelief at what had just happened.

'Close shave, eh, mate?' Scotty made a blowing-out-steam noise and pushed his baseball hat back.

'Just really lucky, I suppose. Fuck, really lucky. I mean it was such a gamble to say that stuff about the woman he was with, you know?'

'It's all a gamble, mate.' He laughed madly, patting me on the back. 'It's all a fucking gamble.'

We drank a cold beer each but never sat down, knowing well that nothing had been sold tonight, and that I'd probably have to go back out and try again. Even if Scotty had suggested that we call it a day I don't think I could have, for I was getting to the stage where every time we went selling, I didn't want to go back to the city unless I had sold at least one. It had become such a game, such a challenge and such a performance that I loved it, despite the risks.

CHAPTER **NINETEEN**

It was dark and beautiful again. Things always felt better after dusk. The evening was a cloak that I wore well, and with it came drinks and loose talk, which helped a world full of strangers feel easy.

Scotty dropped me off in a cul-de-sac in a different suburb altogether, which meant he'd have to race back to get the others, then back to get me again.

'You'll just have to get lucky in the one house, mate, all you got time for.'

I nodded from the pavement.

'Give it all you've got.' He sped off in another unnecessary emergency-like fashion.

I glanced over the houses and chose the wealthiest-looking one, which was in the far corner of the cul-de-sac of seven houses. Its driveway was on a steep slope, surrounded by a white wall. The house was gated, and on the gates was an intercom. All these signs were telling me no, and that even if I did gain entry, the inside would almost definitely contain real works of art on its walls. I pressed my head through the gates, peering at the house. Guarding the front door were two enormous ceramic lions, a strange regal sight for Sydney. It was seven thirty. I rang the intercom, causing the *Doctor Zhivago* theme to resound along the drive.

'Tiff, for fuck's sake, get your ass in here, you're late,' said a man's voice that had smoked a million cigarettes.

'It's not Tiff,' I said, but was cut off. I felt the ground vibrate and the gate mechanism kick in. They opened slowly. I walked up the driveway towards the house, unsure of how to approach the voice that answered. I leant my folder against the wall of the house and waited at the front door, until I realised it was slightly ajar.

'Come in, come in, come in, come in,' sang the same voice as before. As I pushed the door open, I could hear guitar-tuning coming from inside.

'Hello there,' I said, as friendly as possible to a suntanned middle-aged man, in perhaps his fifties, sitting at a wooden table.

'Who the hell are you?' he said, really pissed off.

'I tried to tell you at the gates I wasn't who you thought I was, but you answered too quickly so I thought I'd—'

'Are you a friend of Tiff's? He's fucking late, and a date's a date.' He had half-moon glasses on. He peered over them at me but continued tuning, completely unfazed by my arrival. I laughed at the sight of him. I liked him. He was odd and I knew immediately that I had another lunatic drunkard on my hands.

'You know how to tune a guitar?'

'You know, the basics, but I'm no expert.'

He wore smart shorts and looked like he'd just showered and shaved; his black hair was still wet and combed over to one side, and I could smell his aftershave. He was a never-got-over-the-sixties type, beads round his neck, a leather bracelet of some kind. He'd cut himself shaving and blood seeped through a tiny piece of toilet paper stuck to his cheek. He was totally engrossed in the tuning and let me stand there, as I looked round at what had to be the most salubrious house I'd been in so far.

'What time is it?'

'Just after seven thirty.' I looked at my watch despite the enormous clock on the wall above the fireplace. He reached a satisfactory place with his tuning and started nodding and running his tongue over his top lip.

'Good, good, good. OK, what's going on?'

'My name's Kerry. I'm basically showing my artwork around some of the houses in your neighbourhood. By the way, this is the most beautiful house I've ever seen in my life. I love it.'

'Is that so?'

'Yeah, it's gorgeous.'

'It's the wife's, I'm a mere mortal.' He examined a dead cigar in an ashtray on the table, dusted off the ash and lit it.

'Can I ask something?'

'Sure can.'

'Who's Tiff?'

'Tiff's a mate, and he's let me down badly, got a set to run through. Look at the bloody time.' He worked on his cigar until it was up and running. I looked around some more, embarrassed to move from the same spot I'd been standing in since I'd entered. The place was cool and tiled, and what wasn't tiled seemed to be wood. It looked Spanish and stylish.

'Can you sing?'

I laughed.

'I'm serious, can you sing?'

'I can hold a tune when I've had a drink.'

'Well, I'd better get you a drink, then.'

'What's your name?' I put out my hand.

'Fritz.' He shook it, his grip was tight.

'Good name, Fritz.'

'What are you doing? Refresh my memory.'

'You know, trying to show off my paintings.' I added the 'you know' due to Fritz's extremely relaxed manner.

'Right, right, so you're not anything to do with Tiff?' He went back to the guitar and played a few chords. I laughed at his mentioning Tiff again.

'No, sorry, I told you I just fell upon your house as part of my attempts to show my work around.'

He wasn't listening; his head was down again, his eyes squinting with concentration. In my head I willed him to make my drink.

'There are people arriving later, we have to rehearse.'

I should have left him to it of course, but it was just all so appealing, and once again the urgency to sell temporarily gave way to the pursuit of strangers and their intriguing lives.

'OK, let's get us a drink.' He put his guitar back on its stand and stood up.

'That's very kind of you.'

'Oh, you're not getting away without having to help me out here. I'm in a spot due to that fucking clown. Jesus, no discipline.' He walked towards another room.

'I'll have what you're having, please,' I called after him.

'Sit down, sit down, sit down,' he muttered before he disappeared into the kitchen.

I thought about setting out some paintings around the lounge for his return, but decided against it. Instead I sank down into the most luxurious white sofa and looked at the décor.

I could hear Fritz preparing my drink, the ice hitting the bottom of a glass.

'Where you from, Fritz?' I asked, as he entered carrying two pale green drinks in huge thick tumblers.

'Beatles.'

'What?'

'Everybody knows a bloody Beatles' number, right?'

I sipped my drink; it was a new drink to me, intensely sweet. 'Yeah, that's true.'

'Chains.' His face became animated.

I nearly spat out my drink, trying to suppress laughter; the guy was a grade-A lunatic.

'Sorry?'

'Chains.' He gulped from his tumbler then picked up the guitar.

'This is nice, what is it?' I said, moving my ice around.

'Caipirinha and vodka. We could do the "Chains" harmony.'

'When are these guests arriving, then?'

'*Chains, my baby's got me locked up in chains.*' He began belting it out. '*And they ain't the kind, that you can see ee ee eey,* this is your bit.' He gestured towards me with his forehead. I wiped the drink from the table that I'd let dribble from my mouth when I was laughing. 'You do the harmony, right?'

'I see.'

He started banging the guitar in between strumming it. '*Wow wow these chains of a luuhuvve gotta hold on me he.*' He pointed up with his finger. 'That's when I go down, you see, and you go up.'

'Fuck's sake, Fritz, what do you want me to—'

'From the top.' He started again. I felt like I had no choice. Besides, I knew the song.

'*Chains,*' we both began, me taking the high road, him taking the low one. At the end he was ecstatic, jumping up punching the air.

'Wow, baby, we got ourselves an opening number.'

'What are we opening?'

'OK, OK, let me look at my list.' He brought out a piece of paper from his back pocket. I could see lists of songs, some scored out.

'Hey, hang on. I'm not doing all these – not unless you buy a painting.'

'What?' He reviewed his set list, making notes with a pen.

'I am trying to earn my living here, Fritz, you know?'

'I'm going to try Tiff.' Completely ignoring my agenda, he went over to the phone and dialled his friend. 'Just ringing and ringing.' He looked over at me, shaking his head.

I shrugged, then finished my drink. I figured I would sell him a painting without even getting one out of my bag, and then I'd do what he wanted in the way of entertainment. This was the best situation I had encountered since I began the job, and I had a very strong feeling that it was about to get even better.

'OK, here's the score,' he said still holding the phone. 'The wife and I are having a few guests over, in about an hour. Bob is a big shot, OK, blah blah, so I want this to be right. Understand?'

'Yep. Where's your wife then?'

'Exactly.'

Finally he put down the phone. 'I hope that idiot is on his way to the gig.'

'What gig?'

'THIS GIG, LOVE! This one.'

'OK, Fritz, I'll cut a deal with you here.' I thought he'd like me saying cut, I was talking his language.

'I'm listening, but we haven't got long, we need to rehearse. Fuck poor old Tiff, he just lost his place.'

Now I knew for sure that Fritz had lost his place a long time ago. I wasn't even sure he had a wife; this could be just an average night in alone for some poor old deluded hippie with more money than sense, who had taken far too many drugs a long time ago.

I would have put Fritz around Mac's age; in fact, they would have hit it off big time, and could have enjoyed each other's completely different strands of conversation. Fritz had jet-black hair swept back, he was very brown and looked quite Mediterranean; his body was weak, not the build of anyone who had ever worked, and his hands were long and thin like an older woman's.

'OK, Fritz, please can I speak with you quickly?' I stood up and he sat down, strumming the guitar again. 'I am here to sell paintings, it's my artwork and selling them is my job, OK?'

'OK, OK.' He finished off his drink then looked at me, for what felt like the first time.

'So I'll help you out and do the gig with you but I need you to buy a painting, otherwise I'll let myself and some other people down. So you can have a look and buy one, then I'll rehearse with you, but not until then, and if you don't want to, that's fine, but I'll have to head off.'

'Fuck.' He shook his head and blew out, like it was a really big problem. 'How much?'

'Hundred bucks to you.'

'Oookayeeh.' I laughed again, which he didn't ever respond to.

'OK, I'll look through and you fix us a drink – it's through there.'

I could not believe how relaxed he was about a stranger coming into his house. This was the thing I was beginning to understand and love about Australia; the rich people in the big houses were very different from the ones back home. They seemed less affected by what they had become. If I were to go back to Scotland and knock on the door of a huge house in Morningside, they probably wouldn't have even answered it, let alone allow me to fix us both a drink within my first half-hour of being there. I looked over at Fritz thumbing through my folder muttering to himself, then headed into the kitchen.

'Lime-sugar-mix in fridge, and vodka in the freezer compartment, yeah?' He called as I went.

'Okayee.' I mimicked Fritz.

The kitchen was huge with a massive solid wood table in the middle. It opened through a glass screen to a lit-up lush garden, with a giant hammock attached to two trees. Through the garden was a path that finished at the edge of a built-up platform area made from strips of wood.

I found the vodka in the freezer; it was Russian or Polish, probably good stuff, as I didn't recognise the brand. I fixed us two generous drinks and closed the fridge. As I was stirring them, my eye caught a framed photograph on the wall. It was Fritz with a woman about the same age as him on a boat, with Sydney harbour in the background. The woman wore huge hoop earrings and seemed familiar to me. I took a sip from a drink that could have been Fritz's or mine because I'd mixed the glasses up accidentally, and stared at the picture trying to figure her out. I could have sold her a painting – I'd met so many people by now – but she felt like more than that.

Back in the lounge Fritz looked pleased with himself, and seemed to have slowed down slightly from his earlier mania. He sat on the sofa lighting up a big new cigar. Leaning against my portfolio was a painting turned away from us.

'So, Fritz, how you doing? Got a painting?' I was being very cheeky, but it really didn't matter.

'Yes, I have.'

'Thanks. Which one is it?' I could see cash on the table.

'OK. We have a deal, right?'

'Yes, we have.' We both drank at the same time, and made refreshed noises.

'Want to extend that deal?'

'What do you mean?' Although this was the most unorthodox selling situation, I felt I had failed to observe the most important rule. NEVER LEAVE THE CLIENT UNATTENDED.

'Want to double the deal?'

'Fuck! OK, explain please, Fritz?' Fritz was an old friend already, and saner than I had thought, plus the existence of a wife did seem to be authenticated by the sighting of the coupley photo in the kitchen.

'You said that if I buy a painting, you'll do the gig with me, right?'

'Yes.' I breathed out the yes in a tired fashion.

'Now I'm saying you can up the stakes, if you like.' He paused for a puff.

'Why do people want to play such games?' I pleaded.

'Because it's fun.' He had a fair point. 'If you guess the painting I have laid aside over there, then I will not only buy one painting, but two. But if you fail to guess, then I get two free.'

I thought about it for as long as I could, which wasn't very long because the caipirinhas tasted so good.

'And if I don't take part?'

'Then you are free to go and I'll perform alone, although there might be a big fuckin' problem because I could never sing.' He mumbled to himself the bit about singing like it was an aside.

I looked at the clock. It was after eight. I wouldn't have the time or energy to start afresh in another house. Scotty and Jim would be rounding us up by nine thirty; I was half cut and had already had a taxing evening dealing with Bruce earlier.

'What about, if I guess wrongly you get one painting?'

'Sorry, life's a bitch and all that. It's two or nothing.'

'Life's been no bitch to you, has it?' I looked around in an exaggerated fashion.

'I'll drink to that.' He raised his glass, I clinked it.

I thought about losing two hundred dollars, and then I thought about winning it.

'How can I trust you?'

'My money's on the table. Take it, and if you're wrong, then put it back.'

'OK, Fritz, you have a deal, but I'll need some time.'

'Five minutes, that's all I can afford. Audience get in at eight thirty.'

I laughed, expecting him to join me, but he didn't. I felt powerful with my big chunky glass full of ice and drink. I lit a Marlboro, sank back and tried to work it out, while Fritz played some tunes.

I had nothing to go on whatsoever. There were no other paintings in the house from what I could see, just a couple of plates that looked Japanese, and some rubber plants. I could only find one more photo in addition to the one in the kitchen. It was near the door as I came in, on the wall. It was a racehorse with a young woman and another man. I had a horse and a boat and that was all.

I sensed Fritz had done very little over the past few years and that perhaps his wife was the driving force behind their luxurious lifestyle. The house would probably have a study packed with clues, but I was restricted to the minimalist entrance room.

Did they have a boat and a horse? In which case, it would have to be Peter Bloody Stuger. The only horse featured was a unicorn – surely Fritz wasn't that wasted, and the house was in far too good taste to go down that route.

'Three minutes left,' said Fritz, loving the other two that just passed.

'Shit.'

I would have to do it by a process of elimination. There was no way the mountains, the triptych and the landscapes were in the race. I wasn't sure why but my instinct said no. The abstract would be suitable for the house, but I didn't take Fritz to be the home-furnishing type. He loved music and was obviously in a band of some sort at one point. So I had him as a sentimentalist, therefore his choice was connected with something personal – otherwise why suggest a game based on guessing? I went back to the bloody unicorn against all odds.

'Time, please.' Fritz pointed at the clock.

In a desperate last-second attempt to secure the deal, I scrutinised the back of the painting to see if there were any bits of paint overlapping, so at least I would have more of an idea what colour scheme was used. But it was clean. Which is why I had a slight chance in saying what I thought it was.

'Is it the unicorn drinking from the lake?'

Fritz let his head fall back over the sofa, which confirmed it for me. I jumped up and down; I was having so much fun.

'How did you know, you bastard?' Fritz downed his drink.

'I think you maybe have a racehorse, that's all.' I gestured to the photo. What I didn't tell him was that I always kept the unicorn at the back of my folder, as it was the last one I was likely to get out because it was so shit. Most of the paintings had some paint on the back because they were often still wet. But the unicorn only leant against the folder so it was spotless in comparison.

'Unicorn's Trust,' said Fritz, swirling his ice.

'What?'

'That's the name of our horse.'

'Fuck, that's weird, really weird.'

'So, it's all yours.'

'Guess so. What about your other choice? The deal is you get to buy another one.'

'Let the wife choose that. Here she is now.'

An engine purred in the drive. I was apprehensive about meeting his wife, and afraid that she might change the evening, which was turning out to be better by the minute. I stood up in anticipation of her arrival.

'What's the plan, Fritz?'

'Plan is, you're Tiff's replacement. Joyce will understand, she's used to last-minute hitches.'

I was registering the name Joyce with the face in the photo and the fact I'd felt I'd met her before, when she came in, all bright and breezy, just as I'd imagined her. Her arms were laden with shopping and gold bracelets. She was no taller than me, with big brown eyes and smudged mascara from a hot day; her handshake was warm and long.

'Hi there, love. Joyce Cane. Pleased to meet you.'

CHAPTER **TWENTY**

I could not believe for one moment that I was in the house of carpet mogul Joyce Cane. It was not the house I had imagined her to live in. I had imagined her to have a house full of carpets like the ones she advertised on television.

'Fix me a bloody drink, will you, darl'. Been on my feet all day,' said Joyce.

Fritz mumbled and walked through to the kitchen.

'So what's he got you doing, love?'

'Nothing – I mean, I was going round the houses selling my artwork when he thought I was his friend Tiff at the door, so he let me in.' I stared at her, as I spoke.

'And you couldn't get away ever since, uh?' Joyce lifted her hair up at the back and stretched her neck before kicking off her shoes and sitting down.

'No, I've actually really enjoyed myself.'

'Typical bloody Fritz, flamin' maniac, he gets so over the top. Don't let him bother you.'

Fritz came back with the drink and Joyce took a generous gulp.

'That's better.' She put her feet up on the sofa and played some more with her hair. 'So, you one of these travellers who sell the paintings, yeah?'

'Yeah, I've been doing it pretty much since I came here.'

'Oh yeah, got a few mates who have bought some of that stuff; some of it's OK. Bet you get around a bit, love?'

'I do, yeah, going up the coast tomorrow with the people I work with.' I was nervous in Joyce's company, like I was a fan. I wanted to know about her life and I couldn't stop looking at her, while Fritz played guitar softly in the background as we continued to chat.

'So watch this, he'll go berserk,' she whispered, but needn't have because Fritz was oblivious to anything we were saying. 'Fritz, love.' She winked at me playfully.

'Mm, yes, my darling wife?' he said sarcastically, looking up.

'Got some bad news, I'm afraid. Well, I happen to think it's good news but then I've been working all day. But the Harrisons have cancelled, Sheila's got crook.'

'What's crook?' I asked.

'It's Aussie for *ill*, love.'

'Oh, right.'

'Cancelled!' yelped Fritz. 'Why didn't they let us know earlier? A lot of thought and hard work went into this gig, you know.'

'Calm yourself now, love, I'm not in the mood for one of your tantrums.'

'What, they just blew us out, like that?' Fritz clicked his fingers, then got up and started pacing. 'Bloody flakes, the lot of them.'

Joyce rolled her eyes at me. I sniggered.

'WHY-ARE-PEOPLE-SO-UTTERLY-UNDEPEND-ABLE?' He threw his arms around.

'Fritz, calm down, babe, we'll rearrange for next week, I promise. Now why don't you go and give me five minutes of peace and quiet to chat to the girl?' She shook her head into her drink.

As soon as Fritz left the room we both laughed.

'Men! Uh, who needs them?' she said.

'Fritz is a fairly unusual man though, is he not?'

'You can say that again.'

'How long have you been together?'

'Twenty-four years, just passed.'

'Long time. Hey – that's when I was born.'

'There you go.'

I couldn't stop staring at Joyce; her presence felt so warm and reassuring, like nothing else I had experienced before.

'Let me tell you about Fritz, love.' She paused for self-editing purposes. 'Fritz had a rotten life by the time I met him, I mean we all did then, but his was about as low as it gets. Amazing that I've still got him with me. Anyway, to cut a long story short, he ends up becoming a muso.'

'What, sorry?'

'Muso – you know, musician – in a band. The Hideaways – real top band in the sixties, made it number one over here. They had a big hit with a song that Fritz and his mate Tiff wrote. Tiff's a bloody nutcase by the way, can't bear him. He's bad for Fritz. Anyway they wrote the song, it was number one for six weeks, and Fritz has never got over it. He's always harking back to those days, and on a night like tonight when he wants to put on a show, when we have guests coming over, he loses the bloody plot.'

'Poor Fritz.'

'Don't you worry about him, he's OK, but I've got to keep my eye on him, and I've got to watch him with this stuff.' She shook the glass. 'Speaking of such, fancy another?'

'Yes, please.'

She winked at me again.

'Fritz! Fritz!'

Fritz came back in looking dejected.

'Can you get us another couple of these, babe, please?'

He picked up our glasses without speaking.

'Come here, you big idiot.' She pulled him down onto the sofa and cuddled him, to which he responded reluctantly. She pulled back strands of his hair that had fallen onto his face and kissed his forehead.

I watched with fascination, for here was the perfect wife, and the perfect mother. I wanted to stay there for a long time and be Fritz under the care of Joyce. But why? Why had I felt this connection with her from her television adverts, beamed into my life from her Parramatta Road showroom? Was there more to her and this than coincidence?

As she petted Fritz reassuringly, I traced back the path that led me to Joyce.

First, if I had not gone and sold a painting to Bruce and his wife, I would have had no cause to meet Bruce again and argue about the sale. However, if I had not been at the house at Watson's Bay at the time I was, I may never have run into Bruce again. Let's not forget that Bruce would not even have been there at that time himself, had he not been having an affair with the woman whose house it was. But they were both there and it caused us all to row, which made Scotty collect me and take me to this suburb, which he said in the car was not one that he had really ever considered targeting, and certainly one I would not have been targeting at all if I had not argued with Bruce, forcing me to find another area before the night was up. And tomorrow I would be going to the Gold Coast, and may never have come back to this side of Sydney.

Then there's the house and what attracted me to it. Admittedly, it was the largest house in the cul-de-sac, with an intercom, so that the person who answered it, in this case Fritz, had no way of seeing that I was not in fact the person he was anxiously waiting for. Had he seen me face to face, he may not have let me into the house so readily. Once there, I did present him with knowledge of the words to the Beatles' 'Chains', and although we both agreed that everybody knew a Beatles' song, that would not necessarily be the obvious choice. And the song kept me there, led me right into the path of Joyce whose house it was all the time, whose face I felt compelled to watch whenever I saw it on the ad and whose voice I heard in the background in many of the homes I visited, saying, 'True blue bonza bargains.' And that took me back to this strange job that I fell into accidentally, a job that took me into the homes of strangers.

After petting Fritz and consoling him about the cancelled performance, Joyce asked me questions about myself, which I loved. All the time I watched her closely.

'So you're from Scotland, are you?'

'Yes, Edinburgh.'

'Got cousins in Newcastle, that's close enough, isn't it?'

I had to stop myself from exploding. 'WHAT? Oh my God, that's just too strange, I have too, I mean, I just found out that I know someone, well, am related to, from there, and now I think she's here. That's why I'm here, oh my God!' I messed with my hair and shook my head.

'Well, I've got to break it to you, love, as much as I'd love to be, I'm sorry but I'm not your mum.' She laughed a little which made me feel stupid, and I didn't want her to break it to me. And I only just got over her saying that, when I had to get over her knowing what I'd meant without me telling her.

'No, obviously, I didn't think you were, but I had a feeling about you when I first saw you on the advert. I felt as if I was going to know you or something, but how did you know about my mother? I haven't told anyone here, how come you knew?' My head was bursting with all of this.

'I don't know anything, love.' She put down her drink, and searched my face with her eyes. 'I just feel something from you, dear, and I think I'm on the right track.'

I bit my lip.

'You'll find what you're looking for, love, I promise.'

I wanted to cry, but turned it into ice chewing instead.

'You won't always be lost.' Her eyes looked watery.

I couldn't take another mouthful of ice, so I brought my foot up on to my other leg and began massaging it.

'I saw your sadness, love, the moment I walked in.'

'What do you mean, Joyce?' I loved using her name.

'I can see things, my mother was the same, and so was my grandmother.'

'You mean, like, psychic?'

'Uh-huh, I'm afraid so, runs in my family whether you want it or not, and I tell you something else, love, you have it as well. It's not developed yet, and I don't know if you'll ever want to, but it's there. Probably what you picked up when you saw me.'

'Do you really think so?'

'Could be.'

'Do you believe in fate, Joyce? Because I do. In fact it's the only thing I think I believe in at all.'

'I do too. I know there's such a thing. I know because when I was a little girl, I dreamt about a big boat that would take me and my mum and dad and little brother far away to another place that was dry and hot. I would dream this maybe every week, and each time I dreamt about this place I would know the place more and more, like I would add things on, so that when I went back to it I had built up a life almost, that I knew my way around. I started these dreams when I was very little, as young as four years old I started having them.'

'When did you come here?'

'We came in from Manchester in the mid-fifties. It was my dad's idea – he hated what had happened in the war and was never the same when he came back – seen too much. He stuck it out at home for a few years, "then one day he stood up and he told us that either we all went to Australia with him or he would go himself. My brother said, "What's Australia?" And my dad said, "It's the furthest away from here you can possibly get." That's when I knew we'd be on the boat I'd been dreaming about, that's when I knew what fate was.'

'That's like me, with here. I always felt I'd have to make some big journey, to find things out about myself, like how I began, how I was made.' I felt young in my explanation of things with Joyce, and excitable.

'So, is it both your parents you are looking for? Or just your mum?' It was strange to hear this, as I had never thought about both of them much. My obsession was with the search for my mother only.

'No, just my mother,' I said tearfully. 'I was adopted.'

'Yep, I figured.' She shook her head. 'Like so many little babies of the fifties and sixties, and long before that too, you know.'

'Yeah, I know,' I said mournfully.

'What do you know about your mother?' She sipped from her drink, the whole time looking into my eyes, reading my face. I composed myself in order to answer that question, a question I had never been asked before.

'Nothing much, other than what I was given when I first went to Register House on my eighteenth birthday. And that was just an address given by her at the time of my birth.'

'Uh-huh.' Joyce smiled at me through tear-filled eyes that I tried my best not to be affected by.

I continued. 'A few years later, when I was twenty-two, I got on a bus for Newcastle and went round knocking on the doors in the street where she used to live until I found out what I know now, which is that she came here soon after I was born, and married an Australian serviceman called Duffy. I don't even know what part of Australia, for sure, or if she's still here, but he was from Sydney, and the neighbours I spoke to thought it was here or Brisbane. I could go to Births, Deaths and Marriages and do a proper search, I suppose, but I don't, and I don't understand why I don't. It's such a long story, Joyce, and it's a weird story, and I found it all out myself.'

'Course you did, love.' She took another drink, this time a larger one, and watched me unravel the page of Duffys from my pocket, as I began to tell her about Hank, and the odd way I found him.

'None of this surprises me, you know, love?'

'Really?'

'Nuh, none of it – you being here, phoning up that cowboy fella who's going to help you – it's all for a reason, like I said. But it makes me laugh because Australia is a big place, as you know, nothing quite like it, and here you are with nothing to go on, floating around but you know you'll do it, don't you?'

'I do, I suppose. Sometimes I just feel that it will come and find me, no matter what I do.'

'One step forward, two steps back – that's you, isn't it?'

'Yes, yes, that is me.' I had only been in Joyce's company for about half an hour, and already I was worrying about how I would leave her. Everything before her seemed to pale into insignificance; she was *it*, so far.

'What about your real mum?'

'No, that is my real mum; the one I think's here.'

'No, that's your biological mum, your birth mum. The mum that stayed with you, the one that brought you up, that's your real mum, love.'

'We really don't get on. Not for a long time, anyway.'

'Of course you don't get on, she's your mum! You're meant to fight, and get on each other's nerves. But that will change, love, believe me, that will change.'

Joyce put a new slant on everything, her words were magical.

'We don't get on – I've hardly spoken properly to her since I left home, or to my father. He's fucking useless, and she just goes along with it.'

'We all hate our parents for a time, you know, you're no

different there. But don't you forget, she's the one that brought you up, that fed you and clothed you and taught you things. And she seems to have done something right, eh?'

I didn't want to respond to that.

'But your other mother, the one you're looking for, she's here, love. I think she's not too far from here.' She put down her drink on a coaster made from cork designed as a slice of orange, and asked me to come closer. I moved up the sofa and turned to face her. She took my hand and held it in hers for a while and looked closely into my eyes. I wanted to laugh out of nerves but managed to control it. Then she said something that really shook me.

'You're closer to your granddad than anyone, even though you haven't spoken to each other for a while.'

I didn't say anything, wanting to test her. She stroked her left arm then clutched her chest.

'He had a stroke, didn't he?'

I nodded, dumbfounded by her findings.

'Yeah, he can't talk, but you understand him. But he wants you to get on with your life.'

I clenched my jaw, fighting back tears.

'You're going on a journey somewhere away from here very soon.'

'That's amazing. Fuck, I am. Tomorrow I'm going to the Gold Coast, that's so weird.'

'Listen, love, a lot of this is up to you, but you'll find what you're looking for, that's all I can say.'

'What else do you see, Joyce, please?' My mind was racing, I was thinking about Hank again and how I accidentally got hold of him because he happened to be in his sister's house overnight, and how he was a DJ so he could reach people on the radio. It seemed that trail had gone dead because he hadn't contacted me, but it was strange, anyway. Then I thought again about how I found this job, and how I came here. All these things raced in my mind and I felt so utterly charged and totally convinced that finding my real mother would be the missing piece in my fucked-up, crap jigsaw of a life.

'Listen, there's no big, secret, bad thing I'm keeping from you, so don't worry.' She had hold of both my hands and moved them up and down in time to 'don't worry', which no one had done since I was little. 'But this is your life, and you need to sort it out yourself. I know what loneliness is, love, and, please, I could write a book about heartache, I tell you.' Her eyes filled with tears. 'I know you've been so very lonely, but you can change all that, you're on the right track.'

What track was that? I wondered what track I was on that led me to money-lenders, bars and one-night stands with strangers, or worse still, not even the overnight part of the one-night stands, just momentary stands.

'Someone's seriously looking over you, love.'

Joyce let go of my hands in that way that someone you hardly know has to let go of them, and looked over to the other side of the room, except she wasn't looking at anything, she was staring into space.

'Are you all right?'

Here it comes, I thought, here comes the big one.

'Do you know anyone with a tattoo?'

'Well, probably yes. I mean loads of people have tattoos, don't they?'

'Maybe. I don't like this person, I feel that they're trouble. I think this one is a bird, like an eagle maybe, maybe not.' She came round out of her deep state of thought and sat upright. 'Now then, that's enough of that. Come on, tell me some other stuff about yourself. What about these bloody paintings and how many has my husband bought?'

'Joyce. Can I ask you something?'

'Course you can, love.'

'Why don't you have any carpets in your house?'

Joyce burst into fits of laughter that broke out into a wheeze, and she slapped the tops of her legs as she laughed, which made me start laughing with her. Fritz came in to see what all the hilarity was about, and the sight of him looking so puzzled as he walked in caused us to erupt even more.

I stood at the edge of the cul-de-sac, trying to get Jim's attention as he drove through the surrounding streets. Finally he flashed his lights and pulled round to get me.

'Hey, all right?'

'Yeah, just finishing up in that house.' I pointed to Joyce's.

'We were worried about you, what happened?'

'Just got caught in conversation, I'll just get my folder – it's in the house.'

I ran back to the house and went inside to say my goodbyes to Joyce. I really didn't want to go, I wanted to ask to stay overnight, but I had to be up early to go to the coast. I also thought about trying to get the others an invite inside for a while, but I didn't want to share Joyce with anyone.

She and Fritz were cuddling in the hall when I got back; they were both pissed.

'I meant to ask, who's that in the photo with the horse?' I pointed.

'That's my daughter, my first one. I've got two.'

I studied her face close up.

'That's Samantha. I had her when I was very young, to a different man from Fritz. My other daughter Carol is a lot younger. They both live and work in the city.'

'They're lucky to have you, Joyce.'

'Hey, they've had their fair share too, you know.' She put her hands on both my shoulders. 'Listen to me, sweetheart. Life is so bloody quick, love, it really is. You've got to go out and grab it. Don't waste it being unhappy. Let yourself go, Kerry. Let yourself feel good things in your heart when they're there. I know you think I sound like a silly old woman.'

I shook my head.

'I know that you're too young to feel this just now, but I'm telling you: it is short, and this is it.' She clicked her fingers. 'We all have shit to deal with, some more than others, I know, but nobody has this life without it, OK? You remember that.'

'OK.'

'Someone told me something, a long time ago, and it's always stuck with me.' She grabbed my shoulders. 'Someone throws you lemons' – she let go and opened up her arms – 'make lemonade. OK?'

I nodded, but felt sad to leave her. I could have stayed all night, listening to her.

She grabbed me again and held me. I cried and put my

arms round her, trying to let myself go, like she said.

'It's all right,' she said, rocking me gently back and forth. 'It's all right.' I pulled away after a while, worrying that I would never stop.

'Just make the most of it, and most of all, enjoy it. That's it, I'll shut up now.' She wheezed away again.

'She knows what she's talking about, you know,' said Fritz. Jim gave a short blast on the horn. Joyce waved out to them.

'I've got to go. Listen, thank you so much for your hospitality, and for buying my paintings.'

We hugged and again she held me so tightly that when we broke off I felt covered in her perfume. I kissed Fritz on both cheeks, picked up my folder and walked outside.

'Listen, when you get back to Sydney, pop round and see us, or come to the showroom – you can catch me there every day except Monday. I'd be interested to find out how you do.'

'Really?'

'Of course, love, but just you look after yourself and enjoy your trip, you'll be OK. But watch out for men with tattoos.' She sniggered at the last part.

'What?' I was at the gates.

'I'm pulling your leg, love, that's my own shit. Have fun, sweetie.'

Scotty jumped out and opened the boot and I threw my folder in.

'Nice house,' he said, tossing his cigarette on the ground and stamping it out. His voice immediately annoyed me.

I got in the back next to the Danish and watched Joyce and Fritz kiss, then close the door.

'How did you do, then?' asked Jim, watching me in the mirror.

'Sold two,' I said, leaning against the window, not wanting to talk to the others quite yet.

Back at William Street, Anaya and Greg handed out the beers. Greg and Jim discussed routes and areas while Scotty lingered on the outskirts of their conversation, half his attention on entertaining the giggling Danes. I stood leaning up against the kitchen units opposite Anaya, as she painted her nails.

'So, hey, Kerry, you're quiet tonight, uh?' she said, taking the excess varnish off the brush.

'Got a few things on my mind, that's all. Also conserving my energy for the trip.' I rolled my tinny of chilled VB on my forehead, trying to get some relief.

'Oh my God,' she said, stopping what she was doing. 'I forgot to tell you but your mother called this morning, like really early, but I never got to the phone so she left a message.'

'Fuck!' I took a big drink. 'Which one?'

Anaya looked at me quizzically.

'I mean, which phone?'

'There is only one phone, stupid.'

'Yeah, sorry, I wasn't paying attention. What did she say?' I put down my beer.

'She sounded just like you. I think she wants you to call your grandfather.'

'Shit, something must be wrong.'

'God, I'm so fucking stupid to forget, sorry, man. Is somebody sick, do you think?'

'Something like that. I haven't spoken to her for a long time, but I left this number with the nurses at my grandfather's home. I need to call, or hear the message – do you still have it?'

'Yeah, sure, it's on the office machine, come with me.'

The office was cooler than the rest of the building and offered some relief from the increasing humidity. Anaya sat on the desk and rewound the machine.

I sat in Greg's chair; I felt I needed to be sitting for what I feared might be terrible news.

'No, wait.' I put my hand on top of Anaya's as she was about to press 'play'. 'I'm scared, I'm dreading this.'

'Do you think something bad has happened?'

'Why would she phone me here? This could be one of those moments you want to reverse in life, so I want to stay for a while before it happens, do you know what I mean?'

Anaya ran her thumb along the side of my hand, which despite the dread of the current situation sent my body into some sort of drug high, and an ache directly between my legs.

'You know something, Kerry, I do understand.'

This was a rare moment with Anaya, and I felt better equipped to deal with it after my talk with Joyce. She was being unusually real and I liked her this way; up until now I had had nothing from her but inconsistencies and games.

'Let's switch the fan on,' I said.

Keeping our hands the way they had been, she leant over the desk and turned the switch on. The fan purred and moved back and forth between us, blowing our hair over our faces.

My heart was pounding, and the anticipation of what my mother was about to tell me, mixed with the excitement of a nearby Anaya, was giving me a dry, thirsty mouth. I swallowed and tried to moisten my lips with my tongue.

'Here, have some of mine,' she said, noticing.

I'd left my beer in the kitchen. I swigged from hers, happy to be near her mouth. I had never been sure what I liked or hated about her. She had been nothing but cold and annoying and deeply untrustworthy since we'd met. But she was extremely beautiful, far more than anyone I had met before, and I suspected it was her beauty that allowed her to get away with so much.

'Come on, play the message now, then you can phone home,' she said, realising I had gone off into a trance.

I released the pressure on her hand and she pressed 'play'. I heard a beep, then the voice of my mother. I sat back in the chair and listened.

'This is a message for Kerry Swaine, it's her mother phoning from Scotland. I'm not sure if this is her number or not, the nurses gave it to me – I haven't got long.'

My heart was in my mouth – who hasn't got long? I couldn't bear anything happening to my grandfather when I was away. I would fly home immediately and borrow money from my mother, if I had to.

'I've only got so much change, I'm calling from the home, you see, and the nurses have been telling me that she's desperate to speak to her grandfather. He's with me now, we're using the pay phone at the home. I thought I would try and get her to speak to him. Never mind, I'll try some other time. Tell her she can call if she wants and I hope she is enjoying herself and looking after herself, that's all.'

There was a delay before she put the phone down. I heard my grandfather make a gargled speech noise, of one word, which he repeated three times before my mother said 'yes' to him in the way you would speak to a child. Then the line went dead.

I fell back into the chair and sighed relief.

'You see, it's OK, yeah, they are both OK.'

'Yeah, they're both OK,' I mumbled.

'OK.'

'Anaya?'

'What?' she said, more softly than usual.

I wanted to ask her how she felt. About me, about here, about Greg and about life. I nearly did, but couldn't quite let go, just yet.

'Nothing, nothing, it's OK.'

'Come on then, better go and have a drink with the others, and gear up for the trip.' She smiled warmly, and then clicked her tongue in the roof of her mouth.

'Sure,' I said, wondering if I'd missed the moment for ever.

I switched off the fan, and we left the office. She led the way and I watched her perfect body move down the corridor and back into the lounge area with the others. Tonight of all nights, I could do without them. Somehow I felt weary of all the jokey bullshit, at least for the time being.

CHAPTER TWENTY-ONE

Everybody talked non-stop at the start of the car journey, and then quickly ran out of steam. Even though we'd been in the car together many times, it felt different because we were going away on a big trip, which made us feel like kids. Scotty reading out our names from an imaginary clipboard, to which we all replied, 'Here, sir.'

The Danish and I agreed to have turns sitting in the middle, as it was less comfortable than being able to lean against the window. I went first, to get it out the way before I got sleepy.

Jim joked at 'I Spy' and started with W, which right on cue I guessed was windscreen. The Danish pretended to be little children in the back and stuck their fingers up at various motorists. Scotty went a joke stage further and showed his arse out the window. Then Jim said something uncharacteristic.

'Listen, it's a beautiful day, why don't we drive to our first place, which is about two hundred Ks away, check into a site, get ourselves sorted out, because we'll be staying there for the next few days, and then just have some time off and a laugh?'

We all cheered and clapped.

'Now you're fuckin' talking, mate, and I like what you're saying,' said Scotty.

'Can we stop at the bottle shop and pick up some beers for the journey?' I asked.

'Oh God, what have we let ourselves in for?' said Jim, which we all took to be a yes. Scotty howled like a mad dog. I nudged the Danish, who seemed like they could take it or leave it, either way. They were normal drinkers, they liked to have their version of a good time, but they had, like most normal people, a cut-off point. There was no madness there.

In the car I felt secure, surrounded by the others; I was filled by a rare sense of belonging. Jim was the dependable parent/teacher who would rescue Scotty and me no matter what happened. Scotty was my cheeky annoying brother, and the Danish were quiet, weird cousins visiting for a short while. I wondered what Greg and Anaya would be if they were with us. I decided Greg would be a sleazy alcoholic uncle, whom I didn't ever want to sit next to. And Anaya would have to be an overseas exchange student visiting for the summer, whose humour nobody got. She couldn't be related, because the scenario would end with us being in bed together.

My turn at the window caused me to daydream happily, watching the road signs pass overhead on the Pacific Highway. They said one hundred and fifty kilometres to Newcastle, which was bizarre. I asked Jim about it, who was a constant source of information on almost anything. He explained that nearly all Australian places were named after areas in Britain because of the original settlers, and most of the strangely pronounced names were linked to Aboriginal words. I imagined him chalking it all up on a board, and then switching on an overhead projector.

I longed for the day that I would be settled enough to take all that stuff in, and go to libraries and look up things about the places I was about to visit. I went to an art exhibition with my mother once, but I felt anxious about other things and couldn't concentrate. I looked over at the others immersed in the paintings, and felt envious of the ones with the headsets on, with that taped information stuff being piped into them.

Jim had some golden oldies station on which was perfect. Scotty complained that he never got to play his Red Hot Chili Peppers' tape. Jim told him to fuck off, then apologised to the back seat for his language. Then Freda Payne's 'Band Of Gold' came on, and halfway through Jim switched it off and said Scotty could go ahead and put his shite on. I watched Jim's eyes in the mirror blinking more than usual, and his jaw tensing in the way that mine does.

Scotty kept the case of Castlemaine that we'd picked up

from a bottle shop on the floor of the front seat underneath him, where it was slightly shaded, and the two of us helped ourselves. Jim stuck to one can because he was driving, while the Danish refrained from having any at all, even though they'd eventually joined in the excitement over getting some beers in the first place.

I slumped down in the seat and closed my eyes, leaning my face against the window until the sun on it made me drift off. Later, the sun streamed down on my thighs. The Danish and I all wore shorts, our hot legs resting against one another, a familiar occurrence by now.

I woke up just as I sensed the car was pulling in over some gravel, and opened my eyes when the engine stopped. Jim stretched out over the steering wheel.

'Shouldn't have had those beers last night. I'm shattered and we haven't even come that far.'

Karin rubbed Jim's shoulders in a half-sleep state, and he moaned appreciatively. We all looked as though we'd woken up at the same time. I leant forward and messed with Scotty's hair. He was still asleep on account of the four beers he'd had in a hundred and fifty kilometres. He looked out of the window as he came to.

'Fucking Newcastle, man, what a dump,' he said, all red-eyed and stinking of booze-sleep breath.

'Scotty, you stink like a bloody brewery,' said Jim, shoving him over towards the passenger door. Scotty farted, and we all quickly got out.

'I'm not putting up with that on this trip, let's get that straight, right now.'

Everybody except Jim was in fits of laughter.

'You're not sleeping in the same van as me; you're sleeping outside like a dog.'

Scotty howled again. Jim waved a map around, fanning the area.

We sat on a picnic bench overlooking the sea, eating burgers and fries and Coke in the Stockton Beach tourist park, which prided itself on its vans being fifty metres from the beach itself. It was late afternoon, with a slight breeze coming off the water.

I asked Scotty why he was called Scotty.

'A lot of people think it's because my folks were Scottish, but it's not.' He had beetroot stains on the side of his face, and ate with his mouth open. I could see Jim suppressing laughter as he spoke.

'No, it's because when I was a kid, me and my old man used to watch *Star Trek* repeats, that's all. My old man would sit in the armchair like the captain, yeah. But I would be pretending to fix it, like, 'cause I wanted to be a mechanic – that was what Scotty did – so the old man started calling me it, and it stuck. Just got used to it.'

'He piloted it, didn't he?' I asked, jokingly, knowing full well that it was Chekov.

'What, the fuckin' *Enterprise*? No, mate, he was the mechanic, the engineer, wasn't he?'

'Thought he was up front, all doom and gloom, always going on about being doomed.' Jim spoke in a bad Scottish accent.

'No, that's *Dad's Army*, you're thinking of Frazer. You're getting your Scottish characters mixed up,' I said.

'Do you mean, "Beam me up, Scotty"?' asked Andrea, which was the only thing she'd said in about four hours.

'You sure Scotty wasn't the driver? Thought he was always worried about where the ship was going,' said Jim.

'Mate.' Scotty was the last to finish his burger, chewed his final mouthful, scrunched up the paper it was in and wiped his mouth with the serviette, then looked directly at Jim like he meant business. 'Do you know what?'

I could see Jim was winding him up.

'What's that, Scotty?'

'Not being funny or nothing, but I know you're a teacher and all the rest of it, and you know loads of stuff, like, but I'm telling you, Scotty was the fucking mechanic, all right?'

'You sure? Thought he sat with the Russian guy, driving.'

The three of us were laughing a little, as well as Jim sniggering, but Scotty appeared to have lost his sense of humour during the car journey and his post-beer nap.

'Just lay off, mate, you're buggin' me now. I mean, do you think I was flamin' named.' Scotty slurred a bit.

'"Flamin' named"? I thought you were named Scotty, not flamin'. Are you sure about this flamin' naming?'

Karin and I rolled our eyes at each other over Jim's bad dad's joke. Scotty looked like he was going to kill Jim. But the more he got annoyed, the more Jim kept winding him up, all the time covering his mouth with his hand and shrugging his shoulders with laughter.

'I think I know what the person I was named after did, mate. He was the fuckin' mechanic, all right? Now back off.'

Jim turned his back, pretending to look out to sea, but we could all see him wiping the tears away from his eyes.

Scotty shook his head in disbelief, muttering, 'Fuckin' smart-arse-know-it-all.'

We were all forced to look out to sea to try and avoid Scotty's expression, which was too funny to look at by now.

'Ah dear.' Jim coughed in an attempt to compose himself. 'I tell you what, we're lucky we found this place; the view.' Jim could no longer make polite pretend conversation, and spluttered all over his last few words about the view, breaking out into full and open hysterics, which set Karin and Andrea off. I wasn't laughing with quite the same gusto as the others. I felt sorry for Scotty, who played the part of the group moron so well, because he tried so hard all of the time.

'Ah, mate, that's it, you've really pissed me off now. I'm going for a fuckin' lie-down.' He got up to walk off but Jim kept at him.

'It's no good, Captain, I'm giving her all she's got.'

Scotty turned in his tracks and walked back to Jim and kind of squared up to him.

'So if you knew what Scotty said, how come you didn't know what Scotty did?'

The problem was, there was not one part of Scotty that could see anything funny whatsoever about the conversation and the levels of animosity he was putting out to Jim.

'I'll tell you why, cause you think you're fuckin' smart, that's why.'

'I thought your name was Scott,' I said, trying to diffuse things slightly.

'Yeah, everybody does.' He didn't move away from Jim, and didn't look over at me.

'What is it, then?'

'Anthony.'

'Weird. I just see you as Scotty.'

'Yeah, me too.'

They both just stood their ground; Jim's slightly shakier than Scotty's, with him still laughing.

'Fuckin' teachers, they're the fuckin' worst, fuckin' boring pricks as well.'

'Is that so?' Jim stopped laughing.

'Come on, for fuck's sake, what's going on?' I said intervening, pulling Scotty away. Karin touched Jim's arm but he didn't respond.

'Really, guys, we've only just got here.' I was no peacekeeper by nature but I could see a potential fight and didn't want either of them to get hurt.

'I'm taking Scotty for a drink,' I said dragging him away, winking at Karin to look after Jim, who by now was standing serious and upright, hands out of his pockets, looking through Clint Eastwood in a *Fistful of Dollars* squinted eyes.

'So. Anthony, eh?' I said, with my arm around Scotty, walking in the direction of the site bar.

CHAPTER TWENTY-TWO

We all sat in the car waiting to be dispatched to various streets. Jim traced a line on the map with his finger.

'You know, in the mid-nineteenth century, Newcastle was the centre of all shipping and industrial commerce. Strange, when you think about that,' he said, still tracing as though he was reading it from the map. 'It has the largest coal port in the world.'

'Really, how come?' asked Karin politely. The 'really' I could live with, someone had to offer up a 'really', but the 'how come' was unacceptable.

'I know, it's not something you would immediately associate with Australia, is it?'

'No,' she said, looking out of the window.

'You'd think all the coal in the world was from my neck of the woods. Most people have no idea what goes on beyond their own street.' Jim was more enthusiastic now he'd found a pupil.

'Imagine the transportation,' Karin piped.

'Yeah, let's fuckin' imagine for a moment,' Scotty mumbled, which made me laugh and have to turn away, avoiding Jim's gaze in the mirror.

'Well, everything was by boat of course. But can you imagine being one of the early settlers? I mean, what a journey. All this way.' Jim went off into deep thought. Karin leant over his shoulder and looked at the map to further his interest, while Scotty chewed the gum he was never without, and I fixated on the word Newcastle.

'It's the sixth most populated city in Australia.' Jim tried so hard with his class.

'Jim?' I asked.

'Mm.'

'Can I ask you, seriously, to explain to me what interests you about that kind of information, and how you came to learn about it?'

'You taking the piss?'

'No, I'm seriously curious, because I want to be interested but I'm not.'

He looked at me with raised eyebrows.

'I mean it.'

'How can you not be interested in history?'

'No, I am, I agree, but all the information, the statistics, buildings ...'

'It's maybe an age thing; I'm a lot older than you.'

'Only about ten years.'

'I think it's the twenties and the thirties thing, there is a difference.'

'But I think about other stuff more – people, love, death, sex.'

'I think about those things too, obviously, but this is all the stuff of life as well, how this got here.' He swept his arm round the limited space.

'Who cares? It's a fucking dump,' Scotty said, stretching. Jim laughed at his response, which was a relief to us all.

I admired Jim's ability to rise above all that happened to him and continue to move forward, while maintaining an interest in the developing world around him, and decided to talk to him further about this at a later date, perhaps when the others weren't around. Maybe he could teach me how to be enthused about buildings and history, how to be more like him.

I suddenly panicked that my real mother might be in Newcastle; it would make sense, after all, if you were going to leave the city that you were brought up in for another one on the other side of the world, that you would choose its name-sake. I had thought that the moment I knew of Australia's Newcastle but hadn't wanted to dwell on it, for I had already convinced myself that she was in Sydney or Brisbane. Based on what, though? An old woman I had spoken to on the doorstep of the house she once lived in, who thought she went to Sydney in the sixties. Or the psychic vibes of carpet mogul Joyce Cane after a chance encounter, or Hank White the country and western DJ, who, because he was based in Brisbane, led me to think that she'd more than likely be there. I was expecting fate to do all the work. How lazy and ridiculous my search was. I talked myself down. Jim's mouth had been moving but I hadn't listened for the last few minutes. I felt rage again, I felt it burning inside. Why the fuck should I be looking for her? Why wasn't she looking for me? Just as well I wasn't really looking for her, otherwise I'd feel really fucked over. I thought back to Joyce Cane's parting words to me, about trying to look for the good things around me, and felt slightly calmer. I decided that after ten, I would get some change and call the home.

'Don't you wonder about how this place was built, how it was developed, how hard the people worked?'

'I don't, but I want to. It's just I've got these things I have to do that distract me.'

'At least the poor fuckers didn't have to sell these pieces of shite paintings,' said Scotty.

We all laughed. I faked mine.

My heart wasn't in the game for the time being. I had grown tired and easily distracted, if it was possible to be any more easily distracted, and found the hours not drinking more and more difficult to inhabit. I dragged my folder round the corner of a street I paid no attention to, and chose a house to knock at. So far I'd already had five no-answers, and two not interested. One of them had the potential to be persuaded otherwise, but I just couldn't care. I wanted to go and live with Joyce Cane, or go back to the caravan site and get drunk with Scotty or with Jim, maybe in a cosy bar on the edge of the beach where I could smell the sea and hear the waves lapping over the edges of the sand.

The hour dragged so slowly. I wondered if the others had sold any, if the area just wasn't working, or if it was all down to me.

Eventually I got into a house, but only because the woman who let me in was a bit desperate and down on her luck. The outside of the house was normal and suburban, except for the garden, which was neglected, and therefore not entirely in keeping with the rest of the area. I didn't have to talk to her for long before being allowed in. Always a bad sign, easy entry. She was thin and pale, looked like she'd never been in the sun. Her house smelt smoky with a trace of dope lingering. She had a big old Border collie dog, that wasn't long for the world. The dog was blind and walked into the walls. I felt sad for her the moment I walked in, and realised she was lonely. This was all unusual stuff, perhaps because I'd only sold in Sydney so far, to comfortable suburban areas. I had begun to think there were no poor fucked-up people in Australia, except for Aboriginals whom I'd run into around Redfern and King's Cross. I didn't understand much about their plight other than they'd been really fucked over by the Australians a long time ago and never recovered. I'd seen a few of them wandering around with bottles of spirits. They would not have looked out of place in Scotland, where the sighting of displaced and broken drunken lunatics is part of everyday life, but here, where the people really did look like the cast of *Neighbours*, they looked bizarre.

I sat down on her sofa, which was covered with a sheet on account of the dog hairs. She listened intently to my routine; worse than that, she looked really genuinely interested and almost flattered that I'd chosen her house to rip off. She offered me a cigarette immediately, which I accepted, and asked me if I wanted a drink of some sorts, to which I asked if there was a beer. She came back with two mini VBs.

I pointlessly went through the motions with the pictures and laid them out. The dog sniffed them, its eyes all grey and weird-looking. Then, like a slow train coming down the track, she told me about her money situation.

'You know it's real weird that you've come here, because we were just talking at the weekend about the house, yeah?'

'Uh, uh.' I wondered who 'we' meant.

'Yeah, and we were just saying I should get a painting up or something, brighten the place up a bit, you know.'

'Really?' This was ridiculous.

'Yeah, I do really want to buy one – it's just I don't get my social security cheque until the end of the week so you would have to come back.'

'The end of the week, mmm.' I had no intention of coming back, but played along out of politeness.

'Would that be a problem?'

'Well, I'm actually on my way back to Sydney, and these are all the paintings I have left, I'm afraid. So a week from now I would have let these ones go. I've only just picked them up from our art warehouse in Brisbane. This is new work, but it really won't hang around.'

'I like that one.' She pointed to the girls in a field. 'That's real cute.'

Her use of 'cute' in the circumstances made me too sad. I had to get out.

'Listen, if I'm back up this way in the next few weeks I'll drop round, I might have something that you like, or even that one, we'll see.'

'Yeah, OK, sorry about that, but I'm really stretched just now.'

'Don't worry about it.' I made my peace with this being a quick beer stop.

'Yeah, I get my cheque next Thursday. I've had bloody vet's bills as well for Glen. He's real crook.' She stroked the dog and spoke to it. I drank down my beer in one and left.

When I got outside, the car was circling, with Jim, Scotty and one Dane in it. I made the thumb-down sign at them.

'Crap, isn't it?' said Jim, leaning out of the window, looking tired.

'Not good, I've shifted nothing at all.'

'Andrea hasn't either. There just doesn't seem to be anyone around.'

'Told you, it's shit, mate,' said Scotty, leaning over Jim in the passenger seat.

'Yeah, all right, we get your point. Come on, let's get Karin and go back.'

I threw my folder in the back, delighted that we were calling it a day.

Back in the van, things felt better again. We got a pizza take-away and some beers and sat and listened to the radio, our only source of music. We all shared a six-berth: the Danes got the double bed in the living area that by day was a table; Scotty and I got the bunks in a separate room; and Jim was next door in the double. He put up a very strong argument as to why he should sleep there, mostly based on him driving and his ongoing back problems. Nobody disagreed with him.

'Come on then, let's show each other our tricks of the trade. I'm intrigued as to what you're all like,' said Jim.

'Yeah, that's always fun,' said Scotty.

'What, every group does this?' I asked.

'Course, yeah, 'cos there's always a part of you that wonders how the fuck you sell them, right? We all work our nuts off, yeah, in the houses, I mean. And then there's people you just can't imagine getting anywhere, but they do – so you wanna see what they do, yeah?'

'I want to see you first, Kerry.' Jim lay on the single sofa at the back of the van, stretched out, peeling the label off his beer, while the rest of us sat round the table.

'I don't have a particular thing, I just learnt as I went along.'

'Yeah, that's what we want to see. What you learnt.'

'Well, it's down to the individual, you know.'

'You've sold the most, know that?' said Jim.

'What, you keep a record of everyone?'

'Oh yeess,' said Scotty.

'I suppose I'm good at playing around with people – like, if they say they don't like something, I'm good at making them want it by the end.' I sipped on my beer, and thought about some of my highlights, including the Arab man and the barbecue. But I didn't really want to do my thing in front of the others – it was personal, and I didn't want anybody stealing my technique. Besides, I wanted my success to be a mystery to them, and would enjoy my new aloofness.

'What about you girls? I want to know what you get up to.' Scotty sank down in his seat like a gormless idiot and pulled his hat down when he spoke to the Danish, which was a sure sign that he had a thing for one of them, and my guess it was Andrea. I'd also had the feeling for a while now that Jim and Karin were pairing off slightly. Where did that leave me? I wondered.

'Wouldn't you like to know?' said Karin, playing it up.

'For a start we're blonde, so we gonna say we're Swedish, right?'

'Swedish, Danish, same thing,' I said, trying to wind them up.

'Hey, you!' shouted Karin, pretending to take a swing at me.

'If the husband answers, then we are Swedish,' said Andrea, in an unusually playful manner that I'd only ever seen the night of truth or dare.

'Yeah, not if it's the lady, she wouldn't like that.' They both burst out into fits of laughter. I looked over at Jim and Scotty who were loving every second of it, and wondered if perhaps I wasn't the only one who played games in some of the homes.

Mosquitoes buzzed around the light at the top of the phone booth. I smoked with one foot in the door, one foot out, waiting for Jim to finish the call back to Sydney. I could hear the distant squeak of Greg's voice in response to Jim's report on how bad a day it had been for selling.

'Yeah, yeah, sure,' he said, rolling his eyes. 'Yeah, I'll tell her. OK, bye, Greg. Will do.' He mouthed fuck off at the receiver and put down the phone, which was very out of character. 'Sometimes Greg talks such shite, you know? Like he's a total space cadet.' Jim burped intentionally really loud.

'Hang on, I need to make a call. Do you have any bucks? I've got four but I need to call home quickly.'

'Sure.' He fumbled in his pocket and gave me what he had. I took out the piece of paper with the nursing-home number and dialled. Jim waited outside, inhaling as much sea air as he could.

'Hello, Fernburn, can I help you?'

'Yeah, hello, it's Kerry Swaine trying to get a message to her grandfather.'

She sighed.

'Hello?'

'Yes, how can I help you?'

'I just said I want to talk to my grandfather, please. I've called before and my mother tried to call with him a few days ago.' She spoke over me, which caused some confusion in the delay; I was trying not to overreact but was finding it hard.

'Can you please at least tell him I'm sorry I wasn't there when they called and that we are twelve hours ahead here.'

'Your grandfather had a little fall yesterday, but there's nothing to worry about, he's much better today, he just got a little fright, that's all.'

'What? Fuck!' I slammed the coin box, causing Jim to turn round and press his face against the glass; I could see him mouthing was I all right.

'Old people just fall, it's very distressing, I know, but it's part of them getting very old and frail. I think in your grandfather's case, he was reaching over from his chair when it happened.'

'Is he hurt?'

The delay of me asking if he was hurt ran over the beginning of what she said, plus I was half cut and was getting more and more frustrated.

'Few bruises, that's all.'

'It's that fucking window, I told you, he hates the sun directly in his face, it gives him a headache. You need to pull the curtain over to shade him …' Beep beep beep. The line went dead; I had been too caught up in the conversation to notice that my money was running out.

I slammed my fist down on the phone.

'You OK?' asked Jim.

'My grandfather. He's in a fucking home and he's had a fall.'

'Yeah, I gathered that. OK?' Jim put his massive arm round my shoulder, causing me to well up.

'Yeah, I'm all right. Just can't do anything.'

'Oh dear, all part of them growing old, I'm afraid.'

'Yeah I know, but I am really close to him, I was brought up by him for a while and I feel so guilty that I'm here. Fuck!' I grabbed my hair. 'I told him a long time ago that I would come here, and he understood, he told me to go and do what I had to, but I feel so bad that he's in that fucking home. He hates it.' I shook my head and stopped trying to explain things to Jim. I felt exhausted and frustrated.

Jim and I walked back to the van, I let his arm remain round me, he tried to joke with me to take my mind off things. I thought about telling him that it was my birthday in two days, and that I was hoping to find my real mother.

'My divorce came through this week, it's official.' He kicked the gravel on the path that wove round the caravan park.

'Shit, what do I say to that? I've never met a divorcee before. Do you say congratulations?'

He took his arm away and put his hands in his pockets. 'Maybe to her.'

I didn't know what to say, I had always been crap when other people needed comfort. Being better at it was another thing that I was hoping to improve on, just like the building and scenery appreciation. I could see the hurt in Jim, though; most days, despite his enthusiasm, it exuded from him and had done since the day we met. But Jim had to be left; he was the kind of man that would only say things when he really felt like it.

'Come on, let's get a beer and forget all this shit.'

'Can't argue with that,' I said, patting him on the arm.

I thought about the Tammy Wynette song 'D-I-V-O-R-C-E', then I thought about an old song that was a hit when I was young, by Peaches & Herb, called 'Reunited'. I sang it in my head and thought about Joyce Cane, my main focus of motherhood, then Anaya. Then we reached the van.

The atmosphere had changed since Jim and I left for the phone. Scotty and the girls were more subdued. Jim announced that we should all get some sleep, because we had a much earlier start than we were used to in the morning. He stretched the map out on the table while I moved through the stations on the radio.

'You see, I think we'd be mad when we're up that way not to stop at Hanging Rock. We could do it, you know.'

'Oh yeah, gotta do that, haven't even been there myself.' Scotty leant over the table showing great interest in Jim's plans for once.

'What, you live here and you've never been to half these places?'

'Working, mate, haven't had the time. If I'm not down in Sydney, then I'm off up working the ski resorts for the winter.'

'Oh yeah, it's supposed to be amazing,' said Andrea, loading another film into her complicated arty camera.

'What do you do at the ski places, Scotty?' I asked, still moving the radio dial.

'Fit boots and shit. It's cool, loads of chicks.'

'We could stop off at Hanging Rock. It's possible but it's out of the way.' Jim was in a map dream. 'Tamworth, give that a miss, but then double back.' He made clicking noises with his mouth as he thought out the route.

'Sound like a bloody 'roo, mate,' said Scotty.

'Yeah, when we gonna see some kangaroos?' asked Karin.

Jim stopped map reading and gave her his full attention. 'Listen, you, we'll see all the sights but we have to work a bit as well, OK?'

'Plenty everywhere, don't worry,' said Scotty.

I hadn't seen kangaroos during my time in Sydney, only dead ones at the side of the road on the journey up. You knew you were approaching one because there'd be the terrible stench of rot. Its stomach swelled up like a balloon and would eventually burst in the sun, Scotty told us.

'We've seen some at the zoo in the city, but I'd love to see a pack of them wild,' said Andrea. The Danish were such swots and never ceased to annoy me, but in a bearable way.

Jim went back to his map. I wondered how he did it, how he just kept on organising us, how he would drink with us then retire early to read a book, then wake up early and eat a proper breakfast and walk, and learn things. No matter what went on in his life, what fucked him up before, he didn't let it run him.

'Mmm, Port Macquarie. We could in theory still get there by night ... yep, that's the best bet,' he said.

I flicked past a song I recognised. I went back to find it. The reception was bad; excitedly, I held up the radio, trying to get it fixed on the station. It was crackly and soundwaves pinged in between the verses but I could make it out.

'FUCK!' I said. 'What are the fucking chances? 'Reunited'!' I shouted with my hands clasped round my head.

I turned it up full; the others looked at me clueless as to what was making me pace up and down the van.

'It's a fucking sign, I'm telling you.' I shook my head and grinned. 'A fucking sign.'

I slumped down next to the radio and listened to the rest of the song. The others kept quiet, just watching me. When it finished I went outside and leant against the van, looking out into the night, wondering who was running this show, and how it would end.

CHAPTER TWENTY-THREE

I woke up feeling thirsty and bloated from a mild hangover, exacerbated by the sun streaming directly onto me through a small orange porthole in the van roof.

Scotty was still snoring underneath me on the bottom bunk. I had slept badly due to the excitement of Peaches & Herb, but despite everything I felt strangely optimistic at the bizarre way things were shaping up.

I reached up and opened the porthole, letting in some air to override the smell of my and Scotty's stale beer breath, and his general sweaty demeanour. I lay back with my hands resting behind my head, listening to the sea birds outside and enjoying the feeling of the van rocking as Jim and the ever-keen Danish moved around in the other room. For a moment it felt like childhood when the three of us, in happier times, would go caravanning, before it all went wrong, before they told me, and before they became so unhappy together.

'Morning, children.' Jim knocked and came in. 'Fuck me, what a stink, Scotty, is that your arse?'

'Do me a favour, mate?' Scotty mumbled.

'How are you, sir?' I joked.

'I'm good. It's a beautiful day.'

'What time is it?'

'Eight o'clock, Australia time.'

Scotty and I both complained in sync. Jim threw a tea towel at me and was about to leave when he turned back.

'Shit, Kerry, I'm so sorry. I forgot to tell you that last night Greg said there was a message for you back at William Street, from a friend of yours called Hank. Sorry, completely forgot.'

I leapt out of the bunk, grabbed my shorts and some change from the floor from Scotty's jeans, and ran out to the call box.

'Hey there, we're not in just now, leave a message.'

'Greg, Anaya, it's Kerry, please pick up if you're there. It's important.'

Anaya answered. 'So, how are you?'

The excitement of some possible news took over from my usual interest in her.

'Yeah, please listen, this is important.'

'Oh, OK.'

'The man that called for me, what did he say? Did you tell him I was on the way to Brisbane?'

'He left a voice message. We didn't talk to him, we were lying down.' She laughed, trying to draw me in, but it was the wrong time. I had no interest.

'And what did he say?'

'That he was a friend of yours and that he had to go to a music festival for a few days but would try again soon, and that he had some news.'

'That's all?' My heart was in my mouth. I let out a big breath. 'OK, if he calls again, please tell him where we are going and that I'll call him, and get him to leave a number, OK?'

'OK. That all?'

'Yeah, gotta go, Anaya, speak another time.'

I only had fifty cents left in change; I dialled Hank's number in Brisbane.

'Come on, come on.'

It rang for the longest time. Just as it went beyond the limit when anybody would answer, a woman's voice did.

'Hello, how can I help you?' The voice sounded oriental.

'Hello, is Hank there, please?'

'Hank left yesterday. He's gone down to Tamworth for the music festival, he'll be gone for the rest of the week. Can I give him a message?'

'Did he say anything to you about a message for me about some relatives? He's helping me, you see. My name's Kerry.'

'Oh dear, I am sorry I cannot help, I have been away and have not spoken to Hank properly. It would be better if you call back on Friday, or maybe you can try his hotel. I'm sorry I could not help.'

The fucking beeps started.

'WHERE'S HE STAYING, WHICH HOTEL?' I was getting hysterical.

'Station Hotel, he alwa—' The line went dead.

I called directory enquiries and got the number for the Station Hotel in Tamworth.

Hank had checked in that morning but was out for the time being. I left a message saying I was on the way to Brisbane and just a couple of hours from Tamworth. I said I'd call back when I could, and asked him to tell reception when he would be in his room so that I could call him.

When I got back to the van, the others wanted to know why I was so excited. I told them an old friend was in Brisbane and that there was a chance I could meet up with him. Then I realised saying 'old friend' sounded ridiculous coming from a twenty-four-year-old.

We left the Pacific Highway to go inland, which was my first real taste of the Australian countryside. We drove through towns with wide unmarked roads, where all the shops lining the front had striped awnings to act as shade. All the store names were painted blue or yellow; everywhere was so very bright and dry. Miles of nothing but parched trees lay between each town, which all seemed to have a name ending in Creek or Brook. When we reached our first stretch of countryside, we all had turns standing on the car seat with our bodies half out the sunroof. Jim drove fast and we screamed and howled as our hair swept back and our faces distorted with the force. Even the Danish let themselves go and made some noise. Jim laughed each time one of us did it.

We didn't talk much for the stretch between Newcastle and the last town before Hanging Rock. It was early and we were tired from talking so much to one another the night before. The journey was only about two hours, and in between bursts of the sunroof, we listened to the radio and sang along to the odd song that we all knew. Jim changed the channel again during another song; this time it was Tracy Chapman's popular dirge 'Sorry'.

I felt the car jolt forward and I woke up.

'I reckon we should stop here and use the toilets, get a sandwich, some cold drinks and then we'll go on to the rock, OK, folks?' said Jim enthusiastically.

I asked Jim to get me a cheese sandwich and went straight to a pay phone.

'Mr White said to send his regards and that he will be back in his room between five and six,' said the Irish receptionist.

We stood on a porch outside a bakery, reminiscent of something I'd only ever seen in cowboy and Indian films, and ate our lunch.

'Hey, some fucking picnic, eh?' I said. Jim laughed.

It was boiling hot by the time we parked up in the small, woodland, dirt car park at Hanging Rock.

'Okayee, this is us,' said Jim, stretching at the wheel.

'Hey, wouldn't it be funny if a couple of us got lost, eh?' said Scotty, nudging Karin, who rode the last part of the journey up front for some reason. We all rolled our eyes at poor old Scotty; he didn't deserve the treatment he got, but he was just so predictable.

We climbed uphill on a well-worn path, passing some Japanese people, lots of Scandinavian backpacker types and men with sandals. Jim was one of these at-one-with-nature people; he took long slow strides, his head back, looking up at the sky and the top of the trees, taking in exaggerated breaths. I hoped that soon after being reunited with my mother, I too would be able to concentrate on any surrounding beauty; everything would fall into place, all problems alleviated, all gaps filled. However, for the time being, I loved and appreciated being free of the intense heat of the city mixed with car fumes.

The walk to the top took about forty minutes; Karin and I were slightly behind because we wore flip-flops. I had come to Australia with one pair of shoes, and bought the flip-flops soon after my arrival, and had subsequently worn them almost the entire time. When we reached the actual picnic spot, it was packed with tourists. Many of them, including

Jim, stood round a tree watching a koala chewing on some leaves. A ranger-type man with a hat and safari clothes explained to his group that the koala was eating eucalyptus leaves, which sedated them. The koala paid no attention to the chattering, photographing group of Japanese.

Scotty sat drinking a Coke from the log cabin café that advertised guided tours of the rock and surrounding area. A couple of American girls asked him to take a photo of them.

'Pleasure's all mine, ladies,' he said, rubbing his hands.

'I'd watch him,' Jim said to them. 'He's not to be trusted.'

The girls giggled and Scotty acted out an 'I'm innocent' routine, and took their picture. After they'd gone he said, 'Hey, you can see why them schoolgirls got lost, eh, mate? 'S flamin' packed up here, probably got on the wrong bus home.'

'Nice one, Scotty,' I said, giving him the credit he deserved for one of his funnier comments.

We all grouped together and Karin and Andrea snapped away with their big lens cameras, stopping to hand them over to competent-looking tourists who took some of us all. Scotty chewed on leaves and looked stoned, pretending to be the koala; Jim stuck his fingers up behind Scotty's head. I bought a disposable camera at the Hanging Rock gift shop, the first I had owned since coming to Australia. I once owned an old Russian Zenith, and took pictures of my gran and grandfather leaning out of their flat window; I framed one and gave it to them for Christmas. The Zenith ended up in the pawnshop, along with some other things.

The gift shop sold picnic baskets, and tablecloths with maps of the area emblazoned on them. The Danish bought tea towels for their mothers; Jim bought more postcards, which he was always writing in the evenings and posting off in the mornings. As I took my first picture of us, the marker on my camera moved to thirty-five, and I wondered if perhaps the last few exposures in the film would contain pictures of my real mother.

After a while we wandered around the actual site itself. Jim told us it was sacred and belonged to the Aborigines, and that the film *Picnic At Hanging Rock* was based on a novel. I berated myself for not keeping up the notebook entries that I had been writing quite frequently when I first arrived in Sydney. I had only written a couple of pages in the last month, and it was unreadable because I'd been drunk at the time.

I looked at my watch; it was only a couple of hours before I would speak to Hank. I was tired and my eyes were stinging from not enough sleep. I was keen to get back to the Kingswood and get my head down until five.

Soon after Hanging Rock, we stopped for gas. Jim spoke to the owner about routes and laid out the map on the car roof. The rest of us used the toilets and bought some gum. In the shop, I got talking to the lady behind the counter. She asked us where we were heading.

'The Gold Coast. Brisbane,' I said.

'You'll be passing Glenairdane Creek, then?' She smiled, her sunbeaten face all lined and scrunched up. I shrugged. 'You have to be – you heading back to the coast road?'

'Yeah, think so, think we're going to Port Macquarie.' I thought about trying to sell to her, which would have been so impressive in the circumstances, but I was so hot and without a beer I didn't feel geared up enough. It was an after-dark thing with me, definitely. I had sold in the afternoons but in the evenings the art had really shifted.

'Listen, when you head off to the coast road, at the end there, there's a sign for Glenairdane Creek. You have to tell your friends to go there, everybody does that passes through, it's beautiful.'

'What, like a place to swim?'

'It's a natural waterhole. All the kids go there in the holidays, it's a part of growing up here. Some people jump in from high up, the stupid ones, but you'll be all right there.'

'There's no crocodiles?' I asked.

She laughed and wheezed and went into a splutter. 'Oh dear, excuse me. No, there's no bloody crocs. There's a waterfall nearby, the water's fresh, don't worry. Oh dear, you pommies make me laugh with your croc thing. Is that what they warn you about here, is it?'

I politely laughed, though saw nothing odd about my concern. Back in the car, I told the others about the conversation. Scotty laughed as much as she did. After he stopped laughing he said, 'Yeah, fuck it, got me togs with me. What about you guys?'

'How about you?' I asked the Danish, expecting them not to want to get their hair messed up or something.

'Sounds cool,' said Karin.

'Oh yeah, I'm in,' followed Andrea, who pretty much always did anything Karin did.

Only a couple of kilometres up the road we reached a small wooden sign with a hand-painted 'Glenairdane – 1km' on it. We went off the road, the old Kingswood creaking under the strain of five people, a bootful of luggage and a roof rack with piles of paintings bound together by orange polyethylene and bungee ropes.

'Fuckin' tank, this old beauty,' Jim said, as he hit the accelerator and the car skidded off, shifting clouds of dust behind us. The Danish shut the windows coughing, while Scotty and I squeezed up together through the sunroof, cheering and urging Jim to put his foot down even more.

When we reached the end of the track there were some bikes piled against a tree, but no other vehicles. We opened up the boot and got out our bags, pulling out various items of swimwear, except for Scotty who said he was always prepared. There was no obvious place of water nearby. Jim told us all to be quiet and still in order to listen for it. A sound of gushing came from behind the trees, slightly downhill from the bikes. We each went behind the car and changed and set off in the direction of the sound.

CHAPTER TWENTY-FOUR

The waterhole was like nothing I'd ever seen before. It was like a film set. It didn't look real. It lay in a clearing, through a thicket of trees; the soil was dry and crumbly. Massive rocks surrounded the water, which lay perfectly circle-shaped but not as big as I had imagined. At the other side was a small waterfall, the water running down from the hill and trees. A dark rough-looking man sat on a rock, watching a kid I took to be his son standing high up in the trees above some rocks, on a jagged ledge that jutted out, holding onto a Tarzan rope and looking down into the pool.

'G'day,' said the man.

We all said g'day back except the Danish, who said hi there.

'Is he going to jump off, do you think?' asked Jim.

'Dunno. He's tryin', though,' said the man, not taking his eyes off the boy.

I thought back to a time when I loved my father, when I was very little and he'd take me to the swimming baths and watch me swim. I loved him watching me play and show off. It felt like a very long time since my father had really watched me out of love.

Nobody jumped in, not wanting to put the kid off.

'How long has he been standing there?' I asked, sitting on the rock next to the man.

'Dunno. About half an hour, I reckon. He'll do it.'

Scotty made a funny face at me after the guy spoke.

'GO ON, MATE!' Scotty shouted up through cupped hands.

'How did he get up there?' I asked, seeing no way of climbing up over the rocks.

'You get up round the back of these trees, there's a path up there.' The man pointed to no particular landmark.

'JUST CLEAR THE ROCKS, MATE, YOU'LL BE RIGHT!'

The boy swung forward and we all gasped except for the man. The drop itself was enough to scare anyone, but what made it really treacherous were the rocks beneath it; they had to be cleared before letting go of the rope and jumping in. He swung back, managing to grab hold of the tree and scramble back up to the top again.

'Phew, he was lucky,' said Jim, sitting next to the guy in an identical position to him, pulling his knees up to his chin with his arms round them.

'Yeah, he's got to clear the rocks. He'll have to do it this time.' The man was completely unfazed by any potential danger. The boy went back to his original push-off position and waited again.

'You from round here?' asked Jim, trying to obtain even more geographical information, no doubt.

'Yeah, couple of Ks that way.' He moved his head to the left.

'How old's the boy?'

'He's ten today.'

'Ten? Whoa.'

'Yeah, it's kind of a tradition round here, the waterhole, like.'

'How do you mean?'

'Well, I did it when I was a kid as well. You get to an age, usually elevenish, and you come here with your mates and try and jump off and not flamin' kill yourself.'

'God, aren't you worried for him?'

'Naw, he'll be right. Everybody does it, eh.'

'Is it like a coming-of-age sort of thing?'

I was embarrassed by Jim's question; he had to turn everything into a lesson or an interview where he could acquire information.

'Could say that, I suppose.' The man quite rightly laughed a little.

'Anyone ever been killed here?' Andrea asked, like a dumb tourist fuck.

'Yeah, long time ago. Wasn't even a kid, just some guy did

it full of grog.' The man never took his eyes off the boy for a second.

'What is grog?' asked Karin.

'Aussie for drink,' I said, beating anyone else to it.

'Kids are fearless, though,' said Jim.

'Yeah, or stupid,' said the man.

The boy let out a scream, pushed off the ledge, his legs dangling, and jumped clear of the rocks straight down into the water. We all applauded him, but the father remained motionless except for a slight smile when the boy surfaced.

'You all right, mate?'

'Yeah,' said the boy, coming out of the water with new red streaks down the front of his legs.

'Stung your legs a bit?'

'Yeah.'

The boy dried off and put on some trainers. His father made a roll-up and bid us farewell. Jim pushed Karin in the water first, then the four of us dived in.

We swam about, ducking under the water for long periods of time, finding each other's legs and grabbing them, or trying to pull down each other's swimming bottoms. Me, Scotty and Jim pulled ourselves out and dived in again a couple of times, then we all trod the water in a circle, or floated. After a while, once we calmed down, we were quiet. We looked up to the rope above the ledge. I knew we were going to have to go for it, and so did everyone else.

'Come on. We gotta, eh?' said Scotty first.

'Absolutely, we'd only kick ourselves if we didn't,' I said, splashing the water with my fist.

Jim said, 'Hey, listen, I don't feel any big need to do anything like that, all right? One of the great things about being older is not having to prove things to people.'

I was hoping Scotty wouldn't push Jim on this, but of course he did.

'So is that your way of telling us that you're a pussy, mate?'

'Hey, less of that, you,' said Karin, splashing him, jumping to Jim's defence. Jim laughed it off.

'Come on, we can all do it, we have to, come on.' I tried to avoid any arguments starting.

'What do you say, Andrea?' asked Scotty, continuing his now rather obvious pursuit of her.

'I don't know. I'm not liking the rocks, they look dangerous.'

The rocks didn't look too bad from where we were standing; besides, I was indestructible so far. I never got hurt despite the state I would get myself into. I'd never been attacked or in a bad accident. These things only happened to people least expecting it. I'd wandered through dangerous areas at night alone, got into cars with strangers for a ride home, then ended up drinking with them, or let people I'd only just met come back to wherever I was staying and had sex with them. I drank a full bottle of rum once and took lots of pills from the junkie that used to live across the landing from me, and slept it off in my bed for two days, without a front door, because the fire brigade had knocked it down when a neighbour found me sitting on the window ledge shouting down that I was going to jump off. Nothing ever happened; someone was watching over me. I felt it was safe to take risks. It's people who love their lives who are most at risk.

I felt all this as we climbed the hill to the rope.

When we first got up there, without even pausing, without edging forward to check out the drop, Jim walked straight to the rope and swung off, plunging into the water. He made an enormous splash, much bigger than the boy. When he came up, which seemed like ages, he made lots of noise, cheering and laughing.

'HURTS YOUR BLOODY CHEST! BETTER WATCH OUT, GIRLS! FFFUUCKK!' He swept his hair back off his face, blew out his nose into his hand and generally made a big song and dance. You had to admire the big fellow though, he was harder than the rest of us. Then I looked at the Danes and Scotty, and thought that they didn't take much beating.

After Jim's jump, the rest of us edged forward to look at the rocks. They looked treacherous now that we were on top of them. The drop appeared much further than from down in the pool, maybe some fifty feet or even more, and the pool looked tiny and narrow. The rocks formed a craggy ledge that seemed as long as a diving board, and could only be cleared when in full mid-swing, otherwise you would fall back and bang into them, doing some serious damage. Once out on the rope, if you missed the opportunity to drop at the right time, you couldn't expect to let go later because the rocky ledge would be jutting out beneath you.

'HA HA! YOU'VE BROUGHT THIS ON YOUR-SELVES, YOU LOT!' Jim basked in his own glory.

He was right, we had brought it on ourselves and we'd look foolish not to complete it. I was still fairly confident, if a little less gung-ho than on the way up. I noticed that Scotty had gone quiet since Jim had jumped, and we began examining the surrounding area. I could feel my heart pumping with adrenalin and my mouth getting dry and thirsty.

'What do you think?' I asked Karin, as the three of us edged forward as far as we could before we started sliding down. We held onto each other slightly. Scotty stood behind, leaning against a tree, his hands down the front of his shorts, shivering slightly, looking like a little boy at the side of a swimming bath.

'I don't fucking like it, are we crazy?' Karin muttered.

I loved it when the Danes let loose a little.

'Why the fuck are we doing it?' said Andrea.

We were all charged up now and exhilarated by the danger and anticipation, though I knew there was no way the Danes could do it, not unless Jim held their hands. Even then, it was so unlikely.

'Seriously, be careful, guys!' called Jim, changing tone and moving to the side of the rocks.

'Scotty, you go next,' I said.

But Scotty wasn't budging.

'Don't like it, mate, don't f-u-c-k-i-n-g like it one bit.'

'Hey, you started this, you idiot, you go next,' commanded Karin, which I quite liked her for.

I was trying to ignore the nauseous feeling I had growing in the pit of my stomach. Scotty leant forward towards the rope. I could see his feet and toes gripping the earth like claws, turning white as they scraped around for grip. He had also lost all signs of humour as soon as we got a real view of the drop. He was leaning forward, his hands raised about to swing on the rope, and stopping himself from moving any further by pushing his right foot against the bottom of a tree. It hadn't been possible to notice the additional danger of the rope pulling you forward as soon as you got hold of it, when Jim was standing in the way. But with Scotty, I could get a sense of where the real danger lay. Once you were holding the rope, you were unable to linger on the top of the hill and the safety of flat ground it provided, for it was too much of a stretch to reach, as it was placed far out in order to help with clearing the rocks. That meant you had to jump onto the rope and commit once there. The moment Scotty tried to do this, the Danes and I upped our fear level. He shouted as he leapt off. He swung out to the middle to the point of letting go, and swung back again towards the rocks.

'CUNT!' he shouted, his leg scraping against the side of them.

'Grab him! Don't let him swing back!' I shouted, realising that if he had any chance of being pulled back in with minimal injury, it would have to be on the first swing, before it got smaller. It all happened so quickly. I crouched down holding onto a root in the earth, leant out as far as I could and grabbed his legs, while Andrea grabbed me to secure me to the spot, allowing me to stretch forward as far down the drop as I could. Meanwhile Karin grabbed his shorts, then waist, and he held onto some of the tree and pulled himself up until he was able to let go of the rope. He landed on top of Karin, and we all piled up on the edge, scrambling with our hands for something to grip.

'Are you all right?' shouted Jim, from below.

Scotty mustered an 'OK', but his leg was bleeding down the shin and his ankle was cut. We all lay panting.

'Right, this is crazy,' said Karin.

'Yeah, she's right,' I said. 'Go down and wait with Jim.'

'Fuck off, it's just a little cut.' He composed himself and started play-acting again, like he'd enjoyed the thrill, but we all knew he was shitting himself.

'Let me look at your cuts,' said Andrea. She hissed in through her teeth. 'Looks sore. Is it?'

'It's a scrape, don't worry. I'll fix it up when we go back to the car.'

'Leave him, it's up to him if he wants to hurt himself,' said

Karin, standing up and picking the twigs and leaves off her arms and legs.

Scotty was freezing by now, though he denied it, and although it was hot, his teeth were chattering.

'What's happening? Shall I come up?' yelled Jim, getting worried; he lifted himself out of the water and began drying himself.

'No, fine, mate, we'll be down in a minute.' Scotty made an appearance over the edge, waving at Jim to let him know he was OK.

I was starting to feel uncomfortable and, if I was really honest, wanted someone else to suggest we call it a day and go down the way we came up, but nobody did. Not in the next five or even ten minutes. We stood there, each taking turns to peer over as near as we could get to the edge without having to use the tree.

'This is fucking crazy,' Karin said again, for about the tenth time in the last five minutes.

'I know, so why don't we go back? Because Jim did it, and we are a group, I suppose. It's weird, isn't it?' I was hoping someone would instigate our descent after my comment.

'Just forget about it, you lot! Come on!' shouted Jim, waving us down.

'Come on, we're freaking him out, maybe we should go down,' I said, expecting the others to agree instantly. They stood silent, looking down, Scotty breathing out short rapid breaths into his cupped hands.

'Nope,' said Karin after a minute.

'What? You going to do it, then?' I was startled.

'You're right about us having to do things that each other does, it's like being kids,' said Andrea.

'Karin? You going to jump?' I asked.

She ignored me, rubbed her hands and let out a big puffed-out cheeks breath, and jumped onto the rope shouting, 'SSHHHIIIIT!'

She started to come back a little after passing optimum jumping point and so leant forward slightly almost like she was going to dive off the rope, and let go, falling almost flat onto her front.

'Fuck me!' said Scotty, as we all rushed to the edge in line to see she was OK. Her splash was much bigger than Jim's, causing a rippling effect for a while afterwards. Jim dived in immediately. She came to the surface, gasping for breath and wheezing, clearly winded. Jim swam to her and pulled her back to the edge like a lifeguard. We could hear him telling her that she was OK and her breathing would be normal in a bit, and to try to take it slowly.

'YOU OK, KARIN?' I shouted.

Andrea shouted something in Danish. Then it hit me. Karin had jumped before me and was much braver than I had thought her to be, which meant I was wrong about her, which meant I would have to jump next, or look and feel like a complete failure.

A good fifteen minutes must have passed, as we stood at the edge looking down, which had become our pre-jump routine. Down at the pool, Karin had recovered and was sitting on a rock with Jim looking up at us. Nobody had spoken for a while. Jim had stopped his attempts to dissuade us from jumping; even Karin, as soon as she regained the power of speech, shouted to us that we would feel better once we jumped, but not to hesitate for a second once on the rope. Scotty stood leaning against the last tree before the slope, while Andrea and I stood together staring at the stillness of the inviting pool. We watched Karin running her hands over her legs – even from where we were, the red streaks were visible. Jim spoke to her and touched his chest; they seemed to be comparing injuries. I was still stunned by Karin's feat of bravery in comparison with my own cowardice. Still, I hadn't officially taken my place at the rope so wouldn't be judged yet. So, she had shown some kind of strength or spontaneity I didn't know she had, but surely there was no way that Andrea would be able to jump. Or had I read everybody wrongly, and was I full of shit, not as tough as I thought I was?

Andrea edged forward. 'This is so fucking dumb but I'm gonna do it.' She stared intently into the pool.

'Oh fuck,' said Scotty, running his hands through his hair.

'You sure? I mean, I think I'm going to go.' The truth was,

I wasn't sure, but I couldn't let Andrea go before me, so I moved towards the rope tentatively.

'OK, sure? You go before me, then, let's get this stupid thing over with.' Andrea's words just made me panic and doubt myself even more.

'OK.' I leant down to grab the rope, Scotty moving to the side so I could use the tree. I did the foot thing against it. I felt as though I was going to throw up.

'Hey, Scotty, did you feel sick when you went to do this?'

'Yeah, mate, and thought I was going to shit myself as well.'

'Then you would have had to jump in the water.'

Andrea laughed, which meant she was so much more relaxed than me. Jim and Karin watched me, silently. I was committed now, I was holding the rope. I could stand as long as I wanted but I couldn't go back, it would just look so bad. I wasn't sure if they felt as strongly about it as me or if this was all in my head, but the jump seemed to be a necessity to all of us, otherwise we wouldn't still be standing here. I didn't understand why I was so hesitant, so shit scared. I was strong and physically very confident. Andrea and Karin wouldn't even pull themselves up onto the roof of the car and let their feet dangle through the sunroof like Scotty and I had. I hated it that I was grouping myself together with Scotty. I had always seen myself as being more with Jim: strong, hard, wise, with a heavy, heavy past. I watched him down on the rock examining Karin's red legs and wondered if he felt shocked at my cowardice.

I urged myself to swing forward, I visualised myself going for it, it was so near, just a push-off. I was a strong swimmer and, in addition to that, would learn from Karin's belly flop. Yet none of these things would help me let go of the ground beneath me. It was the most out-of-character experience I had ever encountered.

I withdrew, letting go of the rope, watching it swing back empty to the middle.

'Fuck. FUCK!' I squatted down, holding my face in my hands. What had this turned into, what were we doing? Why did no one stop it? 'What do you think?' I asked Andrea. Suddenly, her opinion was of importance to me.

'I dunno.' She leant into the rope, hooking her foot under

the root protruding from the dirt that I'd used earlier in order to anchor herself. I couldn't believe what I was seeing. 'Maybe I'll understand when I've done it.' Then she swung off, leaving me with Scotty. Her drop was the best so far. She even whooped as she swung. Her arms tight by her side just before she entered the water. She surfaced completely unscathed to a round of applause that Scotty and I reluctantly joined in.

'Right, that's fucking it!' he said, taking his hand off his balls and grabbing the rope while it was still swinging. This time he let himself move a little further down the bank than before, maybe just one foot or so, and for a second he looked a dead cert to do it, but bottled out again, losing his balance and landing backwards on the slope, his hands and feet desperately scrabbling for anything to hold onto. He lay on his back, his arms out behind him, screaming upwards.

'FFFFFUUUUCCCK!'

'COME ON, SCOTTY, MATE, YOU CAN DO IT!' shouted Jim, now joined on the rock by two jubilant Danes.

'GO ON, IT'S FUCKING FANTASTIC. YOU'LL LOVE IT! JUST CLEAR THE ROCKS, GO ON!' Andrea had become one of them.

There were more of them than us now. We were a duo, a duo of no-jumpers. No-takers. No-can-doers. I helped Scotty back up, holding onto the tree and pulling him with my left hand.

'Oh mate, we're fucked,' he said, exhausted at his own hopelessness. I hated it that he automatically put me with him now, even though I had too as soon as Andrea let go. I worried that my inability to jump would lose me some of the respect I had gained as the best seller. I wanted to ask Scotty what he thought but was afraid he'd say more 'we' things. I decided to zone Scotty out and concentrate on my own jump. I stood at the edge again. Scotty spoke to me, but I wasn't listening. Instead I looked down. Down at the three of them, and longed to get it over with so I could join them, and feel free from this ridiculous burden of our own making.

I was so cold. We had no way of telling how long we'd been up there, or how long I stood at the edge poised, inches away from the rope. My teeth were chattering too now. It was a hot afternoon, and although the trees offered some shade from a vicious sun, it was by no means cool. I think maybe forty-five minutes had passed since Andrea jumped, but since then Jim had gone back in the water a few times, as had Karin. Andrea lay flat out on a rock sunbathing, looking up at us, and using her hand as a peak on her forehead to shield from the sun. Scotty had had another two goes of trying to go for the rope, but didn't even progress to holding onto it. I had held the rope once, and felt another wave upon me, a surge of adrenalin. I clenched down on my jaw, desperate for any part of my being that was a fighter, a survivor, to kick in and say fuck it, I'm afraid of nothing. I felt it rise up, I moved onto the balls of my feet and started breathing rapidly and loudly. Scotty said nothing, Jim shouted once more.

'GO ON, YOU CAN DO IT, COME ON, KERRY!'

'GO FOR IT!' shouted Karin.

I could feel me doing it, feel that jumping onto the rope was the hardest part; the landing would be easy for me, I loved water. I got diving and swimming badges when I was a kid, I had no fear with water. It was clearing the rocks. I started to get burning cramps in my lower stomach. Then a bubbling, gurgling feeling in my arse. That's when I shat myself. I could feel it filling my swimming costume. I wanted to cry. May as well go the whole hog, I thought, and cry my eyes out like a fucking baby. I knew it was over.

'GUYS!' Jim shouted. We didn't react. Scotty was staring at me, like he knew about the shitting.

'GUYS!' Jim waved his arms around. 'THERE'S GOT TO BE A POINT WHERE YOU CALL IT A DAY.'

He was right, and I think we had reached it. 'IT DOESN'T MATTER. COME ON.'

'Scotty?' I squatted down on the ground, not wanting to sit, wishing I was alone so I could empty out completely.

'Come on, mate, let's fuckin' forget this pile of shite.' He helped me up, but I shrugged him off, not wanting him to get too near in case he could smell me.

'You've lost all your colour, mate, pure white,' he said. I felt exasperated and could only manage a nod.

We walked away, dumbfounded at our failing.

When we got down, we joined the others in the pool. I was keen to dive in straight away and wash off without anyone finding out. Jim and the Danes splashed around. They seemed to me to be unburdened, unlike me, who felt extreme self-loathing and deep regret. I was shocked at my failure, but even more shocked at Karin and Andrea's success. I wondered how long these pointless feelings would last, and wondered if Scotty felt the same. I watched him lying on his back floating around, using his hands to change direction while he stared up at the jump. It looked so easy from where we were now, and the rocks looked entirely manageable.

CHAPTER **TWENTY-FIVE**

'Mr White left you a message. Hang on a second, I'll get it for you.' The line played country music.

I had to wait half an hour after leaving the waterhole to find a pay phone, as we didn't drive past the garage on the main road.

'Hi there.'

'Hello.'

'Yes, he said he waited as long as he could but had to leave earlier to go to do something at a radio station, and that he would catch up with you in Brisbane, and not to worry.'

'That's all. He didn't say anything else?'

'No, that's all, that's it. Would you like to leave him a message?'

'Yes, I would, thanks.'

'Go ahead, please.'

'Tell him that Madeline Thomson is my mother, and that's who I'm looking for.'

'Madeline. Thomson.'

It felt so odd telling the receptionist this, and I almost detected some pity in his voice.

'Is that everything?'

I laughed ironically through my nose. 'Yes, that's all, thanks.'

We arrived in Port Macquarie around eight. Jim and the Danish complained that they were starving.

'Steak and chips and an ice-cold beer,' said Jim, stretching. 'What about you two?'

He turned around; Scotty and I were now sharing the back seat, where we'd slept most of the way, while the Danes rode up front in the big old-fashioned one seat.

'Are we staying here?' asked Karin.

Jim shook his head, mid-yawn. 'Think we should go further up, nearer the coast. There's a campsite and a hostel right on the beach, in a little place called Macksville.'

'Macksville?' I said. 'This gets weirder.'

'How come?' asked Jim.

'Just the names, people I know.'

'So do you know anyone called Port or Macquarie?'

'Yeah, very funny.'

'We're near Kempsey, aren't we?' asked Scotty, who hadn't tried to be funny for a record three hours.

'Yes, hang on.' Jim reached for the map, which he kept folded behind the driver's seat visor, and put the light on.

'Kempsey's just a few Ks up the way. Why? Do you think we should stay there?'

'No, it's the longboard capital, mate, that's all, just sayin'.' Scotty couldn't muster a smile.

'Hey, look at this.'

We all leant in.

'Scotty's Head, look at this!' Jim pointed and passed the map around.

A little further up the coast from Kempsey, just before Macksville, was a stretch of beach called Scotty's Head. We all started laughing.

'Told you there's a names thing going on,' I said.

'Scotty's Head! Tell you what, that's surely a place to avoid.' Jim roared with laughter.

'Yeah, you don't want to go there, mate, trust me, I have to live there, and it's not fucking easy.' Scotty was easing back on form, I was glad to see.

'I've heard there's not much going on there at all,' said Jim, all smug.

'Too much goin' on, mate, too much.'

'Oh my God!' screamed Andrea, like her lotto number just came up.

'What?' Karin grabbed the map from her because she was

laughing so hard and talking Danish. Karin examined the part she'd been pointing to, and became infected herself.

'You're not gonna believe this, but right next to Scotty's Head is another place, guess what – GRASSY HEAD!' They both said the last bit together.

The whole car burst out laughing, even Scotty.

'Looks like they named the whole flaming place after you and your hobbies, mate,' said Jim, drying his eyes.

'Grassy fuckin' Head, that'll be fuckin' right.' Scotty shook his head, and lapped up the attention.

Scotty and I felt increasingly bitter about the waterhole. As the evening progressed, the whole incident was starting to have some kind of negative effect on our personalities. I felt resentment towards the others for their ability to jump, and I knew Scotty did too. It was none of their fault, of course, and although the laugh in the car was good fun, I could sense that we were both beginning to separate ourselves from them. The three of them had initially attempted to console us, but it didn't take away any of my darkness. Plus they didn't really understand how badly it was affecting us. Why should they? They were normal, and this was our losers' shit. The rot was well and truly setting in for us both now, and bringing out our demons. So we stuck together after that afternoon, and it started to become very much an us-and-them situation.

Jim and the Danes ordered schooners and steak and chips from a small restaurant down by the boats in Port Macquarie. Scotty and I found a pool table in a bar next door and made do with a packet of chips. We started slamming tequilas and drinking Coronas, a bland, thin beer I had only sampled since being in Australia, and although the bottle was attractively designed, it didn't exactly hit the spot, unlike the cheap European beers I had always enjoyed since I started drinking. We talked about beer brands as we shot some balls, and agreed Foster's was the best Australian beer, but I still stood my ground with Carlsberg, which was in my opinion the best lager in the world. I enjoyed the lightness of our conversation, and felt a little more brought out of myself than in the car.

We hadn't spoken much about the waterhole since first

leaving it, except for begging Jim to drive us back, because we were both sure that given the chance to face it again, we would have been able to jump. Jim had refused to turn round, instead appeasing us with a 'perhaps on the way back'. What we hadn't really talked about was how bad and disappointed with ourselves it had made us feel, and I certainly hadn't told Scotty, or anyone, that I'd actually physically shat myself while up there.

Scotty was the first to mention the jump.

'Fuckin' bummer, eh?' he said, then gulped some beer and burped.

'Stupid, isn't it, Scotty? That we're so fucked up about it. I hate that about myself, you know? I get so fucked up over things. Fuuck.' I felt a bit man-to-man with Scotty, half expressing what we wanted to say, with our beers.

'Nah, mate. Natural to be pissed off.'

We began talking about our lives, now that we were temporarily inseparable. I wanted to know more about my new best friend.

'What are your folks like?' I asked, knowing nothing about him, other than the fact he lived with his mother.

'My old dear, she's cool. Love her to bits,' he said, putting another fifty in the slot in the pool table.

'What about your dad, do you get on with him?' I leant over the table watching him set up.

'My old man. Nuh, don't wanna go there, mate, fuckin' prick,' he said, slamming into the break. I didn't push him on it. I let him have a couple of gulps and just play the game with me, and then he opened up some more.

'My old man is a fuckin' turnkey.' Scotty spoke in hard street-life talk, without ever having lived it, I knew that. However, it was his way of disowning his parents, and I couldn't blame him for that.

'Yep, prison officer all his life, tough as fuck, I'm telling you.'

There were no big surprises, really, as I learnt more details of his life and childhood. He was the eldest of four and his parents were strict Catholics. Scotty had been an altar boy for a while, which we both had a good laugh at and a toast to. His dad was a massive drinker and had beat his mother all the time Scotty was growing up; his mum was a total victim. The story went on, down the usual depressing path, leading to how Scotty came to be Scotty. Except he didn't refer to anything as being depressing, and did all that 'You make what you can in this life' and 'You gotta laugh' bullshit, and drank onwards and upwards, but I could see him for what he was. He was sad already at a young age for what had happened, and fearful of what lay ahead, with no conception of how to run things. Exactly like me.

I thought again about my reliance on fate as a life plan, which wasn't really a plan, but something desperate to hold onto, and felt that in moments of truth, it was wearing rather thin.

After a while, the others joined us for doubles, but we were way too pissed to be on the same level as them. Jim told some funny stories but I couldn't stay with the plot. I could see the Danes laughing but didn't understand why. Jim said it was a beautiful sunset and that we should go drink some wine or beers on the beach. Scotty and I were reluctant at first, seeing no draw in the outdoors at that particular time, and we both agreed about the need to be around music. Andrea persuaded Scotty otherwise, and I just went along with it, so we ended up on the beach, making a fire and drinking a couple of cheap boxes of red wine with the plastic tap at the bottom, until way after midnight. I went back from the shore towards the trees to have a pee and decided not to come back for ages. Something had clicked the wrong way inside my head with the drink, and I became convinced that I was separate from all of them and had to get away. I became highly suspicious of them, and thought they thought I was an idiot. I lay on the sand, flat out on my stomach in the dark, watching them at the fire. I lay still like a soldier on a night mission. I waited until they started talking about me, and enjoyed viewing their concern and frantic search along the beach for me, when I failed to return. I lay in the sand, and laughed and muttered to myself that they would never understand things, no matter how much they tried.

Later they found me when Jim combed my area, and I was too slow to slither away back into the trees. He gave me a talk about self-pity, which I took for the time being. Then my shrunken goldfish brain forgot everything and Scotty and I started taking the piss out of modern dance, and began entertaining everyone by throwing each other around. We all went back to the campsite, where I unfortunately phoned the nursing home and told the nurse to fuck off. Then I called my mother and hung up when she answered. Scotty and I shared a van, as the others wanted some peace and quiet from our hysteria. We listened to the best music we could find on the radio, which was a Doors' retrospective. Then Scotty did a crazy thing by getting out a bottle of whiskey from his bag, which he said he was keeping for the last night. It was Bushmills, and we drank it and went to bed well after the sun was up, and normal people were beginning their happy campers' day.

Jim knocked on the door what felt like ten minutes later, and as we were moving on to Grafton early we had no choice but to get up.

The morning was a haze; we dozed in the back of the car, still completely drunk, miles away from hungover. They had breakfast in Port Macquarie, but Scotty and I sneaked off and had really badly made Bloody Marys in the same bar we had been in the night before. We stopped at a service station, and I sold one painting to the people who ran the garage next door. They were sitting round the table with some other family visiting. It took about half an hour, and the others stayed in the car – I could see them laughing through the windows. The people I sold to found my state hilarious and they began laughing. I can't remember anything I said, though I didn't have to say much because they were actually looking for something to hang in a small granny flat extension they'd just had built out the back. I went back to the car for the credit card-forms and brought Jim in, getting him to take a photo of me with my crappy disposable camera. We all leant into the table and held up the picture, and I gave the thumbs-up sign.

I was a big hero again for selling *ad hoc*, especially when pissed, and suddenly everybody enjoyed the state of Scotty and me again. We started pleading with Jim to take us via Scotty's Head beach and wouldn't give up our chants, like children in the back, until he partially agreed. We stopped at

Grassy Head and looked at the surf, and then drove on to Scotty's Head, renowned for its surfing competitions, and stopped for lunch. Scotty and I slept in the car in the place called Kempsey while the others went selling, but the sleep did us no good, making us moody and humourless on their return. We had headaches and nausea that we wanted to postpone, so we went off to a bar again while the others had food. When Jim got back he'd had enough of us, and dropped us at Scotty's Head because we 'wanted to go there so fucking much' and left us on the beach with a blanket, telling us to sleep it off, and that he'd check in to the backpackers', in Macksville, and come back later. I phoned Mac's bar in Sydney from the call box at the edge of the beach, before passing out. But by that time I could barely speak.

CHAPTER **TWENTY-SIX**

It was dark when I woke up. What woke me was the cold and the water on my legs. There was a blanket over us. I was doing spoons with Scotty, me behind him. He came to at the same time as me, as his legs were also soaked with mine. We were on a beach. We didn't speak for the first minute, we were so disorientated. I had to genuinely think very hard about where I was. Then I remembered I was in Australia. I told Scotty immediately.

'Yeah, I know,' he said, coming out of the spoon.

Marathon drinking vapours filled my nasal cavity, making me keep my breathing shallow. My first concern was that I'd fucked Scotty, but no matter how much I'd drank I couldn't see it happening. We scrambled onto our knees, crawling away from the water which we now knew was the tide coming in. We were both unable to stand. We had our arms round each other to help as best we could, at least for balance, and moved back away from the shore. It was pitch black; I was unable to see any landmarks or lights of any kind. This was my biggest blackout.

'What's going on, Scotty, please?' I slurred.

'Fuck knows. Hang on.'

We stopped crawling and slumped on the sand. Scotty tried to look at his watch; he had a waterproof sports watch with a luminous dial. He held his wrist and pushed it back and forth trying to read it, but couldn't.

'Hang on, hang on.' I tried to help him by squinting my eyes then opening them wide, but the yellow lines added up to too many.

'Fuck.' I collapsed back on the ground, as did Scotty.

'This-is-bad.'

'Man. Fucked. Totally.'

It was impossible in the state we were in to deal with the sheer density of the blackness. Amazingly I was able to process this and realise that we must be out of the city and in a remote part of countryside, as there were no lights anywhere, not even the tiniest sign of one, not even in the distance.

'Sssh,' said Scotty, not that I was saying or doing anything at the time except lying back with him, panting, as the effort involved in crawling back from the water's edge had taken all the strength I had. 'No traffic.'

'Have we got money?'

We both felt in our pockets. I found a coin in the front pocket of my jeans. I vaguely remembered being in a call box, unable to talk for slurring, but I couldn't be sure. In my back pockets were my flip-flops. I stopped for a moment and tried concentrating, for I thought the flip-flops may lead somewhere, but they didn't.

'Nothing,' said Scotty. 'Remember nothing, d'you?'

'No, not really.'

I wasn't afraid; I wasn't anything really, except drunk. I could confirm with myself that this was the most drunk I had been in a long time. Whatever had gone on, whatever it was, felt like much more than just one heavy night of drinking. The night I slept with the barman of The Naked Drinking Club was the worst I'd been since coming here, but this even beat that. I remember someone telling me a story once of a truck driver who got so drunk he had to look at his passport when he woke up to see who he was. I felt just a stage behind that, on the beach in the dark. At least I knew who I was with and what country I was in.

We sat up. I rubbed my face. I just wanted to sleep this off, but we kept on trying to move. We put our arms round each other's backs and stood up. I had a feeling whisky was involved; I would never ordinarily be this drunk with beer or wine. Still, whisky rang no bells. At this moment I had no understanding of how we came to be sleeping by the sea. As we wandered in the dark, mostly within a small radius, there was a feeling of nothing except Scotty and me on the entire planet.

'Look!' I pointed into the blackness, to what I thought was a tiny flicker of light.

'I see it.' Scotty pulled me tighter to him.

'Is it land in the distance?' I asked.

'Think so.'

It was hard to talk and walk; my body was so uncoordinated and trying to control it was exhausting, plus we were walking on sand. I took the light to be streetlights in the distance. I had no idea how far the distance was from us, but thought it might be the nearest town. Anyhow, it was something to aim towards. We walked as fast as we could, which seemed extremely fast. The sand beneath me passed under my feet so quickly I felt as though I was on coasters, or on that long, fast, conveyor belt that takes you from one airport terminal to another. Scotty was leaning on me a bit, which weighed me down and made me breathless, but I needed to feel him close to me, so I didn't complain. We mostly stumbled along in silence, except for the odd bit of giggling.

The light got nearer; it was brighter but still flickered. The closer we got, the more I thought it unlikely to be a streetlight because it was too shaky. If it was a town in the distance then it was very far, and we had a real struggle ahead, moving all the way there as we were. We started stopping every so often to recharge for a moment, then immediately after we would make a half-run advance, often falling over, then starting again, frustrated at not reaching the mysterious light we were banking on. The darkness was getting more claustrophobic as I was forced to accept its permanence; I wanted to unzip it, and return to daylight. It was the oddest thing to have nothing around, not even an out-of-focus object to fix on. I couldn't even make out Scotty's face; there was no reflection of the water, no moon. I was generally bad at reading the moon, and the sun. If only Jim was here, he could tell us moon things. Then I remembered Jim.

I stopped and grabbed Scotty. 'Scotty.'

'What?'

'Jim, Jim, the paintings – think we were with him?'

'Fuck, yeah. Think you're right. Dunno, come on, keep going.' He was right. We had to follow the light and work out the rest later. There was definitely a Jim though, and a group we were with not so long ago, in a car. I remembered someone shouting at us, then throwing us a blanket.

The nearer we got to the light, the more it wobbled around, but never really got much bigger. At first it seemed straight ahead, many miles away, but now as we were approaching we made a direction change uphill and far left.

'Sssh.' Again I was saying nothing when Scotty stopped me, holding onto my shoulders. I wondered what his face looked like, or mine for that matter. 'D'ye hear?'

I strained to hear as best I could. He was right; there was something other than the waves gently lapping the shoreline. There was a slight breeze building that was carrying some guitar chords over us. The sounds were coming from the light. It spurred us on even more, and we made another ridiculous attempt at running.

'Come on!' I shouted, as encouragement for us. We kept on moving and moving, sometimes falling and crawling for a bit, then back up, always attached to each other. As we approached, the music was clear, though gentle. The flicker had lit up some of the beach; I could just make out tall blades of beach grass on the bank up to the left. I was so relieved to be coming out of the darkness.

'Hello!' Scotty called out, slightly ahead of me now, pulling me by the hand. I had slowed down a little, trying to establish whether part of my wet jeans was seawater or piss.

'Hello!' I called out. Nobody called back. We kept moving towards the light and sound, which was a huge relief.

Three people, their faces illuminated, sat in a dip in the sand; I think two male, one female. One had a guitar; the light came from two candles stuck in wine bottles. I don't remember what we said but we joined them for a while, and they seemed friendly if monosyllabic. They were smiley and stoned, I thought. They passed a joint round; Scotty had some, I said no thanks. They were singing something unrecognisable as the man strummed away. The woman wore a poncho. None of us reacted very much to each other. Scotty asked about a town, and bummed a cigarette. A man with blond hair, who I tried to focus on but couldn't, swung his arm round behind him and pointed. We thanked them and left. I thought the pointer had a tattoo. Maybe not.

What if he did have a tattoo? I worried, remembering something about a tattoo warning from someone.

'Did he have a tattoo?' I asked Scotty, as we cleared foliage out of the way, trying to move inland.

'Fuck knows.'

I put on my flip-flops as the ground was changing and had now become gravelly.

After the foliage we could see a light as tall as a tree, and stumbled upon a small road. There was a wall by the road; we leant against it, and tried to focus again. I could feel my head rolling as I looked at Scotty, although I didn't feel as out of it as when I first woke up.

I had never so far had a hangover that stopped me from drinking again. Nor had I vomited through drink, unless you count the alcoholic poisoning I had when I was fifteen, which my father thought would teach me a lesson – that I don't count. And while I knew that drinking to excess, as I often did, could endanger my life or certainly hold it back, there really was little incentive to stop. Somehow I always landed on my feet, and was certain that it would be the same in this instance.

Scotty lit up the bummed cigarette and we shared it, swaying and wondering what to do. He took a pee, without turning round. It was after all too late for all that now. Across from where we were standing was a road sign, a small country-type one, no more than a post with an arrow-shaped piece of wood at the top, with white-painted information. While Scotty peed I went over to try to read it. I held onto the post and looked up, opening my eyes wide trying to concentrate, but no luck. I grasped the post with both hands and squinted, which was better, and barely made out '3km' to some place I stood no chance of understanding.

'I don't care if it rains or freezes, long as ah got my plastic Jesus/hangin' on the dashboard of my caaagh.' Scotty started singing something I'd heard before.

'Next car, Scotty, we'll stop it, yeah?'

'Sure, yep, that's it.'

'Got any money? I haven't.'

Scotty felt around then exploded. 'Yes, you fuckin' beauty!' He pulled out a note folded tightly from somewhere in his jeans.

'What is it?'

'Fuckin' ten bucks. WHOOOA!'

We grabbed onto each other and swung around, falling on to the road. The way I saw it, it was unrealistic to think that the situation would be sorted out tonight; it was late and we were fucked. We might as well continue drinking and start again tomorrow in the daylight, when we would be clear-headed. I shared my thoughts on the subject with Scotty and he wholeheartedly agreed. While we waited for a car, we talked about a campsite and felt that the others must be there, and must have left us on the beach, or perhaps we had refused to go back with them. Maybe we'd had our own party with some beach people like the three with the candles we'd just encountered. Whatever had happened, we now had a plan, which was excellent. To go to the next town and have a beer, then find the nearest campsite.

Scotty tried to teach me a verse of his song, until a car arrived. As soon as we heard an engine, we placed ourselves in the middle of the road, which was hardly wider than the both of us anyway, and outstretched our arms, just in case he tried to drive past.

The car approached with a light on top. As soon as we clocked the light we dropped our arms, worrying that it was a police car.

'Where you headin'?' said the man, leaning out.

'Next town.'

'Got your fare?'

'You a taxi?' I asked, thinking I sounded charming and he might let us in.

'Mate, you'd really be—' Scotty began.

'Come on, get in, I'll sort it,' I said, pushing him in. 'Course we have,' I said to the driver, whispering to Scotty that he must trust me and to not mention money to him. We got in. I told the driver then that we had no money but he could see and touch my tits if we got a lift. Of course, he agreed. I indicated for him to drive off first, but gave him a flash as a taster.

The road swirled round and round from where we sat in the back. I lifted my top up for most of the way. The driver had the radio on; we shouted for him to turn it up. The Rolling Stones came on, which woke us up a bit more. When we drove round a bend, we made an excited noise like kids. He smoked, and I saw his eyes watch us in the mirror, then his hand go down to his crotch. By the end of 'Sympathy For The Devil' we came to a town, of some sorts. There were some motorbikes outside a bar. He pulled in, stopped the car and switched his inside light on. I nudged Scotty and put my finger over my mouth.

He twisted round in his seat.

'Doesn't your boyfriend mind?'

'He's not my fucking boyfriend,' I said, letting him have his feel.

CHAPTER TWENTY-SEVEN

It was easier to see by now, with the air sobering us up slightly. The town had only three things as far as we could see from where the car dropped us. A phone box, a shop that was closed, and the bar we were about to walk into, which had a large board outside with 'Talent Night' written in yellow chalk. The bar was half full. There were some beardy men, who must have owned the bikes outside. Rod Stewart boomed out, which was quality in the circumstances. We jigged around at the bar, as we drank down the schooners that Scotty bought us, feeling as if we were now an inseparable duo; therefore, we agreed to stay together for ever, travelling from one bar to another, then we toasted to it. We attempted to recall the events that led to us becoming a couple of some kind, but found it to be too much effort to concentrate.

'Does it matter?' I asked him.

'Not one fucking bit,' he said.

I swung my head round, taking in the bar and its customers, who were mostly men, almost all of whom seemed to have tattoos on their arms; a couple of them wore them on their chests.

'Notice anything?' I asked, pulling him towards me so no one could hear. 'All these people are ugly.'

We laughed.

'Tattoos!'

'What, mate?'

'They've all got them. I think it's a club. Do you think it is?'

Scotty glanced around. 'Could be.'

Scotty was less concerned with the tattoo theme than I was;

I could see that, even in my state. I finally remembered Joyce
Cane's tattoo remarks, which explained my obsession. Her
vision had clearly been a warning, even if she'd told me not to
worry. People only ever say things in the way she did, when it
is meant as a warning. Odd, that on the beach I met a man
with a tattoo just out of nowhere, who points us to the road
that leads us to here, this bar, the only bar for miles, full of
tattoos. Was this fate again? Had I been led to this bar for a
reason? I wondered about that for a few moments in my own
world, as Scotty talked to the old man next to us about his
lighter. The man was as drunk as us, so the conversation went
on; the man sang a completely different song from the one
playing in the bar. I couldn't hear him, but I could see him
looking ahead and swinging his head from side to side and
contorting his face. Scotty moved the guy's lighter slowly
along the bar, making it do somersaults. Soon I completely
forgot my concerns over tattoos and the possibility of me
meeting my fate tonight.

I soon worked out that we were in the interval of the talent
contest. The music quietened down as various men took their
positions at their instruments at the front of a makeshift stage.
There were six or seven men, all wearing white shirts. The
drummer began to warm up, rattling his moves. I was bored
with Scotty and the man next to us, and wandered off towards
the band. I mumbled to the saxophonist, who had a tattoo on
his forearm. It had a date on it; I tried to read it but spilt some
of my beer on the cables on the floor coming from the
keyboards, which caused a bad-tempered big guy to run over
and grab my arm and usher me back to the bar.

'Have you got a tattoo?' I slurred, as he marched me. He
didn't reply. His angry silence made me giggle, which made
him tighten his grip, which only made me giggle even more. I
didn't care about anything, and felt increasingly mischievous.

I wanted to get back to the saxophonist and read the date
on his arm. I looked to Scotty for help but he had joined in
singing with the old guy. I grew tired of the restrictions, and
decided to enter the talent contest, which seemed to be pretty
relaxed. I walked up the steps onto the stage with my
schooner in my hand, and grabbed the mike.

'WHAT'S THE SCORE WITH THE TATTOOS?' I boomed out over the music and the band tuning. The big guy looked up from the bar and gestured to the bar man.

'LET'S FUCKIN' LIVEN THIS—' The mike went dead. I put down my schooner on the stage and removed my vest, swirling it round my head. A couple of instruments began the familiar, world-famous opening bars to 'The Stripper'. Very soon the whole bar was watching me, even the few women that were there, many of them joining in the notes. They seemed happy with the situation, which gave me no reason to stop.

'Na, na, na, naah! Na, na, na, na.' I threw my vest into the crowd; Scotty lunged forward and caught it. The drummer joined the saxophonist; I moved my hips to each side in time to the thud of the drums.

'Na, na, na, naah! Na, na, na, na!' I kicked off my flip-flops; again Scotty caught them and clutched them tight to his chest. I pulled down my jeans, to which I got the biggest cheer. Hands were clapping above heads. I felt numbed-out nothingness. I took off my bra to almost a full band, bar the keyboard player. Everybody seemed to accept my topless dancing, which was now in full swing. I felt the crowd was with me, so I pushed things further, and began shaking my tits a little, much to everybody's amusement.

'Na, na. Na, naah! Na, na, na, na …!'

I caught Scotty's face: he was making the finger across the throat sign, but I ignored it, feeling no danger, just stupid fun. I began taking off my pants. I dropped them to my ankles at first then kicked them up into my hand. Some men from the back moved the crowd forward, pushing people out of the way to get to the front. I circled my pants above my head before throwing them out to the crowd.

Two large men in matching T-shirts, advertising a beer I'd never heard of, moved to the front and climbed the steps to the stage to grab me. Scotty waved for me to follow him. I was completely naked. The men didn't know what to do. They wanted to be forceful; I could see the intent in their faces, but they couldn't touch me. I loved the feeling of being so free and naked and open, yet my nudity felt like a protective force-field. Nobody wanted to grab me; it would be seen as too intrusive. It was bizarre, and I loved it. The band played the final chords of 'The Stripper', as I jumped down onto the floor. Other men pushed forward to grab me, while the rest of the bar just watched and cheered as the chase began.

I ran behind a table with Scotty, who still had hold of my clothes. It was hard to run for laughing. The bouncers and Scotty were not laughing. I noticed Scotty looking scared, but I had no idea why, and no sense of danger. Instead, when the two men moved one way, I moved the other, using the tables and chairs and the circular central bar to avoid them. I was too absorbed in the chase to notice that Scotty was gone. I ran round the bar for the second time, this time running to the right. Then someone grabbed me from behind and twisted my arm, and marched me out of the bar, a different way from where I came in. I was walked through a small kitchen and outside to a yard where beer barrels lined the wall. I expected we were going to be thrown out, and that all my clothes would follow behind us.

In the yard, Scotty was being held by two men, while another two stood around; with the one escorting me, that made five of them. I registered that as soon as I entered the yard. Then I saw Scotty punch some guy, and it all degenerated into a chaos that we were just too out of it to deal with. Three men set upon him as he lay on the ground, trying to curl up against the kicks. There was blood near his face. The other two gripped me. I struggled to break free but couldn't. I saw my clothes in the corner beside a garbage bin but didn't care.

'How do you like your boyfriend now?' said the one holding my left arm.

'He's not my fucking boyfriend,' I said automatically.

'Not so fuckin' big now, is he?'

Everything happened so quickly, it was hard to know what to do next. There seemed little point in pleading with them to stop, as they wouldn't stop until they felt satisfied. I felt no fear for my own safety, because my nudity was still protecting me, but I felt really bad for Scotty. They took a break from kicking him and threw me my clothes. The guys holding me let go. The others moved away from Scotty, and I felt relief that it was over.

'Put them fucking on,' one commanded.

I put on my jeans and vest and flip-flops, and stuffed my underwear in my pockets. Scotty stood up and spat out blood, wincing in pain.

'Scotty, you all right?' I said, breathless from adrenalin. He was bent over, spitting onto the ground, his hands on his knees. He stood up, and wiped his hand across his mouth, and looked straight at one of the men.

'Fuckin' small-town cunts!' he said, signing his own death warrant.

'Scotty ...' I ran over and held Scotty, trying to get between him and the man I suspected was about to hit him. He tried to push me off. I tried to resist but the big man behind pulled me away from him. The moment I was moved away, Scotty took a massive blow to the face at close range and he fell to the ground, before hitting his head on the fence behind him.

The man beside me laughed as Scotty slid down. I hated the ugly big fat fucking laughing face of the man, and the switch just clicked inside me. I delivered him a right hook with everything I had. It didn't quite make the impact I had hoped, but it was enough to make him hold his mouth and drop his head forward, swearing at me. The other two men laid into Scotty again; he was trying to stand but finding it harder than before. A man lunged towards me, and I jumped up and headbutted him. I felt the crunch of his nose, or teeth, I wasn't sure which. He fell backwards, his nose flattened across his face, blood spraying out. While he was holding his face with both hands, I kicked him in the balls as hard as I could. I felt as though I'd broken my toe in the process but kept going. He fell onto his knees, alternately clutching his balls and his face. The remaining three men grabbed my wrists and ankles and picked me up despite my wriggling around and shouting.

With all the grappling and pulling, we fell back inside the kitchen. Things smashed around. The man gripping my right wrist moved in close to my head to get through the doorway, and I tried to nut him as well. A punch landed across my face, and knees and feet kicked my back and ribs. I didn't feel much pain; I just kept going, kept kicking and punching out best I could.

'Fuckin' kill the cunts!' screamed the headbutted man from the yard. Scotty appeared behind me and hit one of the guys over the head with a bottle, which shattered everywhere, bits flying into my mouth. I felt the grip loosen round my other wrist, as the man holding me struggled to deal with Scotty at the same time. Scotty was screaming like a mad man, his face covered in blood. I wrenched my wrist free, and punched the man in the balls. He bent over double, then Scotty punched him. A red light swooped through the kitchen from outside.

'FUCKIN' COPS ARE HERE, YOU'RE FUCKED!' Scotty screamed, as Eric Clapton's 'Layla' belted out from the bar next door, making it impossible to hear anything of what was going on. Somehow I got to my feet but rammed my back against a fridge door handle. I looked for a knife or some weapon, for I truly would have fought on to the death – I didn't give a fuck. I felt nothing but heart-pumping madness with no time to think of how bad things could get. There was nothing lying around, but it was hard to take anything in because of all the bodies pummelling each other and the glass, and the blood, and the floor being most of my view. Most of the violence was aimed at Scotty again; so I decided to make a run for the door, back out to the small yard with the headbutted man in it.

I swung the door open; the man was gone, and another door round to the front of the building was open. I ran out, I saw walls, blurred lights; a police car parked outside; and an empty, lopsided road, which I ran onto, like in a dream. I was running full pelt but the trees alongside me were not really moving. I shouted out loud to myself, as I ran, a mantra: 'Come on! Keep going! Come on!'

I was free and heading back along the road the cab had brought us from the beach. Then I stopped to breathe, my hands on my knees, panting. Momentarily, I was feeling pretty pleased that I'd escaped relatively unharmed. I was right, I was truly indestructible. I expected to see Scotty running towards me as I waited at the bend, and I planned that if anyone ran after me, I could climb up the verge to my left, or cross over and run through the trees down into the blackness of the beach, where I would just lie and wait until it all passed. I longed for the security of trainers, loathing combat in flip-flops. I turned again to look for Scotty. I had been sure he would make a run for it as soon as I was safely out of the kitchen, but he didn't show. I had two options:

1. To run back into the main bar area and find the police, but risk arrest, jail for the night and possible deportation.

2. To keep on running to the beach where I would sleep off my drunkenness and start again in the morning with a clear head.

My breathing eased slightly. I looked up to the night sky. It felt quiet and peaceful where I was standing, and it was some-what surreal that in the bar down the road Scotty was getting the kicking of a lifetime. I breathed in slowly through my nose and shut my eyes, wanting it all to be imagined. I knew I would have to go back, and just wanted a few seconds of pretending things were not as bad as they were before they got worse.

I couldn't leave Scotty there alone, no matter what. Whoever the hell he was, he was with me, and I was with him, and leaving him was against the rules. I wouldn't do that to someone. I ran back with newfound resolve, cursing my flip-flops as I went. Out front the police car was still empty. A man leant against the wall vomiting. I ran round the back, increas-ingly fearful of what I might find by now. I could hear shouting and banging and scuffling from the yard; when I got there the numbers had doubled and about eight men were kicking the fuck out of Scotty, who was rolled up in a ball on the ground. I jumped on top of the crowd and punched anything I could. The tight group round Scotty broke up slightly, in an attempt to deal with me. Scotty crawled towards the door under an assault of assorted footwear around his head and body. There was no time to get a good look at him, we just had to get out and back onto the road. The kitchen door swung open just as I received the worst blow so far from a fat man in a checked shirt with curly hair. As he punched me in the side with enormous force, I felt something crack and fell down onto Scotty.

Two policeman burst into the yard, but the size of the yard and the fact that there were now twelve of us in it meant they had some obstacles in their way before they could get to us. Two of the men pushed the police out the way and tried to run back inside, making one officer chase them back inside to the kitchen and out to the bar. Two other men ran out the back door onto the road. During the chaos, I grabbed Scotty, trying to help him up.

'This is it, Scotty, come on, NOW!' I yelled. We both lunged up towards the back door and out along the side of the bar towards where the police car was parked.

We didn't talk, we were in such pain, and Scotty couldn't stand upright. I made a split-second decision to head behind the bar through the trees, despite how dark it was, and back towards the sea. We ran, bent over like apes, with no idea of what ground was under us. I caught my leg on something and felt wetness trickle down my ankle onto my foot. We moved branches out of the way as we headed downwards, until we felt sand, then we dropped down and lay as flat as we could. Voices came closer, first from behind us and then from nearby, slightly downhill; a torch light swooped over us and the trees we'd just run through, and I pushed Scotty's face into the sand to muffle his moaning and his wincing. I held onto him tightly, trying to keep us as still as possible. His T-shirt was soaked through with sweat that stuck to my hands. He began sobbing and I pushed his head further into the ground and held him even tighter.

'Must have headed back onto the road,' said a voice. A radio clicked on, as another voice spoke through the fuzziness.

'Nah, mate, one female, another male, copy.'

The torch swooped to the right of us.

'I'll head up there now, over.' The voice spoke some more but I couldn't hear what was said; it became fainter as whoever it was walked back to the bar.

Scotty's body was shuddering as he sobbed.

'I'm fucked, mate,' he cried. It was too dark again to see anything.

'Listen,' I said, suddenly feeling lucid. 'We've got to try to stay near the road, to get some help – a lift or something.' I tried to hold his face in my hands but I could tell it hurt him too much to be touched. I kissed his forehead and dragged him up.

I couldn't move my right hand, something had happened to my thumb. My forehead felt numb in the middle, and when I felt my nose, there was an enormous lump above the bridge.

We stayed close to the road but in the safety of the trees. We waited for a while in case the police drove past, but they didn't. Scotty threw up a couple of times; I watched the road. It was still dark, the few streetlights being back nearer to the bar. Scotty stayed further back, sitting on the ground and resting his back on a tree. He kept complaining he was cold. I told him it was because he had been sweating and now he'd cooled down, but I hadn't had a proper chance to take a look at him. We must have waited half an hour, maybe more. Then I heard the big old meaty Kingswood's exhaust chug past where we were hiding on the road, heading in the direction of the bar. I thought I'd heard it twice before but wasn't sure, and we had been too far back from the road to catch it, but this time I knew it was there.

'Stay there,' I said to Scotty, before I ran out onto the road, waving my arms in the desperate hope that Jim would see me before he disappeared round the bend, but I was too late. The putt had faded and the car gone from sight. I crossed back to the tree side for protection, and tried running as best I could after it, but it was hopeless. There was a terrible pain in my ribs now, making it too difficult to run. I gave up, and leant against a tree panting, trying to figure out where I had left Scotty. I stumbled back the same way again, wondering how many times Jim had driven back and forth to find us, and what chance he'd have of sighting us, out here in the dark.

When I got back to Scotty, his head was resting forward on his chin, like he'd fallen asleep.

'Scotty! Scotty. It's Kerry, wake up. Wake up.' I shook him gently but he didn't answer. I searched in his jeans pockets with my left hand, my right hand now throbbing in agony with what I took to be a break, and found his Zippo. I lit it up and lifted his face with my elbow under his chin. I didn't recognise him.

I couldn't see his eyes, they were so swollen and cut; his nose was broken, there was no doubt about it, for it lay well over to the left of his face, and his chin was elongated and out of shape. His ear was torn at the bottom. The worst thing for me was his T-shirt, which was saturated with blood, not sweat. All the time I had thought sweat was pouring out of him, he was losing blood. I remembered him complaining about being cold. I began shaking and crying, and felt for the first time ever that things had gone way too far in a bad direction, and that I was completely unable to cope. I felt paralysed with fear that Scotty might die. I prayed in panic to anything; I made quick promises of change, if Scotty were saved.

Then I heard what I thought was the Kingswood coming back towards us, and I ran back to the road crying and begging.

'Oh God, please, please!' I waved my arms. 'Jim! JIM!' I screamed.

Jim pointed to the trees from the driver's seat, indicating that he was pulling in there, as it wasn't safe to stop just after the bend. When he stopped, I slumped down onto the bonnet until he got out. His face was white; his eyes darted all over my face as he asked me where Scotty was.

'Fucking hell,' he said, about to touch my head with his thumb, then deciding not to. He looked as though he was going to explode, but bit his hand instead and composed himself.

'It's not good, Jim. Scotty's not good,' I blubbered, as I led the way to the tree he was resting against. As soon as Jim caught sight of Scotty, he ran to him and crouched down.

'Scotty.' He shook him but got no response. He started feeling his pulse under his jaw. That's when I lost it.

'Oh fuck, oh fuck, oh fuck, no, please, I'm so fuckin' sorry.' I paced around, convinced Scotty was dead.

Jim said, 'I need you to go into the boot of the car and get the first-aid kit, it's in a green box with a cross on it, OK?'

'Oh fuck, Jim, what the fuck.'

'Just do it, please.'

'The fuckin' police are looking for us, we can't stay here, Jim.'

'I'll do it.' Jim stood up and took me by the shoulders. 'I need you to be calm now, Scotty needs our help. Stay here and breathe, OK.'

I nodded through tears, then fell to my knees in front of Scotty, praying while trying to stifle my sobs.

I heard Jim shout 'Fuck!' from the road. He ran back to us.

'Fucking took the box out to make room for all our stuff in the boot, didn't I?'

'Jim, we were in a massive fight in the pub down there. Scotty bottled someone, the police came, please, we have to get him in the car.' I looked up anxiously to the road.

'FUCK!' Jim clutched his head, then grabbed me to steady me and get my full attention. 'Right now, I need to ask you some things, OK, so I need you to listen.'

'All right.'

'Did he hurt his neck?'

'I don't know, Jim, he was fuckin' set about by eight blokes. He's lucky to be alive, if he is, I don't know.'

'What about his legs, back? Do you know anything?'

'Look.' I bent down and flicked on the Zippo at Scotty's face.

'FFFFUCK!' Jim lifted him up under the arms. 'Take his legs, Kerry, we have to get him to hospital, now.'

I stood rooted to the spot by the shocking sight of Jim trying to drag a limp, lifeless Scotty.

'TAKE HIS FUCKING LEGS!'

We moved him back to the car. I stayed in the back seat with him. Jim told me to keep Scotty's head up, then he hit the gas like he did on the dirt track on the way to the waterhole. I would have given anything to be back there now, before it all went wrong.

CHAPTER TWENTY-EIGHT

I looked in the mirror above the washbasin in the hospital toilet and surveyed the damage to my face for the first time. My left eye was closing up and my brow swollen and cut, pressing down on it. My top lip was all puffed out like I'd just had plastic surgery, and cut inside from where my tooth went through the gum. I had a tooth mark in my forehead from the headbutt, half a tooth chipped, and my left cheek looked so swollen and felt so big that it didn't feel as though it belonged to me. Above the bridge of my nose as it met my forehead was an enormous egg, which was bruising already. And my hand was swollen to the point that I couldn't see my knuckles; my thumb stood out at a right angle, clearly broken or dislocated.

I lifted my top to see if my ribs were bruised; they were OK, but it was hard to breathe in or out without pain down my left side.

I was thirsty and starting to feel nauseous. I should have been repulsed by the sight of my face, I should have felt utter revulsion for myself and the mess I had got us into, but a part of me liked what I saw; it felt and looked like a fitting punishment for all my behaviour, not just that evening, but for ever. I now looked on the outside how I had always felt on the inside. Ugly, and fucked up.

I waited along with an assortment of injured people in a seated area in Coffs Harbour A & E. I waited with Karin, who Jim had organised to sit with me while he registered Scotty himself, in a bid to keep us separate and not attract any police attention, just in case. Jim sat in the next section of seating, staring ahead. People looked at my face whenever they thought I couldn't see them. I felt hard. I was the only facial injury in the waiting room. Someone had a bloody towel on top of their head, but other than that, it seemed to be mostly relatives of the injured, and a few hand and leg casualties.

While we waited for news of Scotty, I imagined the accidents that had brought those other patients here. Despite how pleasing feeling hard was after my beating, now that I was safe again, I would have traded my disgraceful incident for any of the innocent accidents that sat around me.

'I just want to ask him how he is,' I said again, for the fourth time.

Karin shook her head.

'I don't know what to say. Is he all right?'

'Leave him for now, it's best. We'll talk later. Let's just get through this, OK?'

That was it. It was all over with the group and me. I'd fucked that all up, and now Karin was this expert wife of Jim's, and I was taking polite orders from the Danish.

I focused on a checklist poster for hepatitis on the wall next to the water machine opposite, to distract me from my anxiety. I mentally ticked four out of six of the symptoms, and then decided to bury the information. Next, I tried to piece together what had happened from our arrival in Port Macquarie. Of course, there was the bar down by the harbour that we all went to soon after arriving. I remembered Jim ordering food – I thought they all had prawns – but I was sure Scotty and I had nothing. Small patches of detail were coming through, and I didn't want to ask Karin quite yet, didn't want to weaken my position even further.

What fucking position is that, Kerry? I asked myself, in one of my most sober moments of the last few days, as I returned to the hepatitis checklist.

'Mr Crown. Mr James Crown?' shouted a doctor with a clipboard. Jim jumped up and disappeared behind a curtain with him. Karin and I both let out a big breath through our noses at the same time. We waited for about five minutes, and then Jim came back out and gestured to Karin to meet him at the end of the corridor.

'Stay there, I'll be back soon, OK?' she said.

Jesus, I felt like a convict and she was my parole officer. It annoyed the hell out of me to have that soapy-clean fuck telling me what to do. My remorse and temporary meekness seemed to be turning into anger and resentment as usual. Then I was disappointed at my knowing that I was angry and resentful but not being able to change it. My head was buzzing and all my thoughts were racy and weird; it made me think of my report card at school, which was the same every year: 'Kerry is her own worst enemy'.

I needed to get away from my head; I needed to know that Scotty was all right, then get away, face my come-down alone, then start again in a few days. I'd give myself a few days to patch everything up, then I'd make my apologies and leave them, before they asked me to leave. I'd then find my mother and get better.

I got up and headed for Scotty's cubicle before Jim and Karin came back.

He was conscious, which was an enormous relief, but the sight of his mashed-up face made tears well up in me again.

A nurse swept back the curtain. 'Can I help you?' she asked officiously.

I had to stop myself from saying, Yeah, I'm fuckin' lost, and thought this was the toilet. 'We were staying in the same back-packers' a few nights ago, I saw him in here and just wanted to, you know, see he was OK?'

'It's a wonder you recognised him, poor guy.'

'Well, I didn't.'

She searched my face suspiciously, and then I remembered I'd been beaten up and that's probably why she was searching my face.

'I know his friend outside from a' – I desperately tried to think of a respectable, happy-go-lucky travelling-around-Australia activity – 'from a parachute jump.'

'Well, you won't be doing any of that for a while by the looks of things. What happened?' She opened some swabs and wiped Scotty's ear. His eyes were sleepy, fighting against closing.

'I was really stupid and went surfing at night, when I had too much to drink.'

She raised both her eyebrows.

'And smashed into the rocks.'

'Yeah, you won't be the first pom to do that.'

I tried to smile, a sideways smile from the less swollen side of my face, which immediately felt entirely inappropriate.

'What rocks are they? The surf's kinda flat tonight, isn't it?'

I really couldn't deal with a Miss Marple at this juncture. 'Not at Scotty's Head, it's not.'

Scotty moved a little in response. The nurse wasn't to know that I could lie and bullshit my way through anything.

'Anthony has to rest now, he's in quite a bit of pain I should imagine, and I've given him a shot.'

I stroked his hand, which was puffed out and bleeding across the knuckles, then stroked his forearm instead. 'Yes, sorry, I'll just be a second.'

She hurried around, tidying stuff away, and wheeled a trolley back in from outside the curtain before leaving. I bent down close to Scotty's OK ear. I had to clutch my side to hold the bend.

'Scotty,' I whispered. He grunted. 'Fuck, Scotty, I'm so sorry, I'm so fuckin' sorry.'

He swallowed and nodded slowly. I kissed him on the side of his face. He was trying to say something. I stood up, looking for his mouth to produce something audible.

'You fuckin' …' He was breathless between each word.

'Don't say anything, just get better. Please.' I moved a piece of hair back off his forehead.

'Came … back.'

'What?' I didn't quite understand him.

'You came back for me, mate.'

They felt like the saddest words I had ever heard. Scotty tried to smile, which broke my heart. My head dropped down, and I sobbed.

'I'll see you soon, Scotty,' I said, grabbing some plasters and disinfectant wipes on the way out.

Karin had her arm round Jim in the hospital corridor as they drank from paper cups, just like in all movie hospital scenes. She rubbed his back as I approached.

'Where are you going now?' Jim was near boiling point. He hadn't looked at me since we got in the car at the roadside. He scared me like this; I didn't know how he was going to react. I've always been afraid of simmerers, you just don't know where you are with them.

'To get some air. I had a quick look in.'

'For fuck's sake, nobody saw you, did they?'

'No, don't worry, I just looked quickly.'

Karin said, 'It's just we'll have to fill in an accident form and we don't want the police finding out that you're together. Otherwise, there will be big problems for you both—'

'Yeah, I know.' I cut the Danish off; she was annoying me with her new high rank.

'He's got, eh, how do you say it? Semi-conscious problem?' said Karin, struggling with her wording.

'Concussion,' said Jim, looking at the ground, swirling the dregs of his coffee round in the cup.

'Yeah, thought so,' I said.

'Broken jaw, broken nose, broken teeth.' Jim read out his injuries like a shopping list. 'He's going to need stitches in his ear, his head, his *mouth*.' Karin stroked him again when he boomed out 'mouth'. 'And he's got a small stab wound in his chest, inches from his heart and lungs.' Then he looked at me for the first time in ages, his suntan completely gone. 'He was very, very lucky.'

It was only a matter of time before someone mentioned luck. He looked away again, which I was glad of.

'I'm angry at you both, Kerry.' He looked up again, and sighed. 'I can't very well bollock Scotty, can I? I want to know what happened up there, but I think you should just go and sort yourself out for now.'

'Sure,' I said, very much the told-off child.

'Bloody take a look at yourself, for Christ's sake.' Jim looked ashen.

'You had better go back and see the nurse, otherwise you'll miss your place,' said Karin, trying to force a flat-lined smile.

'I'm not seeing the nurse. I'll cope – and it's better anyway, because of the police. What did you say about Scotty?'

'That he was attacked in Coffs Harbour and mugged.'

Karin was doing all the answering now. 'You need to see a doctor, Kerry. What about your ribs?'

'What are they gonna do, anyway, uh?' I felt like a total delinquent as I walked out of the hospital. Karin ran after me. We pushed open the double swing doors of the entrance. I winced with pain as I pushed into them.

'Kerry, please stay here with us, no more trouble, please. Jim is like this because he's very worried, there's stuff about him I will tell you later, or maybe he will. He's like this just now because it's his way of coping.'

I stood listening to her, full of irrational hatred for her and everything she stood for, which so far had only ever been nice and boring; even though I knew what she was saying was right, I just hated it so much that she had jumped in at the waterhole and I hadn't. That's why we were both here at this moment.

'You really need medical attention, please, go back inside.'

'Where are you staying?' I asked, like a robot.

'You don't remember?'

'Obviously not.'

'We were in the backpackers' in Macksville, but we thought it best if we moved here tonight. Andrea has checked us into the Shore caravan park, she is waiting there.'

I walked away.

'Where are you going?' she called after me.

'Nearest bar. I'll wait for you there,' I said, without turning round.

'Kerry?' she called. But I just kept on walking.

I went into a small bar I'd found a couple of hundred yards down the road, and walked straight into the toilet, keeping my head down so as not to freak everybody out. I pulled out the medical stuff I'd taken from the nurse's trolley, and began fixing myself up as best I could. I wiped the cuts above my eye and head with the antiseptic stuff, and used the one plaster for the tiny tooth hole in my head, which I sealed first with strips of ready-made stitches that I didn't realise I'd taken. I also used them above my eye, which made me feel like a boxer. At least I didn't have blood all over my face now. I put

THE NAKED DRINKING CLUB · 259

water on my hair in an attempt to make it look a bit better. I could do nothing about the blood all over my T-shirt, however; I would just have to live with that.

My options were extremely limited and I was always dependent on others due to my lack of money, which made storming out of places for dramatic effect rather pointless. I pulled up my top again to check on my ribs, but there was no change. There was little you could do for cracked or broken ribs, anyhow. I knew that much from a time when I persuaded a nutcase friend of mine to let a couple of Algerian guys buy us dinner, then do a runner when they were paying. My friend got caught and they beat her up and broke her ribs.

I would check my suspected cracked or broken ribs again in the morning. Meanwhile, I could go back to the caravan park and wait with Andrea, or ask Jim where my wallet was. I didn't want to do either of these, so I had no option but to do the Tampax machine fixed to the wall to the right of the mirror. So I did.

I bought some cigarettes from another machine, put three songs for one dollar on the jukebox and pulled out a stool. There were only a couple of old guys in the bar, and a rough-looking woman drinking alone. But they all looked at me.

'Car accident,' I said, looking at the barman.

'Strewth, you all right?'

In all the time I'd been in Australia, this was my first 'strewth'.

'Yeah, but one of my friends is hurt. That's who I'm waiting for just now. Some of them are back at the hospital with him; they'll come and get me. I had to get away, hate hospitals.'

'I'm with you there, love,' said the barman.

'Yeah.' I didn't want to make small talk for long, I wanted to have a smoke, one drink to straighten myself, and listen to some music, and try and figure out what had happened after the waterhole.

'Have a drink on the house, love.' The barman was warm and kind, and I felt guilty for raiding his Tampax machine. I felt guilt piled on top of guilt, and couldn't afford to sink down any further, so I had a word to myself to justify my actions: after all, it wasn't his Tampax machine, his Tampax, or his money in it. Just like it was not my fault that the bar we got beat up in was full of a bunch of small-town retards. After all, it's not the law of the land that if you remove your clothes on a stage to a musical accompaniment, you deserve to get a complete kicking, and your friend has to get battered to within an inch of his life.

I ordered a whisky and Coke just in time for some other shit to finish on the jukebox, to make way for my excellent choices. I dragged slowly on my cigarette, listening to The Moody Blues' 'Nights In White Satin'. The music, the drink and the atmosphere of the bar changed me. I began to enjoy the way my wounds felt. I started to feel heroic with them, and almost sexy. Everything felt slow motion as I dragged on, and the song built.

Sitting at the bar, smoking out of my swollen hand and listening to the music, I felt like this was an ending, but of what I wasn't sure. Perhaps I had just given up. I found it so hard to change. I changed people, houses, jobs and countries but nothing ever changed inside. All I knew was, I could live like that, right here at the bar, living it all out in my head, in this state for ever. Now I realised what it was that had drawn me to Mac – he was how I would turn out. It was like looking into the fucking future. Maybe one day I would live above a small bar and own nothing but a pyramid of lighters. Then one night I'd just fall over, fall asleep and never wake up, really easily, like that.

I couldn't taste the alcohol in the Coke; I had reached new levels of immunity to drunkenness. I wondered what would actually stop me from going the extra mile this time, and decided, if anything, it would definitely be sleep, but I was dreading what would come after sleep. I ordered another whisky and Coke but made it a double, which was just about all I could afford, and could only stretch to that because the barman had given me a free one. My second song came on; I turned around to make sure that no one else was infecting the jukebox. Santana's 'Samba Pati' began and I raised my glass to the fucked-up woman at the opposite side of the bar, because she'd been grinning at me like a loon the whole time. I felt unreachable and untouchable again. If I ever woke up after this, I would get my things from the van, take a portfolio, and hitch to Brisbane and find my mother. She would be like Joyce Cane, and I'd live there with her, and start again, the madness finally leaving me.

Some car keys landed on the bar next to me.

'Let's have a look at you, then,' said a Germanic voice behind me. I turned round slowly, taking the room with me. It was Anaya.

CHAPTER TWENTY-NINE

'Wow, what a mess, uh?' she said, taking her time, enjoying the shocked look on my face.

'What's going on, why are you here?' I raised my hand for a moment to fix my hair, but dropped it again, deciding that in the circumstances it would be ridiculous.

She clicked her fingers, got the barman's attention, ordered herself a beer and helped herself to one of my cigarettes. She lit up, sucked in on it for ages before exhaling, then rested it between her fingers and looked all over my face.

'I didn't order you a drink because I think I have a lot of catching up to do.' She gulped her VB as soon as it arrived, drinking half of it. 'I drove so fucking fast.'

'What, from Sydney?'

'No, Byron Bay. I was going to meet you all there as a surprise, but I spoke to Greg and he told me Jim phoned earlier to say he had lost you and Scotty or something, and wouldn't be there, so I drove down. I went to the caravan park and Andrea told me that you were all at the hospital because you and Scotty had been in some accident. I've just been there now and spoken to Karin and Jim.'

'Where's Greg?' I asked, mesmerised by her smoking; she was a beautiful smoker. I just wanted to watch her now that she was here, and listen to the music.

She finished her drink, ordered another, and put her foot up on the rail that ran round the bottom of the bar. 'Greg's not here, Kerry.' She sucked on her cigarette. I didn't say anything, just watched her through my puffed-up eyes. She was such an actress.

'I'm on my own,' she said, blowing out again.

I was dead beat, but still nervous and uncomfortable in her presence, now more than ever. I had no energy any more for games and flirting, or word play. That left me feeling raw and in touch with all that really mattered, which at that moment was the desire to lie down next to her and sleep.

'That's some face you have now.' She moved some strands of hair back from my face and ran her fingers round my jaw on the outskirts of my swelling. I didn't move.

'Do you want to tell me what happened?'

'No, not just now.' I drank some more from my glass.

'OK,' she said, nodding slowly. 'You can tell me later.'

My third and final choice came on the jukebox and nothing could be more perfect.

She pulled up a stool next to me and got on it, her body mostly turned towards me. Rod Stewart's 'Boulevard Of Broken Dreams' began, that song that I'd always loved so much. I loved the way it came back, again and again, when you think it's gone, each verse better and bigger than the one before; a long, winding life-pain song. She knew that song; of course she knew the song. She moved her head to the guitar break in the middle. I shut my eyes and felt her near me. I opened them again, half expecting her not to be there, like I'd just drunk her into existence. We looked at each other each time it slowed down and went back to a verse. The song faded out on a crescendo of electric guitar. She leant in before the fade, her hand on my leg to steady her as she bent as far forward as she possibly could, to get right next to my ear.

'I've told Jim that I'll look after you tonight. We will stay at the caravan park beside the others.'

I couldn't speak, I was so nervous. I had fantasised about being alone with her from the first day of meeting her. I had planned so many moments and showdowns in my head, but none of them were like this. In the scenes I invented, I was on 'top form' and in control, the drinks just arriving. Not cut, mashed and stinking from a two-day bender that nearly killed someone. This seemed, however, to be my night with Anaya, and now that she was here with me for possibly its entirety, I was terrified, and she knew it. She moved nearer to my face, narrowing her eyes as she examined my injuries. I could smell her, she was so close. I could smell her shampoo, her beer, and traces of gum, and freshly applied lip-gloss that smelt of sweet fruit. When she'd finished scrutinising me, she stubbed out her cigarette in the ashtray on the bar.

'Let's go,' she said. Then she grabbed her keys and the bottle she was drinking from, and we both left before the next song finished.

We drove past the hospital. In the wing mirror I saw an ambulance arrive and thought about poor old Scotty, holed up in there with all the injured and crazies and vomiters.

I watched Anaya's legs move back and forth on the pedals; she wore a denim skirt. She was a one-handed driver, smoking with the other one, her arm leaning out of the window, and every so often she would cock her head to the right and let her hair blow around outside. She was such a cliché, and I loved her for it. She looked at me a couple of times, but we didn't speak once on the way to the caravan park. I loved Anaya for her lack of small talk and her ease with silence.

Just as the tyres rolled onto the gravel at the entrance to the site, huge spots of rain dropped on the windscreen. She drove slowly along the track until we saw the Kingswood next to a van with the curtains pulled, but lights on. I saw three heads silhouetted inside. Anaya parked her car beside the van next to it, which was dark. As we backed in, Karin's face appeared from behind the curtain and gave us a quick wave. I lazily raised my hand, knowing that Anaya wouldn't bother. I wondered what she was thinking and feeling, and if it was anywhere near matching the intensity of longing that I was feeling for her.

She yanked up the handbrake. 'Hang on, I just need to get the keys.'

I nodded. She reached behind the seat for her bag. I watched her twist round, and then watched her get out and walk over to the van with Karin in it and knock on the door. As I watched her talk to Karin and then Jim at their van door, and take some keys from them, I wondered why she was here, and what she truly wanted from me. She scared me, and always had, and tonight I had no strength to deal with it.

Inside our caravan, Anaya drew the curtains and put on a small lamp by the window. I slumped onto the seating beside it, still watching every single thing she did. She checked out the toilet and the two bedrooms, and then sat down opposite me, with the table between us. The rain began hammering down on the roof. I loved the rain beyond all other weather conditions, the way it shut you in and gave you the right to be indoors, with no one questioning your lack of go-out-and-get-it drive. Everything felt ridiculously perfect.

She rolled a grass joint, taking her time inserting the roach, carefully easing it in with a match, stopping every so often to look up at me, half smiling. When she finished, she offered it to me, but I declined in this instance, because I wanted her to have it all. That way we might be more level with one another's head states.

'I know you'll think I'm fucked for saying this.' She dragged on her joint. 'But I kind of like the way you look right now.' She spoke softly.

'Yeah, you are fucked.' I said, not knowing what else to say, yet understanding what she meant by it. Anaya was a strange person with her reactions; nothing seemed to shock her, move her or anger her. With so little going on, she should be boring, yet I found her utterly absorbing.

She came over and sat next to me, lighting up, and then ran her fingers over my mouth.

'Is it sore?'

'Getting sorer,' I said quietly. I felt calmer than before, partly due to overwhelming exhaustion.

'You know, in the morning it will hurt more than now.'

I nodded. She'd only made a single skin joint, so she soon finished it. She put it out in the ashtray slowly and gently. I could see her now, more than before, I told her.

'And I can see you,' she said dreamily.

'What will happen now?' I asked, wanting her to take control.

'Forget everything tonight, it's too much. Let's just get some rest, tomorrow we can sort things out, and you can tell me everything if you want to.'

I didn't know what there was to sort out. I had fucked the

others off, and would be asked to leave by Jim in the sobering conversation that no doubt he'd want to have with me when I got up. And although I wanted to apologise to everyone and see Scotty again, I had already decided that I would say my goodbyes in a note, before boarding a bus to Brisbane.

'Come on.' She got up, took the hairband out of her hair and walked into the bedroom at the back of the van. I followed. We both took our things off and left them on the floor and got into the bed. I was exhausted beyond all other times of exhaustion and was dying to lie down. We lay on our sides facing each other. We lay for the longest time. The rain eased off a little, just enough to hear our breathing.

'You need to sleep all this off, don't you?' she whispered.

'Is this the end of something, or the beginning?' I asked, not caring what I said any more.

She didn't answer. Instead, she circled the bruising on my cheekbone. I felt attractive behind my swollen eye, with my boxer cut.

I could have asked her a million things, I was dying to. I wanted to know about Greg, and what kept her with him, why she was here with me, why she had come to Australia, how and where she grew up, what she liked about me, and what she was going to do next. I tried to say something more but she wouldn't let me speak. She covered my mouth with her mouth, and kept it there for what felt like ages. My heart pounded, and she slowly took her lips off mine, and held the side of my face in her hand. I ached for her and tried to fight the tiredness, but my eyes were closing. I didn't want the night to end, but I was starting to see shapes in the room that I knew didn't exist, through needing sleep so badly.

'OK, now sleep, ssleep,' she hissed slowly, like a hypnotist.

'What if when I wake up you're not here?' I said, already drifting in and out of consciousness.

'Ssh,' she said, 'ssh.' Then she moved her hand down to cover mine, and I went home for the very first time.

CHAPTER **THIRTY**

I had been scared to fall into sleep with Anaya next to me, scared of what the day would bring, and scared that she would not even be there. But at some point I did.

I had strange dreams about small rodents that grew into birds, attaching themselves to the sleeves of a jumper I was wearing. I was trying to shake off the creatures that bit at my arm and held me back, while being chased by an angry mob with guns. I'd been shot a couple of times, with large rubber bullets that the birds had produced like eggs. As I ran, the eggs dropped from the rodents-cum-birds and filled the path behind me, supplying the mob pursuing me with more ammunition. I ran into a house where my grandparents used to live. I could hear them talking, but the house was empty. Anaya arrived in an ice-cream van, which I jumped into, trying to get away from my chasers, except the van was slow, and Anaya didn't seem to notice. There was no blood from my wounds, only pain. Just as the mob caught the van, I woke up.

I was lying on my side, clutching my ribs in agony. What I had thought was the thumping of rubber bullets hitting the ice-cream van turned out to be rain again, heavy rain on the roof. I didn't move, I didn't want to feel any emptiness in the bed, any lightness on the mattress from a space where she had lain. I moved my foot, feeling behind me at the bottom of the bed, worrying that there would be no Anaya's feet. I turned round. She was gone.

An intense depression set in immediately, and I was also disorientated to the point of panic. My hand throbbed and my head was splitting. There was a sharp pain running from the top of my head, through my eye and down into my cheek-bone. There was blood on the pillow from my mouth. I didn't feel anywhere near as attractive as the night before, instead I felt puffy and bloated, with slits for eyes.

I hated the fact that I'd woken up, but I was way too anxious to sleep any more. I was more sober than I had been, but the drink was still hanging around me, and my mouth tasted foul.

I studied the contours of the other pillow, running my hand over the indentation her head had left. I moved over to her side and lay on the spot where she had slept. There was sand in the bed, and some of her hair just below the pillow – her hair was a lighter brown than mine. I moved on to my stomach, smelling the bed for traces of her.

I realised I had lost my watch, so had no idea of what time it was. I staggered through to the living room of the van and sat at the table, picking up the hairband that Anaya had left there, placing it on my wrist. I pulled back the curtain to find Anaya's car had gone, as had the Kingswood from next door, and all the curtains were open in their caravan. They had left me.

I thought about what I would do next. I picked up the radio, moving the dial back and forth until I hit something newsy. After an item there was a jingle, then a voice saying it was nine o'clock. I had no money, no watch, no portfolio, no car, no clothes other than the ones lying on the floor in the bedroom, no phone numbers, and no friends. I knew I was in Port Macquarie, and regretted not paying attention at any time to maps and geography. I was surprised that Jim of all people would leave me out here, but when I traced back the events of the last forty-eight hours I couldn't blame him.

I would wait in the van until I was thrown off the site – by that time I would be in less pain; then I would go to the hospital and find out what was happening with Scotty. Maybe the others were there. If not, then I'd hitch to Brisbane and track down Hank White, easily traceable through his country and western radio show. If the worst came to the worst, I would do several Tampax machines and take a bus, or phone Joyce Cane, and tell her she was right. I had found the tattoo she had predicted and it had left me in a tricky situation, and I could see no alternative but to beg for her help. So I had my back-up plans, but first I'd lie down until the pain subsided slightly.

A car pulled up outside between the two vans. I lay out horizontal on the sofa seats round the dining table, rubbing Anaya's hairband between my fingers. I didn't hear the meatiness in the exhaust you got from the Kingswood. The handle on the front door turned up, then down, and Anaya walked in.

'I got us something to drink,' she said, offloading a carrier bag with a 7/11 logo onto the table. She brought out two bottles of spring water, unscrewed the top, passed one to me and sat down. I hid my delight at her return, and appeared as casual as I could be in the circumstances.

'You thought I'd gone maybe, uh?' she said, smiling. Was this kindness, or was she playing with me? Was this how our great love affair would be?

'I thought everybody had gone.' I gulped the first water I had drunk in days.

She sat opposite. This was strange new territory with Anaya. In fact, with anyone. I had rarely stayed the night with anybody, certainly never spoke with them the next day, in daylight, without any of the devices that had got us there in the first place. She looked different to me now. She looked real. It had nothing to do with make-up, for she only wore a bit of lip-gloss and mascara in the evenings if we all went out to the pub. It was something else, I couldn't be sure. All I knew was I wanted to say things to her, like: 'I love your face, it's the sexiest face I've seen in my life. I love your cheekbones, and your perfect olive skin and your blue-green eyes.' But I daren't say those things, not quite yet.

'Where are the others? How's Scotty, do you know?'

'Did you really think that we had all just run away?' She laughed.

'Well, you know, I mean after yesterday.'

'Is that what people do in your life, Kerry? Run away?' She held my gaze.

'Maybe,' I said, trying to play down my elation at her return.

'I've bought some tea and milk. I'll make some.'

I nodded.

'I've just spoken to Jim and Karin.'

'Yeah? What's happening with Scotty?'

'Jim wants to have a break today, just to be alone. They are at the hospital just now. Scotty is doing OK, but they're not sure if he will go back with them or stay in hospital for a bit, then go back in an ambulance. He won't know until tomorrow.'

'What about the trip, what does Greg think?'

She filled the kettle as she spoke. 'I've spoken to Greg, don't worry. He wants you to rest today and start again tomorrow. He wants everybody to do that.'

'Do you love Greg?' I asked cautiously.

She turned round, looking right at me. 'I don't expect anybody to understand me and Greg. I'm OK with that.'

'Why were you going to Byron Bay, Anaya? What was the real reason?' I wanted to hear the truth from her, whatever it was.

'Like I said, a trip up north' – she lit a match to the stove – 'a surprise.'

'Well, it certainly is a surprise,' I said, smiling out of the less swollen side of my mouth.

'So today's a kinda limbo, yeah? We can start again tomorrow.' She put teabags in two cups she found in the cupboard, while I wallowed in her use of 'we'.

After drinking tea and staring out at the bad weather, we both took showers and went back into the bedroom. I showered first, and washed my hair with my OK hand. Afterwards, I lay in bed waiting for Anaya. I felt awkward without the bar, the drink and our soundtrack. Instead we had only rain, washing over us in the van.

She came into the room naked, towel-drying her hair. Then she sat on the edge of the bed with her back to me, running her comb through her hair. That's when I noticed that at the base of her spine she had a tattoo.

'What is it?' I said, reaching over and touching it, my heart thumping again.

She bent over so I could get a proper look at it. 'It's a swallow. You like it? I got it done when I was sixteen.'

'Do you believe in fate, Anaya?' I asked, tracing it with my finger.

'I believe that we can all have whatever we want, if we want it bad enough.' She got into bed beside me. My mind raced. It was all leading to this, all of the time, everything that had happened so far. This is what Joyce saw; this had to be my fate. She would become my life now. Maybe she would come with me to find my mother. Maybe I could stay in Australia with her, and we could run the selling together. Or we could live like this, moving around caravans until we ran out of options. But what would a life with Anaya be like? How could I live with the all-consuming desire that I finally had to admit to myself I'd felt for her from the second I saw her face in the bar?

We both lay down facing each other again.

'Forget what's in here,' she said, touching my head lightly.

'There's so many weird coincidences going on I need to tell you about, Anaya,' I said, my eyes darting anxiously over her face.

'It can wait,' she said, pulling me towards her. We started kissing but my mind was racing and worrying about other things. I felt sobering, terrible remorse over Scotty's beating, and my general body state was causing my heart to pound. I hadn't eaten since our arrival in Port Macquarie a couple of days ago, and although I was exhausted, I resisted closing my eyes as it caused me to see lots of tiny spiders climbing down from long fine pieces of web, then multiplying and scattering as they landed.

Kissing was painful and had to be light; we moved our tongues around harder than was normal to compensate for the lack of mouth pressure. We kissed the longest kiss I'd ever experienced, maybe half an hour. I could feel her breathing, and the noises she made vibrated through my nose, which hurt the swelling at the top of the bridge. Our bodies didn't touch, just our mouths. I moved my injured-thumb hand against her stomach lightly; my hand felt big and hot and ugly in comparison to her smooth tight skin. But I knew it felt good to her.

She reached over with her hand round to the bottom of my spine, and spread it out there. I pulled her towards me more, all the time kissing. My body had reached new levels of agony, probably because I was sobering up and starting to feel my injuries. The ribs and the headache were the worst, but I had to persevere with the agony-ecstasy tightrope I was treading.

I pulled away.

'My fucking ribs, it's hard to move,' I moaned.

She breathed out a kind of half-laugh. She started kissing me again, and she positioned herself on top of me, sitting looking right at me and moving around. Then she leant down and kissed my fucked-up hand, and started licking it. It was hard to reach without straining my neck, which hurt my ribs, so she put her hand around my head and helped pull me up to where I wanted to be. She pushed her weight into me as she sat on me, sliding back and forth. I lay back, resting from the agony of my straining. It was so hot in the cabin and sweat had begun pouring from us.

As Anaya moved more and more, I threw back the sheet that was starting to entangle around us, and put my hands on her hips, my injured one only half resting on it, protecting my broken thumb.

I looked up at her; I wanted to tell her I loved her completely, whoever she was, but thought it best not to, afraid that she might hate it. From what I knew of Anaya so far, I figured she would hate people that wanted her too much.

She bent down and kissed me again, then whispered in my ear. 'Let it go.'

I tried to let go, tried to forget my anxieties about how if I let her in, she might go. But my vicious circle of a life pattern kept moving round in my head. I worried that the hell of the hangover would never leave me, but promised myself that when it did, I would get better – eat, begin exercising, be normal like the others, and enjoy only the odd mad night. I couldn't wait to start afresh, free of this pain and the ridiculous spider hallucinations.

Anaya increased the pressure of her grinding into me. My thoughts and worries began to shrink, as I melted into her. Her face was completely different to me now, it already felt like it had been a part of my life for ever. She reached round and put her fingers inside me. I was tense at first, not wanting to let her before I had fucked her first. She sensed my apprehension, as I tried to sit up.

'Let it fucking go,' she said again.

I wanted to so much. I had always wondered what it would be like to try and truly let someone in. Half my mind was against it, but she pushed further in until I weakened, and let her fuck me until I came.

We lay on our backs recovering, from the heat and the effort.

'How're you feeling?' she asked.

I winced as she secured the strip of micropore that had come undone above my eye. I felt a surge of overwhelming sadness engulf me and couldn't understand why. I had just had sex with someone I had desired for a while now. Why was I not happy? Perhaps it was the melancholy and paranoia of the drink in my system. But it felt deeper than that. I felt almost breathless trying to push it down. She could see me struggling, but said nothing, just watched me closely and held my face in her hands, which made me feel small and stupid and even more upset. My eyes filled with tears that were to big too hide, but I fought them off, blinking for as long as I possibly could. She put her hand on my chest, just below my throat, and I lost it, just like when Jim arrived and rescued Scotty and me.

'It's OK,' she said.

That made me even worse, and I began crying for everything: for my grandfather at the end of his life, for the death of my grandmother, for my parents and how miserable they had become. I cried over happier times with us all together, before we were scarred and changed for ever with unhappiness, times when my grandparents would take me on the bus down to the seaside every summer, and how we would always sit upstairs at the front and look out at everyone, laughing at all the funny things we saw. I thought about me desperately walking around the streets of Newcastle alone a few years ago, trying to find clues that would lead me to my mother. I cried about my fear of being close to others, and how I saw what was normal to most as a weakness with me. Eventually, the crying fizzled out, and we lay quiet for the longest time, until I drifted off.

'I gotta pee, OK?' she said. Running her thumb lightly over my forehead. Sometime later I felt her move off the bed and I felt immediately afraid that she was leaving.

I listened to her pee trickle down into the toilet, the only sound anywhere now that the rain had stopped.

We slept for five hours, which took us into the late afternoon. A firm knock on the caravan door woke us, and I checked the time on Anaya's watch. I got up and moved along the furniture, clutching at things to make it to the door. I felt in much worse shape now; every part of my body ached, my stomach felt as though it was eating itself, and I had a headache like I had never known before.

I opened the door. The rain had begun again and was pelting down. Jim stood outside with a waterproof hooded jacket on and a pizza takeaway box in his hand. 'Come on then, let me in.'

'Is it the next day?' I asked, letting him into the caravan.

'No, it's bloody not the next day.' He shook off his coat and threw the pizza box on to the table. 'Still got company have you?' He rolled his eyes.

I pointed to the bedroom. 'Yeah, Anaya is, eh, sleeping. I think.'

Jim mumbled that he didn't want to know.

'I thought you wanted to be on your own today,' I said, wanting him to go.

'Get some of that in you.' He pushed the box towards me; I opened it up and ate a slice of Hawaiian. I was ravenous.

I said, 'I keep seeing these spiders, imagining them crawling around.'

'I'm not bloody surprised. Look at the state of you.'

I chewed and talked. 'Jim, I'm sorry about the pissed-up behaviour, I really fucked up.'

'Pissed-up behaviour! That's what you call it, is it?' he said, half laughing.

I felt embarrassed at my appearance, and could see Jim looking at my nails and hands, which were filthy despite the shower I'd had earlier, no doubt from scrabbling on the ground, hiding from the police. I was disgusted at the sight of my swollen hand holding the pizza slice, and the appearance of it next to the ham was making me feel sick. I had never been sick before with drink, and vowed to myself that this would not be the start of it.

'How's Scotty?'

'He's much worse than you, but he'll be OK, he's a young lad, which is probably what saved him.' Jim spoke about Scotty as though he had survived a plane crash, living for days on top of a dangerous mountain. 'He's coming back to the site tomorrow, all going well.'

'Thought he was going home?'

'Nope. He's refused. Doesn't want to worry his mum.' Jim shrugged his shoulders. The bedroom door opened and Anaya walked out wrapped in a blanket.

'Hey, Jim, how are things?'

Jim changed his mannerisms when Anaya came in, and began punctuating his Scotty update with two-handed thigh slapping, then he drummed on the table, while Anaya sat next to me, helping herself to the pizza.

'Right, you,' said Jim, pointing at me. 'I've been thinking, and you and I need to have a talk.' I saw the teacher in him again. 'Get your bathers or whatever and meet down the beach in ten.'

'Why?' I looked out at the rain, which now appeared torrential.

'We're going to sort out this bloody state of yours. You're no good to anyone like this.'

'There, that's you told,' said Anaya, eating her second slice, apparently without a care in the world, and back to her old self again.

I did feel better on the beach. The battering rain took away my mental claustrophobia, waking me up a little. There was no wind and no surf, it was humid to the point of the rain feeling warm, but it was hard and pounded off my head, hurting my facial injuries when I looked up.

'Breathe in that beautiful, fresh sea air.' Jim took huge breaths, striding ahead of me towards the edge of the ocean. I copied him. 'This'll sort your bloody head out.'

Now that my breaths were exaggerated, I could taste the levels of stale drink in my system, which made me want to throw up. I staggered along, waving one arm around, unable to match Jim in his enthusiasm. We reached the edge of the water. I turned to look along the shore, almost expecting to see Anaya heading down to us. But there was no one in sight. The beach was deserted from where we stood for a mile in each direction.

Jim started to strip, just as some lightning appeared. 'Right then, get your kit off, come on.'

'Isn't the lightning dangerous?' I said, a little apprehensive.

'Fuck's sake, after what you've got up to, you're worried about the lightning?' He had a fair point. 'It's not lightning that's going to bloody kill you.' He threw his jacket and shoes away from the tide and ran in.

I winced as I peeled off my top and shorts, and waded in behind him. The tide was full in, making me waist deep in a few strides. Jim swam front crawl fast and furiously out to sea. Thunder grumbled over us, as I lay on my back and looked up to the darkest sky I had seen in any daytime: a thick charcoal sky that looked as if it was about to swallow us. The waves started to build slightly and bobbed me around. I kept looking up, trying to faze out the spiders; I'd only seen a couple since entering the water. I tried to clear my mind of Anaya, of the night before and what had happened today, of the panic I felt about her, and of my increasing remorse over the bar fiasco. I ducked under the water, and swam down to the bottom. Hundreds of little fish darted around, moving out of my way. The shape of Jim swam towards me. I surfaced. The spiders were gone.

'Much better, eh?'

'Yeah, thanks. Jim?' We both stood facing each other.

'No, listen to me, you!' He firmly grabbed my arms with both hands. 'I'm going to tell you this once, and never again, OK?'

I nodded. 'Yeah, of course.'

'Chris, my brother, was always trouble, ever since he was a lad. Always in trouble, always pushing things with everyone. He had a massive chip on his shoulder, always thought he was the worst off. I didn't tell you when I spoke about it before, that my brother ended up dead.'

'Fucking hell, I'm so sorry. Fuuuck.'

'Yep, and I spent four months in hospital with this.'

'Now I see why Scotty was pissing you off so much that night we played truth or dare, when he kept going on about it.'

'Scotty's all right, but he's a fucking idiot as well, and the annoying thing is he reminds me of our Chris.' Jim cupped seawater.

'Is that when you decided to come here?'

'A lot more stuff happened after Chris died. Some things have a knock-on effect, you see, and then everything else seems to slide away.' He trod around a little. 'I hated teaching, it was so bloody disheartening, but that's another story. The way I looked at it was that I had another chance after that fight, another crack at it, so why spend my life doing something I hated?'

'No point,' I said solemnly. 'What happened to the people who stabbed him?'

'Seven years, reduced to five in the end.'

I shook my head.

'Destroyed almost everything, wrecked my mother. My father worked twenty years in the pits and survived them, but the shock of Chris killed him a year later.'

'Fuck.'

'Look, I'm from a good family, you know. I mean, there were five of us, so it was hard at times, but we were well brought up. Chris was the youngest. There was a time when my mum and dad nearly separated, and my mum had an affair with someone and got pregnant with Chris, so he was my half-brother, yeah? It was tough for him because he only discovered it when they had a massive row, and my dad shouted at my mum about the last child not being his.'

I listened, willing the story to bring me closer to my own destiny.

'We all loved Chris and never thought about him as anything but our brother, and their son. But Chris was on self-destruct from that moment. We loved him, but he didn't like himself, couldn't accept his life the way it was.'

A bird swooped down in the background; my gaze followed it.

'Are you listening, Kerry? Because this is important, and it's the one and only time I'll talk about it. My life's about moving on, do you understand?'

'My life is too.' My eyes filled with tears, and suddenly I felt ugly and small, and such a misguided idiot for thinking I looked good in the bar, all beaten up, and fucked in the head.

'I don't know you well, Kerry. I think I do, but I don't know what's eating you. 'Cause I see Chris in you as well, and it's very hard to let it happen again.'

I nodded, too choked up to be able to speak.

'Listen to me.' He grabbed me again, his jaw tensing, his eyes watery. 'I made a mistake, Kerry. I was angry and I made a mistake.'

I looked at him quizzically.

'I should never have left you both on the beach that night. I'd just had enough. I could see what you were doing and I just couldn't let it go on, but it was really wrong of me to leave you both there. I wasn't thinking. You see, it reminded me of stuff. I'm sorry.'

'Please, I don't blame you. We were being very annoying, really, I know that.'

'Well, I'm deeply sorry for what I did.'

'Forget it. Not your fault, you know?'

'I know you're still young, but if you don't sort some stuff out now, you'll go the wrong way, and there'll be a point when it's all irreversible, do you understand?'

I understood more than he could imagine. Thunder clapped again, this time nearer, and a fork of lightning appeared on the horizon.

'There was nothing I could have done for Chris, he made sure of it. It was the worst thing, to see someone I loved destroying their life.'

'Yeah – but poor Chris, not being told the truth by your parents. No wonder he went fucking mental, that's enough to destroy everyone.'

'NO! Life deals you stuff, Kerry. I've said this to you already. It deals you stuff, fuck knows why, but it does, and either you chose to let it ruin you, or you make the most of it, and move on.'

'That's not true, not everyone has difficult stuff to deal with. Look at Andrea and Karin, they're OK, aren't they?'

'Yes, I agree they seem reasonably happy girls, but that doesn't mean to say that they have got through life without any mess or pain. Besides, they're young. Who knows what kind of hand they'll have been dealt by the time they're my age or older? By the way, Karin is the first person I think I've met in a long time who's not fucked up. That's why I like her.'

'Yeah, well, I was dealt a shit hand to start with.' I wasn't buying any of that there's-loads-of-people-out-there-worse-than-you crap; it didn't make me feel any better, or any better equipped to deal with what was happening in my life at this moment.

'Listen. You make the most of the hand you've got, and that's that.' Jim ducked under the water and came up again, sweeping back his hair.

This felt like the right time to tell him my story, to open up to him, and so I started. I began with the morning of my eighteenth birthday, when I took the bus into Edinburgh to Register House, and waited in a library-style silent queue for an hour, and was then taken into a small room with tall ceilings. How I showed my driver's licence as ID and paid a clerk five pounds. A while later, the clerk and a second person brought an enormous ledger into the room and laid it on the table in front of me, with a piece of paper acting as a marker sticking out from one of the pages.

'There you go,' said the clerk, opening the book at the marked page and turning round to face me. My heart was thumping through my chest.

In faded black fountain-pen writing was the date of my birthday in 1965. Next to it was written 'Mother' with a line under it. The name read 'Madeline Thomson'. It gave her occupation as a nurse, and her age as eighteen. It said the father was 'unknown'. There was another name underneath: Joanna Thomson. That was me, that was the name I had been given for the purposes of my birth. It only stayed with me and was used by my mother for the three months before she handed me over to my new parents, who would know nothing of my old name or the people who made me. There was an address for my mother at the time of my birth. It was in Newcastle. Then there was a signature belonging to my mother. I ran my fingers over it. It was the first thing I had ever known about where I was from and perhaps the only thing I would ever see that came from my mother, except for myself.

I asked the clerk for a copy, but she said that was not allowed. I got out my notebook and wrote down the information before my allocated time was up. As I left, I looked at the queue of people still waiting – most of them were around my age – who were about to go through the same thing I had just experienced. They looked at me; we all knew how it felt to be each other.

I tore out all the other pages in my notebook that had already been written on and decided that the book was only to contain notes and findings regarding the search for my mother that began that day.

I began drinking heavily. Then one night, three or four years later, quite unplanned, I boarded a bus for Newcastle. I spent a day and night there wandering around asking questions, going from house to house in the streets around my mother's original address. I spoke to an old woman who had been a neighbour for many years of a woman whom I thought might be my grandmother. She was the one to tell me that there was a middle daughter called Madeline, who'd lived in the house with her seven sisters after her parents died. In the mid-sixties she met an Irish soldier by the name of Duffy, whom she married and emigrated to Australia with within a matter of months. The woman thought the daughter had mentioned Sydney as their destination but she could not be sure. I slept in the bus station before returning to Edinburgh, and from that day on planned that I would eventually take up my final search in Australia itself.

'Why did you leave it so long before you came here?' asked Jim, who hadn't moved for the duration of my story.

'I don't know.' I splashed water on my face. 'It's hard to explain to anyone who hasn't experienced it. You just try to get on with things the way they are, I suppose. Then every so often a bad thing happens, and I think, I'm like this because I need to see who she is, I need to meet her, and learn how I was made, where I come from.'

Jim looked at me, shaking his head, then throwing water up over himself. The rain was even heavier now.

'Come here,' Jim said, but I didn't want to. I was too wired with my story and telling it out loud for the first time in that detail. It made me more sure than ever that I had something to complete before I could get on with my life. I went on to tell him about Hank and Joyce Cane, although he kind of laughed at the part about her going on about tattoos and fate. I'd let him have that though, I thought. It's something you either believe in entirely like me, or like him, think is a pile of shit. I told him Hank had a radio show, which was bizarre, because it meant the person I had chosen to speak to on the phone could reach thousands of people across the airwaves. This still didn't convince him about fate, but he did think it was an amazing story. I reached the end of it and punched the water.

'Listen, you.' He moved towards me for a second time. 'I'm shit at things like this, I know I am, but have you thought about what your mother might say? I mean, I don't want to sound harsh but she might not want to meet you. Have you thought of that?'

The truth was, I had never given that possibility one thought, and wasn't about to. I had presumed she was waiting for me all this time, unable to contact me. This was what I held on to.

Jim touched my shoulder, laying his hand flat on it. 'I don't want you to get—'

'What, hurt?' I said it for him.

'Yeah. I don't.'

'I'm already hurt,' I said. 'I have to find her now, I think it will take some of it away, you know?'

Jim hugged me tight, my head pressing into his chest; I felt his heart pumping away as fast as the rain. I was scared to put my arms round him, for I didn't want to fall apart completely in the state I was in. I knew he wasn't a hugger and neither was I, and that this gesture had taken a huge effort, so I hugged him back, and we swayed a little as the waves built at his back and splashed onto him, my jaw locked together fighting the sadness.

I couldn't wait to get back to the caravan and be with Anaya. I felt much better for talking to Jim, and my hangover was shifting. I had decided that things were looking up again, and that I had a chance of a new start. I had been wrong not to trust Anaya – she was a little aloof, but from how she'd been since she'd arrived in Coffs Harbour I was quickly learning that she had a big heart.

I planned my conversation with her out loud, as I walked off the beach to the caravan park. Jim had said we could all eat together later that night if Anaya and I felt like it, which I thought would be nice and civilised. But first, I needed to tell her about my search for my mother, and explain why I had fallen apart earlier. Then perhaps she would come with me to Brisbane and help me find her. I was still mumbling to myself when the van came into view, without Anaya's car next to it.

At first I thought she'd gone into town again to get some stuff, but as I got nearer, I started to feel my heart sinking. The curtains were drawn. I let myself in slowly. The van smelt stuffy, but also of her perfume. There was nothing to tell me she was gone in the front of the van, but in the bedroom, on what had been her side of the bed, was a piece of paper folded over.

I sat down beside it, and sighed wearily. I dropped my head down, looking at the ground. Something stuck out from under the bed. I bent down further. It was her hairband. I rubbed it between my fingers, smelling it. I opened up the curtains in the small window next to the bed. I held the piece of paper in my other hand, slowly unfolding it. It read:

If I don't go now, I'll never go. And for other reasons I have to. I'll be in Byron Bay, then Cairns for a while. If you believe in fate or want it enough, then maybe you'll find me. Whatever you do, I wish you well, and I hope you find what you're looking for. Stay out of trouble meantime.
Cheers, Anaya xxx

I lay down on my side, clutching her hairband and staring out through the window at the sun appearing slightly in the distance for the first time that day.

CHAPTER **THIRTY-ONE**

The humidity in the phone box was intense. Sweat poured down my face. Outside the beautiful rain continued, although the clouds had lifted slightly. Hank's voice answered the phone after one ring.

'Hank, it's Kerry, I'm sorry I lost touch with you. I've been travelling around a bit and missed your calls.'

'Heeyy, Kerry. Where are you now?'

'Coffs Harbour. Listen, do you know anything?'

He paused.

'Hank?'

'I do have some information for you, Kerry, love.' He was really dragging this out, which made me suspicious of him. He was enjoying withholding stuff from me; ever since I'd first spoken to him, I'd sensed he was full of himself. He'd have to do, though – right now he was the only lead I had.

'OK, Kerry. I have had some contact with some of your family, all right?'

'NO FUCKING WAY! WHAT? WHAT?'

'But—'

'But what? WHAT!'

'Listen, I knew when we first spoke about this that you were looking for someone much bigger in your life than you were making out to me. I mean, I thought all along that you were adopted.'

'Hank, please, for fuck's sake, tell me everything. It doesn't matter now, I'll tell you everything.'

'OK. I think the sister of this Madeline Thomson came to see me after I put out the call on air. I know one of them was anyway – and your mother is alive.'

'Wow, FUCK! Go on.' I couldn't believe what I was hearing.

'I got a call a few days ago from someone in response to my mentioning it on the radio. I've done it a few times, you see.'

'Uh-huh, go on.' I bit on the nails of my less swollen hand.

'The next day they showed up where I live and they were well, pretty pissed off, to put it mildly.'

'And.'

'Look, Kerry, this Joanna Thomson you told me to mention, it's you, isn't it?'

'Yes, it is.'

'And Madeline is your mother, right?'

'Yes. Why? Have you found her, Hank?'

'They didn't tell me an awful lot, but I have every reason to believe that your mother and her family are living somewhere here in Brisbane.'

I leant my head against the booth, and slammed the wall. 'Hank, listen, please, I need to come and stay with you for a while, is that all right?'

'Sure it is.'

'I'm getting on a bus, Hank, as soon as I can. OK?'

'I understand, kid.'

'I'll let you know what bus I'm on. Did they give you an address?'

'No, nothing. Listen, kid, they were very protective of her – put it that way – and not open to discussing much.'

'I'll call you later, really soon, tonight, tomorrow, when I know the buses, yes?'

'Gotcha.'

I hung up, and gripped my hair in disbelief that I was, at the moment, the nearest I had ever been to meeting the person who made me.

I stood in line to buy my ticket at the bus station in Grafton, the nearest major town to Coffs Harbour. The rain was still lashing it, causing melancholy to ooze from everywhere. Jim had driven me there, on a journey that took around half an hour from the caravan site. The plan was that Jim would go back to Coffs Harbour and see how things were at the hospital, then he and the Danes would drive up towards the Gold Coast and work the tourist strip there for a few days. They would decide how long they'd stay once there. Then we would all meet up in Brisbane in around four days' time, and I would start selling again. I insisted that I take a folder with me, just in case I saw an opportunity, but, as Jim pointed out, no one would want to buy anything on their doorstep from someone with a face like mine at the moment. I said that there was a way round everything, so he dragged one out of the car for me, with the bestselling paintings doubled up, in case things really kicked off. I had known all along, from the second I got this job, that if I did find out where my mother lived, it would be an ingenious way of getting into her or her family's houses, without arousing any suspicion.

We all acknowledged that, because of the amount of time off we'd had, we would have to work hard from now on, until our return to Sydney. I was confident that, although I was lying low for a few more days, I would sell double what anyone else sold when I started again. Jim agreed, which made me feel less guilty.

We didn't speak much in the car on the way to Grafton; we had said all the major stuff in the sea, and were both too worn out for small talk. Instead we listened to the radio, lost in our own thoughts. I leant against the passenger-seat window, fiddling with Anaya's hairband, holding onto the belief that she wanted me to go after her.

The bus driver took my portfolio and put it in the luggage hold of the coach, along with my rucksack.

'Got everything?' Jim stood with his hands in his trouser pockets. Despite the humidity he wasn't a shorts man, which I quite liked about him.

'Yeah, don't have much stuff, but it's in there.'

'Hope that guy's not some kind of nutcase.'

'He is, but he's all right, don't worry.'

Jim laughed. The last in the line boarded the coach, leaving only me. 'I'll call you when I get to Brisbane, on his number, and if you need to leave a message for me, leave it with Greg in Sydney, yeah?'

'Sure, no worries.'

'Good luck, and don't do anything too stupid.'

'Promise. And, Jim, thank you.'

He nodded, and I moved towards the automatic doors. I was hoping he would leave the moment I boarded the bus, but he waited until it pulled out, waving me off, which gave me a lump in my throat.

On the bus, I went over everything, especially my time with Anaya: how she threw her keys on the bar, how she smoked, how she leant her head out of the car window during her one-handed driving. How she cared for me, and held my hand until I slept. How she looked sitting on top of me, moving back and forth. Her telling me to 'let go'. How she had impressed me with her intuition, not to forget her knowledge of the lyrics to most of the songs I loved. I wished I could relive that night again – next time I would be more awake and less mashed up. I hoped there would be a next time, but with Anaya, you just didn't know. In a way it helped that I was too taken up with my plans to get to Hank's and meeting my mother to dwell on the wrench and initial shock I had felt at her leaving.

I thought about my real mother, Madeline. It was impossible to process how I thought she might look; it was something I had never dwelled on until now. The thought alone of two people, maybe more, on this planet bearing some actual resemblance to me was unimaginable. For me, being brought up in a world where you shared your looks with no one was normal. I was certain that meeting her would make me feel filled up with some kind of love, or the sense of wholeness that other people seem to feel, or have felt at least for a time in their lives. I felt a strange sense of hope and optimism on the bus. My journey had a purpose, a definite direction and a happy ending, I was sure.

My most recent bender was spoiling how I usually preferred to travel, which was with a pack of beers, striking up conversation with other transients. This time, as part of my new start, I had promised myself a complete rest from drink for the next three days, at least. I would drink soft drinks for a while, like lemonade, as a tribute to Joyce Cane's advice.

I looked around the coach; it was half empty. I thought

about the half-empty glass, half-full glass shit that people go on about when you end up having a conversation about how shit life is, and began putting everyone I'd befriended since landing in Sydney into each category. I mistrusted half-fullers, yet I immediately put Jim in this group, because of his endless resourcefulness, and constant energy reserve. I also put the Danish and Joyce Cane in with him. I put Scotty, Mac and me in the half-empties, but couldn't place Greg and Anaya, because they disclosed nothing, and displayed nothing of their views or feelings on life. By our first pick-up point, I'd decided Greg was half full. He had to be: he was optimistic in his work, he had a relationship, even if it was with Anaya, and he seemed pretty happy-go-lucky. Anaya had an impenetrable confidence, which I think also made her half full. Now, Fritz was a difficult one, for he was surely looking at a half-empty one, yet Joyce's positive upbeat approach ran both their lives, so did that mean she carried him over to half full? I decided if I got him on his own for long enough, without his rock, he would join me and the other half-empties. My group, I realised, was full of people who were hopeless, and glaringly unhappy. They all had the irreversible-lives syndrome that Jim had warned me about today. I didn't want to play things like that. Not any more.

I checked out the kilometres to Brisbane on the next sign, which said two hundred. Then I curled up on the double seat, happy at the swishing sound coming from the tyres hitting the wet highway, and got my head down, confident that meeting my mother would make my future glasses half full, rather than half empty.

CHAPTER THIRTY-TWO

I was sound asleep when the bus pulled into the station in Brisbane. I got myself together and checked out the people awaiting our arrival. I picked out Hank White straight away. He was perhaps in his early fifties, and dressed like Roy Orbison in all-black clothes, but had a look of General Custer about him, with a huge white moustache and a narrow pointy beard. His hair was wild and swept back, and he wore enormous sunglasses even though it was dark and dusky. I was worried from the moment I saw him. I'd always hated beards and completely distrusted men who wore them; it felt as though they were hiding behind them. It was hard to hide Hank though.

I was last off the bus and could see the others looking at him as they stepped down onto the forecourt. It was probably the black clothes more than anything, for black in Australia seemed to be a big no-no, automatically arousing suspicion among the happy-go-lucky colour-clad.

'Kerry?' He clicked his fingers into a point.

'Hank.' I outstretched my hand.

His Cuban heels clicked towards me as he rejected the hand and forced a hug, with big back pats.

'Ow, careful, I'm a little fragile.' I coughed from the firmness of his pat.

'Yeees, what the blazes happened to you, girl?'

'Boat capsized during white-water rafting, smashed into the rocks.' I scanned the rest of his clothing. He wore a cowboy belt with studs round the leather and an enormous star buckle; he also wore his shiny shirt open at the chest, revealing a huge pendant made of stone or bone hanging by a piece of leather. I couldn't believe this guy was for real, and hoped that he would soon tell me he was on the way to a fancy-dress party.

'You gotta be careful, girl.'

'Shit!' I had nearly forgotten the portfolio in the hold, with the shock of seeing Hank. I ran over to the bus driver as he was unloading the last few items, and dragged it out with Hank's help.

'What you got in here, love?'

'Paintings.'

'Oh yeah.'

'Yeah, I sell them.'

'Is that a fact? Well, don't be trying to sell them to us; we've got far too much stuff at our place as it is.'

I wondered who made up the 'our' in Hank's life, as we walked towards a large station wagon with a 'Country Classics 115 FM' sticker along the bottom of the back window.

'Your face has taken quite a battering, hasn't it, girl?' He put his hand on the side of my face and turned it round, letting his sunglasses drop onto the chain round his neck. I was tired from sober, stranger, small talk already and couldn't wait for darkness to come so that I could be alone in what I prayed was my own room.

'So, Hank, what do you know? I need to know everything.' I imagined I was a detective again, just arriving on the scene, needing to be filled in on the situation by my hapless sidekick.

He laughed, which annoyed me.

'I know you do, love, but we've only just checked in. Let's get you back, get that cut of yours seen to, and we'll sit down with a nice meal and a nice glass of wine, and we'll have plenty of time to chat, OK?' He loaded my things into the back of the truck.

'OK. I'm just dying to know.'

Hank gave me an over-the-top sympathetic look. 'Let's get back, OK?' He opened the doors, and we got in.

'OK,' I sighed disappointedly.

'Have you ever had barramundi fish?'

'No.'

'Do you like wine?'

'Of course.'

'Good, good.' He put a tape in, and we drove away listening to some whiney, wobbly man's voice singing about his wife leaving him.

'Funny, I feel like I know you already, like we're old friends,' he said, smiling at me.

'Yeah, I know, it's weird, uh?' I forced a polite smile, not a hundred per cent sure yet how I felt about him.

Hank's place was a big, old, white colonial house with a porch right across the front. It was in a quiet road in an area called Paddington. I asked Hank why all the names of areas seemed to be the same in different cities and he said it was because the English settlers named them after places at home, and didn't expect people to build others anywhere else, and because the land was so vast they rarely got to know about the settling of other places.

'We're back!' Hank opened the fly screen with wind chimes dangling above it. He took my rucksack, while I went ahead of him dragging my folder, which was extra heavy with the double-ups. I left my folder in the hall and followed Hank through to a room.

'Will this be safe here?' I asked, concerned that there was only an unlocked fly screen between the street and my only source of income and ticket to spy on my mother.

'You're not in Sydney now, love. Of course it's safe.'

Something good was cooking: a warm spicy coconut aroma drifted through from another room.

I looked around. He led me to the kitchen and we pulled chairs up to a table and sat down. The house was old and plain-looking, cool and dark – which I liked – and the furniture was heavy, and dark-stained wood. There were lace doilies on the tables with ornaments on them; the ornaments were all stones, or marble, shells and bits of driftwood. There were pieces of material hanging on various parts of the wall with Asian writing on it. He saw me looking.

'A lot of the furniture's my mum's. She lived with me most of my life until she died two years ago this December.'

'Oh, I'm sorry.'

'Don't be, she had a fine old time. She was OK; just old, that's all. I could sure do with changing the place around. It's a bit dusty, shall we say?'

'Wasn't Slim Dusty a country music star?'

'Very good. You like country?'

'No, not really, bit of Patsy Cline of course, but not a huge fan in general. But we were near Tamworth a few days ago, and there were signs on the road for some of the stuff going on.'

'Oh, yeah, that'll be right.'

'There was one for the Slim Dusty museum.'

'Well, as you can tell, I'm a big country fan.' He pointed to his clothes. 'Now, just you sit down and relax. Can I fix you something? Coke, beer, cup of tea?'

I struggled with my decision; it was a hard one. My kidneys ached and I still felt thirsty and bloated, but the polite chat was killing me, and I was finding it hard keeping my eyes open.

'I'll have a Coke please. Cold, if you've got it.' I'd wait to drink until I'd eaten, that would be my new rule for my stay here.

'Sure thing, let me get that for you, and I'm going to find some plasters and stuff as well, OK?'

'Thanks.'

Hank, although Australian, spoke in a bit of a fake Memphis drawl, which was so corny I was amazed that he didn't notice it. He opened a cold bottle from the fridge and put it down beside me, and began rooting around in the drawer.

'Excuse me.' He left the room and began shouting for someone. 'Pat! Pat, love, you in?'

He came back into the room muttering to himself. I wondered where I would be sleeping, longing for dinner and answers about my mother and an early night. Then in the morning I could start what I came here to do.

A bell sounded from the oven, and a small smiley woman with a round face and straight black hair burst in through the back door, saying, 'Oh my goodness, you are here.'

Pat was Chinese or Mexican, I couldn't be sure.

'Hi there, I'm Kerry.'

'Kerry, this is Pattana.' We shook hands.

'Nice to meet you. Sorry, I was outside picking some coriander but, my goodness, what has happened with your face?' She dusted her hands on her apron.

'Pattana, we need to sort it out, it looks very red,' said Hank, putting on some spectacles and going back to the drawer.

She looked horrified.

'White-water rafting,' I said sheepishly.

She gasped.

'Stupid, I know,' I said, shrugging my shoulders.

'Let me take a look.'

'Yes, Pattana used to be a nurse back home in Thailand. I'm looking for the plasters, sweetheart.'

'Here, I get them.' Pattana went to a different part of the kitchen and brought out a small red box. 'My goodness, such a mess.' She was shocked but laughed and darted around. I liked her, she seemed like fun, and they were an odd couple.

After Pattana disinfected my wounds, she put some more micropore stitches above my eye and cleaned the cut to my mouth with a cotton bud. We had dinner, which was the most fantastic meal I'd ever eaten in my life. The fish was huge and white and lay on my plate covered in a tasty chilli and coconut sauce, with carrot and coriander salad. I finished well before Hank and Pat, and perked up immediately.

'Are you sure you won't have a glass of red, Kerry? Brown Brothers is a good wine, you know.'

'I will now I've eaten, thanks, but only a small one, please.'

Pattana laughed.

After dinner she tidied around us and I thanked her for her excellent cooking.

Hank kissed her on the head and asked if she wouldn't mind seeing to things herself while we 'got down to the nitty gritty'.

I was loosening up already, and feeling happy and appreciative for the special care lavished on me.

'OK, Hank, this is lovely but I really want to know stuff now.'

'I'll get my file,' he said, putting his reading glasses back on from the chain round his neck.

'File?'

'Hank likes to be organised about everything,' said Pattana, laughing away again to herself.

Hank came back to the table with an orange folder and began examining his notes. 'Now listen, Kerry.' He shut the folder and pulled his glasses down onto his nose, looking over at me.

'Hank, this is driving me mad, what do you know?' I leant forward anxiously, drinking from my glass. The wine was the smoothest I had ever drunk, slipping down effortlessly, burning my stomach slightly with the chillies.

'This isn't all your stuff, by the way. I just like to keep notes so I remember things, that's all. I didn't want to miss anything, you understand?'

'Yes, but please tell me, this is killing me. Have you spoken to my mother or not?'

'I've spoken over the telephone with your mum's sister, your auntie.' He read off the file again.

'Fuck!' I quickly turned to Pattana, embarrassed. 'Sorry.'

'That's OK.' Pattana tutted in the background.

'A woman going by the name of Mary spoke to me and from what I can gather she's your mum's oldest sister, and she's married.'

'And is my mum here?'

Hank stared at me. 'Well.'

'Hank, don't be slow with her, she needs to know,' chided Pattana.

'Pat, I'm not playing around, I just don't want her to get hurt. Kerry, your mum is very resistant, she's fearful of meeting you. It's traumatic, you understand that?'

'What!' I shouted, ecstatic that I was now talking to the first person that had ever spoken to my mum, or at least a blood relative of hers.

'This Mary woman said that your mum has been terrified of this happening since the day she gave you away, worried that you might just show up.' Hank took his glasses on and off to emphasise points, but I knew it was nerves because he was unsure of how I would take all this. I didn't quite know how I felt about it, but I would settle for anything at this point, even just an acknowledgement that I did have a person somewhere who gave birth to me, that some part of me looked like.

'Did you tell them I was here?'

'No, I didn't. In fact, they asked that. I told them you were thinking of coming over, but so far were just trying different means of reaching them, or finding out something, and I was just someone you came across when you thought you'd try radio as a way of reaching people. For all they know, you are in still in England.' Hank's glasses were off for the last part. Pattana cocked her head to the side in sympathy.

'You sure?'

'Positive. I didn't want to frighten them off, you see. I wanted to get as much information as possible.' He stopped and read the wistful look on my face, then smiled. 'That's it, that's all we know for now.'

I could have cried, but swallowed it and got back to my questions. 'Is Mary her real name, I wonder? What about her second name?'

'Well, I'm presuming she wouldn't lie about a first name and she didn't tell me her second name.' He shrugged.

'OK.' I ran my hand through my hair, trying to think of what to make of everything and what plan of action to take. I needed one of those plastic boards on the wall with bits of card pinned to it that detectives use on TV.

'Got some other news that might disappoint you, I'm afraid, love.'

I braced myself for something along the lines of, she's going back to the UK this week.

'Your mother didn't marry the man you thought she did, the Duffy fella.'

'No?'

'Not according to Mary.'

'Well, how do you know she isn't double-bluffing?' It seemed to me that Hank was a pushover with this Mary woman.

'Well, I don't, but I just got the feeling that she was telling the truth. She said your mum did marry a military man, but not by the name of Duffy.'

I felt drained. This meant my search would be much harder, and completely ruled out the back-up plan of search by surname – if fate didn't do its magic this time, of course.

'Perhaps who ever told you it was Duffy was wrong; it could have just been a mistake on their part.' Hank smiled kindly in an attempt to console me. I thought back to the old lady on the doorstep in Newcastle, who gave me the information; at the time, she seemed reliable. Now, however, that seemed doubtful and I recast her in my mind as a confused old woman who'd sent me off on the wrong track with her muddled memory.

'Was the man my mum married Australian, even?' I was clutching at straws.

'I honestly don't know, love.' He sipped his wine. 'Like I said, she was resistant and kinda well' – he moved his hand around – 'worked up, you know?'

This was fairly bad news, and threw a spanner in the works, but I wasn't going to be put off that easily.

'Phone book.' I clicked my fingers. 'I should still check the Duffys out up here, in case she was lying.'

'Of course. It's the first thing I did. You're welcome to take a look yourself.' He pointed through to the hall. 'Only three in this area funnily enough, and a couple of pages for the rest of Brisbane.'

I looked at him quizzically.

'I called a couple but none of them knew what I was talking about. That means nothing because a hell of a lot of people are ex-directory.'

'That's right,' Pattana nodded.

'They could be lying as well.' I laughed a little, feeling that the obvious was being overlooked.

'Yes, they could, but I don't think so. One was an old lady who'd never been married, and the other two I could just tell were being honest.'

'OK, tell me the whole thing, please, from the start. About Mary coming to see you and everything she said.'

'Well, I got a call from the station that evening. You see, I do pre-records sometimes, so when the call about you went out, I was at home, yeah?'

I nodded.

'They said there were some people anxious to meet up with me, so I went in straight away and there they were. Almost as soon as I arrived, the eldest one, this Mary, asked me – quite aggressively, I have to say – how I knew about the baby.'

'The baby?' It was strange to hear me referred to as 'the baby', but they hadn't been living with me all these years; to them I was still the baby, I suppose. 'How many people came to see you that day?' Hank was frustrating me now, leaving little bits of information out that I could use as a lead in this case.

'Her husband, James, who was outside in the car.' He sipped on his wine again, which annoyed me this time.

'Sorry, what? Whose husband?' I moved my glass away and leant in.

'Mary's. She referred to the man in the car outside as James, her husband.'

'OK, Hank, don't miss out any information whatsoever when you're telling me this, please.' I became overanimated. 'I need to know every little detail. Who was there? The names. The vehicle registration. That kind of thing.'

'Sorry, love, but I think getting the plates is expecting a bit much, don't you?' He drank from his wine, went red-faced and waited for an answer.

I shrugged, because I didn't think it was too much to take down the car plates. But then, I had tunnel vision now, and all I could see was my faceless mother standing at the end of it. 'What did the car look like, then?'

'Uhm.' Hank pressed the palm of his hand to his head. 'White. A white station wagon of some kind, I think.'

'OK, OK. Who was there again?' I calmed down slightly.

'This Mary.'

'Uh-huh.' I nodded.

'James in the car, and a woman with Mary whom she referred to as a family friend.'

I looked questioning again. 'Family friend! That could have been *her*.'

'No way! I'm telling you, they were shit scared. There's no way your mum would just show up. They want to protect her.'

I felt sad again for a brief moment at the thought of my mother protecting herself from me, but consoled myself with the belief that when she met me, she would regret that feeling, and realise it was just fear of opening up the pain from her difficult past.

'What exactly did you say on air about me?' I took a drink of wine and sat back a bit.

'I told them I was passing on a message from a Joanna Thomson, who was looking for a Madeline Thomson, who married John Duffy in 1966, whom she believed was living somewhere in Australia, possibly Sydney, or Brisbane, or Melbourne even, and that if anyone knew anything, would they leave a message with the show.' He finished reading from the file. 'But I didn't use any surnames, because I felt that would be a little too intrusive, you know?'

Pattana and I both nodded.

'So why did they come forward if they didn't want to know me?' I didn't miss a trick.

'Perhaps they thought I might say more – like, mention your mother's name, which I would never have done, I have to say, because I don't think it's right. And anyhow you hadn't officially told me you were looking for your mother, even though I sensed as much.'

'Then what?' I got up and started walking round the table, taking my wine with me.

'Poor girl, look at her, Hank,' said Pattana, hands covered in soapy water, straining round every so often to see how I was taking things.

I felt awkward whenever Pattana showed concern. 'I'm all right, thanks, just excited. This is massive, you know? Just massive!'

'Tell her what happened after that, Hank.' Pattana looked solemn.

'Well, I thought that was the end of it until I got hold of you. But two days later, there was a knock at the door here and this Mary was there, looking very angry. She was with a tall quiet woman and they walked in, and this Mary lady started having a go at me. What business is it of mine? How I was an interfering busybody, how I should back off, and all that sort of stuff. I looked out and there was a bloke sitting in the car, maybe the husband or a brother I thought, I didn't get a look at him.'

'Jesus, Hank, why didn't you call me straight away? And how did they know where you lived, and who was the other woman with her? I bet it was her. Fuck, Hank!' I definitely needed the board now; there were too many characters involved to keep track of.

'Listen, love.' He took his glasses off and folded them away. 'I had nothing but your protection in mind during all of this. I felt from talking to you on the phone that you could easily be hurt by this, so I wanted to take it easy until I knew more about the situation. I felt a duty, can you understand that?'

At this point I felt that Hank was mistaking me for a fucking moron.

'What about the other woman, Hank?' I wanted to get back to more important matters.

'For the last time, love,' he sighed. But it was too important for me to feel guilty about asking him to go over the details again.

'I doubt if the woman with Mary was your mother, love, given the stink they kicked up about it all. I would have thought that she would have been kept well away. It's like how I felt about you, I wanted to protect you from it – they would have felt extremely protective over your mother.'

'Yeah, well, I don't want to be protected from the truth, thank you.' I felt slightly angry now, and was growing impatient.

'Unfortunately, the truth is often the very thing that people need protecting from the most.' Hank looked sad, glancing over his shoulder at Pattana.

'How did they know where you lived, Hank?' I got back to matters practical.

'It's not hard to track me down, love. I'm fairly well known around here.' He smiled.

'I wonder if they live in Brisbane?'

'Well, I don't know for sure but I'd say they did, based on the fact that they were at the station a few hours after I aired. I would say it's highly likely.'

'How come the woman gave you her name at all if they were so scared of everything?'

'Just politeness. People here are nice people. Besides, it was just a first name, and I said I don't talk to people and answer questions if I don't know who they are. That's when she introduced herself as Mary. I asked if she was a relative and she said she was, but it was none of my business and that she certainly wasn't the mother in question. I looked at the woman with her and she reassured me that she was a family friend.'

'And that was it?'

'You see what I mean, kid? I don't want you getting your hopes up, all this might lead you nowhere.'

'My hopes aren't down, if that's what you mean. An hour ago I knew nothing – now I know they are real, that she exists, that I was made by someone still living. Fuck, it's brilliant. Sorry.' Suddenly I was drinking from a glass that was half full for the first time.

'Tut, tut.' Pattana hung the dishcloth on the cooker.

'So that was it, you just said sorry for freaking them out, and then they left or what?'

'Not before threatening me.'

'Fuck.'

'They told me I'd caused enough trouble and if I didn't watch it, I'd be sorry.'

'Jesus.'

'Yes, Jesus indeed.'

'That's it, then?' I wasn't sure how to play things next, but I felt Hank was being overcautious and that there may be more to this case than met the eye.

'Well, I don't know but they were so resistant, I can't imagine them coming round.' Hank shrugged his shoulders.

'What will I do?' I was concerned but not panicked, for every day was a step nearer to meeting my mother and I wouldn't be deterred now by anything or anyone.

'I'm going to run you a nice hot bath. You need to soak your body, it will help it feel better,' smiled Pattana.

'That would be nice,' I said, closing my eyes and breathing deeply. A bath would be nice and would give me some time to think.

'Let's take our drinks to the porch and talk a little, then I think you should get some sleep. You look like you've been through the wars.'

'I have. I can't imagine sleeping tonight, though.'

Hank offered me a refill but I declined for what felt like the first time ever. I didn't need more wine. I felt high with excitement and hope.

'Relax, no hurry,' said Pattana, putting her hands on my shoulders, still warm from the dishes.

We chatted for a while, Hank being very patient and telling the story over and over until my bath was ready. I agreed with what he said in the truck on the way from the station. He did feel familiar, and we already felt like old friends.

I lay in the water looking up at the ceiling; I felt euphoric yet strangely calm. Nice classical piano music, maybe Chopin, drifted through from the lounge. I played at holding my breath under the water for as long as I could: if I held it for a minute then I would meet my mother. I hadn't played this game since I was a child. The bathroom was nicely tiled, all clean and white, with little pieces of driftwood and shells lining the edge of the bath. I imagined my mother to be somewhere near, in the same city as me, the closest we had been for many years. Perhaps she was in her bath right now. I felt round my face and cheekbone, checking the swelling, and wondering what my real mum would make of the state of me, if we met before my wounds healed.

My mind drifted back to Anaya, whom I had temporarily forgotten. I started to miss her, and longed to have a new, improved night together. Maybe after my search was complete and I'd changed, I could meet up with her. I thought about her sliding around on top of me.

After my bath Pattana showed me to my room.

'Hank asleep,' she said, blowing out the candle on an oil burner next to where I was sleeping, which was a fold-down sofabed at the side porch extension, with bamboo blinds all around to keep out the daylight.

'You like the smell?' she asked.

'Oh yes, very much, thank you.' I stood in my bath towel, waiting for her to go so I could get into bed.

'Geranium and lavender help you sleep and feel calm.'
I smiled.
'Goodnight, Kerry, I hope you feel peace.'
'I'm all right, really, but thanks for tonight, it was lovely.'
She smiled and left.

It was cosy in the room, which was full of books and an old card table. A strange item hung from the roof above me, made up of feathers and string and glistening wire stuff. I sat looking up at a gap in the blinds through the glass, hoping that the room wasn't sun-facing in the morning. I pulled out my notebook that I'd hardly written in, and scribbled away all the information I could remember from Hank's findings. I filled an entire page with Marys and question marks. I was not convinced that revealing only a Christian name would make her untraceable. I had ideas about what to do with that. I switched off the lamp on the card table beside me and lay back. A mild breeze blew the wind chimes outside; the clanking felt comforting. I got Anaya's hairband from my bag and put it around my wrist. I would get some sleep now, then in a few hours, when I could be sure that Hank and Pat were sound asleep, I would creep round the house and find Hank's folder and look at it for myself. Despite his kindness, I felt there was something in it he was hiding from me.

CHAPTER **THIRTY-THREE**

'Hello, Kerry, good morning,' a voice sang above me.

I thought it was the ice-cream-van man in my dream; he looked like Hank. His van was covered in blue paintings of dragons. I was standing in line, my grandfather was there, but everyone else was a zombie slowly moving to the van. I was trying to get the attention of the old man serving before the zombies reached the line. The van was pulled by a unicorn; I tried to get on but kept sliding off, my flip-flops not helping.

I opened my eyes.

'Kerry.' It was Pattana giggling.

'Oh my God, what time is it?' I sat up, and felt the bruising around my face immediately.

'You slept well, it's almost nine o'clock, and how you feel? How is your face?' She placed a reddish drink next to my bed.

'The best I've slept in ages, feel stiff but much better, thanks.' I pulled myself up. I felt good if a little disappointed at myself for not finding the folder.

'I bring watermelon juice, very good for you.'

I gulped it down in one go. 'Mmmm, that's fantastic.'

'You dream?' Pattana smiled away.

'Yeah, loads of dreams.'

'The dream-catcher, that's why.' She pointed to the weird feather-wire thing above me.

'Oh, right.' I didn't want to dismiss her thing by telling her I dreamt all the time, even when I was awake.

I heard a faint bell every few seconds coming from another part of the house. 'What's that?'

'That's Hank, he's chanting. We are Buddhists, we chant every day.'

'Right, I see.' I smiled and nodded. I hadn't met any Buddhists before and didn't know much about it, except that it involved lengthy solitary praying of some sort.

'I gotta go out now, you take your time. Hank will show you around, OK?'

'Thank you so much, Pattana, you're very kind.'

'Not a problem.' She left, taking the empty glass with her. I lay thinking about what to do. I didn't really have very much to go on, and only had three days at the most until the others got here, when I'd have to move to group accommodation and spend my time selling with them. So I would have to maximise my time at Hank and Pat's and do as much ground-work as possible, while enjoying the comforts on offer, which were the best I'd ever experienced.

I put on some clothes and went through to the house. I boiled the kettle and went in search of Hank. The bell clanging was louder as I crept up the stairs; I snuck up gently, not wanting to step onto a creaky floorboard and disturb him. I could hear him speaking in a different language, saying the same thing over and over, half singing it, with the bell that sounded like the old-fashioned kind someone rings by hand. The sounds were coming from the third room at the end, where the door was slightly ajar.

I went back down the stairs to the room before the kitchen, which was closed. As long as I could hear the bell, I knew I was safe to look around. I slowly pushed open the door and felt for a light switch as the curtains were still drawn. As I had thought, it turned out to be a study. There were certificates for physiotherapy and massage on the wall with the name Frank White on them, mostly dated from the early eighties to eighty-seven. There was a map of China in a frame, and a picture of an old lady in a garden surrounded by bright flowers, whom I took to be Hank's mother. The bell stopped and my heart thumped, but then it started up again, with Hank repeating something starting with 'nam' and ending in 'kyo'.

I turned my attention to the desk. There were many folders

on a shelf above but none of them orange. I tried the drawers of a filing cabinet behind the door but it was locked. The bell hadn't chimed in the last few seconds; I put out the light and snuck back through to the kitchen as quickly as I could without creaking. I switched the kettle back on and waited as Hank made his way down stairs.

He was wearing a white medical top buttoned up the side of the neck, white trousers and slip-on white sandals, his hair held back in a ponytail.

'So it's all black and white with you, Hank, isn't it? No in between.'

'Good morning, love, I like your style. You're a smart little thing, aren't you?' He laughed heartily.

'Oh, you know.' I made myself some tea and sat down. Hank joined me, opening up his mail with a letter opener. He had his glasses down on his nose again, peering over them. He looked much bigger than the day before; I could see his build more in his white tunic, and he was well built and muscular-looking. As he stretched forward to pick up some more mail from the table I could see the bottom of a tattoo under the white of his sleeves, which stopped at his elbow.

'Oh my God! Have you got a tattoo?'

'I'm afraid so. Got it done when I was a kid in the Navy.'

'Can I see it?'

'If you like.' He put down the mail and the opener and rolled up his sleeve. 'Got it done in Thailand, we all got them done, it was the thing to do at the time.'

I sat speechless, looking at the faded mini-sunrise, which began at his shoulder and spilled out over most of his upper arm.

'You all right?'

'Where do I begin? This is getting more and more bizarre.'

'Well, I'm sorry, love, you might have to hold that thought until later. I've got to get to work.'

I realised that, with me being so preoccupied with the other stuff, I didn't know much else about Hank, apart from his radio show once a week.

'Why don't you come with me into town? I'll drop you off and you can see the clinic, then have a wander round town if you like. I could meet you at lunchtime, if you fancy?'

I really wanted to stay at home and root around but I didn't want to be impolite, so I quickly got dressed and jumped in the car. It was, after all, right to stick with Hank; he wore the eagle and would therefore lead me to my mother.

Good old don't-have-to-do-much fate plan, I thought, as he put on another dreadful country tape.

Hank was a physiotherapist and sports injury masseur, while Pattana ran the office, booking appointments, answering the phone and doing the books. Their premises were a run-down, cramped little place between two shops somewhere in town. It was called 'Healing Centre' and advertised physiotherapy and reflexology on handwritten signs stuck on the window, with rainbows drawn on the top in coloured pencils.

Inside it was hard to move around with three people. Pattana sat behind a tiny desk with barely any surface space left, an enormous old-fashioned till taking up most of it. There were shelves selling crystals and incense. Hank showed me around, proud of his empire.

'Took me years to build this up,' he said, leading me into the treatment room. It was cold in the room and badly in need of a paint job. On the wall were charts of the body with lines directed into various points, and pictures of feet divided into areas in different colours, with names of organs written in them. In the middle of the room was the massage bench, next to it a table of clean towels. The room had a bluish light to it, from a half-torn piece of blue plastic cellophane taped on the striplight above.

'This is great,' I said politely, feeling like a child going to her father's work for the day.

'You like it?'

'Yeah, I do.' It was nice being with Hank and Pattana, they were very warm and generous, but I couldn't afford to play visitor for much longer. I would have to move things along. I had no idea what Hank wanted with me if he couldn't help with the search, but I had an increasing sense that he knew more than he was letting on.

'Hank, can I talk to you?'

'Hang on.' He popped his head next door and asked Pattana what time his first client was.

'Not until ten.'

'OK, thanks, love.' He closed the door of the treatment room and gestured for me to sit up on the massage table. He moved some things from a small stool in the corner and sat down, arms folded, all ears.

'Hank, I told you last night, my friends with the paintings are arriving in Brisbane in the next few days and I have to join them, and they're only here for a short while after that. So I really have to find my mother. I don't want to stay here when they're gone if she's not here. I told you my visa is running out, and I would have to find someone to marry if I want to stay in the country, so I need to know everything you can tell me. Please, Hank.'

'OK, OK. Listen, I know you're anxious, anybody in your shoes would be, and I want to do everything I can to help, honest I do. But I don't know any more. I think you should stay for as long as you can and get some rest, and I'll tell you another thing, I'm going to work on those shoulders of yours. They've taken some impact with your accident.'

'Why wouldn't you let me see the folder, Hank? What are you hiding?'

'I like to keep track of things, so I wrote it all down. I don't want there being any complications and me not being able to be clear about things, that's all.'

'Do you believe in fate, Hank?'

'I believe a great many things and fate is definitely one of them.'

I grew excited, having hardly met anybody who agreed with me on this subject. I thought Hank and Joyce Cane would make a great couple, better than Fritz, but that would leave Pattana. I couldn't see Pattana and Fritz together.

'Sixty-five, when you were born, isn't it?'

I nodded.

'Year of the snake.'

'What does that mean?'

'Well, the snake is very cunning, very sneaky, slithering around into people's lives trying to find out stuff.' He laughed again, taking the subject away from the folder, no doubt. I recalled my snake behaviour on the beach in Port Macquarie when I drunkenly mistrusted the others, and crawled round the sand on my belly trying to hide from them. Perhaps I had snake leanings. But all this new Chinese stuff was confusing me and interfering with my search. I didn't need symbols at this point, I needed a phone number or an address.

But Hank had the eagle, so I was obliged to stay for the time being.

He said, 'We'll think of a plan tonight, I promise. Meanwhile, why don't you wander around, buy a map and meet us back here at five? It's a short day today. Bank holiday.'

'OK.' I swung my legs like a ten-year-old.

'You'll find plenty to do, it's a wonderful city, Brisbane. And the snake is very resourceful.' He hissed and wiggled his arm, laughing.

'Great,' I said, jumping down.

I wandered around the centre, which was different from Sydney, in that it looked newer, and hillier, until I found a café I liked the look of. I sat outside and ordered poached eggs on toast, a pineapple smoothie and tea. I was feeling half recovered from the Scotty's Head incident, and my system felt rested from the bender. I wanted to be fully OK by the time I met up with the group, so that I could have a few beers and a laugh with them. The swelling had gone down considerably on my face, but the bruising and cuts were still bad, leaving me no choice but to stick to my white-water rafting excuse when I took up selling again.

I brought out my notebook and drew up a plan. I counted my money; I had one hundred and fifty dollars in cash that Jim had advanced me, and some loose change. I had no idea how much the company owed me, as I'd stopped keeping a record of it in my notebook of late, but it couldn't be more than another hundred bucks. I wrote two lists, one practical and one emotional. The practical one read:

Do washing.
Buy mouth-ulcer gel.
Send airmail to granddad.

Buy phone card.
Buy maps. Learn local area for good places to sell.
Don't drink before food. Must keep head clear to think.

My emotional list only consisted of:

Find mother, follow all leads.
Keep spirits up.

I paid for my breakfast and left to find a chemist. I had a sore mouth, as some of the cuts from the fight had ulcerated. I paid for some mouth gel while worrying about the possibility that my mother might be in a state other than Queensland or even New South Wales. I lingered at the counter of the chemist wondering whether to buy some Remegel or not, because my stomach was burning since I'd had the chillies with the red wine the night before.

I couldn't deal with having to find out about all the other states in Australia. I didn't know how many there were, but decided if it came down to it, Jim would help by looking it up or I would go to a library or something. The phone rang behind the counter. A staff member shouted to the pharmacist about a delivery, the pharmacist shouted back to get where he was calling from and I began thinking about Hank, and how he was contacted by this Mary woman at the radio station, wondering whether the calls went through some kind of switchboard that might have logged area codes. I jotted down in my notebook to follow that line of enquiry when I got back to Hank's later.

The day dragged. I bought a map and lay under a tree in a park, examining the areas with the widest roads, which I took to represent comfortable suburban areas, and good places to sell. It was hard to concentrate on anything, knowing that there were officially alive and breathing family members out there somewhere, perhaps nearby, and I couldn't do anything about it right now.

I wandered around some record stores, bought an airmail letter and went to a bar for strictly lemonade only, while I wrote to my grandfather. I told him I was bored with the hot weather, and found people to be friendly but that I was starting to miss him too much, and that I was trying to find what I was looking for and couldn't come back until I did, but wished that he was with me, and how the warmth here would be good for his arthritis. I imagined a nurse sitting on his bed reading my words aloud to him, and hoped it would be her and not my other mother who would do it, as I wanted to hide my search from her. Despite how badly we had fought over the years, I didn't want to hurt her. I would protect her from my quest to find my birth mother, until the time was right for me to tell her. I thought about all the protecting going on from everyone around me, including myself now, and wondered if it really was protection. Or just fear of the truth.

I posted the letter, feeling like a new improved person, being so in control that I could make use of the postal service for a change. On the way back to Hank's, I stopped off at a grocery store and bought the ingredients for one of the only two meals I knew how to cook, deciding that cooking for Hank and Pattana would be the right thing for me to do, and also a way of feeling able to ask Hank for the use of his phone, if I left him money.

I arrived back at the clinic too early for going home, as Hank was still with a client. I helped Pattana stick stamps on envelopes until the groans and cries of pain from the room ceased, and a big rugby-playing type came out of the room, paid and limped off.

Hank was a little more downbeat on the journey back; I put it down to the end of a hard day at work. Pattana chatted away, oblivious to his fatigue. I asked him if I could have a look at his phone book when we got home, as he'd offered the night before. But he suddenly seemed unsure whether he had thrown it out or not. As we pulled into the drive I felt part of their domestic routine already, and wondered how it happened that I ended up in short-burst situations of speeded-up familiarity with people I'd only just met.

I told them I was cooking pasta and ratatouille. They seemed concerned, and I felt the need to reassure them that although my repertoire was limited, it did, however, taste very good. I helped them unload some stuff from the back of the car and carried it into the house. I was starting to feel the need for a

'Why are you helping me?' conversation, and so planned to have it later, once we'd eaten. All I had, as always, was my instinct, and so far that was telling me that something was not quite right here.

CHAPTER THIRTY-FOUR

'That bone just under the eye, part of cheekbone.' I winced with pain as Hank prodded around as gently as he could. He insisted that he take a look at it after dinner, as he felt it was looking worse today. 'Ugh.'

'It's broken.'

'What can I do?'

'Nothing, it's too delicate, you just have to let it heal itself.'

'And the rest?'

'Your ribs aren't broken or cracked, just badly bruised. The rest looks nasty but you'll live.'

I sat at the table after dinner, drinking some wine with Hank and Pattana. Hank stood over me, holding my face in his hands in the direction of the light.

'Such a shame to do such a thing to your face, it's so pretty.' Pattana contorted her face while Hank prodded.

'Yes, it was stupid.' I was starting to believe the white-water rafting story myself, and even pictured Jim at the front of the boat with the man from the rafting centre, all of us screaming madly as it bounced down mini falls. I said, 'Hank, could I please look at your phone book?'

Pattana began tidying around us.

'Sure. Might have to have a good dig around first. Would you mind if we sat outside for a bit and let your lovely cooking digest?'

'Sure,' I said, going along with it, fascinated to see what he'd do next. He opened a cupboard, brought out a wooden box and took a cigar from it, running it under his nose, savouring the smell.

Hank and I sat on deckchairs out on the back porch. It was getting dusky and Hank put on some lights that were strung through the trees.

'This is my little haven,' he said, putting his feet up on a sawn-off tree-stump stool and lighting up. 'Everybody needs a sanctuary, you know?'

'I guess so,' I said, longing for the day I would have one.

'What's it like back home?'

'Grey, I suppose, but familiar grey.'

'My grandparents were Irish, came over here after the First World War.'

'I think my grandparents were too.'

'We're all from the Irish somehow, kid.' He laughed, staring out to the end of the garden, to the city lights in the distance.

'Except for Pattana.'

'Yeah, not Pattana, she is one hundred per cent Thai. You ever been to Thailand?'

'No. I should really drop off on the way back but I'm not really a traveller, you see. I'm on a mission.'

'A mission to save your soul, eh?' He chuckled.

'Or to find it. How did you meet Patt?'

'Well, she's not a Thai bride, if that's what you mean.'

'I don't even know what that means.'

He swung his head round. 'You're kidding?'

'No, why would I be?'

'Well, there're some blokes who can't get a woman through the normal ways, shall we say, so they buy themselves a Thai lady. There's millions of them that want to get away and have what they think is a better life, and an Aussie, British or sometimes American is the only way.'

'But I thought it was a great place, Thailand?'

'It is, it's very beautiful, but some people are so poor they have to get out. Same old story.'

'Were you in the Navy there?'

'Yes, I was, for a long time. Pattana is not my first wife, though.'

'Oh.'

'I was with someone when I was very young and we had a child.' He sighed deeply and played around with his feet, trying to get them to pick up an old beer can next to the tree stool. 'Yep, mucked that up but there you go.'

'How old is your child now?'

'She would be about twenty-six, I guess. I haven't seen her since she was a toddler.' He played with his cigar ash, flicking it with his fingers and turning the cigar round. I left a deliberate pause in the conversation.

'I'm lying. I've never met her.' He leant forward and looked straight at me. 'Her mother gave her up for adoption, Kerry, just like you. I know it's awful, and I worry, I worry that there are others.'

I must have looked horrified.

'I know, I know, it's terrible. It's what happened in those days, you know. Women got pregnant and they couldn't keep the baby. It's wrong but that's how it was.'

'Oh God, this is fucked. What's wrong with everyone? Is anyone normal?' I couldn't honestly say I was surprised at what I was hearing; it seemed that anyone I ran into these days had some other life that had produced children, a life that they were running away from.

'Hey, maybe you're my father, Hank, you ever think about that?' I was joking, but it was all so ridiculously closely linked.

'I'll be honest, when you first called, I thought that it might be you. I mean, her, the baby I never knew. I've always expected a call at some point.' He laughed the comment away.

I didn't. I felt sad again. 'So that's why you're so sympathetic to my real mum and her family?' It made sense now, all his talk of what a shock it must be for her.

'Well, the curious thing is, I feel for all of you. I know what it's like to be afraid of your past catching up with you, because you feel such guilt and such a sense of failure. But on the other hand a huge part of me also wants to know this little girl I made, and know how she is and what she looks like.'

'Look, Hank, do you ever wonder why we've been thrown together like this? I mean, you were at your sister's when I called, your name isn't even Duffy, yet I phoned you, and the radio, I mean, come on, why?'

'Of course I've thought about it, and I know what it means.'

'Well?'

'We are all on this earth to learn about what we did wrong the last time.'

'What, like reincarnation and all that stuff?'

'Yes, past lives. Each time we give it another go and see if we can do any better, but there's some stuff that feels familiar in our current lives. That's what I felt with you when I picked you up at the station, like I'd met you already – that's past lives, kid, that's what I believe.'

'Oh God, I don't want lots of lives, not unless I have no feeling or memory of the ones before, or not unless they're easier than this one.'

Hank laughed like a man pretending to be Santa Claus. 'You're a young soul, that's why you find it so hard. You're new to this, this is maybe your first life.'

'No, I find it hard because my mother left me when I was born, and that's fucked up, and I've felt odd and broken since I found out, although I felt odd before anyway and that just confirmed it.'

'You'll find your way, but you and I were meant to meet. It must be to help you and it must be to help me, help us both move on in this life.'

'You really believe this stuff?'

Hank took a few puffs on his cigar before answering. 'Yes, and you know what? You do too – you just won't admit it to yourself.'

'Want to know what I think?' I said, like an old hand.

'Go ahead, but you won't tell me something I don't know.'

'I think desperate people throw themselves into the paths of strangers, because they are the lost ones, who need to search, and to search you must be open to others, and open people open themselves to like-minded lost people who too take comfort from their paths crossing.' I went over what I'd said, not sure if I'd made any sense.

Hank started laughing again. 'How did you work that out?'

'Because I've had quite a bit of a life already, OK?' I liked what I said; I liked myself for the stuff I came out with at times. I felt hopeful again. I liked being with Hank and Pat, I loved the people I got to meet, all the strangers who were most kind, unlike my experiences with most of my own family members.

Maybe I had read Hank wrongly; maybe he just didn't want me to get hurt, like he said, or maybe he wanted me to hang around because of his past-life feelings, and his lost child. He had his chanting and his crystals, Pattana had the dream-catcher, Scotty had his bong, Anaya had her aloofness and I had my wine. We all had our things to get by with, what the fuck.

'Let's open another bottle, eh? Pat's having a soak – she won't know.'

'Doesn't she let you drink?'

'It's not like that. She doesn't like me to overdo it. I guess I did when she first knew me – it was the Navy you know, we were all drinking. I just don't like to overdo things now. I like it quiet.'

'I'm good at quiet drinking,' I said.

'Excellent, then we shall have another.' He got up and left, rubbing his knees as he stood.

I stared up into the Brisbane night, under the same sky as my mother.

'Hank?' I asked, when he got back.

'Yes, love?'

'I need you to be honest with me about what you know. I know you're lying.'

He was standing holding the wine; I could see his chest heave up and down as I spoke to him. He let out a long breath through his mouth.

'What makes you think I'm not telling the truth?'

'Let me see your phone book and I'll show you.'

He began taking out the cork.

'Don't be daft. Why do you want to do that just now?'

'Hank, please get me one and I'll show you.'

He stopped what he was doing, put down the bottle and walked back indoors to the study. I was nervous. I didn't want to look a fool, but if my instincts were right, I wouldn't. He walked back shaking his head and threw the phone book down on the grass in front of me.

'Okayee,' I said, flicking through to the Ds. He continued opening the wine, and refilled our glasses.

'As I thought.' I dragged it out like Colombo, certain I had found no Duffys, until I turned a page, and found three at the top.

'As you thought, nothing.'

We laughed together. He was right, he was telling the truth, there were only three Duffys. I was way off track with my last hunch. He just laughed and laughed, until it annoyed me a little.

'Jesus, kid, is that how that mind of yours works?' Hank coughed and spluttered and laughed some more.

'What – what's so funny?' I laughed some, to be friendly, then I became serious and stood up. 'You're not getting off that lightly. I know you're lying about something, and tomorrow I'm going to leave and follow my own line of enquiries, until I get what I want.' I felt pretty smug. Hank had stopped laughing, and became as serious as me. 'Listen, I didn't come all this way to get fucked around. I'll find out with or without you, but I will find out, at any cost, do you understand me, Hank?'

'I do. OK, just keep it down, love.'

'Don't fuck about, Hank, please. I am really grateful to you and Pattana for letting me stay here and everything, but I won't let people mess me around with the facts. I was half-arsed before about finding her, but lately I need to do that more than anything. I won't stop now, until I find out who and where she is.'

'Sssh.' Hank pointed to the steamed-up bathroom window upstairs. I was leaning over him, bending down. 'OK, OK, I think you should calm down.' He did the flagging hands sign for slow down.

'Calm down! I'm trying to find the person that fucking made me, and right now you are the only living soul that knows more than I do.'

'OK, OK, fair enough. Sit down, love, sit down, there's stuff you need to know.'

CHAPTER **THIRTY-FIVE**

I didn't move from the spot until Hank began to explain his big mystery to me.

'Look, I lied about Pattana,' he said. I rolled my eyes. 'We've not been together for as long as I've made out. I didn't meet her in the Navy, I met her here, OK?'

I nodded, mystified at the connection between the details of how they got together and me.

'About ten years ago, no, not about, I know it was ten years ago, I got a girl pregnant. She was young, seventeen, although to be fair she had always claimed to be twenty, but that's another story.'

My heart began pounding in anticipation of some head-fucking announcement that would knock me off my feet. 'Fucksake, how many children have you got out there exactly?'

'I know, I know, but ten years ago I was a very different person, Kerry. I was very unhappy with myself, had been all my life, and I drank a bit too much. It was just after my first divorce and I was really low. Things are very different now, very different, and I'm very happy with Pat. I'm a changed person and—'

'Anyway and ...' I was impatient and increasingly anxious that I might perhaps be related to this nutcase unravelling before me. After everything I'd heard so far it wouldn't have surprised me.

'I had to move away from the area. People gossiped and I was very unpopular. My name then was different, it was Frank Coleman. I had some trouble when people found out, and I owned a shop at the time, a small business. It got in the local paper, because her uncle and her brother burnt the shop down and got charged with arson. Well, the girl kept the kid and I had to move away and start again, different name.' He looked up remorsefully. 'When I tried to help you initially I didn't think I'd get involved. Thought I'd maybe get some information for you, a phone number and I'd pass it on, and I wanted to help, really I did. With hindsight, maybe I shouldn't have, but I felt responsible, probably because I skirted responsibility years ago with my own situation. Can you understand that?'

Hank kept a watch on the bathroom window, lowering his voice every so often.

'Of course I can. I'm not stupid.' Hank *was* a lovely man, but I found it disappointing to learn that he too, like so many others, abandoned a child of his own, and I found it hard to be as sympathetic as he would have liked me to be. I just stared at him blankly throughout his confession.

'But I wasn't thinking. I thought it was all forgotten about, but when the people you're looking for got in touch, and I found out they knew who I was, I just wanted to back off.'

'Shit, so they remembered you from before?'

'Exactly. So they started threatening me, that if I didn't butt out they'd cause trouble for me, and I don't want to hurt Pattana with any of this.'

'So you weren't going to tell me.'

'I didn't know what I was going to do, to be honest, and I still don't. I mean, I told Pat about you and that I wanted to help, but I got scared when that lot turned up and started getting heavy with me, so I thought maybe if you came here and I told you a little bit of information, you might either be satisfied with that and decide to leave it, or not bother turning up at all. I don't know. I've been so worried, to be honest, I've been trying to not think about it.'

I looked at him, thinking he'd lost his mind.

'I know, I know. Crazy.' He looked at me directly. 'Kerry, seriously, aside from all my problems, they are very pissed off. They're very protective of your mother, whoever she is. I know it's hard to accept and it's wrong, but they don't want to meet you. To them and to her, you are a terrible secret, I suppose.'

Nothing affected me about what he was saying. It didn't hurt me in the way he worried it would. I was more shocked at how people were trading in lies about children they'd made. I was also determined that whether my mother liked it or not I was going to meet her, with or without her knowing. It was all something she'd thank me for in the end.

'Where did you live before, when all this happened?'

'Ferny Hills, the other side of Brisbane, but it was ten years ago.'

'The chances are that if they remembered you, then they probably still live there.' I started looking through the phone book. 'And you know nothing else about them, no more names, nothing? Please, Hank, I need you to be honest, I really do.'

'No, honestly, that's all I know.' He put his hand on his chest. Maybe because he was a Buddhist, which I thought must give him some kind of integrity, I believed him. I don't know why, but I did.

I lay looking up at the dream-catcher, trying to figure out why Hank would encourage me to come here then withhold information from me. It made no sense whatsoever, if I was honest with myself. I was glad Hank had levelled with me, obviously, but all the same thought it best to rely on myself for the next part. I planned to make some calls in the morning and move this situation along, hoping to attract no more flaky people in the process.

I lay back with my hands behind my head thinking about Anaya again, wondering when I would see her again. Then I thought about my real mother and wondered if she had a suntan like me. Somehow, despite the load on my mind and the strangeness of the evening, I drifted off.

The morning started the same way as the day before. Pattana brought me a drink, tea this time, while Hank chanted away upstairs. She asked me about my dreams again, but this time I had nothing to report.

'Your mind,' she said, tapping her temples, 'too busy with all the other things you worry about just now.' Then she ruffled my hair, and left ahead of Hank for work.

I got up quickly as soon as the door closed and sneaked into Hank's study without touching my tea. I tried his filing cabinet but it was locked, so I started looking around for a key, all the time keeping track of the chanting, ready to race back through at any break in it. I ran my hand along the top of the door frame and knocked something off that fell onto the ground behind the cabinet. I crouched down and slipped my hand in between it and the wall and scrabbled about as best I could. I found the key and quickly opened up the cabinet. The orange folder lay flat in the top drawer under other paper stuff. Hank went on upstairs.

'Nam you ho rangy kyo.'

I could see the notes Hank had made about the phone conversation. He had scribbled my name over and over in pencil; next to it was written 'Ferny Hills', the area we had talked about. And the words 'Mary, sister of mother' written next to a question mark. So far, from what I could see, Hank had told me everything he knew. The chanting stopped suddenly and a door closed upstairs. I took the piece of paper, put the folder back in the cabinet and shut the drawer, being careful to lock it. But before I had a chance to put the key back on top of the door frame, the phone rang in the study, making me jump. I closed the door and ran back to my bedroom. I could hear Hank moving down the stairs to answer it.

'Kerry!'

'Coming!' I shouted, breathless from the adrenalin. I walked back through with my tea, trying my best to appear casual.

'It's your friend, Jim.' Hank looked at me, and mouthed was I OK, to which I nodded and smiled.

I took the phone. 'Hey, Jim, how are you?' I could hear traffic from where Jim was calling.

'Yeah, good, good. How's you, more to the point?' It was good to hear his familiar voice.

'Yeah, better thanks, but I'll tell you everything when I see you, yeah?'

'You sure now? You sound odd.' I had my eyes on Hank

who stayed in the study, which made me nervous in case he tried to look for his key.

'No, I'm not, just at someone else's house, you know?'

Hank turned round at that point.

'Well, listen, we've made an early start so we'll be in Brisbane in a couple of hours, OK?'

'How's Scotty?'

'He's a pain in the arse again, so – much better. Dropping him at a friend of his up there. He wants to stay there until he's all fixed before he heads back down the coast.'

'So what's the plan?'

'We'll be staying at the One World backpackers', on Highgate Hill. From around, let's say, twelve – OK?'

'Sounds good. OK, see you soon.'

'Yeah, take care and good luck.'

'Thanks, Jim.' I put down the phone.

'Is that your friends arriving, then?' asked Hank, opening some mail.

'Yep, so I'll be meeting up with them today and staying where they are.'

'Shame, feel as though we were just getting to know one another.'

'Yeah, I know, but I'll be in the city for a while, so I'll drop by, OK?'

'Sure, sure, that would be good. What are you going to do about the other stuff?'

'Don't know just yet, have a think. I'll let you know later, yeah?'

'Yeah sure, but, Kerry, I think you should have a think about everything, talk to your friends. Don't rush into anything, you with me?'

'Yep.' I smiled and nodded, trying to get us both out of the study. 'I'd better get my stuff together.' As I walked towards the door, the phone rang again, giving me just enough time to slip the key up on top of the door for the second or two Hank had his back turned. I smiled and walked out.

Hank drove slowly into town with some boring Jim Reeves' cassette blaring. Still, I was happy to have music as a way of avoiding much talk with him. We reached the backpackers' where he had agreed to drop me and we pulled up outside.

'Now, Kerry, I mean it, if there's anything you need and I mean anything, you know where to find me.' He pulled up the handbrake and patted my thigh twice.

'Thank you, Hank, for all your hospitality. Please say thanks to Pattana, won't you?'

'I will, love, look after yourself, and good luck round the houses.'

I dragged my folder and bag out from the back seat and got out, leaning in through the window for the final goodbye.

'Listen, before I head back down to Sydney, I'll drop in and see you and Pat and let you know how things are.'

'I'd like that very much, Kerry, and do you know what?'

'Oh God, what now?'

He laughed. 'No, don't worry, nothing bad. I've decided after all this that I'm going to talk to Pat about everything.'

'I think that's a good thing, well done.'

'You reckon?' He winked.

'Definitely.'

'You see, Kerry, we were meant to meet for a reason. Guess this must be part of mine.'

I winked back and patted the roof as he drove off tooting.

I found a pay phone with a phone book not too far from where I was and began calling the Duffys as a starting point, just to make sure. The first two, a Mr and Mrs N. Duffy and a Mr D.M. Duffy didn't answer; the third one, a Miss R. Duffy, was an old woman, just like Hank had said.

'Hello, sorry to bother you but I'm looking for a Mrs Madeline Duffy, formerly Madeline Thomson, or her sister Mary someone.'

'No, there's no Mary or Madeline here. Just me.'

'OK, well, thanks all the same.'

Then it came to me, and I cursed myself for not acting on it sooner. I had in all my time here failed to follow any leads as far as RSLs went. I remembered Barbara and Norman, the old couple I had encountered when I first began selling, who first told me about the Royal Servicemen's Leagues that were all over Australia. If my mother had settled here with an ex-servicemen, then surely they were members of one in Brisbane.

I abandoned the Duffy list in favour of directory enquiries, which I hoped would supply me with the numbers of all Brisbane RSLs.

'You kidding?' said the whiney Australian voice on the other end. 'Do you know how many RSLs there are here?'

'How many?'

'Well, we have two hundred and fifty sub-branches alone in Queensland. That's bowling clubs, social clubs, the lot. It's a massive organisation throughout the whole of Australia.'

I felt overwhelmed. 'OK, how many social clubs in Brisbane only?'

'Forty.'

I sighed. 'Look, give me the first four.'

I took them down and hung up. I panicked. There was no time to go through everything I needed to in the few days I had in Brisbane. I thought about staying on after the others had gone but couldn't bear the idea of trying to find another job and place to live, and new friends and all that stuff, although I was sure I could have stayed on with Hank and Pat.

My mind raced over what to do next. I thought about asking the entire group to take, maybe, so many phone numbers each and go to separate booths and make the enquiries. My fate plan was wearing thin; it looked like hard work ahead, and hard work was and always had been my enemy.

I didn't know why I'd asked the operator to give me four numbers, rather than three or six or any other amount; maybe it was because it seemed not too many to ask for on the call, but enough to work with; but mostly I think it was because my grandfather's birthday was on the 4th November.

I lit a cigarette and tried the first two. On the first call, I tried out an Australian accent.

'Oh yeah, hello, love.' I deepened my voice and used 'love' to sound older. But the man on the other end seemed a lot older, which made me feel that my use of 'love' was inappropriate.

'Yes, I'm wondering if you can help me, I'm trying to track down an old school friend called Madeline Thomson, that's her maiden name, but I can't remember her husband's first name so I can't find her number, but her married name is Duffy.'

'Oh yeah, and how can I help?'

'Sorry, yeah, I think she may be a member there. I moved away a long time ago when we were first married.'

'And her husband was in the forces, you say?'

'Yes, he was, but it's the name I've forgotten and I've lost touch with our other friend.'

'What's your name?'

I looked outside for clues, and saw a Sue Ryder charity shop across the road. 'It's Kerry Ryder.'

'Hang on, Kerry; I'll see what I can do.' He went away for a minute then returned. 'Nope, sorry, can't help. Had a look at the members' book and there are no Duffys and I can't help you with the maiden name, sorry.'

'OK, thank you all the same.'

I hung up and tried the next one, which was an answer-phone; I didn't leave a message. Then I called the other two, going through the same routine as the first, but with no joy, as they too reported having nobody by that name. Then I gave up on that approach.

I decided to go back to the name pages in the book and exhaust that before trying again with the RSLs, which would have to be done another day when I could sit down some-where comfortable and get through all the calls. Then I came across a club listed as 'Ferny Hills British Working Men's Club'.

My heart was thumping. This would be an extremely long shot to some people, but to me, it felt like the next piece of the puzzle, and that it was all falling nicely into place. I dialled. It rang twice before a woman answered.

'Ferny Hills.'

'Hello, is the manager or club secretary there, please?'

'Hang on.' I could hear the phone being put down on the table. I hadn't exactly worked out what I was going to say, so this gave me some time.

THE NAKED DRINKING CLUB · 329

'How can I help?' said an older man's voice.

'Hello there, my name is Sue Cook' – a mixture of Sue Ryder and Captain Cook, which I'd thought of at the last minute – 'and I'm looking for an old friend of mine, Mary. Except I know her and her sister Madeline from their maiden name, which is Thomson. Do you know either of them at all?'

'We're not at liberty to divulge information about our members, I'm afraid.' The man sounded officious. 'And I certainly wouldn't have a clue what our members' maiden names were.'

'Of course not, I wouldn't expect you to. I'm an old school friend and we've lost touch. I have something very dear to her that I know she would love to have passed on to her.'

'Well, like I said, I can't see how I can be of any help to you, Miss.'

'Do you have many Marys as members?'

'I honestly couldn't say.'

'Could you have a look, please? I've come all the way from Scotland to find her.'

He laughed a little, which made me feel more hopeful.

'We have only got three Scottish couples that I know of, and two Geordies.'

'Sorry?' I interjected immediately. 'Geordies, you say?'

'That's right. But not a Mary. Patsy and Ken.' He spoke slowly, reading from a list I presumed. 'Have been members for years, they are from Newcastle; then we have a Margaret and James, they're from Newcastle too.'

I would have to trust my instinct on this one, for all this time I was convinced that given how uptight and pushy this Mary character was, she was probably not using her real name. Perhaps she was using her middle name, but even if that was confirmed to me, it would be useless without her married name. I decided to stick my neck out and have one last try.

'That's Margaret and Neil Black, right?' I'd just seen the name Black & Sons on a van passing by outside.

'No, Brotherstone,' said the man, falling directly into my trap.

'Listen, I must have it all wrong, I'm sorry, but thank you so much for your time.'

'All right then,' he said.

'Bye now.' I slammed down the phone and thumped the glass shouting 'Yes!', causing two passers-by to stare in.

Even if this wasn't her, and I had no concrete reason to believe it was because she wasn't even a Mary, but, at the very least, it was a couple from Newcastle, and I reckoned they would all stick fairly close together and would more than likely know the Mary I was looking for.

Must be nearly eleven. Jim and the others would be arriving shortly. I tore the page from the phone book, which consisted of only two Brotherstones, then jumped in a cab and headed downtown to Highgate Hill, to check in to the One World backpackers'.

When I got there, it was teaming with new arrivals, plus a group of school children from Japan. Enthusiastic, cheerful, bronzed Scandinavian types lingered in the reception area. I got the attention of a bloke behind the desk and explained to him my friends were on their way to check in, and as I was ahead of them could I leave my bags. He checked the list of names on the counter and confirmed with me that a Mr Crown and four others had reserved space there.

A traveller returned a map to reception that read *Brisbane Suburbs* on the front, so I asked him if I could look at it. I traced the area of Ferny Hills with my finger, and then jotted down a couple of streets in my notebook, including the one with the club in it. Map concentration was an entirely new area for me, and I struggled with concentration of any kind. But I was becoming obsessed with the idea that I must track down my mother a.s.a.p., as though my sanity depended on it.

'That's all right, we have plenty. You can take that if you like,' said a man with cropped hair and a bandana saying 'One World' across it.

I thanked him and stuffed it in my pocket, then wrote a note for Jim, which I left with the guy, and hailed another cab. I'd never had so many cabs in one day, but I didn't care; besides, I always had the Tampax machines as back-up.

My note read:

Dear Jim,

Hope you are well. Found fantastic area called Ferny Hills, great for selling. Gone ahead of you, meet me on the corner of Ferguson Ave and Spring Street at two, please. Any problems, or if you can't make it, will meet you back here at four! Use this number as a base if we lose touch.

K x

CHAPTER THIRTY-SIX

The moment I walked into Weaver Avenue, I felt all eyes upon me. There was no evidence of this, of course, but it was my feeling. I felt nervous and conspicuous, as though I looked like a girl searching for her mother, hiding behind the pretence of selling paintings, with a beaten-up face that was so obviously not acquired through a white-water-rafting incident. It felt as if the way I walked or what I wore told them my story.

I was heading for Mr and Mrs N. Brotherstone of 15 Weaver Avenue. I thought about Dennis Weaver, the seventies cowboy detective Sam McCloud, as I climbed the uphill path to the front door. I knocked at the fly screen; I could smell warm food and cleanliness.

Outside were two enormous flowerpots with children's shoes leaning against them. Were these the shoes of my young blood relatives? If so, then they were the first things I had ever seen of my real family in my life. And if they were indeed the shoes of the children of Mr and Mrs N. Brotherstone, and Mary Brotherstone was my auntie, then what would that make me to the children? And how would I be explained to them? I would be their great-aunt, I supposed, or was it a cousin thing? I wasn't sure. They were girl's shoes, perhaps belonging to a ten-year-old. Ten years ago I was fourteen, dying to be eighteen so I could look up my adoption records.

I was nervous and my mouth was dry. I felt quite sick as I knocked, but the moment I did, I sensed it was quiet inside the Brotherstones' house, and that perhaps no one was home. I had, after all, been standing on the step for a few minutes, staring at the shoes and gathering the courage to knock.

'Hello there, are you all right?'

I jumped. An elderly man with a sunhat on leant over the fence to my right.

'Sorry, no, I'm OK.' I was startled.

'I didn't mean to frighten you. Are you looking for anyone?'

Great – this was all I needed.

'No, thanks. I'm travelling around showing some paintings.'

'You're what, dear?' He leant in closer, cupping his hand at his ear.

'Paintings. I've been here before and I've been asked to come back.' I hadn't used that one for a while.

'No, don't need anything.' The guy was deaf and struggled with everything I said. I didn't want to hang around on the doorstep having an extra loud conversation for all to hear, so I decided to grab the bull by the horns.

'OK. Do Mary and her husband – whose name I've forgotten – live here?'

'WHO?' he bellowed.

'MARY?' I bellowed back. Surely if Mary, or whoever she was, was nearby, then she would now hear me.

'Sorry, love, haven't got my hearing aid. Yes, Mary and Neil, they'll be back shortly, I expect. Can I help?' He strained further.

He was only being neighbourly but I wanted to tell him to fuck off for the time being.

'OK, sorry to bother you.' I walked away, embarrassed by the volume of our conversation. I moved a few blocks out of the area to a shaded tree with a bench, where I sat down to recover and mentally regroup. This was mad. I was feeling stressed and agitated, as well as worn out and hungry, as I'd had no time to eat at Hank's, what with my hasty departure and the study anxiety.

I thought about passing the time by trying my luck in some other houses, but decided against it. I knew what I looked like – I'd been examining my facial injuries in the driver's mirror in the cab on the way over. Although they had improved in terms of swelling, they wouldn't help with my gaining access into the houses. I waited for twenty minutes, which in the circumstances felt like far too long. I was confident that the Brotherstones would be back soon, given the shoes outside.

I got up and wandered off in the direction of a wider, busier street that I hoped would lead to shops, food, phones and a beer, perhaps. Around fifteen minutes later I found a parade of shops and a tiny, cute, toy-looking train station.

I was hot and tired from carrying the folder that I had now lost complete interest in. My selling days felt over; I'd lost my spark, I was worn out inside and tired of feeling rootless. I longed for the foundations that the other people – who went to and from the shops in their family cars, carrying newspapers and bread – took for granted. I went into a bakery, feeling stressed at the light banter exchanged between the vendor and his customers.

'And how are you today, love?'

The 'happy love shit' was wearing me down every day now, and I felt myself turning against Australia by the second.

'Yes, all right, thanks.'

'What can I get you? That looks nasty.' He was referring to my bruised face.

'Yes, it is very nasty.' I deliberately missed out an explanation. 'Just a cheese roll, please.'

He bagged me one up without saying any more and I left. Outside I looked for a place to sit. I walked back to the train station and wandered onto the platform, where I took a shaded seat and ate my roll, watching people around me. A train pulled up on the dinky little platform opposite. I saw a handful of housewife-types and mothers with babies get off. I looked for any potential relatives and fixed on a woman around my height, maybe in her mid-forties, with dark hair like mine, watching her as she walked along, oblivious to me.

I longed for dusk, and a post-selling-day drink with the group. I hated this bright domestic day shit, and all those no doubt settled and fulfilled people waiting on the platform for a train to take them somewhere they felt they belonged. The lady who looked the most like me was the last to climb up the stairs and then she disappeared out of sight.

I scrunched up the bag my roll was in into a ball and threw

it at a garbage bin by the station steps. If it landed in it, then I would meet my mother today.

It landed inside, and I found some new resolve.

'Excuse me,' I said to a man standing in the waiting shelter. 'Where is the nearest bar?'

'Oh, now, that'll be the Fern.'

'Oh yeah? Near, is it?'

'Just few minutes down there, second on left, right next to a dairy.'

When I got to the gate at the entrance to the station, the lady I had been staring at was waiting, and I got a closer look at her. She wore a uniform, maybe of a hospital auxiliary nurse or dental assistant. She had a name badge and was obviously waiting for someone. I tried to move nearer to her without making her aware of me. We were the same height, and she had glasses and short brown hair.

As I stopped and pretended to rummage in my folder, she looked over at me. My eyes flicked up but I couldn't make out the name on her badge. A green station wagon pulled in with a Garfield stuck to the back-seat window. She smiled, got in, and it drove off.

I knew I was clutching at straws with this kind of behaviour, but I felt that I had little choice now but to go with it.

The Fern was a typical small suburban pub with no character or golden-oldie section on its jukebox. I had noticed that the old-style jukebox that had been around from the seventies and early eighties was being phased out in many places in favour of a depressing, futuristic-looking one, which looked like pages of an open book. I put on the Bangles' 'Eternal Flame' (the best of a rum lot) and ordered a midi of Foster's. There was only me and two old guys in the bar, but however substandard it was, it offered me some sense of peace and respite from the outdoor daytime world I didn't fit into.

I paused before my beer, thinking that perhaps it was a bad idea, on top of the state of me, to smell of drink on the doorsteps – but then I ignored those concerns in favour of feeling more reassured by its effect. I lit up a Marlboro Light and took a long slow drag on it and an even longer blow out.

I gulped the midi almost in one, as I wanted an immediate result, then ordered another, which I vowed to sip.

The jukebox volume was disappointingly low and drowned out by a fruit-machine jingle and some clutter from the kitchen, no doubt the noise of making the roast-chicken lunch advertised outside on a chalked board. I looked up at an advert on a turned-down TV attached to the wall in the right-hand corner. A man stood on a doorstep with a box of washing powder, charming a smiling housewife who let him wash her clothes with it. The old men looked up at the screen with me. I felt so much better after my beer, warmer and safer inside, and more positive again.

I got out my notebook and the piece of paper from Hank's folder with the name on it and the suburb I was in. I prayed inside for guidance to whatever I prayed to, which wasn't a god, but more like my strength and my beliefs in things leading me to things. I looked back up at the TV to find Joyce Cane advertising her carpet showroom, which appeared to exist in Brisbane also. That's when I knew I was back on track and in the right place.

I asked the barman to look after my folder while I went to the toilet. In less urgent times I would have tried to palm off some of its contents on him, but decided instead to use the time productively by raiding his Tampax machine, which contained a well above average amount of coinage. I downed the rest of my beer, thanked him and left.

I leant against the wall across the street, chewing gum and staring at the white station wagon, which earlier I'd seen pick up the nurse woman. It was now parked outside the Brotherstones of 15 Weaver Avenue. I longed to have someone with me to witness and experience all this coincidental madness. I was so close now, and glad of the beers that had steadied my nerves slightly.

I crossed the road, walked straight up to the house and knocked on the now opened fly screen. I waited but a radio from inside was drowning out my knocking, so I rang the bell.

A figure walked up the hall towards the door and pushed open the screen. She had an oven glove on one hand, and still wore her uniform, and her badge said 'Margaret'. It was the lady from the station. I felt the colour drain from me, and struggled to get words out.

'Can I help you?' She had a warm smile and nicely applied make-up.

'Yes, my name is Anaya and I'm from Denmark. I am an artist trying to bring my work to people, for I cannot afford a gallery.' I was pretty pleased with my accent, even if it was a little ropey at first.

'Did I just see you at the station?'

I felt my hands shaking. 'I think, maybe yes, I was there with my friends. We all show our work around the place. I live in Sydney but I'm trying to sell work further afield.'

'What did you do to your face, Anaya?' She spoke slowly to help me with my accent.

'White-water rafting.'

I decided to try the oldest trick in the book; but she seemed kind and I felt sure it would work. 'Could I trouble you for, please, a glass of water?'

'Eh, yes, hang on.' She took her foot away from the fly screen, causing it to ping shut. 'Oh, sorry.'

I opened it again.

'Come in, then and just wait there, I'll get you a glass.'

I was anxious to look around and see some photos maybe, but the other rooms were too far down the hall, and she was back in a second. I smiled and gulped the water.

'That better?'

'Yes, thank you, I've been walking around for hours.' I examined her face for signs of my own as I drank from her glass.

'Have you seen someone about your cuts? That one above the eye looks bad.'

I dragged out the last of the water, convinced that we had similarly high cheekbones.

'Yes, it's OK really, looks worse than it is, that's all. So, you are a nurse?'

'Yes, in the city hospital. Just come off a shift. So, what are your paintings?'

'Well, a mixture, but I need to spread them out somewhere.'

'Uh-huh. Listen, if you were to come back later maybe, but I've got to get lunch on, my husband and I are going back into town. Sorry, it's not a good time.'

I felt all my powers of concentration had gone on my accent and trying to appear calm, and therefore I was not in full possession of my usual charm, personality and ability to control the situation. An oven-timer went off in the background.

'Hang on.' She ran down the hall, and I took a couple of steps inside and swung my head round the door, trying to take in the room and any clues. There were two photos above the fire but I couldn't make them out. I moved quickly back to my folder. She came back, looking more agitated.

'Like I said, I'm sorry, but now is a bad time.'

I looked at her, willing her to recognise me. She didn't feel like my mother, although I had no idea what that would feel like; she felt like a stranger, and her eyes were blue, while mine were green. I realised that meant nothing after thinking about it, but I was at odds over what to do next.

A man walked up the drive with a Border collie behind him, sniffing around.

'OK, thank you, not to worry,' I said politely.

'Yes, sorry, dear.'

I looked for signs of worry or suspicion in her face, but she had quickly moved on, and began talking to her husband about some hosepiping and did he have any joy. The man went to the station wagon and rummaged in the boot.

'G'day,' he said, as he walked past.

'Yeah, hi there,' I said, dropping the accent. I swung my folder over my shoulder and walked away.

The pub was fuller than when I last had been there. A few younger men played pool, and two women ate lunch.

'Is there a phone?' I asked speedily. The barman brought one out from under the counter.

First I dialled the backpackers' and asked if there were any messages for me. The reception guy told me my friend Jim had left a note for me. I asked him to read it. He sighed and said they didn't usually do that, but I begged him, told him I was in a spot.

' "Kerry, got your message, can't come to Ferny Hills, been some car trouble, got to go to garage. Disaster. Plus some news from Sydney. Meet back here at four, like we said. Jim." '

'If you see him, can you please tell him that I got the message?'

He sighed a bigger sigh and I hung up. I turned round; a man was waiting to use the phone.

I got out the piece of paper with the phone number of the house I'd just been in and dialled the number.

The husband answered. 'Hello.'

I felt sick. 'Can I speak to Margaret, please?'

'Who's calling?'

'Kerry.'

'Maggie! It's yours!'

I heard her ask, 'Who is it?' and then she came to the phone. 'Hello, who's speaking?'

I detected concern and slight panic. 'It's me.'

'Who?'

'You know, don't you?'

The bloody fruit-machine jingle went off in the background and the boys around it cheered. I had never imagined it to be like this.

'No, I don't. How can I help you?'

'By putting me in touch with Madeline Thomson, my mother.'

She was silent, although I could make out the slight mouthing of words to her husband.

'I don't know what you're talking about. Now, I'm putting down the phone.'

I cupped my hands round the receiver, trying to block out pub noise and cover what I was about to say. 'Now, this is what is going to happen. Unless you take me to my mother, I will kill myself but leave a letter for the local paper and contact my radio friend, so everyone will know the truth one way or another.'

'Where are you now?'

'In the Fern, down the road.'

'She doesn't want to know you, I'm afraid.'

'Well, she can tell me that to my face.'

Someone leant over me and ordered a roast-chicken lunch.
'I'll call you back.'

'I mean it, I'll do it, I have already prepared a letter.' The line
went dead. I passed the phone to the meathead behind me.

I ordered a whisky, drank it straight down and waited for
the phone to be free. The man made a quick phone call to
order a taxi, and the second he put the receiver down, it rang
again. The barman answered.

'It's mine!' I grabbed it.

'Is that Kerry?' This time it was another voice.

'Yes, who are you?'

'I'm your auntie Carol.'

'Who?'

'I'm your mum's sister.'

'Who was Margaret?'

'That's our eldest sister, Margaret Mary; she's very protective
of your mam. Now listen, Kerry, this is important' – I was
reeling from the shock of speaking to my very first self-confessed
blood relative and the use of 'your mam' in her sentence – 'your
mam is not very well at the moment. She's had a hysterectomy
and is just out of hospital yesterday, so she should be taking it
easy, and I'll be honest – she doesn't want to meet you, she's
terrified.'

'Tell her not to worry, tell her I won't be trouble if she
meets me.'

'Well, I'm going to bring her to meet you, OK?'

'Oh my God, oh my God, I mean.' I wanted to grab
someone in the bar and tell them.

'But listen carefully. Once she meets you, then that's it,
finished, OK?'

'OK, fine, anything.' I didn't care, I just needed a fix of her.
Once in my life would do.

'Now, do you know Brisbane at all?'

'No.'

'Well, there's a pub down at the water, off Rowan Avenue
on Shore Walk, right at the water, on the corner. It's called the
Last Drop. Meet me there at six o'clock, OK, pet?'

'Yes, I will, OK.' I didn't have my notepad out but I didn't
need to. I would remember those words for ever.

'And don't expect too much.'

'I won't, I don't,' I said, lying.

I put down the phone and wondered how on earth I could contain myself for the next five hours, and started by ordering another beer, staring ahead. People nudged me as the bar filled up with workers ordering food, and going on and on about their fucking 'chooks'.

CHAPTER **THIRTY-SEVEN**

Everything I was feeling was new. It was the most bizarre and totally amazing feeling I had ever experienced in my life. I was so excited and happy, ecstatically happy, nervous, but bursting with complete and utter joy.

I immediately decided not to drink again until later – I didn't want to be too drunk to forget everything – but I didn't know what to do in the meantime. The pub was a trap, I decided, and left.

Outside in the street, as I walked down to the train platform, I wanted to stop strangers and tell them, I was so high and so sure that my answer was near, that there was an end in sight to my oddness. I had actually heard the voices of two of my mother's sister. It was mind-blowing.

Back at the backpackers', it was hard to be around people. I needed to be in a place of my own to sit it out and hear some music and have a glass of wine that I'd make last in these special circumstances. I tried to find out where the others were at reception. The man wasn't sure, but he thought they were taking the car to a garage and trying to get a rental car. I went to my bunk and lay down, but it was impossible to rest. I had four more hours to kill. I wanted to call an old friend back home, a girl I grew up with, and the only other person apart from my grandfather that I'd ever spoken to about my plan to find my mother. I decided against it, thinking it would seem odd, given that I hadn't spoken to her for six years, plus she'd be asleep.

I decided to shower and get changed to kill another half-hour. That meant three and a half to go, but I'd be at the pub on Shore Walk an hour before – so that meant only two and a half hours, and it would take me half an hour to get there if I walked, so that meant two hours. I would lie on my bunk for another half an hour, hoping that Jim would return and come with me. I waited as long as I could, but left around three thirty, leaving another note for Jim.

Jim,
Waited but had to go. Think I found my answer! MY MOTHER!!! Meeting her down at the riverside at six. See you later tonight; tell me where you will be.
K x

The Last Drop was an old English-looking pub with small, yellowish, mottled-glass windows along the front. I went in and ordered a Coke, wanting to pace myself. I wanted to tell the barman my story but restrained myself. I looked at a clock above the bar every minute, willing the hands forward. I moved my seat so I could look out of the window at the spot where in a while I would see my mother arriving. I tried to process everything but it was impossible, as it was incomparable with anything before it.

The last hour was unbearable; I walked outside up and down the quay, then gave up and came back inside and ordered a large glass of white wine, reapplied my lipstick for about the tenth time, and started oversmoking. I put a song on the jukebox and asked the man behind the bar to turn it up.

Time moved more quickly once I'd ordered the wine and I found the song that I would play to mark the occasion: Jimmy Ruffin's 'What Becomes Of The Brokenhearted'. I sat on a stool by a tall table with a window view, as the song belted out. I felt all its words:

'*I know I've got to find, some kind of peace of mind ...*'

Of all the moments in my life, this was the one I was made for. I was going home, going back not to a place I remembered but to something new. Something that everybody else had that I couldn't imagine. My pain and oddness would soon disappear. I needed to scream, but instead sat rocking on the stool, gulping my wine and ordering another, feeling the song throughout.

At five fifty-five, a car pulled up outside and parked at the edge of the dock, and a woman with bright blonde hair got out. I knew it was who I was waiting for despite our completely different hair colour.

I ran to the door of the bar and stood watching her walk towards me. She was smiling, I was smiling, and I could see me around the age of ten in her face and in her smile. She was petite like me, maybe in her late forties, well dressed and pretty with blue eyes. She spoke before she got to me.

'Hello, I'm your auntie Carol, Kerry.'

I burst into tears.

'All right?'

'You look like me when I was ten,' I blurted.

She laughed a little and hugged me. 'You all right now?'

I felt awkward in the hug, but kept it up way past what felt natural.

'Now listen, Kerry, I know this is hard for you but your mum doesn't have much time. It's not easy for her to get away, you see.'

'What do you mean?' I stood back from her, taking her in more, now that the initial shock had subsided.

'Well, she hasn't told her husband and her family about you.' She shrugged her shoulders.

'Never told them?' I found this so hard to believe.

'Complicated stuff, eh?' She smiled warmly again and rubbed my arm reassuringly, as I started to cry again. I was shocked by my crying and had not expected to be this way. Nor had I expected my auntie Carol to be so friendly and light.

'She's dead shocked, you see, so you have to think about that when you meet her. This is what she's been afraid of for years.'

'That's fine, that's OK, I know, I just want to meet her.'

'Well, I'm going to take you to her now.'

We left the pub for some reason and walked back to her car. She told me we were driving to another pub nearby. I went along with their high-security pub plans without questioning them, but felt them unnecessary.

There was little conversation on my part in the car. I

watched her ankles move off and on the pedals; her ankles were shaped like mine. She and my mum occupied the same womb in my grandmother. That's all I kept thinking as she drove. She attempted to make humdrum small talk, which I was unable to take part in.

'What do you think of Brisbane, then?' She turned to me smiling, searching my face and hair. 'I daren't ask about your face, it looks nasty. You haven't been in a scrape with someone, have you?' she joked.

'White-water rafting accident.'

'Where are you from?'

'Scotland. Edinburgh.'

'How long have you been here, then? And how the devil did you find us?'

'It's a long story, a lot to do with coincidences.'

'There's loads of us out here.' She laughed, and kept looking round at me.

'How come?'

'Well, we are a big family. I mean, there were ten of us, and there's four of us out here.'

I shook my head in disbelief.

'It's mind-boggling, isn't it?' She was so smiley and warm and normal.

'Are you my auntie?' I said for about the tenth time.

'Are you my niece?' she said back, which I loved.

We didn't drive far, just a bit along the riverside in the other direction until we reached a car park. There was a car waiting outside another bar called The Shore. There were two women in it. One hid her face with her hand.

My auntie Carol ushered me out of the car with her hand on my shoulder and into the bar, straight upstairs. She thanked the bar lady on the way up as if she knew her.

'Can I get you something?' she asked, going into her handbag.

'White wine, please.'

'Go on then, you sit down, I'll bring them over.'

I sat down in the corner, my back to the wall, looking out.

'You all right?' She brought over the drinks and put them on the table.

'I'm nervous.' I gulped my wine.

'Well, course you are, pet. You're going to be, aren't you? I think we all are.'

Footsteps climbed the stairs. I heard two sets, one of them surely my mother's. Two dark-haired petite women shuffled into the room. I didn't know which one to look at. I fixed more on the one behind the one with glasses. Everything became slow and odd and not at all how I imagined. There was no running over and hugging, no shouting or cheering, no ending music; instead, the woman with glasses arranged stools round my table and ushered the shorter, silent woman to sit opposite. She was reluctant until the woman with her pushed her down onto the stool. It seemed ages before anybody spoke. I was breathing as though I'd just finished running.

'Hello, Kerry,' said the woman with glasses. 'I'm your auntie Deb and this is your mum.'

My mum looked ashen. I stretched out my hand but she refused it, instead shaking her head. Auntie Carol brought drinks back from the bar for my mum and her sister.

Auntie Carol said, 'Double brandy,' as she put it down.

I looked at my mum but she didn't look at me; instead she rummaged in her handbag, then brought out cigarettes. I noted my mother's brand was menthol. Once she lit up and took a drag, she fixed on me, putting her mouth to the side and chewing on it. I watched her mouth smoke and her eyes dart around. She and I had the same shape to our faces, and the same mouth, although she had smoker's lines. She had freckles and a tan; her face was quite lined for her age and her eyes were beautiful, like mine. She wore a gold bracelet, a watch and a wedding ring. I watched her hands – her nails were bitten down. She wore a frosted lipstick that, like me, she had freshly applied. Her hair was fairly short and highlighted; I wondered if we had a tendency to grey early in our family.

'Go on, say something,' said auntie Deb to Madeline Thomson, my mother. But she refused.

'It's all right,' I said, smoking. I felt strong again. I could see she was terrified and I didn't want to scare her away. I wanted to show her that I could be calm and controlled in a crisis.

'Your mum hasn't been well, you know, so she's pretty

worn out, and the shock of this is a bit much at the moment,' said her sister Deb.

My mum flicked her ash into our shared ashtray. 'I mean, am I never going to be able to forget this? Is this never going to leave me alone?'

Those were the first words my mother spoke to me. They had little effect on me; I was too carried away by the excitement of seeing who made me, a face like mine, for the first time. I used to draw pictures when I was young, in primary school, of my face with different hairstyles, and sometimes like a man with beard and moustache, trying out different ways to make me look, but here was the face that made me. She drank half her brandy down and did not smile once, despite my constant smile.

'We'll leave you to it,' said Auntie Carol, moving away to another table with Deb.

'No need,' my mother said firmly. My aunties moved away all the same.

'Is it brandy that you like, then?' It was a dumb thing to say but I was just trying to find a way to talk to her.

'It is, yeah.' Everything she said was an attempt to close down our talk. She seemed to have no interest in me and how I felt, she seemed to have no curiosity – but I knew that would change in time. The sisters kept away from us and talked among themselves, keeping an eye on us all the time.

'I call it D-day,' she said, dragging hard. She smoked like a bitter person. She sounded pretty Australian with a slight hint of Englishness in her vowels. Her voice was a heavy smoker's voice and quite husky.

'Sorry?'

'That's what I've always called today. D-day.' She stubbed out her cigarette for much longer than she needed to. I was looking at her like I was in love. Even her harsh words were beautiful to me.

'When I heard the call on the radio, I said to Carol, that's bloody D-day. I've always said the day you found me would be my D-day.' She finished off her drink and lit up another cigarette. I reached for mine; she pushed hers towards me, offering them up. I thanked her and took one, excited to be smoking my mother's cigarettes.

'So.' She paused to inhale, and she seemed calmer. 'How did you manage to find me then?'

'It's such a weird and long story.'

The aunties were silent, listening to everything that was said between us.

'First of all I went to Register House when I was eighteen, so I had your name and address at the time of my birth, then I went to Newcastle and asked around in your street.'

'So, someone shopped me?' She looked angry again, increasing her drag rate.

'A neighbour said you went to Australia and married an Australian soldier called Duffy, and the rest was my own detective work and pretty much fate.' I smoked, waiting to see what she'd make of my story.

'I bet I know who told you.' She looked over at the sisters, and they both nodded.

'Do you believe in fate, Madeline?' This was the first time I'd used her name.

'There's certainly something else going on out there, there has to be.'

Auntie Deb asked us if we wanted another drink, we both said yes. I became aware of how limited my time with her was tonight, so I tried asking the essential, must-know questions.

'What are my relatives like? I mean ancestors, what do they do?'

'Just ordinary people – builders, electricians. Just workers.'

'What about my real father?'

'I haven't seen Robert since before you were born. We were both very young.'

'Did you love him?' I wanted to know the circumstances under which I was conceived.

'At the time, I suppose I thought I did, but like I said, we were young.'

'What does he look like?'

'He was very good-looking, what you would call a catch. Dark like you. You look like your father, I thought that as soon as I saw you. I got a shock.'

'What else about him?'

'He loved Bobby Darin, I remember that, and he was always very well turned out.'

The aunties came back with the drinks.

'Look, I understand, I know they made you give me away, I know that's what they did in those days.' I felt myself turning into this understanding, kind, selfless person. I didn't recognise myself, but I wanted to be nice. I felt sorry for her; she was as fucked up as I was.

'If you knew how they treated us in the home, made us feel like we were so dirty. And we felt grateful that we were given a place to go and have our babies, and glad that our babies were going to a good home. It was just what happened, you had no choice if you had no money, and we were poor, everyone was.'

'What about your family now? Have you got children?'

'Two boys and a girl. Andrew is twenty-three, Calum is twenty and Linda is eighteen.'

I felt a little depressed momentarily as I calculated my half-brother's birth at being the year after mine or even less.

'So you got married quickly after me.'

'After what I'd been through, I just wanted someone to come and take me away. I was lucky, he was my saviour at the time, he really was.'

'What does he do? Is your married name Duffy, then?'

'No, it's not, but I can't tell you anything about them, OK? Not my married name or anything else, OK?'

'OK, that's OK.' It annoyed me slightly, her telling me this, but I could find out anything I really needed to. 'What happened to my father, then?'

'He went off to sea.' She looked down. 'He was in the merchant navy. He said he would come back and get me and the baby, he wrote to me in the home saying that he'd be back but ...' She shook her head and downed half her new drink.

'Did he see me, then?' I hoped he hadn't; it would make me feel better about him leaving us.

'No, he left before you were born. He came back on leave to see me when I was in the home, brought a big lovely bunch of flowers and told me that he was going home to tell his mother that he was marrying me and that everything would be all right, and that he'd come straight back when he could. He didn't show. You were born, and I got a letter from his mother saying that he was marrying someone else.' She stubbed out her cigarette firmly again. When she looked up she had tears in her eyes. 'If you knew what it felt like, to lie to everyone, to have to write back home saying that I was happy and had a job and all that crap.'

I looked down now.

'All the time, I was lying to everyone, 'cause I was sitting writing letters from a bloody home, waiting to give my baby away.'

There was a pause and then she said, 'Is there anything else you want to ask me?'

My mind raced to think of more questions and categories, so that on leaving I would feel no regret about missing stuff out I wanted to know.

Then she said, 'What do you do, then?'

'Just selling paintings door to door. Just a traveller's job for now.'

'So have you been to college?'

This was a family-type question that pleased me. 'No. I was going to go to art college but I messed things up at school. I've had a messed-up life, wasted things, I have lots of regrets already.' I laughed a little.

'Life is full of regrets; I learnt that at a young age, too. That was one of the things they said to us, about our babies going to good homes.' She became quite animated. 'They said the baby would have more chances and opportunities than if it stayed with us. That it would have a nice home and probably go to college, and get a good job.'

I didn't know what to say. I felt like I'd disappointed absolutely everybody in my entire orbit, including myself, with the college failure. But I'd fucked up school in the first place because I couldn't concentrate because I was so unhappy – which was probably linked to feeling weird and adopted.

'Are you staying here, then?' she asked.

'Don't know, haven't decided yet. But I will have to leave soon I suppose. I've got a six-month visa.'

'I just want to forget this. I had no choice, you know.'

'Yeah, I know. Why did you come to Australia, then, what about your family back home?' I knew really but I wanted to hear it from her.

'A fresh start. Nobody knew me. When I met my husband he was in the army in Ireland, and he told me about this place that was warm and sunny, and where the houses were big and new and there was plenty of work, and it would only cost us ten pounds to go there. So I wasn't going to say no, was I?'

'No, suppose not.'

'I've got my two sisters here, and one brother. My mam and dad came out but they're both dead now, and the rest of the family come over and visit.'

'Do you ever go back over there?' I hoped she would say yes.

'Been over three times for weddings and funerals, but it's expensive to fly back and forth, so we only do it when we really have to.'

I wondered if having to see me again would be one of these occasions.

'You've got a lovely mouth,' she said, thawing slightly. Her comment knocked me out; I read it as love.

'Have I?'

'It's a nice shape.'

'Thanks.'

My mother ordered another brandy and I had some more wine.

'What were my grandparents like?'

'Your grandfather was in the army, he was a hard man and a drinker. He gave us a hell of a life, but then his life was pretty grim when he was a boy so ... I lost my mam just three years past. There were ten of us so we never had any money.'

'Fuck, ten? So I've got millions of relatives?'

'I suppose you have.'

'That's weird, you know?' I imagined a formal photograph pose with loads of people who looked like me.

'I can't stay long, you know, I have to get back before my husband gets home from work.'

'Does he know about this?' I said *this*, instead of *me*.

'No, he doesn't. I've kept it from him all this time.'

'What does he do?'

'Electrician.'

'What do you do?'

'Just a housewife.' She gulped her third drink with more urgency than the first two.

'They were bastards in that place, what they did to us, how they made us feel. There were some women who walked up and left before they had the babies, just had enough and decided to keep them, and when they got up to leave we would shout things out to them and clap and stuff, but they were the brave ones. I wasn't, I was too afraid to be brave, I admit that. My father would have killed me, he would have absolutely killed me if he'd known I was pregnant.'

'What, you didn't tell him?'

'No. I said that I was working as a nurse. So was our Carol, she's older than me and was further ahead in the nursing, and she knew of this place in Scotland, in Dundee, where you could go and have the baby, so I told Mam and Dad that I got a job there and I went away. Those bloody letters saying how much fun I was having and how good the job was!' Her eyes grew watery; she sucked on her menthol.

I felt nothing at this point. This was the story of the making and the leaving of me, but I knew nobody in the picture.

She got a handkerchief from her bag and blew her nose but there were no tears, except from the aunties who were both sniffling at the other table.

'What was my birth like? What time? What did I look like?'

'It was a beautiful bright sunny afternoon when you were born, it was half past four in the afternoon, and the birth was straightforward.'

The term 'straightforward' was hard to hear.

'They told us we were doing the best for our babies, you know, and that's what we believed. They said that you were going to a good home with a caravan that you could go on your holidays in. Was that true?'

I could have said a whole lot more at that point but, like her, I chose to focus on the caravan.

'Yes, it was a good home, and there were loads of nice caravan holidays ...' I petered out at the end, suddenly feeling great sadness for the pain I had caused my adopted mother over the years, and the hatred I had for my unhappy and bitter father.

'Well, then, I did what was best.'

I said nothing and helped myself to another of her cigarettes. She lit me up and I touched her hand briefly. I was desperate to go to the toilet but was afraid to leave in case she was gone when I returned. In the end I would have to risk it, trusting that the aunties were too understanding of both our sides to let it end abruptly.

I sat on the toilet peeing, thinking about the Bobby Darin songs I knew, and my love of the jukebox. Someone else came into the cubicle next to me and peed just after me. Outside, I stared into the mirror trying to imagine a male version of me. I looked at my nice mouth and pressed my fingers to it.

The toilet flushed and my mother walked out. I didn't know what to say now that we were alone, so I compared our heights. We shared the hand dryer, both standing there after our hands were dry, moving them around. I strained over the noise of it.

'I'm slightly taller than you – how tall are you?'

'Five three,' she said.

The dryer stopped.

'I'm five five.' I stood close to her, comparing heights.

'They made us do it, you know, there was no choice.'

I held the door open for her and we walked back to our seats.

'Right then, how you both feeling?' asked Carol.

'I have to get going,' said my mother.

We all sat down but my mother put her cigarettes away, which meant my time with her was nearly up. I drank down the remainder of my wine, and considered taking my mother's empty glass as a keepsake in case I never had another drink with her, but thought it would probably get broken during the journey home.

She fixed her smudged mascara with a handkerchief. 'I have to go, pet, sorry.'

This was the first time she had said 'sorry'. I was expecting more.

'Can I have a contact number or address?'

'No, sorry, this is all I can do, and I wish you the very best, really I do.'

I started to feel slight panic. The sisters got up like body-guards, in case things got out of hand, no doubt.

'OK, then please can I have something of yours? Anything?'

'I haven't got anything.'

'Please, could you all look in your bags, and give me some-thing, anything.'

They all rooted around. My mother went into the small zip compartment in her handbag.

'I've only got this. It's just a stupid thing I've had in this bag since Christmas, I think. It's just something stupid from a cracker.'

'Let me see.'

She handed me a tiny silver alien, like the robot thing in the seventies Smash adverts; it was just bigger than my thumb-nail.

'And this.' Then she passed me a small silver aeroplane the same size. 'I got them in a Christmas cracker and they've been in my bag all this time.'

'Just stupid things, like,' said my auntie Carol, offering me a small pillbox from her bag. I put the plane and the alien in the pillbox.

'I don't know what you're wanting with them,' said my mother.

'Just something to keep,' I said, already attaching massive meaning to them. The alien, of course, was me, and the plane was what brought me to her, and what took her from me, and what would take me away from her. The pillbox was for the bitter pill she'd had to swallow all these years. (Plus, 'The Bitterest Pill I Ever Had To Swallow' by The Jam, a song I fixated on when I was at school.) These items were perfect. 'I want to say something important to you.'

She looked afraid again, like when she first entered. 'All right, but then I've got to go, I'm sorry.'

My mum stood up.

'If I can't get in touch with you after this, I want you to

know you can with me. One day I'll get my shit together and do something, and I'll be someone, famous maybe, and you can come to me. I won't mind, OK?'

'I know you wouldn't, but I don't want to get your hopes up. Let's just get on with our lives. It's for the best, really.'

'And maybe now you know who your mother is, you can get on, Kerry,' said Auntie Deb, trying to end things on a positive note.

'Why did you name me Joanna?' I asked, getting some last-minute questions in.

'No particular reason,' she said, my auntie Deb guiding her out. Auntie Carol stretched out her arm for me to follow them.

Outside at the water, it had become muggy and cloudy. Some slight rain was starting, and it thundered in the distance.

'Perfect,' I said, looking up.

Auntie Deb stood by her car beside my mother, and Auntie Carol by her car behind them. I was close to tears, so pressed the pillbox into the palm of my hand as a distraction.

My mother and I hugged in silence, and then broke off.

'Take care of yourself and good luck,' she said, before walking back to the car. I couldn't speak. My auntie touched my arm and I turned away.

'WAIT!' shouted my mother, just as the sky emptied enormous spots of rain that drummed on the car roofs. She ran back to me, in tears.

'Listen to me. I need to tell you this. There is never a day that goes by, never a day, when I don't think of you, you remember that, OK? Never a day when I don't wonder what you are doing and how you've turned out, and your birthdays are hell for me, do you understand?'

I nodded but couldn't speak for crying.

'Listen, I'm sorry, I had no money and I couldn't keep you, *I had no choice!* You're a lovely girl, and I wanted what was best for you. I would have loved things to have been different but they're not, so we just have to get on with it. I hope you find happiness, really I do, and I'm sorry.' She grabbed both my arms and we hugged and cried, then she got a paper handkerchief out of her bag and blew her nose. 'Never a day, remember that.'

I nodded manically, still crying, moved in a way I had never quite felt before.

Yet, as I watched her getting into the car and driving off, I didn't feel torn away from her, or as though half of me was with her or anything; after all, I had no memories of her, before today, nothing to miss. I had longed for something always, since I could ever remember anything, and had always felt an emptiness I didn't understand. I hoped my emptiness would go now, now I knew that she was real, and that I was made like everyone else, and that I came from a body and a face that I had seen with my own eyes.

I just felt I'd see her again, maybe a long time from now. I just knew it. I watched the car go out of sight, my auntie letting me stand there for ages, looking up at the dark clouds, getting soaked, loving the totally appropriate rain.

CHAPTER **THIRTY-EIGHT**

There was a freshness in the air now that the rain had cleared the mugginess, and the sun was already getting bright. You could tell it was going to be a scorcher of a day. We crept around the wooded undergrowth.

'I don't understand, where are they?' asked Karin.

Jim was in front with a stick, prodding and poking at the ground. 'Don't want a bloody snake bite.'

'Mate, the snakes can hear you comin', they're more bloody scared than you are.' Scotty limped along, aided by a stick, still recovering from his injuries.

'Maybe the kangaroos are still asleep,' I said, following Jim, agreeing with his snake caution.

'You'll see some, don't worry, Uncle Scotty's not going to let you down.'

It was just after dawn. Jim and I stayed up all night talking when I got back from seeing my mum. It was so good to see him, and the others. We sat out on the porch at the backpackers', watching bouts of fork lightning. The others had gone to bed around midnight. I didn't want to talk to them much, or to drink much, or go anywhere. I wanted to be quiet with thoughts of my mother, and replay her words in my head. But Jim was good and easy to be with. He listened to me telling the whole story initially, then just sat with me quietly and hugged me when I became tearful.

It was fair to say that the trip was a wash-out from a selling point of view, and we'd all decided that evening that we should return to Sydney the following morning. Just before sunrise, Jim and I woke the others up and told them that we couldn't go back until we had seen some genuinely wild and roaming free kangaroos. The man on reception had told us that we were near a forest, where if you got up before sunrise, you could see hundreds of them running around. From where we were standing, however, it looked extremely doubtful. There was nothing for miles but charcoal trees, grey and brittle, and scarred ground from previous summer fires.

'I'm going home in two weeks, to start back at uni,' said Andrea, slowing down to walk with us.

'We won't talk about leaving just now.' Karin put her hands on top of her head and held them. Jim responded by putting his arm round her waist.

'What about you, Scotty?' I asked.

'Me, well I'll probably kick around at my mates up here for a week, until me bruising goes down.' Scotty's face was still badly swollen, and he had stitches above his eye, and a nose that was broken out of shape. 'Then, I reckon, I'll do this until the end of the summer, if it's still going, or I'll get some work on the prawn boats up in Darwin. Winter, I'll go up to the ski resorts.'

'Yeah? Jesus, I didn't even know there was snow here,' said Karin.

'Oh yeah, we got the whole lot. What about you, mate?' Scotty asked Jim.

'I'm not going back, no way. I like it here, it's easy.'

'I think it's too easy,' I said. 'I think there's something missing.'

Scotty laughed, then sneezed, tripped over a log on the ground and fell. As we laughed, out of nowhere hundreds of kangaroos of all sizes ran in packs up ahead where the edge of the woods met a field.

'SKIPPY!' shouted Jim. They kept on coming from everywhere around us, from out behind trees up ahead: small ones, huge ones, like dinosaurs on the horizon, some with little Joey ears sticking out their pouches.

'WOW! GO, GO, GO, GO, BABY!' shouted Karin.

We all cheered them on. Scotty howled and whooped. Andrea was frightened and clung to Scotty, which he loved. Whichever way we turned, there were kangaroos leaping and darting to join the others up on the field. It went on for ages until the woods were emptied.

'Fuck me!' said Scotty. There was a crack of dry wood behind me.

I span round, to find an enormous kangaroo staring right at me, its tail a good five feet long. I was terrified, knowing nothing about how to approach them.

'Don't move, just be still, take it easy,' said Scotty.

It towered over me and began clicking. A tiny little baby 'roo popped up from its pouch, its ears longer than its little face. It stood rooted to the spot. I moved towards it with my hand out.

'Easy,' said Scotty. 'Take it nice and slow.'

'It's all right, no one's going to harm you,' I whispered.

It looked at me again, and then skipped off in the direction of the fields to join the others. Everybody blew out and sighed with relief.

'Jesus, you were lucky,' said Scotty. 'They can be vicious, especially when they're carrying a Joey.'

CHAPTER THIRTY-NINE

No sale in one week was my all-time low. I was bored and had hit a wall with the whole thing. I sat in the dark on a kerb on Dawson Hill, in the suburb of Manly, smoking and listening to some bird sounds, hoping that I'd catch Scotty circling the area. I'd had some possible interest from the last house on the corner in a pair of Blue Mountains, but couldn't summon up the enthusiasm to push it towards a close. I put it down to losing some of my magic, but Jim said it was simply a job that nobody could do for very long without burning out.

It wasn't just me who'd become slow. Karin had moved nothing much since returning from the trip, and even less since Andrea left a few weeks back.

Scotty parped his horn, which was completely unnecessary given that he and I were the only two beings in the street. He pulled alongside. I didn't get up.

'Nothing happening, uh?' he said, leaning over to the passenger window.

'Nup, sorry, nothing.'

'Wanna beer, mate?' He drummed on the dashboard.

'How about the others?'

'Yeah, new guys did OK. Dirk's rounding them up.'

Dirk, a tall thin humourless South African guy, had taken over Greg's job, after he became just too out of it to function. We had arrived back in Sydney to find him drunk out of his mind, claiming that Anaya had left him, perhaps for Cairns, or Darwin, with a considerable amount of the company's money. I wasn't surprised, and wondered if my path would ever cross with hers again.

When Greg told us the news, Jim said nothing to him about her visit to me. As soon as Greg left, Dirk was quickly dispatched from another team in Melbourne, swiftly springing into action, advertising for new recruits and training up two teams at once. Scotty was elevated to supervisor and drove a bunch of new young hopefuls around, with me reluctantly sandwiched in the middle of two German boys, and Justine, an annoying, uptight English girl who worked in the tennis world.

I was glad Scotty and I were alone and away from the new recruits, and a beer sounded as good as ever.

'What about Jim and Karin?' I threw my folder in the back and got into the passenger seat.

'Dunno, probably crashed early. Come on, let's get going, there's a schooner with my name on it.'

The more I knew Scotty the more I liked him and admired him; he just kept at it the whole time. At first I thought I could see through his act, but lately, since the others arrived, I got the feeling that this was genuinely him. Jim had faded into the background a little, spending most of his time with Karin, organising their trip to New Zealand, where they planned to travel together for the rest of the year. Sometimes they helped out, giving demonstrations to the new sellers, but, like me, their hunger and love of it had gone.

'Do you wanna know what I think?' he said, beaming away at me.

'Of course I do.' I beamed back.

'Think me and you should get a tattoo.' He looked at me, waiting for my reaction.

'I don't believe this.' I covered my face with my hands and slowly dragged them over it.

'What do you think?'

'I've been thinking the same thing.'

'Now that I'm on the mend, could take it, I reckon, little keepsake of our adventure up north, eh?'

I was excited by his suggestion. 'Fuck!'

'What do you reckon we should get?'

'When were you born again?'

'Sixty-five,' said Scotty.

'Yep, me too.' I banged on the roof. 'Year of the snake.'

'Snake it is, then!'

'Fuck,' I said again.

'Get it done tomorrow, if you like, I know a place down town.'

I sat back smiling. 'Where to now?' I asked, as Scotty retuned the radio.

'Usual.'

'Fine by me.' I searched in the glove compartment for the Billy Idol tape; it was at the end of the track that we often played on the drive back from a night's selling. I rewound, hardly listening to Scotty rambling on about the new team and their recent selling accolades. I waited until we reached Sydney Harbour Bridge before starting the song that had become my latest number one.

I slumped down watching the giant steel girders that they called the coat-hanger pass over us, playing a game in my head that involved us driving under certain parts of the bridge during certain breaks in the music. Scotty drove with one hand, thumping the other one on the roof.

'Don't you know that we're hot in the city, Hot in the city, tonight …'

Mac stood at the bar as usual, looking up at a muted TV. He had always looked the same since I first set eyes on him: tired, sad and uninterested. But tonight he looked particularly weary. Now I had got to know him, I failed to find him as mysterious and intriguing as the first few times I drank with him, and had come to the conclusion that he was maybe just a bored and broken old man. We exchanged words now and then when buying drinks at the bar, but never spent any other time together, since the night I stayed in his room.

'Still here, then?' he mumbled, smiling away as though there had been some huge irony or something.

'You mean, since last night?'

'Just still here, that's all, still knocking around?' He looked smarter than usual, in one of his three outfits I'd seen in his strange minimalist wardrobe that night.

'You look smart.'

'Funeral,' he said, his elbow holding him up on the bar, with his front teeth resting on his thumbnail and a spire of cigarette smoke floating up from his nostrils.

'I'm sorry,' I said, toasting his glass with my whisky.

'Here's to the goners,' he said, clinking so hard that his drink spilled over his hand.

'Now, before you start, you're not getting a bloody free one,' said Val, wiping the bar with a cloth. Scotty waved for me to hurry up with his drinks.

'Visa is running out soon,' I said, putting down our schooners and chasers.

Scotty drank half of his down. 'That's better,' he said, checking out a girl crossing the floor. Bruce Springsteen sang about fires and sparks in the background. 'Yeah, how long you got?'

'Month or so.'

'What will you do if you go back?'

'Don't know. I've missed my records, though. If I go back, the first thing I'll do is get them back off my friend, get drunk and play them for days.'

'Good plan,' said Scotty.

'How long will you hang around here?' I asked, finishing half my schooner to level with Scotty.

'Dunno, fuckin' new year or something, head up to Darwin, to my mate's boat, money's good.'

'Yeah?'

'Better than this. Can get you a job, like, if you fancy, but you might have to cook and shit.'

'Yeah, maybe. What's it like there?'

'Fuckin' hot, I mean f-u-c-k-i-n' hot. And the roaches eat your fuckin' undies.'

'No way!'

'I'm tellin' you, mate.'

I laughed. Scotty loved me laughing at things he said, and he glanced round to see if any girls were looking. I felt warmer again and safe with Scotty, filling up with Foster's. Maybe I would go up north with him, maybe I would marry him and get residency and stay here until eventually my mother would get over her fear about having me in her life.

'Are you a happy person, do you think, Scotty?' I asked, putting my arm round him.

'Well, you gotta laugh, mate, don't you?' He downed the rest of his glass and shook it at me.

'Yeah, go on,' I said.

Dirk and the new team arrived with Jim and Karin. The tennis girl pulled up a stool next to me with Karin, while the boys went to the bar.

'So, how long have you been working at the Art place?' she asked predictably. She had an irritating kind of cloth purse hanging round her neck.

'A while.' I felt like a worn-out old hand.

'You still enjoy it?'

'Nope!' Karin and I both said at the same time, then laughed.

Jim and Dirk sat at another table going over maps of Sydney suburbs, Jim showing him the best areas. Dirk scribbled away keenly in a notebook. Scotty brought back two whisky doubles this time and we sank them immediately. The Gipsy Kings came on, which I hadn't heard in ages.

'This is for you, babe, you love this, come on – up you get!' Scotty stretched out his hand across the table and pulled me up. We both lit up cigarettes and danced around the bar to 'Bamboleo'.

I was really happy again. I span round and round. Scotty jumped up on the table until Val shouted at him to jump down, but everybody in the bar started clapping, so he stayed there, dancing, stamping his foot in an attempt to look Spanish.

I took off my vest and danced in my bra, swinging my vest around my head, then letting it go so that it landed on one of the Germans. Jim and Dirk stopped looking at the maps and joined in the clapping. Scotty jumped down and swung me around again, and as he did so I saw bits of everybody in the bar: bits of Mac with his anodyne grin, and bits of angry Val behind the bar; Jim was shaking his head while Dirk was looking at my tits.

'Don't, whatever you do, take all your flamin' clothes off!' shouted Scotty.

'Don't worry,' I said, grabbing his face, thinking how it might be OK to go to Darwin for a while.

But I didn't ever want to be held to anything. I wanted to be free and young for as long as I possibly could. Moments like this, I fuckin' loved it, I loved life.

I thought back to being little, when I would travel on the bus with my grandfather, how sometimes the bus wouldn't go the whole distance and it would pull in, and the driver would come upstairs to where we were sitting and shout out, 'All change! All change!'